piercing
the
Darkness

FRANK E. PERETTI

piercing the DARKNESS

TYNDALE HOUSE PUBLISHERS, INC., CAROL STREAM, ILLINOIS

Visit Tyndale's exciting Web site at www.tyndale.com

Piercing the Darkness

Designed by Jacqueline L. Noe

Originally published by Crossway Books. Reprinted by permission.

Some Scripture quotations are taken from the *Holy Bible,* Revised Standard Version, copyright © 1946, 1952, 1971 by the Division of Christian Education of the National Council of the Churches of Christ in the United States of America, and are used by permission. All rights reserved.

Some Scripture quotations are taken from the *Holy Bible,* New International Version®. NIV®. Copyright © 1973, 1978, 1984 by International Bible Society. Used by permission of Zondervan. All rights reserved.

ISBN-13: 978-0-8423-6372-3
ISBN-10: 0-8423-6372-6

Printed in the United States of America

10   09   08   07
14   13   12   11   10   9

To Gene and Joyce,
my dad and mom,
who gave me my heritage,
and always encouraged me

"The Light shines in the darkness,
and the darkness has not overcome it."

John 1:5, RSV

one

It could have begun in any town. Bacon's Corner was nothing special, just one of those little farming towns far from the interstate, nothing more than a small hollow dot on the AAA road map, with exit signs that offered gas, no lodging, maybe a little food if the place was open, and little more.

But it began in Bacon's Corner.

It was a normal Tuesday evening. The workday was over, supper was on in most of the homes, the stores were locking up, the tavern was filling up. All the employees at the Bergen Door Company had clocked out, and the security guard was checking the locks. Mr. Myers's son was bringing all the lawn mowers and tillers in for the night at the Myers Feed and Farm Store. The lights were winking out in the local mercantile. Two retirees sat in their chairs in front of the barbershop, putting in their idle hours.

The fields and farms right across the Toe Springs–Claytonville Road were getting warmer and greener with each day, and now the evening breeze was carrying a lot of mid-April smells—apple and cherry blossoms, plowed dirt, a little mud, some cattle, some manure.

It was a normal Tuesday evening. No one expected anything unusual. No one saw or heard a thing. No one could have.

But the commotion started behind a dismal little rented farmhouse just south of Fred Potter's place—a flapping, a fluttering, a free-for-all, and then a cry, a long, eerie shriek, an echoing, slobbering wail that raced into the forest like a train whistle through a town, loud, muffled, loud, muffled, moving this way and that through the trees like a hunted animal; then a flash of light, a fireball, blinking and burning through the forest, moving with blinding speed, right behind that siren, almost on top of it.

More cries and screams, more flashing lights! Suddenly the forest was filled with them.

1

The trees ended abruptly where the Amhurst Dairy began. The chase broke into the open.

First out of the forest came a bug, a bat, a black, bulb-eyed thing, its dark wings whirring, its breath pouring out like a long yellow ribbon. It just couldn't fly fast enough, but clawed the air with its spidery arms, desperate for speed and shrieking in total panic.

Right behind it, so close, so dangerously close, the sun itself exploded out of the forest, a brilliant comet with wings of fire tracing a glimmering trail and a sword of lightning outstretched in burly bronze hands.

The black thing and the comet shot into the sky over Bacon's Corner, zigzagging, shooting this way and that like wild fireworks.

Then the forest, like a row of cannons, spewed out more hideous creatures, at least twenty, each one fleeing in utter panic with a dazzling, flaming figure tenaciously on its tail, scattering in all directions like a crazy meteor shower in reverse.

The first demon was running out of tricks and maneuvers; he could feel the heat of the warrior's blade right at his heels.

He spit over his shoulder, "No, turn away, I am going!"

The fiery blade cut an arc through the air. The demon met it with his own and the blow sent him spinning. He corrected with his wings, turned and faced his assailant, shrieking, cursing, parrying blow after blow, looking into the fiery eyes of more power, more glory, more holiness than he'd ever feared before. And he could see it in those eyes—the warrior would never turn away. Never.

The demon withered even before the blade struck its final blow; it slipped from the earth, from the world of mankind, into outer darkness, gone in a tumbling puff of red smoke.

The warrior turned and soared higher, spinning his long sword above his head, tracing a circle of light. He burned with the heat of battle, the fervor of righteousness.

His fellows were consumed with it, striking demons from the sky like foul insects, vanquishing them with strong swords, relentlessly pursuing them and hearing no pleas.

Frank E. Peretti

On the right, a long, slithering spirit took one more swipe at his heavenly assailant before curling tightly in anguish and vanishing.

On the left, a loud-mouthed, boasting imp cursed and taunted his opponent, filling the air with blasphemies. He was quick and confident, and just beginning to think he might prevail. His head went spinning from his body while the proud sneer still twisted the face, and then he was gone.

There was one left. It was spinning, tumbling on one good wing.

"I'll go, I'll go," it pleaded.

"Your name?" ordered the angel.

"Despair."

The warrior swatted the demon away with the flat of his blade, and it fled, gone, yet still able to work evil.

And then it was over. The demons were gone. But not soon enough.

"Is she all right?" asked Nathan the Arabian, sheathing his sword.

Armoth the African had made sure. "She's alive, if that's what you mean."

The mighty Polynesian, Mota, added, "Injured and frightened. She wants to get away. She won't wait."

"And now Despair is free to harass her," said Signa the Oriental.

Armoth replied, "Then it's begun, and there will be no stopping it."

Sally Roe lay in the grass, clutching her throat and gasping for air, taking long, deliberate breaths, trying to clear her head, trying to think. A raw welt was rising on her neck; her plaid shirt was reddened from a wound in her shoulder. She kept looking toward the goat pen, but nothing stirred there. There was no life, nothing left to harm her.

I have to get moving, I have to get moving. I can't stay here— no, not one more minute.

She struggled to her feet and immediately rested against

3

the farmhouse, her world spinning. She was still nauseous, even though she'd already lost everything twice.

Don't wait. Go. Get moving.

She staggered up the back porch steps, stumbled once, but kept going. She wouldn't take much with her. She couldn't. There wasn't time.

Ed and Mose were quite comfortable, thank you, just sitting there in front of Max's Barber Shop right on Front Street, which is what they called the Toe Springs–Claytonville Road where it passed through town. Ed was sixty-eight, and Mose wouldn't tell anyone his age, so nobody asked him anymore. Both their wives were gone now—God bless 'em, both men had pretty good retirements and Social Security, and life for them had slowed to a comfortable crawl.

"Ain't bitin', Ed."

"You shoulda moved downriver, Mose. Downriver. They get cranky swimmin' clear up to your place. You gotta catch 'em in a good mood."

Mose listened to the first part, but not the second. He was staring at a green Plymouth hurrying through town with two upset children in the backseat.

"Ed, now don't we know those kids there?"

"Where?"

"Well, why don't you look where I'm pointing?"

Ed looked, but all he could see was the back end of the Plymouth and just the tops of two blond heads in the backseat.

"Well," he said, shading his eyes, "you got me there."

"Oh, you never look when I tell you. I know who they were. They were that schoolteacher's kids, that . . . uh . . . what's his name . . ."

Irene Bledsoe sped along the Toe Springs–Claytonville Road, wearing a scowl that added at least a decade to her already crinkled face. She kept her fists tightly around the wheel and her foot on the gas pedal, spurring the green Plymouth onward whether Ruth and Josiah Harris liked it or not.

"You two be quiet now!" she yelled over her shoulder. "Believe me, we're doing this for your own good!"

Bledsoe's words brought no comfort to Ruth, six, and Josiah, nine.

Ruth kept crying, "I want my Daddy!"

Josiah could only sit there silently, numb with shock and disbelief.

Bledsoe hit the throttle hard. She just wanted to get out of town before there was any more trouble, any more attention.

She was not enjoying this assignment. "The things I do for those people!"

Sally stepped out onto the back porch, still trembling, looking warily about. She'd changed her shirt and donned a blue jacket. She gripped her wadded-up, bloodstained plaid shirt in one hand, and a paper towel dipped in cooking oil in the other.

It was quiet all around, as if nothing had happened. Her old blue pickup was waiting. But there was still one more thing to do.

She looked toward the goat pen, its gate swung wide open and the goats long gone. She took some deep breaths to keep the nausea from coming back. She had to go into that little shed once more. She just had to.

It didn't take long. With her heart racing, her hands now empty, and her pockets stuffed, she got out of there and ran for the truck, clambering inside. It cranked and groaned and started up, and with a surge of power and a spraying of gravel it rumbled down the long driveway toward the road.

Irene Bledsoe was speeding, but there were no cops around. The speed limits were inappropriate anyway, just really impractical.

She was coming to a four-way stop, another stupid idea clear out here in the middle of nowhere. She eased back on the throttle and figured she could just sneak through.

What! Where did—?

She hit the brakes, the wheels locked, the tires screamed,

5

the car fishtailed. Some idiot in a blue pickup swerved wildly through the intersection trying to avoid her.

Little Ruth wasn't belted in; she smacked her head and started screaming.

The Plymouth skidded to a stop almost facing the way it had come.

"Be quiet!" Bledsoe shouted at the little girl. "You be quiet now—you're all right!"

Now Josiah was crying too, scared to death. He wasn't belted in either, and had had quite a tumbling back there.

"You two kids shut up!" Bledsoe screamed. "Just shut up now!"

Josiah could see a lady get out of the pickup. She had red hair and a checkered scarf on her head; she looked like she was about to cry, and she was holding her shoulder. Bledsoe stuck her head out the window and screamed a string of profanity at her. The lady didn't say a thing, but Bledsoe must have scared her. The other driver got back in her truck and drove off without saying a word.

"The idiot!" said Bledsoe. "Didn't she see me?"

"But you didn't stop," said Josiah.

"Don't you tell me how to drive, young man! And why isn't your seat belt fastened?"

Ruth was still screaming, holding her head. When she saw blood on her hand, she went hysterical.

When Bledsoe saw that, she said, "Oh, great! Oh, that's just terrific!"

Cecilia Potter, Fred's wife, was glad that one of those fool goats wore a bell. At least she was able to hear something and run out into the yard before they ate up all her flowers.

The two kids bolted and ran back toward the rental home. As for the doe, she thought she owned anything that grew, and she wasn't timid about it.

"You, GIT!" Cecilia shouted, waving her strong arms. "Get out of those flowers!"

The doe backed off just a little, but then lowered her head, giving Cecilia a good look at her horns.

"Oooh, you're really scary!" said Cecilia. She ran right up, clamped an angry fist around the doe's collar, and lifted the doe's front legs off the ground in turning her around.

"You're going back where you came from, and right now, and don't you think you can scare me!" *WAP!* "And you lower those horns right now!"

The doe went with Cecilia, mostly on four legs, but on two if she even dared to hesitate, and got more than two earfuls of sermonizing on the way.

"I don't know how you got out, but if you think you're going to run rampant around here, you've got another think coming! Sally's going to hear about this! She knows better! I'm really surprised . . ."

She crossed the field between the two houses and then saw the goat pen, its gate wide open.

"Sally!" she called.

There was no answer. Hmm. The truck was gone. Maybe Sally wasn't home yet. Well, she was late then. She always came home from work before this. But how did that gate get open?

She dragged the doe alongside her and through the gate.

"Back where you belong, old girl. No more of this free and easy stuff—"

Well . . . who was that in the shed?

"Sally?"

The doe, suddenly free, walked out through the still-open gate. Cecilia didn't follow it.

She was looking at the body of a woman, thrown down in the straw like a discarded doll, limp and white.

She was dead.

Nathan, Armoth, and the other warriors made a low, slow pass over the farmhouse and saw a distraught Cecilia running from the goat pen. Nathan gave the others a signal, and with an explosive surge of their wings they shot forward, etching the evening sky with streaks of light.

The fields below them passed by with the swiftness of a thought, and then the green canopy of the forest swallowed them up, the leaves and branches whipping by, over, around, and through them. They rushed through shadows and shafts of fading light, through tall trunks and thick, entangling limbs, and finally reached the clearing where the captain was waiting.

With wings snapping full like opening parachutes, they came to a halt and settled to the forest floor with the silence of snowflakes. The moment their feet touched down, the lightning glimmer of their tunics faded to a dull white, their fiery swords cooled to copper, and their wings folded and vanished.

Tal, the mighty, golden-haired Captain of the Host, was waiting, his fiery eyes burning with expectation, his face tight with the tension of the moment. Beside him stood Guilo, the Strength of Many, a dark, bearded, massive spirit with thick, powerful arms and a heart yearning for a fight. They were dressed in dull white as well, and wore formidable swords at their sides.

Nathan called his report even as Tal and Guilo were stepping forward to greet them. "All the demons were routed except for Despair."

"Good enough," said Tal. "Let him carry word back to his comrades and then continue his work. Any other spirits from Broken Birch involved in this?"

"Several. Formidable, but defeated for now. We didn't see Destroyer anywhere. He sent his lackeys and stayed out of it himself."

"Of course. Now what of Sally?"

"Sally Roe is fleeing. Her truck is several miles down the road, heading south toward Claytonville. We sent Chimon and Scion to follow her."

"The assassin?" asked Tal.

"Slain, by our hand. We had no choice. Sally was close to death."

Guilo rumbled his approval of the action.

"How is Sally now?" Tal asked.

Armoth reported, "A minor throat injury, a welt on her

neck, a shallow knife wound in the shoulder. No immediate physical danger."

Tal sighed just a little. "No, not immediate anyway. What about the near-collision with Irene Bledsoe?"

Nathan and Armoth looked toward Signa, and the lithe Oriental smiled. "Successful, but by a hair. Ruth Harris suffered a small injury on her forehead, but Sally was clearly seen by everyone in the car, and she saw them just as clearly."

Armoth picked up from there. "And now Mrs. Potter has found the assassin, and she is calling the police."

Tal had to take a moment just to shake his head at the immensity of it all. "Just that is news enough."

Guilo expressed his anxiety with a gravelly chuckle. "Captain, we have never before hoped for so many things to go right . . . that can go so wrong!"

Tal looked toward Heaven and smiled a cautious smile. "We can hope for them all to go right as long as the saints are praying, and they are."

There was a mutter of agreement from all of them. They could feel it.

"So," Tal continued, "if all goes well, this time *we* advance, *we* conquer, *we* set the enemy back . . . *We* purchase just one more season of restraint."

"One more season," they all echoed.

"Sally should arrive in Claytonville safely enough with Chimon and Scion as escorts. The demon Terga has much to answer for now; I expect he'll send some spirits after her to tear her down. Even so, Chimon and Scion have orders not to intervene unless absolutely necessary."

"*More* pain, captain? *More* destruction?" Guilo blurted in anger. "One would think these wretched spirits can never inflict enough suffering!"

Tal looked into those dark eyes, so full of the fire of battle, and yet so tender toward God's elect. "Good friend, we all hurt for her. But her suffering will bring about God's purpose, and you will see it."

"May it come soon," Guilo said, gripping the handle of his

sword. He looked at Nathan and prompted sarcastically, "I'm sure you have more joyful news?"

"Yes," said Nathan. "Of Tom Harris. He is at the police station now, trying to do something to get his children back, trying to reason with Sergeant Mulligan."

At the mention of Mulligan's name, Guilo laughed a roaring, spiteful laugh, and the others made a distasteful face. Nathan only nodded with resignation. They were right.

"So now comes the testing of Tom's faith, a real trying of his commitment," said Tal.

"*I'll* be watching the saints," said Guilo. "I'll see how they handle this one."

Tal touched Guilo's shoulder. "This will be one of those things we hope will go right."

"Oh, may it go right, may it go right."

"For Tom's sake," said Nathan.

"For *everyone's* sake," said Armoth.

"Which brings us to Ben Cole," Tal prompted.

Nathan responded, "He's about to walk into it right now."

two

officer Ben Cole pulled the squad car into the lot behind the precinct and sat behind the wheel for a moment after the engine was still. It had been a long day, and he was tired. Bacon's Corner didn't have that much heavy action, but today was a little more trying. The trucker he'd stopped for speeding was twice his size and didn't like being one-upped by such a young officer, much less one who was black; Bill Schultz still hadn't contained that dog of his, and now someone else had been bitten; he'd caught the Krantz boy with some pot again, and his parents still wouldn't believe it.

That was the rub with police work—you always had to see the bad side of people, when they were angry, defensive, self-righteous, drunk, drugged . . . *Oh, let it go, Ben. The day's over. There are some good people in the world, really. You just need to get home, have some supper, see Bev. Yeah, that'll make it all right.*

He got out of the car; he was going to write up some quick reports and get home so . . . *Now whose cars are these?* Two strange cars were sitting in the reserved parking spaces, and wasn't that Tom Harris's little station wagon? The office was closed by now; it was too late for visitors. He'd better check it out once he got inside.

He went in the back door and started down the long hall-way that connected the rear offices and cell block to the front office area.

Oh brother, now who's Mulligan hollering at?

He could hear Sergeant Mulligan's voice from clear down the hall, booming through the open door of his office. "So all right, you don't have to tell me anything! Go ahead and lie! You guys always lie, and I'll be happy to listen to that so I can use it against you!"

"Sir, I'm not lying . . ."

Ben stopped in the hall to listen. That other voice sounded familiar.

"So let's have the truth, huh?" said Mulligan. "You've been having yourself a real party with those little kids, haven't you?"

"Sir, *again*, there is nothing going on at the school, or at my home, or anywhere! This whole thing is a terrible mistake!"

Yeah, that *was* Tom Harris's car out there, and this was Tom getting outtalked by the sergeant.

Ben had to look. This conversation was sounding worse all the time. *Lord, please don't let it be what it sounds like. I was just feeling better thinking about the good people in the world.*

He went down the bare hallway to Mulligan's door, and stuck his head in.

"I'm back, Harold." *No big deal, I'm just reporting in, nice and businesslike, just finding out what's going on.*

Ben stood there frozen, looking at the shaken, upset man sitting across the dented, green, metal desk from big Sergeant Mulligan.

Mulligan was in his overweight, ugly glory, and really enjoying this. He always got his kicks from all the wrong things. "Hey, Cole, look what I caught today! Another Christian! I'll bet you two know each other!"

Ben looked confused. "Hey, Tom. What gives?"

"Child abuse!" interrupted Mulligan, proud of the fact, proud of his catch. "Got a real case brewing here."

"Then you know far more about this than *I* do!" Tom said. He looked up at Ben with tear-reddened eyes. "The sergeant here just . . . just *stood* there while some welfare lady came and took away Ruth and Josiah, just dragged them from the house, and . . ." Tom's voice rose in fear and anger. "I want to know where they are."

Mulligan remained as hard as nails and sneered at Ben. "Wait'll you hear what this creep's been doing with some kids at the Christian school."

Tom rose from his seat. "I haven't been doing *anything!* Can't you get that straight?"

"You sit down, buddy!" Mulligan easily outweighed Tom and made every effort to show it.

Ben's heart twisted in his chest. The Christian school? Bacon's Corner only had one—the Good Shepherd Academy, a little first-through-sixth-grade ministry run by—

"I'd say your church is in big trouble!" Mulligan told Ben.

Ben looked down at Tom Harris, one of the gentlest, most godly men he'd ever met. Tom was in his thirties, with dark curly hair and a young face. Ben knew the guy was more than just honest—he was downright vulnerable. *No way, man. Tom Harris didn't do anything.*

"Tom," Ben said gently, "are you aware of your rights?"

"He's not under arrest!" Mulligan snapped. "He came here himself!"

"And I'm not leaving until I get some cooperation!" said Tom.

"Hey, don't come after me," said Mulligan. "The state people have to check this all out."

"So let's call them!" said Ben.

"You get out of this, Cole! You two are friends and everybody knows it. You're not coming anywhere near this case!"

Tom demanded in slow, enunciated words, "I want to see my children!"

"You're talking to the wrong man."

Tom pointed his finger. "You were right there! You abused your authority and let this . . . this Bledsoe woman march right into my house like some kind of . . . gestapo raid! She terrorized my children and invaded my privacy right under your nose!"

Mulligan remained straight and tall in his chair and said firmly and simply, "You watch it, Harris. Ms. Bledsoe had a bona fide court order to pick up your kids in response to a complaint filed against you!"

Tom was flabbergasted. *"What* complaint?"

"I don't know. Ask Bledsoe. That's her department."

"Then you must know how to contact her."

"I'll find out," said Ben.

"Isn't your shift over?" Mulligan roared.

"Yes, sir."

"Then get out of here!"

Ben had to obey. He told Tom, "Give me a call," and turned to leave.

Just then the police radio came to life. The sound of it always froze time in the station as everyone stopped to hear the message. "Bacon's Corner, Bacon's Corner, possible DOA at Fred Potter farm, 12947 197th SW. Aid crew is en route."

Mulligan jumped from his chair, making it rumble backward and smack against the wall. "Where's Leonard—is he here yet?" Then the phone rang. "Nuts! When it rains it pours. Get that!"

Ben hurried to the front desk.

A man and a woman were sitting in the reception area. Ben recognized the man: John Ziegler, reporter for the *Hampton County Star*; he worked the local police beat and hung around the station a lot. The lady was obviously a photographer. Ziegler had a notepad handy, and was apparently scribbling down everything he heard!

The phone rang again.

Ben kept staring at the news-hounds while he grabbed the phone. "Police Department." The voice on the other end was frantic. "Slow down, ma'am, please. I can't understand you." It was Cecilia Potter. She'd already called 911; now she wanted to make sure the police were coming.

Ben knew where their farm was. "We just got the call on the radio. We'll be right there." So much for going home.

The back door opened.

"Here's Leonard now," Ben reported.

Officer Leonard Jackson was reporting in for the night shift. He was a calm, thin, easy-paced sort of guy in his forties, almost a permanent fixture around the place. Mulligan nearly ran over him bursting out of his office.

"Let's move it, Leonard! There's a suicide down at the Potter place!"

"The Potter place?" Leonard had trouble imagining either of the Potters doing such a thing.

Ben was quite unsettled about an additional matter. "What about John Ziegler out there?"

Mulligan looked at the reporters and started cursing, looking this way and that. "Harris! Get out here!"

Tom stepped out of the office, trying to be cooperative.

Mulligan shoved him forward toward the front office. "Have a seat with those nice people—they want to talk to you! Leonard, we'll take your squad car."

Tom looked at Ben for help. "They were at my house today when that lady took the kids. They took pictures of it!"

Ben could feel his temper rising. "Tom, you don't have to say anything to them. Just go right on by them and go home!"

Mulligan must have seen something he didn't like. "Cole, you're coming too!"

Leonard was ready to roll. Mulligan grabbed his hat and jacket. The reporters were on their feet and coming toward Tom.

Ben asked, "Is Tom free to leave?"

Mulligan rolled his eyes at such a question. "Cole, he came in here on his own two feet—he can go out the same way. Hear that, Harris?"

Ben said quietly, "Tom, just get out of here. You don't have to talk to anyone."

Mulligan growled at him, "Are you about ready, Cole? C'mon, let's move!"

Ben didn't like this one bit, but orders were orders. He headed for the back door again.

Mulligan tipped his hat to John Ziegler and the camera lady. "Just make yourselves comfortable. We'll be back in about an hour, and I'll have a statement for you."

Ben told Tom, "I'll call you," then followed Mulligan and Leonard.

Mulligan muttered over his shoulder as they went out to the cars, "I'm not leaving you in there with that Christian buddy of yours, no way. If you're gonna be on duty, you're gonna work, and you're gonna do what I tell you and no static. We don't need you two fanatics having some powwow in there, no sir!"

Tom went back into Mulligan's office for his jacket and then stepped into the hall again.

John Ziegler was standing right in front of him, blocking his path.

"Excuse me," Tom said, trying to get around.

John was insistent on having a conversation.

"John Ziegler, with the *Hampton County Star*—"

"Yes, I saw you at my house," said Tom curtly.

Ziegler asked, "Mr. Harris, what is your response to these allegations?"

"*What* allegations? I don't even know why this is happening to me!"

"Do you think this will hurt the Christian school?"

"I don't know."

"Do you deny any abuse of children in the Christian school?"

That question stopped Tom cold. He was troubled by it.

Ziegler picked up on that. "You do deny the allegations?"

Tom found his voice for that one. "I don't know of any allegations."

Ziegler scribbled it down.

"Has there been any reaction from your family?"

"Besides the fact that my children were terrified?"

The woman began clicking a camera at him.

"Hey, come on, now . . ."

The camera kept clicking.

Ziegler raised an eyebrow. "I understand you're a widower. So you live at home alone with your children?"

Tom was indignant. "That's it! I'm leaving. Good night."

Ziegler threw questions at Tom's back as they followed right behind him toward the front door. "Is the state considering your children as possible victims as well?"

Tom jerked the door open and glared at them for a moment.

The camera caught his angry expression.

Ziegler was satisfied. "Thank you very much, Mr. Harris."

Just across the street, Despair sat on the roof of the Bacon's Corner Library and Gift Shop, a forlorn beanbag of melancholy filth, whimpering over his wounds and watching the two squad cars speed away.

"Oh, there they go, there they go. What now?"

Several other dark spirits were with him, staying low, muttering, hissing, slobbering in agitation. They were a motley band of tempters, harassers, and deceivers, suddenly half as strong, half as numerous, and full of anguish over the recent, terrible defeat of their comrades.

Despair was living up to his name. "Lost, lost, lost, all is lost! Our best are gone, all vanquished but for me!"

A sharp slap bounced his round head against his shoulder. "Stop that whimpering! You make me ill!"

"Terga, my prince, you were not there!"

Terga, the Prince of Bacon's Corner, resembled a slimy toad with a fright wig of black wire and two rolling, yellow eyes. He was indignant, and kept scratching his gnarled head purely from an itch of frustration. "Failure, that's what it was. An abominable display of ineptitude!"

Murder was quick to object. "Had the mission succeeded, no doubt you would have been the first to praise it!"

"It did not, and I do not!"

Deception tried to objectively assess the debacle. "Our forces were strong, and I'm sure they fought valiantly, but . . . the prayers of the saints are stronger. The Host of Heaven are stronger. They were waiting for our warriors, and they were ready. We severely underestimated their numbers and their power. It's quite simple."

Terga spun around and glared at Deception, hating his words, but knowing the astute demon was quite correct. He paced, he fidgeted, he struggled to comprehend what was happening. "We have moved against Tom Harris and the school! The Plan of the Strongman is unfolding at this very moment. It is underway, right now! But here you are, lamenting a rout and telling me that the Plan could be marching headlong toward destruction, and all because of this . . . this . . . *woman?*"

Deception thought about the question, and then nodded. "That would be a fair assessment."

Terga rolled his eyes toward the sky and wailed his fear and frustration. "Destroyer will have all our hides for this! Those who did not fall in this rout will certainly fall under *his* sword!" He counted the demons around him and came up shorter than he wanted. "Where is Hatred?"

"Gone," they all answered. "One of the first to fall."

"And Violence?"

"In chains in the Abyss, I imagine," said Deception.

"Greed? Lust? Rape?"

He only got forlorn stares. He looked out over the town, and his head just kept twitching from side to side. He could not fathom what had happened. "Such an easy task . . . a simple little murder . . . We've all done it before . . ."

Despair moaned, "When the Strongman finds out . . ."

WAP! Terga bounced Despair's head off his other shoulder.

"He must know!" said Divination.

"Then tell him!" said Terga. "Go yourself!"

Divination fell silent, hoping some other demon would speak up.

Terga snatched a fistful of Despair's baggy hide and held him up like a trophy. "Our envoy!"

They began to cheer, their talons clicking their applause.

"No . . . not the Strongman!" Despair whined. "Is not one thrashing enough?"

"Go now," said Terga, "or the Strongman's will be your *third* today!"

Despair fluttered crazily into the air. One wing was still battered and bent.

"Go!" said Terga. "And be quick about it!" Despair hurried away, whining and wailing as he went. "And when you're through with that, go back to the woman and continue your duty as you should!"

Some snickers caused Terga to spin around. A few small spirits cowered, looking up at him—they'd been caught.

"Ah," said Terga, and they could see the slime on the roof of his mouth. "Fear, Death, and Insanity, three of the woman's favorite pets! You look rather idle at the moment."

The three demons looked at each other stupidly.

"Back to your posts! Follow the woman!"

They fluttered into the air like frightened pigeons, clawing after altitude.

Terga wasn't satisfied. He slapped several more demons with his wings. "You too! All of you! Find her! Torture her! Terrorize her! Do you want Destroyer to think you are the worthless lumps you are? Correct your blunder! Destroy the woman!"

The air was filled with roaring, fluttering wings. Terga covered his head to keep from getting clouted with a wild wingtip. In only moments, they were gone. Terga looked down the street, down the road that would take the squad cars to Potter's farm.

"Our sergeant isn't going to find what he expected," he muttered.

three

It was getting dark when the two squad cars rumbled down the gravel driveway to the Potters' house. The aid car was already there, its doors flung open, its lights flashing. Fred and Cecilia were out on the wide front porch waiting for the police, holding each other close. They were strong, rugged people, but tonight they were obviously shaken.

Mulligan locked the wheels and slid to an impressive, slightly side-skidding halt in the loose gravel, then bolted from the car in time to emerge like a god from the cloud of dust he'd stirred up. Leonard waited for the dust to blow by before getting out—he didn't want it all over the seat when he got back in the car.

Ben pulled to a careful stop behind the first car and got out in calm, businesslike fashion. He was being overcautious, aware that his emotions were on a thin edge.

Mulligan was already talking with one of the paramedics, getting the lowdown. The paramedic had just come from a little farmhouse across the field. Ben could see two more flashlights sweeping about in the darkness over there. Apart from that, there were no lights.

"Deceased," said the paramedic. "Dead at least an hour."

"Okay," said Mulligan, clicking on his big silver flashlight, "let's go."

He headed into the field, swishing through the wild grass with long, powerful strides, his nightstick swinging from his hip, his belly bouncing on his buckle. Leonard and Ben followed close behind.

"It's that Roe woman," said Mulligan. "Sally Roe. You know anything about her?"

Leonard assumed the question was directed to him. "Very little, Harold."

"I think she's one of those weird types, some kind of left-over hippie, a loser. Guess she decided to end it all."

Ben was probing his brain as they continued toward the dark farmhouse. Sally Roe. The name didn't register.

"All right," said Mulligan. "There's the goat pen. Spread out a bit, you guys. No hiding behind me."

They came out of the field, crossed an unused, heavily weeded roadway, and came to the goat pen. The fence was crude and aged, made of rusted wire nailed to split rail posts, with a creaking gate hanging crookedly on one good hinge and one loose one. The gate was still open; all the goats were now corralled over at the Potters'. Two emergency medical technicians were standing outside the pen, putting away their gear.

"She's all yours," said one.

Ben glanced around the pen, shining his light here and there, just checking for anything unusual, not wanting to disturb it. His eye caught a spilled pail of goat feed near the door of the goat shed.

"Hey, check that out," he said, pointing with his light.

Mulligan ignored him and charged right across the goat pen and into the weathered, tin-roofed shed, leaving a big manured footprint in the middle of the spilled feed. Then he stopped short. He'd found something. Leonard and Ben came up behind him and looked in through the doorway.

There she was. The dead woman. Ben couldn't see her face; Mulligan was in the way. But she was dressed all in black, and lay on her back in the straw, her body and limbs twisted and limp as if someone had wadded her up and thrown her there.

Ben shined his light around the inside of the shed. The beam fell on a plaid shirt next to the body. Apparently Mulligan hadn't seen it. He reached in and picked it up. It was stained with blood.

"Hey, Harold, look at this."

Mulligan spun around as if rudely surprised. "Cole! Get back to the Potters and get a statement from them!"

"Yes, sir. But take a look at this."

Mulligan didn't take it—he grabbed it. "Go on, get over there. We can handle things at this end."

Leonard was shining his light at the woman's face and Ben

caught his first glimpse of it. She was young and beautiful, but dead—violently dead. The expression on the face was blank, the eyes dry and staring, the shoulder-length black hair a tangled shadow upon the straw.

Ben didn't know he was staring until Mulligan hollered at him.

"Cole! Have you seen enough? Get moving!"

Ben got out of there, and hurried back across the field to the Potters' house. His mind was racing. This was going to be a bigger case than they'd thought. The appearance of that body, the bloodied shirt, the spilled feed, the obvious violence . . .

This was no suicide.

The aid crew drove away in the aid car, their work completed. Ben put on a calm demeanor as he went up the porch steps. The Potters heard him coming and immediately came to the door.

"Hi. I'm Officer Ben Cole."

Ben extended his hand, and Fred took it.

Fred stared at Ben just a little. "Have we met before?"

"No, sir. I'm new in Bacon's Corner. I've been here about four months."

"Oh . . . well, welcome to the neighborhood. Things aren't usually this exciting around here."

"Of course, sir. Uh, with your permission, I'd like to get a statement."

Cecilia opened the door. "Please come in . . . Ben, was it?"

"Yes, ma'am. Thank you."

Fred and Cecilia took their place on the couch and offered Ben a chair facing them. He took out his notepad.

"How are you doing?" he asked.

"Oh . . . fair," said Fred.

Cecilia just shook her head. "Poor Sally." Tears returned to her eyes. "This is just awful. It's terrifying."

Ben spoke gently. "I . . . understand it was you who first found her?"

She nodded.

"Did you touch her or move her in any way?"

Cecilia was repelled by the very thought. "No. I didn't go near her. I didn't even look at her face."

"About what time was this?"

"About 6."

Ben jotted these items down. "Now, why don't you just tell me everything that happened?"

She started telling him about the goats being out, and about the nanny goat trying to butt her, and then tried to remember what she did to get that goat back to the pen, and then a strong opinion took precedent over her narrative and she blurted, "I think somebody killed her!"

Fred was shocked at that, of course. "What? What gives you that idea?"

Ben had to get control of this. "Uh . . . we'll work on that when the time comes. But for now you need to tell me what you saw . . . just what you saw."

She told him, and it wasn't much different from what he himself had seen. "I didn't want to see her that way. I just didn't stay there."

"Okay. Can you tell me the victim's full name?"

"Sally Roe. She was such a quiet sort," Cecilia said, her face full of grief and puzzlement. "She never said much, just kept to herself. We enjoyed having her for a renter. She was clean, responsible, we never had any trouble from her. Why would anyone want to hurt her?"

"So you can't think of anyone who might . . . have some kind of grievance or grudge against her?"

"No. She was a very private sort. I don't remember ever seeing her having company or visitors."

"Can you think of anything else that may have seemed out of the ordinary?"

"Did you see the feed spilled on the ground?"

"Yes, ma'am."

"Someone may have jumped out and grabbed her."

"Uh-huh. Anything else?"

"I saw a long piece of rope in her hand. Maybe it was to tie the goats, I don't know."

Ben noted it.

There were loud footsteps on the porch. It was Sergeant Mulligan. He let himself in, and removed his hat.

"Well, folks, it's been quite an evening. We've seen a real tragedy here. Got their statement, Cole?"

Ben rose and looked over his notes. "Just what Mrs. Potter saw initially. I suppose—"

Mulligan took the notes from Ben's hand and looked them over.

Ben finished his thought. "I suppose once we check the house and comb the area we'll have more to go on."

Mulligan didn't seem to hear him. "Umm. Okay, I'll get these typed into the report." He pocketed Ben's notes and told the Potters, "Guess she hung herself from the rafters of the shed, who knows why."

"Hung herself?" said Cecilia in surprise.

"How about any suicide notes? Did you find anything like that around?"

Cecilia was still taken aback. "No . . . no, I—"

"Well, we'll be checking the scene over tonight and maybe we'll find something." He headed out the door again. "Cole, go ahead and call it a day. Leonard and I will check the area over and wait for the coroner."

"You say it was a *suicide?*" Ben asked, following him out the door.

"Cut and dried," said Mulligan.

"Well . . . maybe."

Mulligan got impatient with that kind of response. "What do you mean, 'maybe'?"

"Well, you saw what it looked like in there . . ."

"Yeah, I saw it all, and you didn't."

"But Mrs. Potter did. The body wasn't hanging when she found it. It was lying in the straw just like when we first saw it."

Mulligan turned back toward the rental. "Go on home, Cole. Don't worry about things that aren't your responsibility."

Mulligan headed across the field, cutting the conversation short. Ben went back to his car and sat in it with the door open, flipping through his notepad. He clicked his pen and started scribbling some notes to himself, things he wanted to remember: "plaid shirt with blood . . . position of body suggests violence . . . spilled feed . . . rope in hand, not around neck . . . victim not hung . . ."

Just outside Claytonville, Sally turned off the highway onto an obscure, overgrown and rutted road that meandered deep into the forest, winding around trees and stumps, passing under low limbs, dipping into black mudholes, and making the old pickup buck and rock with every new pothole, rut, bump, and turn. This road—or maybe it was a trail—had probably been used by surveyors and developers, but now was kept in existence only by kids on dirt bikes and perhaps an equestrian or two. Maybe somewhere back in here she could find a good spot to abandon the truck.

She finally found what looked like a turnaround or dead end, a short section of once-cleared area the dirt bikers hadn't found yet, quickly being reclaimed by the thick brush. She cranked the wheel hard and let the pickup push its way forward, plowing through the brush and flattening the weeds that rose in front of the headlights.

Far enough. She turned off the lights and shut down the engine.

And then she sat there, her elbows on the wheel and her head in her hands. She had to hold still for just a minute. She had to think, to assess the situation, to sort out thought from feeling. She didn't move for a minute, and then another, and then another. The only sound was her own breathing—she was conscious of every breath—and the steadily slowing *tink, tink, tink* of the engine cooling. It occurred to her how still it was out in these woods, and how dark it was, and especially how lonely it was. She was alone in the darkness, and no one knew.

How poetic, she thought. *How appropriate.*

But to the business at hand: *How about it, Sally? Do you keep going or do you give up? You can always call them, or send them a letter, and just let them know where you are so they can come and*

*finish the job. At least then it will all be over and you won't have to
wait so long to die.*

She drew a long, tired breath and leaned back from the
steering wheel. *Such thoughts, Sally, such thoughts!*

No, she finally admitted to herself, *no—I want to live. I
don't know why, but I do. I don't know how much longer, but I
will. And that's all I know for now.*

*That's all I know. But I wish I knew more. I wish I knew how
they found me . . . and why they want to kill me.*

She clicked on the dome light—it would only be for a
second—and reached into her jacket pocket for a small
object. It was a ring, ornate, probably pure gold. She took a
close and careful look at it, turning it over and over in her
fingers, trying to make out the strange design on its face. It
made no sense to her, try as she might to understand what it
could mean. For now, she only knew one thing for sure about
this ring—she'd seen it before, and the memories were her
worst.

She clicked off the dome light. Enough sitting. She put the
ring back in her pocket, took the keys from the ignition, and
opened the door. In this deep, surrounding quiet, the dry,
dirty hinges seemed to scream instead of groan. The sound
frightened her.

The dome light came on again, but then winked out as she
closed the door as quietly as possible, which still amounted
to a pretty loud slam. Now the only light in the middle of
that thick, forlorn forest was gone. She could hardly see, but
she was determined to get out of these woods even if she had
to feel her way out. She had to get moving, get someplace
safe. She pressed on, fighting the brush as it pulled at her legs,
scratched her with its thorns, jabbed at her out of the dark.
Somewhere ahead was that old roadway where the ground
was still bare and walkable. She only had to find it.

Underneath a fallen log, deep down in a dark and rotted
pocket, two yellow eyes were watching her, two taloned
hands curled in hate. The thing let out a little snicker as she
stumbled past.

In the low, overhanging branch of a tree, another spirit

crouched like a grotesque owl, its black wings hanging at its
sides like long, drooping curtains, its head not more than a
knob above its shoulders. The yellow eyes were following her
every move.

They were out to do Terga's wishes; they hoped to appease
Destroyer.

She made it to the old roadway; she could feel firm, bare
ground under her feet and discern just a little more light
ahead of her. She quickened her pace. She was starting to feel
like a little girl again, afraid of the dark, afraid of unseen
horrors, longing for some light to drive all the spooks away.

Two black shapes hovering just above the roadway waited
for her to pass beneath them. They drifted in little back-and-
forth patterns, floating on unfurled, shadowy wings, their
long, spindly legs and arms hanging down like spiders' legs,
each tipped with long, clawed talons that flexed and curled
with anticipation.

Sally stopped. Did the roadway turn here? *Come on, girl,
don't get lost. That's all you need.*

Three more spirits, some of Terga's worst, sailed down
through the trees like vultures gathering for a feast. They came
in behind her, slobbering and cackling, jostling each other to
get closer.

Sally thought she saw the roadway again, heading off to
her left. She tried that direction. Yes, she'd found it. But her
legs were getting weak. Her heart was beating against her ribs
like it wanted out. *No, please, not again, no more . . .*

But it was fear, all right, the old-fashioned kind—the kind
she'd lived with for years. Just when she thought she'd gotten
rid of it, escaped from it, forgotten it, here it was, back again,
as fierce as ever, digging into her, scrambling her thoughts,
making her tremble, sweat, stumble.

Her old friends were back.

She passed under the two hovering demons.

"YAAAK!" they screamed, enveloping her with sulfur.

The spirits following behind slapped through her soul with
their black wings.

OOF! She pitched forward into the dirt, a muffled cry in

her throat. She struggled to get her legs under her again, to get moving again. Where was that road?

The spirits alighted on her back and dug their talons in deep.

She covered her mouth tightly with her hands, trying to keep a cry inside, trying to keep quiet. She couldn't get her balance. Something was after her. She had to get away. She was still trying to get up.

The demons gave her a stab and a kick, cackling and shrieking with delight, and then they let her go.

She was on her feet again. She could see the roadway and she ran, her arms in front of her face to block the forest limbs that slapped and grabbed her. She could hear some traffic out on the highway. How much further?

The dark spirits fluttered and flapped after her, chattering and spitting. It was a wonderful, cruel game.

But warriors were watching. Deep within the texture of the forest, here and there within the trees, the logs, the thick brush, there were deep golden eyes watching it all, and strong arms upon ready swords.

The Good Shepherd Community Church had a prayer chain, a simple system for spreading prayer requests throughout the church via the telephone. Every participant had a list of all the other participants and their phone numbers. When you needed prayer for something, you called the next person on the list after yourself, who then called the next person on the list, who then called the next person, and so on. The whole church could be praying for a request in just a matter of hours any day of the week.

Tom's request for prayer set the lines buzzing with the news about Ruth and Josiah, and with each phone call, more saints started praying. At the top of the list was Donna Hemphile, a supervisor at the Bergen Door Company; next on the list was the Waring family, then the Jessups, followed by Lester Sutter and his wife Dolly, then the Farmers, then the Ryans, then the widow Alice Buckmeier, then the elders on the church board—Jack Parmenter and his son Doug, Bob

Heely, and Vic Savan. On down the list it went until all the numbers were called.

That started a flurry of prayer, of course, but also a flurry of phone calls back to Tom to find out more. To his great sorrow, he had nothing more he could tell them; and to his frustration, a lot of the information being passed through the chain was wrong.

He tried to call the Child Protection Department, but they were closed.

He tried to find Irene Bledsoe's home phone number; it was unlisted.

He tried the office of the State Ombudsman. The lady there told him to call the CPD or try the Department of Social and Health Services.

He called the DSHS and they told him to contact the CPD in the morning. They had no number for Irene Bledsoe, but weren't free to give out numbers anyway.

Pastor Mark Howard and his wife Cathy were out of town. but would be back sometime tomorrow.

Ben Cole made good on his promise and called, but by now there was nothing that could be done until morning.

After one last call to a state representative who didn't answer, Tom dropped the receiver into its cradle and hid his face in his hands. He had to stop, to breathe, to calm himself. It couldn't be as horrible as it seemed. Somehow, sometime, somewhere he had to find Ruth and Josiah. It just couldn't be this difficult.

The silence, the emptiness of his little house was so odd, almost taunting. Right now he should have been tucking Ruth and Josiah in for the night. But he was alone, and so tired.

"Lord God," he prayed, "Lord God, please protect my children. Bring them back to me. Please end this nightmare!"

Wednesday morning.

The Bacon's Corner Elementary School reeked of demons. As Nathan and Armoth flew high above, they could feel them, sense them, often see them, buzzing and swirling in and out of that brand-new brick and concrete structure the community was so proud of. The playground was full of kids, about two hundred, running, playing, and squealing before the first bell signaled the start of classes. Then they would gather in all those classrooms where the spirits would be busy, more than ever before.

The two warriors passed over the school, continued on for another mile, then banked sharply and sideslipped toward the earth, dropping like stones, twisting slowly about until they were facing the way they had come. Then, easing back their speed, they skimmed across the fields of hay and young corn, across some gravel access roads, right through some sprinklers, and finally came to an old chicken house on a farm next to the school.

Their wings snapped like parachutes, and they went through the old clapboard walls of the chicken house feet first. Inside, a cackling chorus of eight hundred leghorns carried on, pecking at feed, rolling out eggs, oblivious to their presence.

They hurried toward one end of the long house, moving through floating white feathers, fine brown dust, and chickens, chickens everywhere.

Tal stood at a window, looking toward the school.

Armoth quipped, "One might ask why you chose this place."

"For the view," said Tal. Then he looked toward the school again. "They have quite a project going over there, well established."

"The saints are buzzing with the news about Tom's children. They are praying," said Nathan.

"And the Lord is responding, so we're well covered so far. But the real attack is still coming this morning. Place a guard around Tom. It's going to be hard enough for him; I don't want any extra harassments against him while he's down."

"Done."

"Where is Sally now?"

"She made it to Claytonville, and she has a motel room.

31

Chimon and Scion are watching, but Terga's spirits are tormenting her, hoping to regain Destroyer's favor."

Tal bristled at that. "What spirits?"

Armoth had a mental list. "Fear, Death, Insanity. They and some others tormented her last night, and they've followed her today as well, trying to break her spirit."

"What about Despair?"

"Terga sent him to inform the Strongman."

Tal was amused. "How bold of him." He looked toward the school again. "I want Signa and Mota to clear a path into that school, do some screening, some diversions. We'll need to get in and out of there without the whole demonic network finding out about it. As for Cree and Si, they'll need to do the same thing at Omega, which means they'll need twice the warriors just to get Sally in and out of there with her life."

Armoth drew a deep, long breath. "A touchy business, captain."

"And getting touchier with each move we make. What about the room at the Schrader Motor Inn in Fairwood?"

Nathan reported, "We have warriors there now, keeping it open. And the old hiding-place for the ring is still intact."

Tal took a moment to think. "So those fronts are covered. Now all we can do is play the game, one careful move at a time." He smiled with amusement. "So I suppose the Strongman should be hearing from Despair any moment now."

"And who is stationed there?"

"Guilo."

Nathan and Armoth nodded. That was no surprise.

four

GUILO had often noted how the darkest, most horrible evil seemed to choose the most beautiful places to build a nest, and so it was again. The mountains around him were towering, jagged, snowcapped, picturesque. The early morning air was clear, the visibility unlimited, the wind steady and gentle, the sky deep blue. Tall armies of evergreens stood at attention on every hillside, and crystal-clear streams trickled, splashed, and cascaded down from the pure white glaciers. Below him, the little town of Summit nestled peacefully in the green, wild-flowered valley, surrounded by a restful, noticeable quiet.

He whistled at the thought: all those little people down there, surrounded by all this beauty, could not see the horror all around them, the impending storm about to swallow them up, the cancerous darkness that first blinds, then consumes.

He and some dozen warriors were staying out of sight, sticking close to the pines, not showing any light of glory. He didn't want to be spotted by the evil powers that only spirits could see—a cloud of demons that swarmed and swirled like a smoke-black whirlwind on the mountainside only a mile away from the town. Below the guarding whirlwind, almost invisible in the trees, was a quaint, alpine village, a picturesque campus of ornate buildings, fastidious walkways, fascinating trails, stunning gardens. The whole place shouted invitation, exuding a welcoming, embracing sense of peace, beauty, and brotherhood.

It was the home of the Strongman, his outpost, the hub of an ever-widening evil. The sooty spirits were bold and riotous, reveling in a constantly growing tally of victories over human souls.

Guilo stood still, watching their moves, sizing them up, getting an idea of their numbers. Yes, it was nice to see them so cocky; demons in that state of mind were always easier to

catch unawares. But they wouldn't be so cocky for long—
he and his warriors had seen the recent arrival of one little
whimpering demon, one little envoy from one little insignificant farming town, and the news that spirit was bringing was
sure to change things throughout that supposedly charming
village. An assault would have been difficult enough beforehand. Now it was going to be nothing short of a real nightmare.

A cry! A wail, a shaking rippled through the whirlwind. The
ranks of demons began to compress, shrinking tighter, pack-
ing closer, growing even darker, thicker.

"Oh . . ." said Guilo. "Looks like the Strongman's gotten
the news."

"ROOOOOOAARRRRR!!"

Despair's shapeless little blob of a body stretched, warped,
and bulged this way and that, like a big black bubble fresh
from the wand, as he sailed across the chalet and then
dropped to the floor, whimpering loudly, his black body limp
and flat like a sobbing, shuddering bear rug. All around him,
the demon princes and generals were in a chugging, slobbering, sulfurous dither, hollering and shouting out curses and
yellow vapor as thick as cigar smoke. The chalet was filling
with a heavy, putrid fog that almost obscured their shadowy
forms.

They didn't like his news either.

At the end of the living room, the Strongman was glaring
at the pitiful little demon, his huge yellow cat eyes almost
popping from his head, his nostrils flared, the sulfur chugging
out of them in swirling clouds. The immense, hulking spirit
was trying to decide if he felt better now, or needed to hurl
Despair across the chalet again.

The princes and generals—almost a hundred of them—
were beginning to turn on each other, waving their arms,
throwing their black wings in each other's faces, shouting and
hissing; some were demanding explanations, some were
beginning to pass blame, some wanted to know what to do
next, and some just stood there cursing.

The Strongman filled his end of the room with his wings and held out his arms. "Silence!"

He got it.

He took one huge step toward the center of the room, and all the demons backed one step away, bowing, folding their wings. He took a few more steps, and the room echoed with the sound of them.

Then he addressed the little rug on the floor. "Have you anything else to report to me?"

"No, my Ba-al."

"No further casualties?"

"No, my Ba-al."

"No further blunders?"

"No, my Ba-al."

The demon lord considered that for just a moment.

Then the order exploded from his gaping mouth as from a cannon: "Then get out of here!"

The force of the Strongman's breath was more than enough to get Despair started. He was out of the chalet and into the sky before he even opened his wings.

The Strongman paced back to his end of the room and sank onto his throne—the fireplace hearth—with a deep scowl. The demonic ranks on either side of him trimmed their lines, standing straight and tall against the walls. The room came back to order, filled with darkness, shadows, yellow fog, and a deathlike stench.

"She is alive," he mused bitterly. "We were rid of her, we thought for good, but then she popped up again. We sought to kill her, but now she is still alive and . . . under *their* protection."

The princes stood like statues, silently waiting for his next word.

"RRROOOOOOWWWLLLLLL!"

The demonic ranks had to trim their lines again.

"Broken Birch . . ." he continued to muse. "Such a delightful group of people, so unabashed and forthright. So ready to kill. So . . . so CLUMSY!" He fumed, he drummed his huge fingers, he glared at nothing in particular. "These humans . . .

35

these worshipers of our lord are marvelously evil, but sometimes . . . sometimes they stumble ahead of *us!* No subtlety, no caution.

"So now we have a blunder, and a slippery little soul has escaped from our fist, a worse threat to us now than ever she was!"

A prince stepped forward and bowed. "Will my lord consider aborting the Plan?"

The Strongman straightened, and his fists thundered down on the hearthstones. "NO!"

The prince stepped back into the ranks under the condemning stares of his fellows.

"No," growled the Strongman, "not this Plan. Too much is at stake, too much has already been established and prepared. There is too much to be gained to let one little woman, one little pitiful soul, ruin it all!"

The loathsome spirit tried to relax, leaning his head back and letting his amber tongue roll across his lips.

"The town was so perfect," he mused. "The saints of God so few, so penniless . . . and *our* people, oh, so strong, so numerous, so . . . so pioneering! We worked so hard to establish the foothold we have in that town. Ah . . . who knows how long it took . . . ?"

"Twenty-three years, Ba-al," said a well-meaning aide.

The Strongman glared at him. "Thank you. I know."

The aide bowed and retreated.

The Strongman continued his mental review. "And the petty little saints in the town were . . . obscure, don't you see, far from help, far from the mainstream, alone amid the rolling farmlands . . . unknown. It was a perfect place to begin the process." His beastly face grew tight and bitter. "Until they started praying. Until they ceased being so comfortable and started weeping before God! Until they began to reclaim the power of the . . ." The Strongman sealed his lips.

"The Cross?" the aide volunteered.

"YAAAAA!!" The Strongman's sword sizzled through the air and missed the aide by inches. No matter. Several princes grabbed this foul-mouthed vassal and ousted him.

The Strongman settled onto the hearth with a thud. "Destroyer!"

The princes looked toward the other end of the room. A mutter moved through their ranks. Some stepped back.

A shadow stepped forward, a silhouette. It was tall, shrouded in billowing wings. It moved so smoothly, so silently, that it seemed to float. The other demons dared not touch it. Some bowed slightly.

It moved across the room and then stood before the Strongman, its head lowered in obeisance. It remained absolutely still.

The Strongman studied this dark, silent shape for a moment. "You have been noticeably silent during these discussions."

The thing raised its head and looked at its lord with narrow, calculating eyes. The face was not entirely hideous; it was almost human. But it was evil; it was cold and filled with hate.

"Speak, my Ba-al," he said, "and I will answer."

The Strongman's eyes narrowed. "Your minions failed, Destroyer. She is alive and free. What do you say to that?"

Destroyer's face was rock-hard, his spine straight. "Is she still mine?"

There was a strange, cutting tone in the Strongman's voice. "Do you still deserve her, Destroyer?"

Destroyer didn't seem to appreciate the question.

The Strongman spoke clearly, threateningly. "I want you to remove her, so that she will never reappear again." There was a slight tinge of doubt in the Strongman's voice as he asked, "*Can* you do that?"

The thing didn't move for a moment.

SLASH! Red flash! A sizzling sword cut through the air and divided space into burning segments. Black wings filled the room like smoke and rolled like thunder. The princes fell back against the walls; the Strongman actually flinched.

The thing stood there motionless again, the eyes burning with anger, the black wings slowly settling, the glowing red sword steady in his hand.

His low, sinister voice was seething with resentment. "Give me some real warriors, not Terga and his bungling, whining little imps of Bacon's Corner! Turn over your best to my command and let them empower Broken Birch, and you will see what your servant can do!"

The Strongman studied Destroyer's face and without the slightest smile asked, "What about the rumors I hear?"

Destroyer puffed a derisive laugh through his flaring nostrils. "They are rumors spread in fear by cowering spirits! *If* our opponent be this Tal, so much more the thrill of the challenge."

"He is mighty."

Destroyer countered, "He is *clever*. His strength is not in his own sword, but in the saints of God. The ranks have made a legend of his victory over us in Ashton, but they pay him too much respect. It was the prayers of the saints that defeated us, not this wily Captain of the Host." Destroyer waved his sword slowly through the air, admiring the burning after-image that trailed behind its razor-sharp edge. "And so it was in this recent, minor setback. But I now have an advantage, Ba-al: I have tasted the enemy's wiles, I have tested his strength, and I know the source of his power."

The Strongman was dubious. "And just how do you expect to thwart him where once you could not?"

"I will go to the saints first. Already there is plenty in Bacon's Corner for them to be upset about, plenty to divide them. I will keep them busy censuring and smiting each other, and then their hearts will be far from praying." He held the sword high; its red glow lit up the room and his yellow eyes reflected the glow in bloodshot crimson. "I will pull Tal's strength right out from under him!"

The Strongman was impressed, at least for the moment. "I will commission my best to accompany you. Broken Birch is clumsy at times, but totally devoted to us. Use them at your pleasure. Now go!"

Ben sat at his small desk in the front office of the police station and tried to get some paperwork cleared up before going out on patrol. It was a nice little office, with two small desks, a copy machine, some colorful traffic safety posters, and a low wood railing partition. Right now the morning sun was streaming in through the big windows, warming the place up. Under different circumstances he'd always enjoyed working here.

But Ben was far from cheery this morning, and his mind was far from his paperwork. He'd seen Mulligan's final report on the so-called suicide, and found it unbelievable. He couldn't be sure, but the photographs of the body and of the surrounding conditions simply did not match what he remembered seeing. Suddenly there was a rope around the woman's neck—last night Ben saw no rope around her neck, and even Mrs. Potter said the woman had the rope in her hand. The spilled goat feed had mysteriously vanished, and the straw around the body seemed undisturbed, not at all in the trampled, kicked-around mess it was in last night.

Ben didn't like the thought of it, but it was obvious that the scene—and the photographs of it—had been sanitized, as if Mulligan and Leonard had done away with all the evidence before taking the photographs and writing up the report.

As if that wasn't enough to stew about, there was also Mulligan's deriding and accusing of Tom Harris, and in front of reporters. And what in the world was the press doing in the station anyway? A lot of things were looking suspicious to Ben right now.

The *Hampton County Star* was lying on the corner of his desk. He had to go all through the paper before he could find even the slightest mention—and that's all it was—of the death at the Potter farm. The article was more a space filler than any real news, as if the reporter dropped all the facts on the floor somewhere and forgot about them . . . or purposely ditched them there. The whole thing felt wrong, so wrong it turned Ben's stomach.

I've got to get out of here, get out on patrol. I don't want to talk to Mulligan, don't even want to look at him.

But Mulligan was hard to ignore—he liked it that way. He came up to the front, belched loudly, and sat behind the desk across the room like a load of grain landing on a wharf. He had the investigation report in his hand, and started flipping through it for one last look.

"Well," he said, his booming voice shattering the nerves, "that does it."

"Any next of kin we can notify?" Ben asked.

Mulligan pulled a manila envelope out of a drawer. "There aren't any. Roe was a nobody, a loner." He slid the report, along with its accompanying sketches and photographs, into the envelope and folded it shut. "She pulled her own plug, and now it's our job to plant her quietly and get on with business."

"I don't suppose there will be a coroner's report?"

Ben knew he'd overstepped. Mulligan was getting steamed. "Of course there will. What about it?"

Ben wanted to back off, but now he had to answer Mulligan's question. "Well . . . with all due respect . . . the coroner might find some evidence to suggest another cause of death."

Mulligan didn't have time for this. "Listen, Cole, if just being a plain, hard-working, clean-nosed cop isn't enough for you . . . if you just don't feel you have enough responsibility . . . I'm sure I can find you some more important jobs, something you can really take pride in. The place could use some sweeping, and I know you'd be thorough; you'd get that broom into every corner, you'd catch every cobweb, huh?"

Ben knew he was glaring at Mulligan, but he made no effort to soften his expression. "I could be very thorough in checking the accuracy of last night's investigation."

Mulligan yanked a file drawer open and tossed the envelope in. "You just concentrate on doing your job, Cole. I'm not paying you to be my conscience."

five

POSTMASTER Lucy Brandon couldn't keep her mind on her work. Debbie, the postal clerk, had already asked her three questions—one about the Route 2 driver, one about the cracked mailing trays, and one about . . . now she couldn't remember the third question. She couldn't answer any of them; she couldn't recall the information; she just couldn't think.

"Hey," Debbie said finally, "are you feeling okay?"

Lucy removed her glasses and rubbed her eyes. She was usually a strong person, tough enough. A tall brunette in her late thirties, she'd been through plenty of life's little trials by this time: poverty, the early death of her parents, a wild and rebellious youth, a shaky marriage, picking up the pieces after a bitter divorce, and raising a young daughter alone—all in all, a well-rounded package of scrapes. So she'd learned to cope, usually; most troubles never really got her upset—as long as they didn't touch her family.

She looked around the small Post Office, and fortunately it was quiet right now. The midday rush was still a few hours away, the drivers had all left for their routes, the stack of work on her desk was growing, but she could catch up.

She was determined to answer at least one question. "Well, no, not really."

Debbie was young, pretty, and compassionate. Maybe she hadn't lived long enough to develop a tough exterior. She touched Lucy's shoulder tenderly. "Anything I can do?"

"Well . . ." Lucy checked the clock on the wall. "I have an appointment coming up in just a few minutes. Think you and Tim can hold down the fort until I get back?"

"Oh, sure."

A flash of reflected sunlight danced along the wall. A deep-blue fastback pulled up outside.

"Oh, there's my ride."

"You go ahead. Don't worry about us."

The driver of the car was Claire, a wonderful friend and counselor for not only Lucy, but many people of all walks of life around the town. She was a beautiful woman with blonde hair arranged neatly around her head and adorned with combs and pins that twinkled and shined. Her blouse and long skirt, both of beautifully woven natural fibers, draped about her like regal robes, and in Lucy's eyes Claire *was* a real queen. She and her architect male friend Jon were the perfect couple, constantly growing together in self-realization and harmony and becoming an enduring example to all their friends.

As Lucy climbed in, Claire leaned over and gave her a hug. "And how are you, Lucy?"

"Oh . . . coping," she answered, finding her seat belt.

Claire pulled out of the Post Office parking lot and headed down Front Street.

"And how is Amber?" she asked.

"She's doing all right. I didn't tell her we'd be coming by today. I didn't want to cause any alarm before we had to."

"Fine, fine."

"I'm going to take her back to the elementary school on Monday and see if I can get her worked into her classes there again. Miss Brewer doesn't think she'll have too much trouble catching up and just finishing out the year."

"Oh, no, not Amber, and it's so close to the end of the year anyway."

They drove through town and then turned onto 187th, commonly called Pond Road because it passed by a large and popular cattailed pond some two miles west. Along with the street sign naming the road was another sign pointing the direction to the Good Shepherd Community Church and the Good Shepherd Academy.

"I think John and Paula will be there today," said Claire. "I hope you don't mind."

"I guess not. I haven't even met them yet."

"Well, you'll find they're wonderful people. I'm glad we'll be working with them on this thing. Reporters aren't always as courteous as they are."

Lucy was quiet for a moment, just watching the farmlands and small forests go by.

Finally she said, "Why did we have to bring in the press?"

"Oh, it's very simple. In a case like this, public opinion is important. It's the public mind that eventually creates the laws we all have to live by. You see, we fight our battles at two levels: in the courts and in the public arena. A lot of the cases we win today came about because of public opinion that was molded years ago. What we do now to mold public opinion will have a positive effect on legal cases that arise in the future. It's a process."

"I just don't know if Amber can go through it."

Claire smiled with confidence. "Oh, Amber's a strong little soldier. She can do it. I was impressed with how she spoke right up and told everything to our staff, and Dr. Mandanhi, and even Mrs. Bledsoe."

Lucy was bitter. "*Amber?* You mean 'Amethyst,' don't you?"

Claire smiled and nodded. "Yes, you're right. But that doesn't matter. It's still Amber, really. Amethyst is a good friend for Amber because she bears the burden of what happened and speaks so freely, something Amber could never do as herself."

Lucy smiled a nervous smile. "But you know . . . I don't think I like Amethyst."

Claire laughed.

Lucy laughed too, hoping that statement would not be taken as seriously as she meant it. "I mean . . . Amethyst is just so brash and disrespectful . . . And I think Amber's getting away with a lot by blaming it on Amethyst."

"Well, you should put a stop to that, of course."

"But you see what I'm worried about? I think I would trust Amber to tell the truth . . . and I would know what she was thinking and feeling. But I just don't know about Amethyst. I never know what she'll say next!" Lucy shook her head to think she was even having such a conversation. "I need a set of reins for that little critter!"

Claire only laughed again. "Oh, don't be afraid of Amethyst. Inner guides are always trustworthy, and Amber needs that support and fellowship for what's ahead."

"Oh, I can see that."

But Lucy didn't feel any better, and Claire noticed.

"What else?" Claire asked.

"Since we're talking about Amethyst . . ."

"Yes?"

"Did you see that other article in the paper, about Sally Roe?"

Claire knew about it. "Lucy, really that's no concern of yours. You shouldn't even think such a thing!"

Lucy was close to tears. "But how can I help it?"

Claire stole several looks at Lucy as she drove. "Listen to me. It's not Amber's fault. I had some friends check out Sally Roe the moment you told me what happened in the Post Office. From what I've heard, Sally Roe was a deeply disturbed individual. She was tormented with self-doubt and guilt, and she could never break through . . . She was a karmic mess! Amber had nothing to do with her killing herself. She would have done it anyway."

Lucy shook her head and stared out the window. "But if you could have been there . . . if you could have seen that woman's face when . . . when *Amethyst* just tore into her. And I couldn't get her to stop. Amber just wouldn't snap out of it."

Claire patted Lucy's hand. "Let it go. Sally Roe is gone, fulfilling her own path wherever it takes her. You have your own, and so does Amber. You need to be thinking about that."

Lucy finally nodded. They were getting close to the Christian school, and she was feeling nervous. "I just hope this whole thing goes all right. I hope we know what we're doing."

Claire was firm. "I think it's something we must do. Religious bigotry is everyone's enemy. I think we would be denying our responsibility not to do anything."

There wasn't time to say any more. Claire was slowing the car down and signaling for a turn. There, on the left, stood the Good Shepherd Community Church, a simple brick building with gabled roof, traditional arched windows, and a bell tower. It was a landmark around Bacon's Corner, the home of several different congregations over the years; some had died out, some had moved on and new groups had come in, but it remained through it all for almost a century, a steadfast monument to tenacious Christianity. This latest congregation seemed to be setting a new record for endurance; it had been there in the church for almost fifteen years, and the current pastor had hung on for at least eight.

Claire pulled into the parking lot between the church and the Good Shepherd Academy, a simple, shed-roofed portable sitting on posts and piers. There were four vehicles parked in the lot at the moment. Two must have belonged to the school staff; the station wagon belonged to John Ziegler and Paula the photographer, and the large white van was clearly marked, "KBZT Channel Seven News."

"A *television* crew?" asked Lucy in surprise.

"Oh, right," said Claire. "I didn't tell you about that. The people from Channel Seven thought this would make a good news story."

The two men from Channel Seven were already prepared for Claire and Lucy's arrival, and bolted from the van as soon as their car pulled in. The cameraman set the camera on his shoulder and started watching the news with one eye. The other man, a young, athletic sort with suit and tie above the waist and jeans below, stepped up and greeted Claire as she got out of the car.

"Hey, right on time!" he said, shaking her hand.

"Hi, Chad. Good to see you again."

"This is Roberto."

"Hi."

Roberto smiled back, looking at her through the camera. Lucy got out of the car a little hesitantly.

Claire introduced her. "Chad and Roberto, this is Lucy Brandon, the mother."

"Hi there. Chad Davis. This is Roberto Gutierrez."

"Are they going to take my picture?"

"Do you mind?" asked Chad.

"It'll be all right," Claire assured her.

Lucy just shrugged.

John Ziegler and Paula were there, ready to go. Claire greeted them, and Lucy just smiled.

The door to the portable opened, and a man looked out. At the sight of this band of people gathered in the parking lot, his face went pale; he looked sick.

He was, of course, Tom Harris.

Claire raised her hand in greeting, said, "Oh, hello there," and started walking toward the portable, the others following close behind.

No, Lord, no . . .

If I could just close this door and never come out, Tom thought. *If I could just call down fire from Heaven to clear these people out of my life, to make them go away . . . Haven't they done enough to me?*

Tom had been on the telephone most of the morning, riding the carousel of state bureaucracy while trying to teach his classes, and he still had not found his children. The last word he got was from the CPD, and they were emphatically refusing to tell him of the children's whereabouts. Pastor Howard still wasn't back, everyone else was at work, and nothing was happening fast enough.

Lord, I just wish these people would go away. I wish this day would end.

Tom looked back inside. Two kids, one third-grade, one fourth, were getting curious.

"Hey . . . TV!" said the little girl.

Tom was being recorded on camera this very moment. At least addressing the child would give him a chance to turn his back.

"Sammie, go sit down—this is none of your concern. Clay, are you finished? Well, put it on my desk and start the next page. I'll check it right after lunch, all right?"

"Mr. Harris?" said Claire, coming up the wooden steps.

"Yes?"

"My name is Claire Johanson. I'm a legal assistant for

46

Ames, Jefferson, and Morris. I'm here representing Mrs. Lucy Brandon, whom you know. May we speak with you briefly?"

"This has been a very difficult day for me, Mrs. Johanson . . ."

"*Ms.* Johanson."

"I have nothing to say to any more reporters. I've had quite enough."

"This is a legal matter, Mr. Harris."

Oh, terrific. What more could go wrong?

Tom knew better than to embark on any conversation in the presence of big-eared reporters and a television camera. "Why don't you come inside?" Then he made it clear. "You and Mrs. Brandon. These others can wait out here."

He stepped aside and let the two women come in, then closed the door against the reporters.

They were standing in a common lunchroom/coat room/library between two classrooms. Tom poked his head into the classroom on the right. A first- and second-grade class of about ten children was puttering away at some low work-tables, coloring, pasting, and keeping the level of noise just below their teacher's established limit.

"Mrs. Fields?"

A plump, middle-aged woman stepped out of the class-room. Her cheeks were rosy and her hair tightly permed. Her eyes immediately showed alarm at the sight of Lucy Brandon and this officious-looking woman beside her.

"We have some important visitors," Tom explained quietly. "Could you please oversee my class for a few minutes?"

"Certainly," said Mrs. Fields, unable to take her eyes off the two women.

"They're doing their reading assignments right now, and should be finished by 10. Clay's on a special project I gave him; just make sure he puts it on my desk."

She nodded and crossed over to look in on the third-through sixth-graders.

"Let's step into the office," said Tom, and led the way to a small cubicle in the back of the building containing one desk, a computer, a copy machine, and two file cabinets. There was

47

hardly room for three people to sit down. Tom offered the ladies the only two chairs and chose to stand, leaning against the file cabinets.

Claire wasted no time. "Mr. Harris, we're here to remove Amber from the school. We'd like to have all her academic records."

Tom kept cool and businesslike. "I'll check with our secretary and have those prepared for you. You understand that all tuition payments must be current before the records can be released."

Claire looked at Lucy as she said, "All the payments will be taken care of. We'd like to process this as soon as possible."

"Certainly." Tom looked at Lucy. "I'm sorry that we weren't able to discuss this . . ."

Claire interjected, "There is nothing to discuss." With that, she rose, and Lucy did the same. "Now if you'll let Amber know we're here . . ."

The two women went out into the common room, and Tom followed.

Tom just wasn't satisfied. "Uh, this is a bit of a surprise. I take it we weren't able to resolve things to your satisfaction?"

Claire began to answer, "No, Mr. Harris—"

"The question was addressed to Mrs. Brandon," Tom said politely but firmly. He looked at Lucy. "It's been a month since we had that little problem. We talked it through, and I thought everything was settled. If you still had some doubts or misgivings, I certainly would have welcomed another meeting with you."

"Would you call Amber, please?" said Claire.

Tom poked his head in the door of the classroom and quietly called, "Amber? Your mother is here. Better get your coat and your things."

There were eighteen third- through sixth-graders in the classroom, each seated at a small desk, and all the desks were arranged in neat rows. Posters of nature, astronomy, the alphabet, and tips on cleanliness adorned the walls. Against one wall a large aquarium gurgled, and nearby a donated telescope stood poised to probe the heavens. There were pots of pea plants all lined up and labeled on a table, and next to them a family of hamsters in a large, activity-filled cage.

At the second from the last desk, fourth row, was Amber Brandon, a bright, clever, slightly mischievous fourth-grader with a full, often wild head of blonde hair and large blue eyes. She was wearing a purple jumpsuit and pink tennis shoes, and on her shoulder, a little pin of a toy horse.

She was surprised to hear that her mother had come, but also a bit excited. She hurriedly closed her workbook, gathered up her textbooks and her pencil box, and came to the door.

Lucy bent and gave her a hug. "Go get your coat, honey, and your lunchbox."

Those were the first words Tom heard from her today.

As soon as Amber was ready, Tom saw them to the door, opening it widely for them to pass through. The reporters were still waiting outside, of course, and Tom could almost feel the one-eyed stare of that television camera.

"Say, listen," he said to the reporters, "you people are on private property, and I think it would be best if you just move on, all right?"

"Oh, Mr. Harris," said Claire, turning back and joining him in the doorway. The camera caught a perfect two-shot. "I'm also here to serve you this."

She took an envelope from her suitcoat pocket and placed it in his hand. The camera zoomed in for a close-up. Paula's camera clicked and whirred off several shots.

"We'll see you in court, sir. Good day."

She went down the stairs and walked with Lucy and Amber back to her car.

Tom was frozen to the spot for a moment, which was fine with Paula and Roberto. He stared down at the envelope, his stomach in a knot, his heart pounding so hard he could feel it. The envelope was starting to quiver in his hand. He looked at the newspeople. They got some more shots.

"Please leave," he said, his voice hardly audible.

"Thank you, Mr. Harris," said John Ziegler.

Tom swung the door shut and then leaned against it, all

alone in the common room. He felt his legs would collapse under him and he would sink to the floor any moment.

"Oh, God," he prayed in a whisper. "Oh, God, what's happening?"

From the two classrooms the quiet puttering and studying continued. Suddenly that was such a precious sound to him. He looked around the common room and recognized the coats and lunchboxes of all the children, all this dear little tribe. Before long they would be having a prayer and going out for morning recess, filling the swings and playground like they always did. Such simple, day-to-day routines now seemed so priceless because of the envelope in his hand, this invader, this cancer, this vicious, imposing enemy! He wanted so fervently to tear it into a million pieces, but he knew he couldn't.

Now everything was coming together. Now things were beginning to make sense. His eyes blurred with tears.

So this was why they took Ruth and Josiah!

Tal was there, his sword drawn, staying close to the building, out of sight, watching the car and the news van pull away. Only a few dark spirits had accompanied the visitors, and there were no skirmishes, at least for now. The fact that Tom was well-guarded by two towering warriors helped keep things peaceful, plus the fact that Nathan and Armoth were atop the church in plain sight.

"No more harassments for the rest of the day," Tal instructed Tom's guards. "Let him heal up from this one first."

Then he spread his wings and reached the roof of the church in one smooth leap.

"So they've decided to go ahead with it!" said Nathan.

"The Strongman can be inflexible," said Tal. "I expect this will be a fight to the finish. It's—"

FOOM! A sudden explosion of wings! All three warriors immediately formed a close cluster, each facing outward, sword drawn, poised for battle.

"There!" shouted Tal, and they all faced the old bell tower.

It was Destroyer, standing tall and imposing, his expansive wings just settling, his glowing red sword drawn. A dozen warriors accompanied him, six on each side, almost as monstrous as he was. The hot yellow vapor from each demon's nostrils was already collecting in a writhing ribbon that drifted out over the parking lot like a slow, inquisitive serpent.

"If I mistake not, you are Tal, the Captain of the Host!" the demon called.

Tal, Nathan, and Armoth were sizing up this bunch. A fight would best be avoided.

"I am," said Tal.

The black, bristly lips pulled back in a mocking grin, unveiling long, amber fangs. "Then the rumors in the ranks were true!"

"And who might you be?"

"Call me Destroyer for now." Then he proclaimed proudly, "I am the one assigned to the woman!"

Tal didn't stir. Taunts never bothered him. He never fought until he was ready.

The demon continued, his sword ready. "I thought, before the battle begins, the two warlords should meet each other. *I* wanted to meet *you* to see if all the lofty words I've heard are true." Destroyer eyed Tal carefully. "Perhaps not." He waved his sword about. "But please look at this place, this little school! Is it really so much a prize as to be worth all your armies? Be assured, we want no more trouble in taking it as you desire in saving it. Captain of the Host, we could settle the matter sooner rather than later."

Tal answered, "The school is ours. The saints are ours."

Destroyer spread his arms with a flourish and made a pronouncement. "The Strongman has authorized me to give you the Christian schools in Westhaven, in Claytonville, in Toe Springs! You may have them! We will leave them alone!"

Tal remained stone-solid. "No."

Destroyer only laughed. "Oh. It must be the woman. Perhaps you are still bolstered by your recent victory in saving

51

her. Consider that a gift, captain, our last blunder. Yes, you did save her life, but she lives for us. Her soul is ours!"

Tal said nothing.

"And not only the woman, but also all the power, resources, people, minds, money . . . *everything* we will ever need to trample you and your motley little flock of saints into the dust! You are too late, Captain of the Host! The time is past for you and your saints. *We* hold the power now! Surrender, cut your losses, and be content!"

"We will see you in battle," said Tal.

Destroyer looked at Tal for a long moment, shaking his head slowly, marveling at this angelic warrior's stubbornness. Finally he nodded.

"In battle then."

With another explosion of rushing, leathery wings, the demons rose into the sky, whooping and wailing, mocking and spitting until they were gone.

Only then did Tal put away his sword.

"Was that an attempt to frighten us?" asked Armoth.

"A strategic move," said Tal. "He was trying to steal our courage at the beginning."

"So now what do you think of our chances?" asked Nathan.

"Even," said Tal. "Maybe just even."

chimon and Scion remained hidden on either side of Room 12 at the Rest Easy Motel in Claytonville. There were dark spirits about, apparently Destroyer's scouts—slimy, cowardly harassers, swooping down through the trees and power lines, zipping up and down the streets, looking into houses, through windows, down chimneys for the poor, bedraggled fugitive. The two angels were working hard to maintain a hedge about the woman, to screen her from their sight, and thus far they were able to keep her hiding-place a secret from any spirits sent to torment her.

But four spirits still followed Sally Roe wherever she went, and had been her close companions for so long that they could not be separated for the present. Chimon and Scion were just itching to stand in their way, to hack Despair, Fear, Death, and Insanity out of this world, to lessen the pain for that frightened, battered soul. But her life was such that they were there by right; and besides, the pain was necessary. The two warriors had to withhold their power.

Sally gave her head a good rub with a towel, and then straightened up for a look in the bathroom mirror. Her once-red hair now cascaded over her shoulders and down her back in wet, black strands. Well, maybe it would work—if they were only looking for red hair. But her face was still too distinctive; even with her hair dyed black and all pinned up, she still looked like Sally Roe. If she could hide all those freckles it would help. Maybe she could conceal her brown eyes with a pair of glasses, those stylish, tinted kind. Maybe she could wear a lot of makeup.

Her heart sank. This was all so futile, so childish. She was dreaming, groping for hope, and she knew it. If they ever spotted her, they would recognize her. She was finished, through, as good as dead.

She leaned on the sink, let her head droop, and just stayed

there for the longest time, her mind failing her miserably; it just wouldn't function. It was tired, burned out, discouraged. All she could do was stand there, breathing one breath at a time. At least she could breathe; at least *something* was still functioning.

But why was she so glad about it? That bothered her.

Sally, you're too tired to think about it. Let it go.

But then her mind clicked on, just a little, and again, for the millionth time, she tackled the same vexing question: If life was so pointless, so futile, so meaningless, so empty, why was she trying so hard to hang on to it? Why did she want to keep going? Maybe it had something to do with how life evolved; nothing poetic or lofty, to be sure, just that mysterious, unexplained self-preservation instinct, the only reason we hung on long enough to beat the odds so we could walk upright and kill each other . . .

She snapped out of it. It was a waste of time trying to figure it out. It was a merry-go-round, an endless maze. *Keep it simple, Sally: somebody wants to kill you, but you want to stay alive. Those two propositions are enough for now.*

She leaned forward to check the cut in her shoulder. No infection, at least; that was good. For now the bleeding was stopped and the wound was closed, but just barely. She carefully bound it up with adhesive tape and gauze—a nice manual task, no heavy brainwork—then slipped carefully into her shirt.

She came out of the bathroom, sat on the bed, and started tinkering with the clasp on an inexpensive neck chain. It was a good buy down at the local variety store—provided it didn't turn her neck blue—and should do the trick.

She'd been shopping that morning, as quickly and quietly as possible, constantly hoping she would not be seen by anyone who might know who she was, or care. But she had to get that tape and gauze, the hair rinse, this chain, some clean clothes . . . and the morning paper.

The *Hampton County Star* was still spread out on the bed. She'd paged through it the moment she got back to the room. The front page carried some stories about a sewage plant, a local political scandal, and a county commissioner's thirtieth year in office, but no news from Bacon's Corner. The second and third pages didn't say anything either. She didn't find what she was after until the bottom of the last page of the news section. It was a tiny headline and about one and a half inches of story:

> LOCAL WOMAN FOUND DEAD
> Bacon's Corner—The body of a local woman was discovered last night in her home, an apparent suicide. The victim is identified as Sally Beth Rough, 36, an employee at the Bergen Door Company.
> Her landlady, Mrs. Fred Potter of Bacon's Corner, made the discovery after noticing some of Rough's goats were loose.
> "It's a real tragedy," she said.

It was a ridiculous piece of reporting. A run-over chicken would have gotten more copy, maybe even had its name spelled correctly. But that didn't bother Sally. That wasn't the point.

The story was not just wrong—it was incredibly, shockingly wrong.

They think the dead woman is me? The woman who tried to kill me? They think she's me?

She'd brooded about that all through her shower. It bothered her so much she had to read the instructions on the bottle of rinse three times.

At first she thought it could be good news. *They'll think I'm dead!*

But that notion soon faded. *They know I'm not. They have to know. They've lied to the paper, or the paper is lying.*

She finally got the clasp of the chain open and hung it around her neck. Then she reached over to the night table and picked up . . . that ring. She threaded the neck chain through it, fastened the clasp, buttoned up her shirt, and the ring was hidden.

They know who that woman was. They don't want anyone else to know.

And she knew she wasn't hallucinating. The ring around her neck told her that. It was one solid piece of evidence that would help her hold on to reality, bizarre as it may be.

Sally reached for her jacket and pulled another solid piece of evidence from the pockets—many pieces, actually.

Cash. She'd already counted it. Ten thousand dollars, in three bundles: one of twenties, one of fifties, and one of hundreds. The assassin's fee, most likely. Sally found it all in the woman's coat pockets and grabbed it. Why the woman was carrying it all on her person was a mystery, unless she carried the money for the same reason she wore the gold ring.

But the question still remained: After all these years, what had Sally done? How had she gotten in their way?

It had to be what happened in the Post Office. It was the only thing Sally could think of, a frightening experience and now a horrible memory. It was just like being caught, found out, discovered by an old enemy . . . a *savage* enemy! That little girl's eyes! Those taunting, hideous eyes! She could never forget that short moment when every fear, every nightmare from all her previous years came back in a torturous, merciless wave of recollection.

She had looked into the eyes of a devil. She could recognize it; she'd seen that look before, felt the stinging, mocking hate, heard the same vicious lying.

Sally flopped on the bed. No, she couldn't think about it. She was just too tired. She was frightened, her hair was black and looked strange, she couldn't think, she was a hunted animal, and she was just too tired.

Your hope is lost, worthless creature, said a voice in her head. *It's only a matter of time; a very short time,* said another.

"Amber . . ." It sounded so much like her.

Now you can see how big we are, and how little you are! You are dead, worthless creature! You are crazy!

Sally leaped from the bed and grabbed a pen from the table. She found some stationery in a drawer next to a Gideon Bible. She would write things down, that was it! Perhaps her mind wouldn't get scrambled if she put it all down on paper. She could record her thoughts before they melted away. She bent over the table, her pen poised over the paper.

But Despair was wounded, humiliated, indignant, and determined to redeem himself. He hung on her back like a coal-black leech, sucking out her will, whispering confusion to her mind. The other three spirits were with him, circling Sally, taunting her, jabbing her with their swords.

Insanity whipped his sword right through her brain.

Sally stared at the paper. Somehow she'd ended up on the floor. Nothing would come. What was that thought? She just had it, she was going to write it down, and now it was gone.

Give it up. Turn yourself in.

No one will ever believe you. You're crazy.

Crazy. It was a word. She wrote it down.

Insanity, cackling his witchy laugh, grabbed her mind between his two hairy palms and dug in his talons. Death joined in the attack.

Sally's mind went blank. The paper began to grow into a white screen that filled her eyes like a fog, a blizzard white-out. She was floating. She kept writing: "My name is Sally Roe . . . Sally Roe . . ."

She could hear voices in the room, taunting her, and could feel sharp claws tugging at her. They remained invisible, hiding from her, teasing, tormenting.

Then came Fear. Sally was overcome with a numbing, para-lyzing fear. She was lost and falling, spinning, tumbling in space. She couldn't stop.

She willed to think, to form the word in her mind: Sally. Sally. Sally.

Come on, write it. Take the blasted pen in your hand and write it!

We have you now. We will never let you go.

Sally. She could feel the pen moving.

The pen raced over the paper in circles, squiggles, jagged lines, crisscrosses.

It was gibberish. Nonsense.

She kept writing. She had to capture a thought, any thought.

Chimon and Scion had seen enough. It would have to be quick. Scion slipped outside to check the perimeter. Chimon crept like a shadow through the walls, moving in close.

All four spirits were clustered around Sally's head, whipping her consciousness into a myriad of senseless fragments. Chimon got a nod from Scion—he would be able to shield out the spirits outside. Now for these insects inside. It had to be just the right moment, just that one instant of opportunity.

Now. They wouldn't see it. Chimon whipped his sword in a quick, tight circle, a shining disk of light. *WHAM!* The flat of the blade smacked the demons senseless and shattered their tight little cluster. Despair went tumbling backward in a blurred spin and landed outside the motel; Fear, Death, and Insanity were interlocked and fell away together, their arms, legs, and wings a spinning, fuming, angry tangle.

The two warriors ducked back inside the walls.

Despair righted himself with a shriek and a huff, and only then realized where he was. With a flurry of wings, he shot back through the wall into the room. His three cohorts were just recovering. All four flung themselves at Sally's mind again.

But it was too late. She'd slipped from their grip like a bird out of a trap. Her thoughts, though sluggish, were moving in an orderly sequence through her brain.

Sally was suddenly able to read the words on the page. There were only six legible words at the top, "Crazy my name is Sally Roe." The rest of the page was filled with aimless, chaotic scribbles. She got up from the floor and sat at the table to try again. She had to keep writing, first one word, then a phrase, then another word—anything that would capture her racing, fragmented thoughts before they escaped her.

"Death and despair and fear and madness are back," she wrote, and then another thought: "Why kill me? I died years ago."

Sally kept moving that pen, whether her mind stayed on it

or not. She was going to whip this madness. She had to. She was going to get her thoughts down on paper where they couldn't get away. She was going to win.

Ben was beginning to wonder about his gift for timing. He'd been out on patrol and just happened to stop in at the station to pick up some more highway flares. As soon as he stepped through the back door, he could hear Mulligan in his office, talking to someone on the phone, and using a hushed tone of voice that immediately roused Ben's suspicion. Since when did Mulligan ever get that quiet?

Ben got his flares from the supply room. The quicker he got out of there, the better.

Oh-oh! There went Mulligan's chair again, rolling back and hitting the wall. Ben ducked into the supply room, expecting Mulligan to come bursting through his door.

But Mulligan must have jumped up in anger. He stayed in his office, hollering at whoever was on the phone.

"No, Parnell, I'm telling you, there was nothing on either hand! That's what I said, nothing!"

Hmm. Parnell. That was the coroner.

Mulligan gave Parnell time to say something, and then dove into him again. "No, I didn't find anything in her pockets either! What kind of a jerk do you take me for?" Parnell got another two bits in, and then Mulligan answered, "Well, you just go back and check around again! I'm doing my job, now you do yours!" Another pause. "Hey, you're the one who got the body, not me. I delivered it just like I found it. Why not ask the medics, if you've got a problem? Yeah, Parnell, it's *your* problem, and I can make it a bigger problem if you just say the word!"

He slammed the phone down and cursed.

Ben ducked back outside as quickly as he could. Even as he closed the door behind him, he could hear the sergeant still hissing and cursing under his breath.

seven

JameS Bardine was a young, handsome lawyer with black, wavy hair left long in the back and a voice with a lingering adolescent quack. Normally, he was tough and decisive—his associates used words like belligerent and rude behind his back—and in control of his situation. He was ambitious, a real goal-grabber, and flaunted his red Porsche at every opportunity. His suits were specially tailored to project an image of power. He'd perfected his own walk for use whenever he went to court: a quick, intimidating clip, chin high, spine straight, and lots of extra yellow legal pads under his arm. He knew he'd go far. He had the grit for this work. He was good at it.

Right now, he was scared to death. He was sitting in an overly soft couch in the outer office of his boss, Mr. Santinelli, waiting to be called in for a conference. The room had high, twelve-foot walls, dark-stained mahogany trim around, over, and under everything, and a thick carpet your feet sank into. It was deathly quiet except for the secretary's steady tapping on the typewriter and an occasional electronic warbling of a telephone. Bardine needed a cigarette, but Mr. Santinelli forbade smoking in his office. The magazines on the coffee table were either old or boring, but it didn't matter. There was no way he'd be able to read right now.

He was trying to compose a defense in his mind, something persuasive. Surely Mr. Santinelli knew when he had a good man; surely he wouldn't make a big thing out of such a little incident. Surely he would consider the fine record Bardine had accumulated in the past five years.

The big mahogany door opened like the seal of a crypt, and Mr. Anthony stepped out. Anthony was Mr. Santinelli's aide and right-hand man, a tall, thin, ghosty character, something like a cross between a butler and a hangman. Bardine rose quickly.

"We're ready," said Anthony. "Won't you come in?"

61

Such a nice invitation to an inquisition, Bardine thought. He stepped forward.

"Are those yours?" Anthony asked, pointing to some yellow legal pads on the coffee table.

"Oh, yes, thank you."

Bardine grabbed them up and followed Anthony through the big door. It closed after them with a thud of finality.

This was the inner conference room adjacent to Mr. Santinelli's office. The ornate light fixtures were at full brightness, but the room still seemed gloomy. The dark woodwork and furniture seemed to absorb the light; the heavy, floor-to-ceiling, velvet curtains were drawn over the windows.

Mr. Santinelli sat at the other end of the oval conference table, looking over some papers before him and seeming not to notice when Bardine came in. He was an impressive figure, intimidating by his very presence. He was expensively dressed, gray, grouchy, and *in charge.* He was flanked by two of his closest and most powerful associates, Mr. Evans, a tight-faced, iron-fisted attorney who hadn't smiled in years, and Mr. McCutcheon, a man who had so much money the subject bored him. Near this end of the table sat Mr. Mahoney, Bardine's immediate superior, and not an impressive figure at all. One other man was present at the table, but unknown.

"Be seated, Mr. Bardine," said Santinelli, still not looking up.

Anthony showed Bardine to the chair at the nearest end of the table, the one directly opposite from Mr. Santinelli. This was going to be a real eye-to-eye meeting.

Bardine took his seat and arranged his legal pads neatly in front of him. "Good day, gentlemen."

Some of them muttered good day back. Some only nodded. None of them smiled.

Mr. Santinelli finally finished perusing his papers and looked up. "Mr. Bardine, let me introduce you to the gentlemen seated with us. Mr. Evans and Mr. McCutcheon I'm sure you know already."

Bardine nodded at the two men, and they nodded back.

"Mr. Mahoney is here as well, and we acknowledge his attendance. The other gentleman is Mr. Goring, from Summit, here to lend his assistance and expertise."

Bardine nodded at them, and they didn't nod back.

Mr. Santinelli leafed through the papers in front of him. "To quickly review our present situation, we find that a . . . complication . . . has developed, which at first seemed not so grievous as it now appears. Ehmmmm . . . and with each passing moment, the gravity of the complication increases . . ." Then Santinelli looked straight at Bardine and asked, "Mr. Bardine, are you familiar with the name Sally Beth Roe?"

Arrow Number One. Bardine could feel the question go right through him. "Yes, sir."

"And what about the name Alicia Von Bauer?"

That felt like several arrows. "Yes, sir."

"Would it be true to say, Mr. Bardine, that you are *extremely* familiar with the name of Ms. Von Bauer?"

"Well . . . I'm not sure what you mean by that . . ."

"We'll get to that later." Santinelli set that paper aside and perused the next sheet. "I'm sure you are aware by now that Ms. Von Bauer is dead?"

"Mr. Mahoney advised me of that this morning, sir."

Santinelli adjusted his reading glasses and studied the paper in front of him. "Sally Beth Roe . . . How interesting that she should pop up again, and in Bacon's Corner, of all places!" Santinelli looked up at the men on either side of him. "Strange how things like this happen so often. You'd think there was an intelligent mind behind it, the hand of whatever god you may wish to imagine . . ."

It was no joke, and no one laughed.

"At any rate," Santinelli continued, "we have just recently learned that a plan was launched to have Sally Roe murdered, and, of course, to make it look like a suicide. Just whose idea was that?"

Mahoney spoke quickly and clearly. "Mr. Bardine's, sir."

Bardine looked at his superior in horror.

63

Santinelli asked, "You seem to be having a problem with his answer, Mr. Bardine."

Bardine's voice cracked as he said, "Uh, well, yes . . ."

"We'll get to that later," said Santinelli, looking at the paper again. "To continue my recounting—and please correct any flaws as you catch them—Alicia Von Bauer, a member of a Satanist organization called Broken Birch, was hired to perform this murder, and paid . . ." Santinelli bristled as he read the amount. ". . . ten thousand dollars as a retainer, with another ten thousand promised upon successful completion of her assignment. Am I correct so far?"

Mahoney just looked at Bardine. Bardine looked back at him. Neither man answered.

Santinelli continued, but watched both of them. "Apparently Ms. Von Bauer made her attempt on Tuesday night of this week, but found Ms. Roe to be more than her match. Ms. Roe was able to overcome her assailant and escape, leaving the dead body of her assassin behind, where, theoretically, she herself would have been found had the plan succeeded." He set the paper down flat in front of him, folded his hands on top of it, and looked at Mahoney and Bardine over the top of his reading glasses. "In other words, this ambitious, overly imaginative plot was a pitiful failure."

Mahoney looked at Bardine again. Bardine glared back at him.

Santinelli slid that paper aside and picked up the next one. "To further complicate matters, the, uh, planners of this scheme widened the circle of confidence beyond the key players and brought in a local peace officer named . . . uh . . . Mulligan, as well as the local medical examiner—the assumption being made, I suppose, that these two parties are steadfastly loyal to our cause, seeing that they were actually told in advance that there would be a suicide at the Potter farm and to handle it as quickly and quietly as possible."

Santinelli dropped the paper to the table and leaned back, removing his glasses. "Which, much to their credit, they are doing, or at least are trying to do, despite the fact that the deceased who is supposed to have killed herself is dead from an obvious act of violence and is, of course, the wrong person to begin with. By your silence I take it my account is accurate so far?"

Santinelli didn't need the answer he didn't get. He just replaced his reading glasses and went to the next sheet of paper. "Now for the complications—the *real* complications. First of all, the most obvious: Sally Beth Roe is alive . . . somewhere. She is living, breathing, walking about, and I'm sure totally cognizant that there was a ruthless attempt on her life. If she doesn't know who was responsible, I'm sure she has a very good idea. And how am I so sure? Let me tell you the next complication.

"According to a reliable source who shall remain nameless, Alicia Von Bauer was wearing a ring when she committed— excuse me, tried to commit—the murder. At our request, the medical examiner checked the body for that ring, and found that it had been removed from the third finger of the right hand with the help of cooking oil . . . uh, traces of the oil were still on the finger. We sent some people to check the murder site and the house, and the peace officer and medical examiner doublechecked the personal effects of the assassin. The ring is gone.

"And then there is the matter of the ten thousand dollars. That is also gone, without a trace. Von Bauer may have placed it in a secret account somewhere, but that is unlikely, knowing the delicate nature of her mission."

"Uh, sir?" said Bardine.

Santinelli lifted his eyebrows just enough to give Bardine the floor.

"The . . . uh . . . ten thousand dollars *was* laundered. It can't be traced to us."

The eyebrows went up again. "To *us*, Mr. Bardine?"

Bardine stumbled a bit. "Uh, to uh, the . . . to, uh, well, to us . . . myself, and . . . and uh . . ."

"It *is* gone, is it not?"

"Gone, sir?"

"Unless you can make a call or take a drive—just go and get it?"

"Oh . . ." Bardine stalled, but finally answered, "Yes, sir, I would say that the money is out of our reach now, irretrievable."

"But . . . laundered."

"Oh yes, sir."

Santinelli continued, referring to his notes. "The third complication embodies the first two: We have every reason to presume that Sally Roe has both the ring and the money. As such, she presents the greatest possible threat to us and to our plans." Santinelli paused for emphasis. "A greater threat, gentlemen, than she ever could have been had she been left alone."

Santinelli put his notes aside, removed his glasses, and looked squarely at Mahoney and Bardine. "Now, Mr. Mahoney and Mr. Bardine . . . let's return to an earlier question: Just whose idea was this assassination plot?"

Mahoney spoke first. "Mr. Santinelli, I'll have to claim some responsibility. When we heard that Sally Roe was in Bacon's Corner, we knew it could be a serious deterrence. We weighed many options, and I guess it became too high a priority in our minds. When Mr. Bardine presented the idea of an assassination to me, I guess I just wasn't firm enough in discouraging it. But by no means did I authorize the action, sir."

Santinelli could see that Bardine was quite agitated. "Do you have anything to add to that?"

Bardine looked from Mahoney to Santinelli and back again. "Sir . . . I . . . well, I understood that this undertaking had been authorized from the top down. I believed I was carrying out the plan with the full endorsement and authorization of my superiors." Bardine could feel the cold, icy wind blowing his way from Mahoney's countenance. He found himself at a loss for words—appropriate words, anyway. "The . . . uh . . . concept of a suicide, sir. This was not to be a murder, you understand, but a suicide, for all practical purposes. Done correctly, it would never be interpreted as anything else. Sally Roe was already a lonely and wasted individual with a terrible past and nothing ahead of her. Suicide seemed credible."

"I did not authorize it, sir!" said Mahoney. "He acted without my direct orders!"

Santinelli made no attempt to hide the smirk on his face. "We'll get to that later. Mr. Bardine, I do have some questions about the involvement of the deceased, Ms. Von Bauer. How was she brought into this?"

"Uh . . . she . . ." Bardine felt like a badgered witness on the witness stand. "I, uh, was talking to her about this particular problem, and she . . . well, she proposed the arrangement."

"She proposed killing Sally Roe?"

"Yes, sir, for the price of twenty thousand dollars." Bardine quickly added, "As you know, this sort of thing *is* done now and then."

Santinelli's eyes narrowed. He was moving in for the kill. "You say you were talking to her about this particular problem?"

"Well, I . . ."

"Mr. Bardine, do you always discuss such highly sensitive subjects with such questionable characters?"

"No, sir, of course not!"

"You freely discussed top-level concerns with a *Satanist?*"

"Not a Satanist, sir—at least, not in a derogatory sense. She belongs to Broken Birch, yes, but they command much respect, even among our own ranks—"

"And just where did this discussion take place?"

"Well, I suppose . . ."

"Wasn't it in your home, Mr. Bardine? More specifically, in your bedroom?"

Bardine was silent. He was stunned.

Santinelli explained briefly, "We do keep up on things, Mr. Bardine." Then he started attacking again. "You were romantically involved with Alicia Von Bauer, weren't you?"

Bardine was trying to formulate an answer.

Santinelli hit him again. "You'd already had many clandestine trysts with Von Bauer even before this; you'd already revealed several of our secrets to her, and now, at the peak of your infatuation, when she had your complete confidence, you told her about this problem, and the two of you made a pact together, isn't that correct?"

Bardine decided to try honesty. "I . . . I thought it would be safe. I mean, she was involved in a bizarre group, she already had a criminal record . . . I thought that if something went wrong, we could always dissociate ourselves from her, claim no knowledge of her actions. She was . . . she was a disposable entity, purely utilitarian. I was sure it would work."

Santinelli placed both hands squarely on the table, as if bracing himself right before exploding. "I suppose, Mr. Bardine, you never considered what it could do to the reputation of not only yourself but this organization for you to be intimately associated with a convicted criminal?"

"Sir . . ." Bardine tried to lighten things up. "Our people are seen in the company of this kind of people all the time . . ."

"Not this kind, Mr. Bardine! Not Satanists! We do not wish to associate with them because we do not wish to *be* associated with them by the public, do you understand? This relationship of yours with Von Bauer was most imprudent!" Santinelli stopped, not satisfied with the word. "*Imprudent*? Mr. Bardine, it was *reprehensible!*"

Bardine could only sit there, silent and shot to pieces.

But Santinelli wasn't through. "Did it never occur to you that she could be a spy? Did it never once dawn on you that all the inside talk you were sharing with her—no doubt to impress her—would be immediately afterward shared with her cohorts in Broken Birch? Haven't you learned anything about the politics of power? Have you any idea how vulnerable you have made us to those despicable leeches?"

Santinelli was hot and rolling; there was no stopping him. "They want power, Mr. Bardine, just as we all do! They are no exception in this game! We all want it, and we all have our own little machinations and tricks to get it. But be sure of this, Mr. Bardine: power, real power, belongs to the select few, and *we* are that select few—do you understand?" He didn't give Bardine time to answer. "All the others, be they rich, be they royalty, be they gutter rats like these Satanists, will just have to get used to that fact and live by it. We will not allow any more petty power-grabbers to vie for leverage against us, and—" he leaned into this phrase—"we will not allow any more of our people to *give it to them!*"

Bardine's voice was barely audible. "I understand, sir."

Santinelli ignored the reply. "The ring taken from Alicia Von Bauer's finger . . . it was yours, wasn't it?"

Bardine tried to explain. "She . . . she stole it, sir! I did not give it to her! She had to have stolen it from the top of my dresser!"

"And this was, of course, after you had made your pact with her?"

"I . . . I suppose."

"So she took your ring, with your personal inscription on it, and placed it on her own finger, just in case—" Santinelli took a moment to breathe and cut some holes through Bardine with his eyes—"just in case something went wrong, and we tried to dissociate ourselves from her and claim no knowledge of her actions and treat her like a disposable entity. With your personalized ring, don't you see, she would have some recourse against us, some proof that it was one of our own top-level attorneys who hired her and paid her that ten thousand dollars!"

Bardine looked down at the tabletop.

Santinelli had vented most of his anger. Now his voice softened. "Mr. Bardine, it is not my responsibility to think all these things through for you; it is your responsibility to do that, and to always keep the best interests of this organization foremost in your mind."

"Yes, sir. I'm sorry, sir."

"It's too late for that. The damage is done, and by another romantic entanglement! I hope you've learned—and it has been in the hardest way—how dangerous they can be."

"Yes, sir, I have."

"You're a good man, Bardine. I like your record of accomplishments. We're going to keep this quiet, and I expect you to keep it quiet, for your sake and ours too."

"Yes, sir. You have my word, sir."

"We will grant you a leave of absence to . . . pursue some further studies—and please come up with something convincing. In the meantime, we'll just have to see what we can do to straighten this mess out."

By this time, such a sentence was good news. "Yes, sir. Thank you for your kind considerations . . ."

Santinelli began to gather his papers together. "In the future, Mr. Bardine, you will show by your example how such actions as we've discussed are never a good idea for any man in your sensitive position."

"Yes, sir," said Bardine. "I will, sir!"

Santinelli only smiled. "Oh, I'm positive of that."

eight

RANSACKED. The place was a disaster, just like Mrs. Potter said.

Ben stood in the doorway of the Potters' little rental house and figured he'd better have a good look from here before he went inside. The small living room was scantily furnished with an old couch, a rocking chair, a small thin-legged lampstand, and one gray and brown rag-rug.

The cushions from the couch were tossed on the floor, the rag-rug was rolled aside and piled in a corner. In the middle of the floor were papers, books, small boxes, and several items of clothing, apparently the contents of some drawers somewhere, brought in and spilled out.

Ben checked his watch. Yes, he had time to linger a little longer. This sidetrip back to the scene of the so-called suicide was not official, to say the least, and he did have some other stops to make. But he had some nagging questions that drew him here, and he was hoping an answer, no matter how small, might turn up. Mrs. Potter was glad enough to see him again, and gave him the key after preparing him for what he would find.

He stepped inside the house and went into the kitchen. Every drawer had been pulled open and the contents scattered on the old trestle table: some unmatched bowls and plates, old army eating utensils, some aging dish towels, some cookware, and a half-empty box of Saltine crackers. The canisters on the counter were all open—someone had dug through the flour, the tea, and the sugar, spilling much of it. He checked the refrigerator—they'd gone through that too.

He found the bedroom. It was the messiest of all the rooms, probably because it held the most of Sally Roe's few possessions. Ben stood just inside the doorway a moment, noticing the intricate quilt now pulled from the small bed, the beautiful carved horse on the dresser, the pictures now hanging crookedly on the walls—prints of serene countrysides, grazing horses, hard-working farm folk. On the square table next to the bed was a small porcelain lamp, cracked, but decorated with hand-painted flowers and topped with an intricate crocheted lampshade. Apparently this was Sally Roe's favorite room, her private little world. It had received most of her attention and creativity.

The small closet had been rummaged through, but most of the clothes still hung there. Ben noted the blouses, the skirts, the dresses, the scarves. They were all clean, pressed, cared for, conservative. The closet smelled of lavender.

The room was flooded with sunlight that came through the south-facing window. Just below the window was Sally's old walnut desk, the drawers all pulled out, the contents scattered everywhere. Even so, Ben could easily picture how it used to be; a few books, a dictionary, and a thesaurus standing at attention on the left end, a small desk caddy holding a supply of pens and pencils on the right end, and in the middle . . . Well, whatever Sally used to have there, whatever she'd been working on, was now somewhere on the floor, or confiscated. But for a moment he could imagine her sitting in that heavy wooden desk chair with the casters on its feet, rolling this way and that, the sun warming her, the whole sun-washed, green, and growing countryside on continuous display through that window.

It wasn't a long, meticulous thought, just a quick impression, a simple conclusion: Mulligan hadn't captured all that Sally Roe was by such descriptions as "leftover hippie" and "loser."

Ben heard footsteps on the front porch and then Mrs. Potter's voice calling, "Officer Cole?"

"Yes, ma'am, I'm in here."

He made his way through the house to meet her, and found her in the living room, her arms crossed, shaking her head at the terrible mess.

"Just look at this! I've never been so disgusted!"

Ben was quite stunned himself. "These were people sent by *our* department?"

"That's what they said. Sergeant Mulligan said they'd be

coming by to look for clues and things and to just let them in, so I did; and when they left, the place looked like this! Do you think I should complain?"

"Well . . . who were they? Had you ever seen them before?"

"No. They weren't from around here."

"Did they say what they were after?"

"No, I didn't think to ask."

"Well . . ." Ben looked all around, not sure what to tell her. "I'll, uh . . . I'll ask Sergeant Mulligan about it. I wouldn't worry. I'm sure they'll also take responsibility for cleaning the place up once they've finished their investigation."

She shook her head and started slowly for the door. "Well, I suppose they may as well box it all up and give it to a charity or something. I don't know what else to do with all the clothes and things with Sally dead. Poor thing. And tell me, just what am I supposed to do with her . . ." She stopped short, standing out on the front porch, looking up and down the drive. "Well . . . that's right! Her truck!"

Ben went out to join her. "Something wrong?"

She was still looking around. "Well, I was just going to ask you what I should do with her pickup truck now that she's dead, but now I remember . . . it isn't even here."

Ben took note of that. "That's . . . uh . . . that's unusual?"

"Well, she always drove it to work, and she always came home in it every day, and if she was home the other night, it just seems sensible that her truck would have been here. She would have had it parked right over there. See that brown grass? That's where she always kept it."

"Maybe it was already impounded. I'll check."

"But it wasn't here the evening I found her."

Ben made a curious face. "That is a little odd, isn't it?"

"Oh . . . who knows what's what anymore . . ." Cecilia looked through the doorway, surveying the living room again. "But I guess she was terribly lonely. Seemed like the animals were her only friends. I figured she was divorced, or separated, something like that. Can't see how else a beautiful redhead like that could be all alone and single."

Ben didn't think the question was that important when he asked it. "She was a redhead?"

"Sure. Had hair like the sunrise."

No. That didn't make sense; it didn't feel comfortable. "Umm . . . what *did* she look like, Mrs. Potter?"

"Oh . . . she was pretty, but tired, you know? Had freckles, big brown eyes . . . but lots of lines, lots of care in her face."

"How tall would you say she was?"

"Mmmm . . ." She held up her hand, palm down. "About there."

"Five five, five six . . . what about her age?"

"Well, she said thirty-four on her rental application, but that was two years ago, so I guess she's about thirty-six; that would be about right."

Ben doublechecked. "And red hair?"

She looked at him just a little impatiently. "Didn't you see her the other night?"

"Well, yes . . ."

But suddenly he wasn't so sure.

The red Porsche was traveling at better than ninety miles an hour when it failed to negotiate the turn, sailed off the freeway shoulder, and nosed into an embankment. Several cars stopped the moment it happened, and there were many witnesses.

"Yeah," said a retired vacationer, "he was doing fine there, passed my camper like I was standing still, and then, zingo! Right off the shoulder, just like that!"

"He was going too fast," said the wife, "just way too fast!"

The patrolman wrote it all down. There was an adequate crew on hand: two patrol cars, two aid cars, and even a fire truck, flashing their lights, setting out flares, and creating quite a spectacle. All the passing drivers were doing the usual rubbernecking, and traffic on the highway had slowed to a crawl.

The patrolman shouted, "Hey, let's get someone out there to handle that traffic! Get those cars moving!"

His partner came up the bank from the wreck. "Got an ID for you, Brent!"

"So, was I right?"

"Yep, it's James Bardine, the hotshot kid lawyer, your favorite."

"Dead, I take it."

"Oh yeah. Half his body went through the windshield, and he's wrapped up in the hood. They're going to have to cut up the car to get him out of there."

The patrolman scribbled it all down. "Well, now we won't be able to play tag with him anymore. Too bad."

The partner looked down into the gully where several men were cutting and winching the front of the car apart, trying to extricate the body. "Boy, the way he could corner in that thing! Never missed a move! He must have had a blowout or something."

"Probably fell asleep at the wheel."

"In the middle of the day?" The partner frowned. "Not him. He was a good driver. I'm kind of surprised."

"Aw, the other guys will figure it out, so don't worry about it. Let's just do our job and get out of here."

James Bardine was as crumpled and crushed as his car; his blood trickled to the ground even as the medics began to pull his body out of the twisted metal. It was tedious work, and they were taking it slow.

But during their grim task, no one smelled the odor of sulfur, or saw the yellow eyes peering from the rear of the car; they didn't hear the fiendish snicker, or the sudden rushing of black, leathery wings as the spirits soared away.

Lucy Brandon and her daughter Amber got home about 5 in the afternoon, and both of them were tired, cranky, and disoriented. Lucy's day had been traumatic enough with the filing of the lawsuit and everything that entailed, and she dreaded the thought of her face being on television that night. Amber's day had been a shambles; she'd spent most of the day at Claire's house instead of in school with her friends, and she still wasn't entirely sure why.

Lucy found some stew in the freezer. She could heat that up in the microwave and then make some salad, and that should take care of dinner for now. She was too tired and preoccupied to put any big effort into a meal tonight.

Amber took off her coat and plopped down on the floor in the living room among her dolls and toys. She picked up one doll, a blonde baby in a long, pink dress, and cuddled it, rocking it gently.

"Mommy?" she asked.

"Yes, honey," Lucy answered from the kitchen.

"Can't I go back to the school?"

Lucy didn't like that question. It made it all the more difficult to keep her mind made up. "No, honey, not the Christian school. We'll try to get you back into Miss Brewer's class. Would you like that?"

Amber rocked the doll and looked down into its little, painted eyes. "I want to go to the Christian school."

Lucy punched the buttons on the microwave and set it whirring. "We'll . . . well, we'll just talk about that later, Amber. It's been a confusing day."

Amber sank deeper and deeper into a melancholy mood. "I don't want to go back to Miss Brewer's class. I don't want to do those things anymore."

Lucy looked into the living room. "Amber, hang up your coat, please."

The little girl ignored her.

"Amber!"

She sat there very still, her blue eyes staring forward and blank. The doll had fallen from her arms.

Lucy approached her to give the command more emphasis. "Amber, I said to hang up your coat!"

"Aahhh!" the little girl squealed in delight, her face breaking into an ecstatic smile. She was looking at a little toy car on the coffee table.

Lucy froze where she stood. Oh no. It was happening again.

Amber rose to her feet, leaped in the air, and pawed the air like a jubilant show horse. She whinnied like a wild stallion, her blue eyes dancing; she tossed her head, causing her blonde locks to whip about her shoulders. "Indeed! All is well, Amber! Indeed, have no fear, for your friends do go before you!"

Lucy didn't know what to do. She was just getting so tired of this. "Amber, that's enough! You don't need to be Amethyst! I don't want you to be Amethyst! Now hang up your coat!"

Amber trotted up to the coffee table and grabbed the little car. "Varroooom!" She raced it around the table, mimicking the sound of squealing tires.

Lucy was angry now. "Amber! Do you want me to—" She was going to say the word spank, but . . . now it didn't seem to fit.

"Faster," said Amethyst, "faster, faster . . . to your death, to your death!"

Then, with a final squealing sound and a powerful thrust of her hand, she sent the little car off the end of the table. It flew across the room and nosed into the carpet, tumbling end over end.

"And now you are gone, removed from that which is called life!" said Amethyst with a raucous laugh and another whinny. "You were just so clumsy!"

Lucy backed away as her daughter danced and pranced around the little upside-down car.

She took Amber's coat and hung it up herself.

nine

"YOU did *what?*"

Attorney Wayne Corrigan had been patiently listening to Tom Harris's story up to this point and had hardly said a word. This was his first question.

Tom tried to back up a bit to explain. "She was . . . well, she was 'channeling' a spirit."

Corrigan rested his forehead on his fingertips and stared down at his desk, paging through the lawsuit as purely an emotional outlet. Looking down felt safer right now than looking Tom Harris and Pastor Mark Howard in the eye. "Channeling . . ."

"Well, yes. We used to call it mediumism; a person allows a demonic spirit to speak through him or her . . ."

"Well, yes, I know what it is, but . . ." And then Corrigan couldn't think of the right words for his feelings. He could only shake his head.

This was his last appointment of the day, and now it would probably be his worst. He was trying to be pleasant, but it was tough. Oh, what so many people expected of him! Here he was, in his forties, a small-town lawyer just scraping by, a reasonable man with a dear wife, four kids, mortgage payments, and a life of struggles and mistakes just like everybody else. But once again, someone with a need and no funds was sitting there looking for him to perform some miracle and suggest quick, simple answers to a case that was going to be complex and difficult. It just wasn't fair.

Pastor Mark decided to get into this. "Mr. Corrigan, I can assure you that Tom is a reasonable and truthful man. I believe what he's saying, and besides, Mrs. Fields can concur. She was there; she saw it too."

"All right, all right."

Corrigan stopped to think for a moment. Should he hear the rest of this? How far should he let these two go before he turned them down? Maybe he should just tell them how

79

much defending a case like this would cost, and that would end this whole conversation. He wasn't too familiar with Tom Harris, but he knew Mark Howard and liked him. This gentle, genuine man in his fifties had that "gray head found in the way of righteousness" that the Bible talked about. Corrigan considered him a decent man of God, and most everyone agreed that the Good Shepherd Community Church was doing a lot of good for its people and for the community.

Corrigan shook his head. *It always happens to the good people,* he thought.

He leaned back with a sigh. "Okay, go on."

Tom wasn't sure he wanted to. "She . . . well, she came to our school just about three months ago. Her mother brought her in and signed her up."

"Did Mrs. Brandon agree to your Statement of Beliefs?"

"Well, yes. She signed her acceptance of them. She knows our doctrinal positions."

"What about the paragraph in the handbook about corporal punishment?"

"Well, I assumed that she'd read it."

"All right, go ahead."

Tom regathered his thoughts and picked up the story again. "Amber got along fine with the other kids for a while. It took her about a month to fit in. Then, during recess, she started teaching the children . . . how to relax."

"Relaxation techniques?"

Tom and Mark looked at each other with a ray of hope in their eyes.

"You've heard of it?" Tom asked.

"We had a case a year ago involving yoga being taught in a physical education class, and relaxation techniques were a part of it. Some parents—Christian parents—complained the school was teaching Eastern religion."

"So . . ." Mark was curious, "what happened?"

"We complained to the school district, but we didn't get the results we wanted. The school simply changed all the terms and sanitized the program so it wouldn't sound like religion, and then just kept doing it."

"So . . ." ventured Tom, "I guess you lost that one."

"We didn't exactly lose it. We dropped it. Let's hear the rest of your story."

"Well . . . I saw what Amber was doing and I asked her what was going on, and she told me that it was what she learned in Miss Brewer's class—that would be at the Bacon's Corner Elementary—and that it was fun because it helped you feel better and meet special friends, imaginary guides. I didn't know quite how to handle that, so I let it go. The other kids didn't seem that interested anyway.

"Well, then the kids started playing pretend games—you know how kids do. They were playing like they were in a horse show, and some of them were acting like horses and doing tricks while the other kids were the trainers. Kids play pretend games like that all the time—it was nothing odd, really.

"But then . . . Amber became the leader in the group, and her horse—the one she was pretending to be—was showing all the other horses how to prance, and do tricks, and how to . . . well, be good horses, I guess. And that was fine. But after recess, she wouldn't stop pretending to be a horse. She'd prance into the room and sit at her desk for a while, then prance over to the pencil sharpener, then prance up and down the aisles for no good reason, and she'd make horse sounds whenever I called on her, and we started having a real discipline problem. She was disturbing the class and disrupting things at every turn."

Mark prompted, "Tell him about the horse's name."

Tom recalled that part. "Oh yeah, right. I got after her once. I said, 'Amber, now you sit down and be quiet,' and she—" Tom made the motions with his hands—"pawed the air like a wild horse, and whinnied, and said, 'I'm not Amber. My name is Amethyst!'" Tom shrugged. "That was enough. I had to take her into the office with Mrs. Fields and have her paddled."

"Uh . . ." Corrigan looked at the document on his desk. "I think that's the second item on the complaint here."

"I think so. We followed the procedure clearly stated in the

81

handbook and agreed to by any parent who enrolls his or her child. We use a paddle when a child decides to force his will against the teacher's will and we've carefully considered all the circumstances. We get alone with the student, we pray with them, we immediately try to contact the parents—"

"Could you contact Mrs. Brandon?"

"No. We tried her at home and at the Post Office, but she just wasn't available and the situation was getting pretty intense."

"Who spanked Amber?"

"Mrs. Fields. It's our policy that the girls must be spanked by a woman and the boys by a man."

"Oh, that's good. Did you have a witness?"

"Yes, our art teacher was there that day, and she served as a witness. We made a record of the whole thing, and then we finally contacted Mrs. Brandon that night and told her what had happened."

"So what was her reaction?"

"That's the strange part. She agreed with our action. She wasn't opposed to spanking Amber if Amber needed it."

Corrigan looked at the lawsuit again. "Mm. Somebody's changed her mind. But when did you . . . uh . . ."

Tom knew what Corrigan meant. "Just about a month ago. After we punished Amber, things went pretty smoothly for about three days, and then . . ." Tom stopped to think. "I think it must have started up again during noon recess. Amber became a horse again, just like before, and came back into class as . . . as 'Amethyst.' This time I wasn't about to tolerate it, and I got firm with her, confronted her, and then . . ."

Tom had to stop. He looked like he would cry. He forced himself to continue. "And then something came over that little girl. Her entire personality changed. She began to blaspheme, and curse, and mock the name of Jesus, and . . . and I had to get her out of there. The other kids were really being disturbed by it.

"I took her by the arm and had to physically drag her from the room—she was grabbing onto the desks and the chairs and even the other kids. Mrs. Fields could hear the commotion from clear across the hall, and she came running to see what was going on, and it took the two of us to get her out into the common room and hold her down. She was just having a real tantrum . . . no, worse than that. She wasn't herself. She wasn't Amber Brandon."

Tom stopped. Neither Corrigan nor Mark said anything. There were no questions. They were both waiting to hear the rest.

Tom pushed ahead, over the edge. "So, I . . . I discerned in my spirit that Amber was manifesting a demon, and I confronted this . . . this Amethyst in the name of Jesus; I ordered it to be silent, and to come out of her."

Corrigan slumped in his chair and exhaled a long sigh.

Mark interjected, "But she was all right after that, wasn't she?"

"She was herself again, yes."

Corrigan asked, "So naturally you assumed that this demon had left Amber, that you'd succeeded in casting it out?"

Tom was obviously embarrassed. "Yes. I guess so. But she must have told some real tales when she got home. Mrs. Brandon came in for a conference the next day, and by then she was beside herself, accusing me of physical abuse, terror, intimidation . . ."

Corrigan looked at his bookshelf, steadily slumping lower in his chair. "You tried to cast a demon out of a ten-year-old child . . ."

Mark protested, "Mr. Corrigan, you know what the Bible says about demon activity. You know demons are real, don't you?"

Corrigan flopped his arm over his desk and pointed it in Mark's face. "Do you think a jury will buy that, pastor? Go ahead! Pull a stunt like that and then try convincing any jury in this country that your behavior was appropriate!" Now he used both hands because he needed a bigger gesture. "A *child*, a ten-year-old child, and you tried to cast a demon out of her!"

"Well, what was I *supposed* to do?" Tom asked.

Corrigan sat up before he slid off his chair. He leaned over his desk and leafed through the complaint in front of him. "Well, to start out, you shouldn't have acted alone and you shouldn't have gone ahead with this . . . this act . . . without getting some counsel, even *legal* counsel."

Mark said, "He knows that now."

Then Tom protested, "But legal counsel? How was I supposed to know about that? Since when did Paul and Silas seek legal counsel before they—"

"They ended up in jail, remember?" Corrigan snapped, and for him to use a voice that was even a *little* loud had to mean he was upset. "They were beaten and thrown in jail for casting out a demon, and you're up against the civil version of the same thing. A civil suit isn't going to get you thrown in jail, but you're still going to need some kind of a Philippian earthquake to get you out of this. The American Citizens' Freedom Association has their fingerprints all over this thing . . . I suppose you know that."

Mark and Tom looked at each other. The ACFA, that infamous association—one could say conspiracy—of professional, idealistic legal technicians, whitewashed, virtuous, and all-for-freedom on the exterior, but viciously liberal and anti-Christian in its motives and agenda. Nowadays it was getting hard to find any legal action taken against Christians, churches, or parachurch organizations that did not have the ACFA and its numerous, nationwide affiliates behind it.

Mark said, "We thought maybe that was the case . . ."

Corrigan tapped the bottom of the first page of the complaint. "Ames, Jefferson, and Morris are members of the ACFA; they run the local chapter, and they've been the liberal, legal bullies around here for years. Why else do you suppose the press knew about your kids being taken away and were right there to hassle you at your home and in the police station? Why do you think they were right there to record you being served your summons? To create a scandal and smear you in the press, that's why. Why do you think your two kids were taken away in the first place? As soon as the ACFA heard about this case, they leaked the information—probably embellished quite a bit—to the Child Protection people and pulled them into it. They want this kind of spicy news. Now you're branded a child abuser, Tom, before you even get to court. The ACFA plays dirty.

"Well, just look at the complaint here against . . . uh . . . the pastor, the headmaster, the church, and the church board: 'Outrageous Religious Behavior Against a Child'—casting out the demon, of course, 'Physical Abuse by Spanking, Excessive Religious Instruction Harmful to the Child, Harassment, Discrimination, and Religious Indoctrination Using Federal Funds.'

"All this stuff is dynamite; it's going to make the case difficult because the ACFA will use all these hot issues to get the public's attention and stir them up.

"And did you catch those big key words, *federal funds?* That's what's going to get them through the door of the federal courts: 'violating mother's civil rights by teaching religion using federal funds—a violation of the Munson-Ross Civil Rights Act and the Federal Day-care and Private Primary School Assistance Act.'"

"Federal funds?" asked Tom.

"Lucy Brandon works at the Post Office, right? She's a federal employee, and under this Federal Day-care Act she receives a subsidy to help pay Amber's tuition. Didn't you know that?"

Tom was obviously surprised. "It's news to me. She didn't say a thing about it."

"Interesting. Maybe she didn't want you to know. Anyway, if you're getting federal funds, that means you can't discriminate or impose religion or spank or cause mental anguish by suggesting a child is demon-possessed, or whatever else the ACFA wants to test in a court of law. That's the whole point of this thing: they find a vague law and then work up legal cases just like this one to stretch that law as far as they can in the courts. This Federal Day-care and Private Primary School Assistance Act is a big, vague, anything-goes cloud of smoke, a clever move by Congress that most people never heard about.

Now the ACFA's ready to get it defined through case law, legal precedents, maybe a Supreme Court decision.

"That's why they're going federal with this, citing federal law. Look here: 'You are commanded to appear at nine in the morning, two weeks hence, at the department of the Honorable Emily R. Fletcher of the *Federal* District Court, Western District, Room 412, *Federal* Courthouse, blah, blah, blah.' This is a federal case, guys."

"So what do we do?" asked Tom.

Corrigan became quiet and then fumbled through an answer. "Well . . . I would say you need a lawyer, all right, but . . . um . . . I'm not sure whom you should consult on something like this . . ."

"You mean, you won't take this case?" Mark asked.

Corrigan gave a nervous chuckle and shook his head. "Well . . . no. No, I can't." He quickly blurted, "Now before you say anything or ask me why not . . ."

Then he stopped. *Oh brother, here I go again, having to explain this to another bunch of naive martyrs.*

"Listen, no offense intended, please understand. I mean, I can appreciate your position . . ." Corrigan pushed his chair back from his desk, waved his hands around a little, and looked at his bookcase as he tried to find the words. "But I've just about established a new policy in this office not to defend Christians anymore who can't pay for my services."

Mark thought the statement a little strange. "But . . . we didn't think you'd do this for free."

It wasn't a good enough escape for Corrigan to look down at his desk—now he looked down at the rug. "Pastor Howard, you're the last guy on earth I'd ever want to turn down, but . . . Well, let me just share some depressing information with you.

"Okay, I'm a Christian and everybody knows it; the police know it, the local judges know it, the county prosecutor knows it . . . Worst of all, all the Christians around this county know it. That means, when the Christians get into a legal predicament, they call me, because I'm a 'brother in the Lord.'

"But then, because they're . . . Christians . . . they come into it having some convictions about how my services are going to be paid for, if paid for at all; they sit in my office and tell me about faith and God's provision and usually throw something in about God rewarding me for all my time and sacrifice; but in the meantime, my practice goes down the tubes from bad debts.

"But please don't get me wrong. I'm not blaming them. It's just the way the system works: The little people—the Christians—get into legal tangles because the state, or the ACFA, or some other rabid, Christian-eating secularist organization decides to pick on them, and those people always have all the power, connections, and finances they need to win any battle they want in a court of law. Not so with the Christians. They have to put on spaghetti dinners and car washes and jogathons just to hire some poor, minor-league attorney like me who supposedly has such a love for righteous causes that he doesn't care about the money."

Corrigan saw that Mark and Tom were listening without any signs of malice—at least not yet; so he proceeded. "Now that's half of the problem. The other half is that all too often Christians just aren't credible. You know, I've actually instructed some clients not to testify in court that they are Christians because in too many cases that information would damage their credibility! The world out there . . . the system . . . thinks it understands us. It has us pegged, categorized, defined. We believe in God; we believe in absolutes. Therefore, we can't possibly be credible!" He chuckled wryly. "When I was in law school it was the other way around. The perception was that people lacked credibility if they didn't believe in God. We've come a long way, haven't we?

"So anyway, I'm faced with two options: I can be retained by Christians and find out later they can't afford my services, or I can take their case for free or on a reduced basis—usually a drastically reduced basis. In this case right here, there would be about a zero chance of any contingency recovery. I could only hope to receive part of the settlement, but even then the system is already so stacked against me that I have no fair

87

chance of winning, and therefore no chance of being paid that way either.

"Am I making this clear for you? To put it simply, I can't afford it, monetarily or reputationally. I've been too close to bankruptcy too many times to take another case like this. I think what you need is a fresh visionary, a brand-new horse who still has some miles left on him, somebody you can run ragged for next to nothing."

Corrigan stopped. He felt released now, but also a little ashamed. He looked at the wall where his eyes fell on his license to practice law, and concluded with, "Sometimes I almost admit to myself that I hate this job. Look what it does to me . . . makes me dump all my feelings on good people like you."

Mark looked at the legal torpedo on Corrigan's desk and sighed. "So where can we go from here? Tom's children are taken from him, and he still doesn't know where. Now the school is slapped with a lawsuit that . . . Well, it seems to me that our very freedoms are being threatened. There aren't any attorneys in Bacon's Corner; we could have gone elsewhere, but we came to Claytonville to see you because—and I'm not ashamed to say it—we knew you were a Christian. We knew you'd have the right perspective."

Corrigan looked at the minister just a little sheepishly. "Well, I guess I've blown that notion out of the water."

"But what about Tom? He could be bitter right now. He lost his wife in a car wreck just three years ago, his salary is pitiful, but he's stayed right here with his two children and served as the headmaster at our Christian school for four years now, doing an excellent job. And what thanks does he get? His children taken away and a lawsuit against the school that could jeopardize everything he and the rest of us hold dear. It isn't fair. It isn't right. Even so, he's remained true to his calling. He's a righteous man, a man of principle and conviction . . ."

"Hence the pitiful salary. Excuse me. Go on."

Mark was getting disgusted. "I'm through."

Corrigan sat quietly, rested his chin on his knuckles,

thought for a moment, then nodded in agreement to his own thoughts.

"And to think it all started in Bacon's Corner. I guess it had to happen somewhere." He sat up straight and folded his hands on the desk. For the first time in several minutes, he looked directly at Tom and Mark. "Pastor, the ACFA isn't after your little school; Tom, they're not really interested in you either; as for this allegedly traumatized child, they couldn't care less about her. No, what they're really after is a legal precedent, something that's going to affect not just you, but everyone. They have all the money and skill they need to pull this thing off, and they know that you don't, and that's what they're counting on. That's why they chose a little place like Bacon's Corner and a little dirt-poor church like yours.

"And I guess they have me where they want me. I can just see those ACFA lawyers sitting in their office over at Ames, Jefferson, and Morris saying, 'Yeah, hit Bacon's Corner. That Wayne Corrigan is a burned-out tube, he'll never take the case.' Now wouldn't that be just peachy for them?"

He looked at the papers on his desk again.

"All right, I'll tell you what: I'll repent . . . sort of. I'll take this case, but I'll take as little of it as possible. That means you do the work, you do the hoofing, you do the research, you build the case. I'll tell you what to do, I'll write up the affidavits, I'll take the depositions, I'll plead the case and present the arguments, I'll advise you; but any information relating to this case is your responsibility. I suggest you get yourselves a private investigator to help you out. As far as my involvement, you'll get what you pay for, and . . ." He swallowed hard, came to a reluctant decision, and added, " . . . I'll reduce my fee by half, but you must agree to raise the other half."

Tom and Mark exchanged a quick glance and quickly agreed. "Okay."

"So what comes first?" Mark asked.

Corrigan leafed through the papers. "Number One, you've got a temporary injunction here that restrains you from just about everything named in the complaint. Uh . . . I think what it's going to boil down to is that you'll have to cease and desist from spanking and from any further 'outrageous religious behavior.' Guess that means you can't cast out any more demons until the court hearing in two weeks."

"What happens in two weeks?" asked Tom.

"We have to appear in court . . . 'to show cause, if any you have, why you and all persons acting on your behalf or on behalf of the school should not be immediately restrained from spanking, hitting, or otherwise having physical contact with children at the school for any reason whatsoever, and why you and all persons acting on your behalf in concert with you, should not be immediately restrained from any further religious behavior which could prove harmful to the mental, emotional, or social welfare of the child, or any excessive religious instruction, direct or indirect, of any kind, at the school or day-care facility, that could prove harmful . . .' And it goes on and talks about all this other stuff."

"Just what do they mean, 'excessive religious instruction'?" asked Tom.

"That has yet to be defined."

"What should we do?" asked Mark.

"Try to behave yourselves for the two weeks. Don't be outrageous, whatever that means. In the meantime, you need to give me some good arguments why you should be allowed to continue the above-mentioned activities. Then I'll file the briefs and affidavits with the court, and then we'll go in and see if we can turn you guys loose from this restraining order. That's the first thing."

"And then?" asked Mark.

Corrigan suddenly looked worried and careworn. "One bite at a time, pastor. You're going to be busy for a long, long time."

"What about Ruth and Josiah?" asked Tom.

"No easy answers there. It's going to be a tangled mess, and could be even worse, depending on whom you're dealing with in the system. I think you're entitled to a hearing within seventy-two hours to determine if the removal of your children has merit, but that's usually a rubber-stamp session where the judge approves the removal of the children based on the testimony of the social worker. You might be called to appear, you might be barred from the hearing altogether. It just depends on who's running the case. I'll look into it."

"But . . . won't I get my kids back?"

Corrigan hesitated to answer the question. "You'll probably have to go through a trial first, and that could mean a wait of six months or more."

Neither Tom nor Mark were ready for an answer like that.

"That can't be all there is to it!" said Mark. "There have to be other options, something we can do!"

"You can pray," Corrigan answered. "Specifically, pray for some friends in the right places. You've got a fight ahead of you."

ten

SALLY would be staying at the Rest Easy another night. She had the whole ten thousand dollars to spend on this one room if she wanted to, if no better ideas came to her. Right now she had no better ideas.

She'd used up the afternoon and all the stationery in the room just scribbling thoughts down as they came to her. Now, as the day outside the windows gave way to evening, she sat at the table and leafed through page after page, her day's work.

The first page was no masterpiece: "Crazy my name is Sally Roe," followed by a full page of aimless lines and squiggles. Apparently she'd failed to capture her thoughts. But that was depressing. Maybe this *was* an accurate record of her thoughts. She didn't even remember doing it.

The next page had some scribbled words that looked like they might be "Death" and "Madness," but she couldn't be sure. After that, her writing broke down into chaotic scribbles again, and then at the bottom of the page she'd written her name several times, encircled by some strange, dark doodles. She remembered making those in a pit of depression when she didn't feel like thinking or writing anything. It just felt good to doodle, to pour her feelings onto the page without using any language.

The third page sounded so great when she'd first written it: "I am I: I think, I exist, but know nothing of the grasping of the essence of all that is under or over the abysmal attitudes that so wrack our awareness in the last autumns of mayhem upon the earth . . ." Now not even she could decode all that. Apparently her brain had been working while her mind was disconnected.

But she felt encouraged, not because her afternoon's project had produced such drivel, but because she could sit quietly now with her mind clear and *realize* it was drivel. She'd just come through some kind of spiritual storm, some raging, agonizing battle. *Just like the old days*, she thought. So many of the impressions, the hallucinations, the mindless wanderings were so familiar. Her mind had not slipped over the edge like that in almost ten years.

No doubt it was this new, mysterious terror that had brought it all back. She had stepped in the way of an old Evil, and she recognized it all too well. It must have recognized her too, and that was why it was chasing her now. With only a little imagination she could sense it still lurking outside the walls of the motel room, ready to pounce on her again should she ever rest.

But . . . what to do, what to do. What was the next step? How could she free herself?

She picked up that day's *Hampton County Star*. There was nothing new about her own death, and she figured there never would be. That story, her life, her name, were now buried, tucked neatly away in the archives to be forgotten.

She flipped to the front page and studied a large photo. Some blonde lady was handing a guy what looked like a summons. Well, this was more news from Bacon's Corner, a Christian school scandal. Tom Harris, headmaster at the Good Shepherd Christian School . . . accused of child abuse . . . accusations brought by local postmaster—

Sally's eyes froze on those last words. The local postmaster? She read the paragraph again.

" . . . the child's mother, the local postmaster, first became suspicious when her ten-year-old daughter was playing games of pretend and began to recount questionable behavior by her teacher at the school . . ."

Sally checked the time. A little after 5. Maybe there was something on television. She clicked it on.

Well . . . nothing much, just the sale of a pro football team to some unknown millionaire, a cleanup of hazardous waste in some small Midwest town, a new paint job for a historical building in the state capital . . .

She let the television talk to itself while she finished reading the newspaper.

According to reliable sources, Tom Harris's two young children were taken from his home by child welfare workers yesterday afternoon . . . The CPD had what it felt was adequate reason to remove the children from the home . . . "If we must err, we must err on the side of the child," said the source . . . CPD is beginning an investigation into the alleged abuses of children at the school . . . Postmaster Lucy Brandon and ACFA lawyers have filed a suit against the school, charging the school with outrageous religious behavior against a child, physical abuse by spanking, excessive religious instruction harmful to the child, harassment, discrimination, and religious indoctrination using federal funds. The little girl reported that Harris tried to cast a demon out of her . . .

Oh! There it was on the television! Sally turned up the sound just as the on-the-scene footage began to roll. There was the little school, and there was Tom Harris, the headmaster, standing in the doorway. Yes, and there was the blonde lady, handing him the summons.

Chad Davis, reporter for Channel Seven News, was doing his voice-over narration. "The lawsuit on behalf of Ms. Brandon once again raises the question of how much religious freedom is too much, especially where young children are concerned, and calls for a limit to extreme fundamentalist practices that violate the laws of the state."

Next shot: Lucy Brandon, the postmaster, and . . . Amber! Neither of them said anything—they just went to their car and got in. Davis narrated, "The case could have implications at the federal level because federal funds were involved in the child's education at the school. The ACFA argues that the practices and teachings of the school are extreme, harmful, and clearly violate the laws concerning separation of church and state."

The blonde lady came on the screen. Her name appeared below her face: Claire Johanson, ACFA.

"We are concerned for the welfare of our children," she said, "and want to protect them from any more vicious and inexcusable abuse inflicted upon them under the license of religion."

Next came a quick interview with a Child Protection

95

Department lady, Irene Bledsoe. "We always investigate any reports that come to us," she was saying, "and we are looking into it."

Davis pressed a question from off camera. "Have Mr. Harris's children been removed from his home?"

"Yes, but that's all I can say."

"In the meantime," Davis continued in his voice-over, "the Federal District Court has handed down a temporary injunction against the school, barring any further spanking, religious teaching that could be harmful to children, or outrageous religious behavior, pending a hearing to be held in two weeks."

Back came the anchorman, staring soberly at the camera. "Thank you, Chad, for that report. We'll definitely keep working on this one and bring you more developments as they happen. Speaking on the lighter side . . ."

Commercial. Young bucks running and hollering and opening bottles of beer.

She turned off the television and sat on the bed, stunned. Irene Bledsoe . . . that same woman with the ratty brown hair and crinkled moonface. That same scowl.

The woman at the intersection! That was *her*? Those were *Tom Harris's* kids?

Lucy Brandon. Amber. Oh, and just when my mind was clearing up!

Thoughts began to fill Sally's mind with the bursting rhythm of popcorn, carrying it away in a tumbling flood, driving it forward like a wild automobile with no one at the wheel; it raced and swerved headlong from one thought to another, skipping over memories and colliding with replays, snagging and dragging scenes through her consciousness faster than she could watch them, flushing out conversations, facts, faces.

She clapped her hands to the sides of her head as if being attacked by a horde of noises. *Please, one at a time! I can't hear you when you're all screaming at once! Slow down!*

She looked at the news photo of Tom Harris again, standing in the doorway of the little school, getting his big white envelope from the blonde lady.

So he had met little Amber too!

Sally's hand went to the ring hanging under her shirt. It seemed that bad things happened to people who had run-ins with Amber Brandon.

She went to the table and found the first piece of paper she'd scribbled on that day. It was all she had; perhaps some legible writing would show up against all that nonsense.

Unless she just wrote more nonsense. It was going to be a struggle, but she would try again. She would try all night if she had to. Her head was boiling with scattered, unruly thoughts, and sooner or later they would have to spill out in some clear fashion.

Then suddenly, all around the motel, such an unexpected legion of harassing demons began to shower down that Chimon and Scion could no longer hide and had to throw any subtlety to the wind. They were in full glory, bright and visible, swatting and slashing as the demons swarmed around them like vile, biting bees. The intensity of the onslaught was shocking, surprisingly strong. It seemed each spirit would be swatted away only to be replaced by two more, and the air was filled with them. They were bold, brash, reckless, attacking with screams and shrieks, even grinning mockingly.

"For Destroyer!" they screamed as their battle cry. "For Destroyer!"

So that was it. The demonic warlord was trying a new tactic now, and this difficulty could only be caused by one thing: something had happened to their prayer cover.

"Well," said Judy Waring, "you just . . . you just never know about people. I always did wonder about him. We voted on your recommendation, we went along with it, and now what are we going to do . . ."

Mark was trying to end this telephone conversation and get back to the meeting. The parsonage telephone had been ringing all day, and he was about to pull the plug out of the wall.

"Listen, Judy," he said, "we're about to have an emergency board meeting about it right now, so I have to hang up. But let me assure you that Tom's handling this whole thing very well, just really open and forthright. I think we can trust him."

"Well . . . I'm hearing a lot of things . . ."

"Right . . . Let me say something about that before I hang up. I don't want any more gossip going around about Tom or the school or any of these matters. If there's anything to be settled, it will be settled at this meeting, with Tom present and able to speak for himself. Now please—"

"You *did* hear what the news said tonight—"

"Judy! Now listen to me! You don't need to get your information from the news, not when all this is happening to *us*, in our own church. Now you just sit tight and don't listen to any more rumors, and please don't spread any, all right?"

"Well, all right, but I don't know if we can keep Charlie enrolled at the school with this going on . . ."

"We'll have our meeting tonight, and then we'll take care of your concerns. Just be patient."

Judy was about to say something else. She always had the last word in any conversation. Mark quietly and courteously hung up before she could get rolling again.

Cathy Howard was nearby, making coffee for the men gathered in the dining room, and overhearing Mark's end of at least the twentieth conversation. Mark told her quietly, "Maybe you can unplug this thing, or leave it off the hook."

She made a questioning face.

"Or take the calls?" Mark asked.

"Just go ahead and have your meeting," she said with a chuckle. "I'll screen the calls for you."

That deserved a kiss. Cathy, a striking blonde with fine Nordic features, was remarkably serene. She'd kept her composure during this rough time, and Mark was thankful for her, more than he could say. Of course she didn't enjoy tribulation—who does?—but right now, when extra strength and resilience were needed, she was supplying them, and that gave Mark a quiet assurance that they would get through this crisis.

He stepped through the kitchen door and out into the dining room. The four church elders were gathered around the table, listening to Tom's account of what had happened up to this time.

"So what was it this spirit said?" asked Jack Parmenter, a hardworking, durable farmer with silver hair.

Tom didn't enjoy the memory of it. "Oh . . . it said we were all fools to worship Jesus, that He was only a liar, and not God at all, but just an illegitimate child—uh, the spirit used another word, of course—and then it went on to accuse Jesus of sexual perversions . . . in graphic terms."

"All that coming from a ten-year-old," said Bob Heely in disgust. Bob was a Viet Nam vet, a diesel mechanic who kept all the farm machinery around Bacon's Corner running. His hands were rough and grease-blackened.

"Sounds pretty weird to me," said Doug Parmenter, Jack's son and the spitting image of his father. "What do you think, Mark? I've never seen someone demon-possessed before."

Mark took his place at the head of the table. "I have, and I think Tom's impressions were correct."

Vic Savan, who ran the farm right next to the Parmenters', concurred with that. "Well, what that little girl—or that demon—had to say fits right in with everything else the Devil's saying nowadays about Christians and about Christ. Just look at all the slander he's been spreading in the papers and on the television, and I don't mean just our own situation. Seems like it's everyone else's civil rights and freedoms that matter, but when it comes to Christians, people—and I guess demons—can say and do whatever they want."

"Well," said Mark, "like Wayne Corrigan said, a lawsuit, a test of Christian freedom, had to happen somewhere. Looks like that somewhere is here in Bacon's Corner, and at our school."

"But isn't it just like Satan to use a child?" said Jack. "I mean, that's getting really low."

"Well, he can use God's own people, too. How many of

you have heard some destructive talk about this before coming to the meeting tonight?"

Every man put up his hand.

Vic related, "I ran into the Jessups at the filling station, and they were wondering how many other kids got abused."

Tom cringed at that. "Abused? Just what do they mean by that?"

"You can fill in the blank, Tom."

"Well, we have the newspaper and KBZT to thank for that," said Jack. "They've been tossing that word around like it was a fact."

"And that's my point," said Mark. "We're the elders of this church, and we've got to keep a lid on this thing. There are going to be questions flying and a lot of accusations and gossip, and we'd better be thinking of how we're going to handle it."

Vic raised his eyebrows, shrugged one shoulder, and said, "Well, as far as the Jessups are concerned, they're taking their two kids out. They don't want any part of it."

"Neither do the Wingers," said Doug.

"And they said I was a fool for keeping my three in there," said Bob.

The phone out in the kitchen rang again. They could hear Cathy answering it.

Mark commented, "That's probably another family with the same concerns." He looked at Tom. "Well, Tom, let's get the first item covered and then we can go from there."

Cathy peeked in. "Ted Walroth's on the phone. He saw the news tonight, and he wants to know if we're going to have a congregational meeting."

"Tell him I'll call him back," said Mark. Cathy went to tell him, and Mark returned his attention to Tom. "You want to tell them?"

Tom didn't hesitate. "I'm stepping down as headmaster of the school; I'm going to take a leave of absence until this whole thing gets cleared up."

Jack was ready to debate that move. "Who says?"

"The school's in trouble because of me. If we're going to save it at all, I've got to get out of the picture."

He was right. Every man at the table hated to admit it, but he was right. There was a long, fidgety silence. They all looked at the table or out the window or around the room, and only occasionally at each other.

Mark decided to break the silence. "Tom and I talked and prayed about it, and we agreed that all of us have to face the facts as they are: the ruckus is over him; he's the center of the controversy. Now I know we're all standing with him, but the matter of his innocence is secondary. The biggest and most immediate concern right now is the confidence of the parents and the community. That confidence is taking a real beating right now, and it's going to be hard to get it back if we keep Tom in his position."

Jack fidgeted, looked this way and that, and then gave the table a pound. "But, Mark, we can't do that! It'd be like admitting Tom's guilty!"

Doug jumped in. "But, Dad, some people already think that! I've talked to some folks just today who are ready to give the whole thing up, just pull out of the school and let it die. They're knocked on their backs by this thing."

Mark cut in. "But that's part of the warfare, guys. Satan set this whole thing up so he could weaken us with gossip and slander. We need to do as much as we can to protect ourselves from that, or at least provide no fuel for the fire."

Tom explained, "If I stay at the school, we won't be able to convince anyone that we're truly concerned about all this. *I'm* concerned. I'm willing to step down in good faith until we can get all this trouble resolved."

"We'll do all we can to keep the academy open. Mrs. Fields will stay on and teach the remaining kids in her classes. I'll take charge of the remainder in the upper grades. Tom, what's the prospective enrollment?"

Tom had scribbled down a tentative list. "Um . . . I guess we should go for a worst case scenario . . . which would mean that Judy Waring will take out her son Charlie . . . and then there are the Jessups and their two . . . and then the Wingers with their three . . ."

"What about the Walroths?" asked Jack.

Mark answered, "I'll be calling him. I think I can talk him into hanging on for a while."

"So we'll leave those two children in?" asked Tom.

"For now."

Tom wrote them back in. "Okay. That means five kids are out of Mrs. Fields's class. Her enrollment's cut in half. My class is down by one. That isn't too bad."

"So for now we'll be able to survive," said Mark. "But tonight we'll have to talk about Tom's salary while he's out, plus some more volunteer help to keep things running—I won't have time to do all the bookkeeping and administrating. Then we'll have to reassign the bus route now that the Wingers are out and get someone else to organize the hot lunches now that the Warings are out."

"Donna Hemphile called today," Tom remembered. "She's very supportive of the school, and willing to put in any time she can spare when she's not tied up at the door factory."

"Who?" asked Doug.

"Donna Hemphile," said Mark. "She's a supervisor at the Bergen Door Company, a single gal."

"Yeah, she's nice," said Jack.

"Anyway," said Tom, "she says she'll take care of hot lunches, probably two days a week."

"Good enough." Mark wrote it down in his own notes. "Okay, other things to discuss tonight: We need to update you on what Wayne Corrigan told us, and what we have to do to fight this thing in court." Mark looked at Tom. "And there's also the latest report on your kids."

Tom looked tired. He'd been through quite a battle already over that issue. "Wayne Corrigan called this afternoon. He finally got in touch with someone at the District Court in Claytonville. They had the hearing today, in Judge Benson's court. It took about ten minutes, I understand. I guess I didn't miss anything; they would have barred me from the courtroom anyway. The judge approved the removal and set a date for the trial in October."

"October?" Jack exclaimed. "So what happens in the meantime?"

"I'm supposed to get some counseling, but from a court-appointed counselor. I'll be able to visit the kids, I don't know exactly when, and it'll be controlled; a social worker will have to be there . . ." Tom couldn't continue.

"Well, I say we fight this thing," said Jack. "Let the others run and hide. If being Christian is too tough for them, well, they can't say Jesus didn't warn them. But let's fight it! Let's go to our knees, and beseech the Lord to show us a way out of this. Our God is greater than any lawsuit or any bunch of social service bureaucrats! He'll stand with us, and that's . . . well, that's my final word on the subject!"

Mark looked around the table. "So how about the rest of you? Let me hear from you now, before we take another step."

"Let's fight it," said Doug.

"We're in this for the Lord," said Bob. "He'll help us."

Vic raised his hand to be counted. "Hey, if it had to happen to us, then it had to happen to us. Looks like we're first in line, guys. If we fall, all the other Christian schools are going to fall next. We'd better give them a good fight, with the Lord's help."

Mark felt the hand of God upon these men. He met Tom's eyes, and through Tom's tears he saw a quiet confidence.

"Then let's go to prayer," he said, "and let our agreement this night be settled in Heaven."

They joined hands around the table, making their covenant with each other and God.

High above the town, hovering between Heaven and Earth, his wings a soft, blurred canopy, Captain Tal overheard the transaction. The saints had bound themselves together in prayer according to the will of God; the Lord Almighty had received their petition. There was agreement, and that agreement was now sealed.

"Good," said Tal, "good enough!"

In Claytonville, the demons abruptly called it a day. The last of them swooped down, spit out some insults, and then soared off like a crazed swallow into the night, leaving Chimon and Scion alone on the roof of the motel. The sudden silence was jarring.

"Well," said Chimon, "did we get a prayer?"

"Looks that way," said Scion.

They sat on the roof, their swords resting on the shingles, their eyes scanning the sky. Below them, Sally Roe was lying down to sleep.

Perhaps now they would all have some peace for the night.

eLeven

The Bergen Door Company was a noisy, dusty place employing about a hundred people, the only real industry to be found in Bacon's Corner. It was Friday morning, and during the regular work shift the planers, sanders, saws, and drills produced such a deafening din that ear protection was required and also a lot of lipreading.

Ben wore ear protection—little sponge-rubber earplugs—and also safety glasses as he walked through the factory. He'd never been here before, and found it a fascinating place, with the smell of sawdust filling the air, and doors, doors, doors everywhere, some stacked, some standing, some riding the forklift down to the loading dock; small doors, big doors, cheap doors, exquisite doors.

He was catching a few glances from the employees as he passed by. The sight of a uniformed police officer often roused curiosity, as if "something" was up. He just smiled cordially at the hefty women, the sawdusted men, the part-time students, the single mothers. He recognized many of them, including Donna Hemphile, busily supervising a big material sorting project. She recognized him and waved.

"Hey, Ben, what are you doing here?" she hollered.

"Oh, just a little business," he answered, probably not loud enough for her to hear him. He was hesitant to talk about it.

Up ahead, at the center of all the hubbub, was the enclosed office space of the floor supervisor, Abby Grayson. She spotted him through the office window and gave him a wave. The front office had already called ahead, and she was expecting him.

"Come in out of the racket," she said, throwing open the door.

He stepped inside the little cubicle and she closed the door after him, shutting out the noise.

"Have a seat," she said. "You must be that new cop. I don't

think we've met before, and maybe that's a good thing, you know?"

They went through some friendly introductions. Abby was a homely but personable lady in her forties; she and her husband were real career people in this place. She'd just received her twenty year pin, and he his twenty-five.

"Well," she said, "we're all pretty shocked. Sally was a good worker. It's too bad she didn't open up a little more. We thought she might have some deep problems, but . . . Hey, we *tried* to be friends; what can I say?"

"I've heard from several people that she was reclusive," Ben said.

"Yeah, pretty much a hermit. We invited her to the last Christmas party, and I think she almost came, but then she found some excuse and stayed home. She didn't get out much as far as any of us could tell."

"You wouldn't have any photographs of her, would you?"

"Funny you should mention that. I guess she hated having her picture taken. We were all going to pose for a company picture . . . When was that? I think around Labor Day, and I remember she just kept hiding behind people and turning away. Ehh, some people are like that."

"So what kind of person was she really? What were some of your impressions?"

Abby took a moment to consider the question. "She was bright and intelligent, good with her hands, and caught on to the job right away, really easy to train. But there was always something a little strange about her." Abby smiled about a thought that came to her. "Well, I suppose I can say it now. You know . . . I think she was hiding something. A lot of us thought that."

"Hiding something?"

Abby shook her head and chuckled. "Oh, we came up with all kinds of silly notions, talking about her maybe being a fugitive from the law, or an ex-con, or a witch, or a hooker, or a lesbian . . . It was pretty silly, but when people are that secretive, that quiet, you wonder about them a little. It's only natural."

"Well?"

"Well what?"

"Was she any of those things to your knowledge?"

She laughed. "No. It was talk, nothing but talk."

"But still you think she was hiding something . . ."

"I don't know. She just acted like it, I guess."

Ben chuckled to keep the atmosphere relaxed. "Well . . . how about a description? What did she look like?"

"Oh . . ." Abby's eyes drifted about the room as she reconstructed an image of Sally Roe in her mind. "About my height, and I'm 5' 6". Red hair . . . long . . . I saw her brushing it out once; it went down to about the middle of her back. But she kept it bound up in a checkered scarf when she was working here, so you never saw much of it."

"Color of eyes?"

"Color of eyes . . . Boy, I never gave it much thought. Seems to me they were brown."

"How old was she?"

"Thirties. Maybe a little older."

"How about her weight?"

"Pretty good," and with that comment Abby laughed. "I don't know, she looked all right to me, enough to be jealous about, anyway."

Ben had heard enough for now. He stood up. "Well, thanks a lot. If I think of any more questions I'll give you a jingle. Oh . . ." He scribbled his phone number on a piece of paper. "If you come up with anything you think I'd want to know, just give me a call at home. It'll be fine."

"Sure thing." She stood and shook his hand. "Well, it was a real shock, just really tough news."

He nodded.

"And then that news this morning about the Christian school and what that teacher was doing! What a world, huh? You just never know about people . . . It's kind of scary."

Ango was nothing significant, nothing to bow to, worship, revere, or dread. He was small, thin like a spider, and ugly. Oh, he knew it. He lived with it. He put up with the taunts of the other spirits who lorded it over him, ordered him this way and that way, took his glory, gave him their blame. Ah, it was all part of the warfare, all part of the master's plan for the earth, and each spirit had his own role, his own station, his own level of power. He knew his was a lowly station. To the rest of the demonic kingdom, what was the Bacon's Corner Elementary School? What did it matter among all the schools in the world?

His lips stretched open, and his jagged teeth clicked and gnashed as he hissed a giggle. Oh, this place *did* matter now! The other spirits had laughed and chided, but somewhere, seated loftily at the peak of power, the Strongman himself had chosen this place to begin the Plan. He had spoken the name of Ango as the spirit to be placed in charge! Now little ugly Ango had the Strongman's favor—and the other spirits' envy!

But why not? He deserved it. It took years to take control of this school—to oust the resisters, to implant the sympathizers, to blind the parents to what was happening to their children. It was no small task.

But it happened, and all because of Ango! Let the other spirits call him little and ugly. At this school he was *Ba-al* Ango, the beautiful and mighty. All the deceivers who flitted, darted, and hovered around that place were at his command, and through them many of the teachers, as well as the principal and the vice-principal. That was a precious power, a constant titillation, a marvelous reward for all those years and all that work. As he sat on his haunches on the expansive tar roof, he indulged himself in some hacking, sulfurous laughter.

He was thinking of all those young, impressionable children sitting in all those classrooms down there, and what they must be learning right now. As usual, most of his spirit underlings were occupied with that task. They were the best, and he reveled in the fact that for the past several years, ever since the laws had been changed, their job had been so much easier. Oh, how quickly men could accept the most outrageous of lies once the Truth was removed from consideration!

Yes, there were still some bold saints of God lurking about like stubborn weeds in this otherwise flourishing garden, causing trouble with their protests, parent-teacher conferences, telephone babblings, and notes, notes, notes to the teachers, but . . .

Ango wheezed out another sulfurous laugh and rolled like a playful pup on the black tar. No matter. They were losing. Let them protest. *He* held all the power here.

Mota, strong, tall, and deep bronze, stood with his sword in his hand, his piercing eyes on the Bacon's Corner Elementary School, and his feet in about eight inches of chicken manure. His oriental friend and fellow-warrior Signa stood beside him, as deep into the same predicament. Were they not angelic spirits, it would have been most unpleasant. As it was, they were not disturbed by their surroundings, and the eight hundred cackling leghorns were not aware of their presence in this old chicken house.

It was Friday, and almost time for lunch and the noon recess.

"She's on her way," said Signa.

"Now," said Mota.

They were gone.

The bell rang for lunch. Ango could hear all the classroom doors opening and the mobs of children filling the halls. Recess would be an enjoyable time, just like always. What corruption the teachers could not spread in the classroom, the children could spread among themselves on the playground.

"Hail!" came a booming voice behind him.

"Aaaak!" Ango's sword was immediately in his hand as he spun to face the heavenly warrior. Oh, he was a big brute! A massive Polynesian, shining like lightning, with wings that scattered the fire of the sun. His sword was drawn, and it glimmered with a living light, but he held it downward, the tip resting on the roof.

"Forces!" Ango screamed, and fifty demons popped up

through the roof like startled gophers with squawks and hoots of surprise and rage. They surrounded the big warrior.

"What brings you here?" Ango demanded.

But Mota wanted a little more space. He raised his sword, held it straight out at waist level, and began to sweep it in a wide circular arc around him. The seething, hissing spirits backed off when the tip of the sword passed under their chugging noses.

Now he was more comfortable, and spoke. "I'm looking for a petty little lizard called . . . Ankle . . . Inkle . . ."

"You seek Ango!"

Mota smiled and raised his index finger. "Yes! Ingo, that's it!"

"Ango!" the demon corrected.

Two guards were at their posts by the main door when Signa dropped out of the sky like a ball of lightning and knocked them both to the ground by his sheer presence.

"Forces!" they screamed, struggling to their feet, grabbing their swords. Twenty demons were immediately on hand, swords drawn, eyes gawking at this visitor.

One spirit shot out of the school in careless haste, not wanting to miss anything, his sword waving, his wings whirring. He got too close to the warrior.

Whoosh! The sword moved so fast it looked like a disk of light. Shredded particles of the spirit fluttered and floated in all directions, trailing red smoke and dissolving out of sight. The tip of the sword was now poised and ready for the next brazen attacker.

No one felt that brazen. They remained like statues, their eyes on this warrior. He remained motionless as well, watching them with his fiery eyes.

Sally Roe reached up and pulled the bell cord. The little bell at the front of the bus went *ding,* and the driver slowed for the next stop along the Toe Springs–Claytonville Road. She could see the Bacon's Corner Elementary School just ahead. She'd never been inside, but somehow she'd just have to find her way around without being seen by too many people. She'd done as much as she could to look unlike Sally Roe; she had her hair—black now—braided and pinned behind her head; she'd found some sunglasses that could pass for tinted eyewear, although they bothered her; she knew her old factory clothes would not be a good idea, so she'd managed to purchase a casual outfit—slacks, blouse, loafers. Apart from that, she could only hope that no one at this little school had ever seen her before or knew who she was.

The bus pulled to a stop, and she got off right in front of the school.

Mota still seemed unsure. "No . . . it cannot be Ango. I see no one here who fits what I have heard of him. I seek Ango the small, weak, and pitiful."

Ango could feel the stares of his subordinates. Of course they wanted to see what he would do. He raised his sword, and they all did the same. "The Ango you seek is mighty! He is Ba-al of this place!"

"Ba-al?" Mota asked. "A spirit with only half a heart, and less of a brain?"

"Gaaaa!!" Ango cried, raising his sword over his head. "*I am Ango!*"

He brought his sword down in a red, glowing blur. The huge sword of the warrior was there instantly and took the blow.

Mota was surprised. This little demon could strike hard, with much greater strength than Mota expected. He hid his concern, however, and only acted as if he finally realized whom he was addressing. "Ooohhhh . . ."

"Forces—" Ango screamed.

Mota thrust his sword right under Ango's nose. "Before you attack . . ." Ango swallowed the order. "I would like to state my business with you."

Signa had the attention of the guards in front of the school and at least half the demons from inside it.

"And now," he said, "we'd like to take a look inside this school."

The guards spit sulfur at him, and for a moment he was blinded. He raised his sword in defense and tried to clear his eyes, stumbling backwards out onto the school lawn. The guards followed him, pushing him back, waving their swords. The other spirits felt a new courage, and moved in closer, hissing, spitting, holding their swords high.

They were not watching the door.

Sally walked briskly up the front walk and through the door. The clock in the main hall said she was on time; it was 11:50, time for lunch break. Now to find Miss Brewer's classroom, Room 105. It was either to the left or the right, but first she'd have to pass by the school office. There was a receptionist standing behind the counter, and several office personnel working at desks behind her. *Well,* she thought, *if I just look like I know what I'm doing, maybe they won't ask to help me.*

She headed for the hall, walking by the reception counter, keeping her eyes ahead, not slowing her walk, not looking bewildered. *Come on, Sally, make it convincing.*

"Don't you move!" said the demon behind the counter. "Don't you come one step closer to me!"

Chimon and Scion had come in with Sally, and were now standing at the counter, their wings unfurled, totally blocking any view of the hallway. Their swords were drawn, but at their sides. They didn't speak, but just looked at this slimy creature yelling at them.

"How did you get in here?" the demon demanded. "Guards!"

Suddenly Scion's hot blade rested right between the demon's yellow fangs. He thought it best not to pronounce another word.

The receptionist looked at the clock. Hmm. Miss Brewer was expecting a visitor today; the receptionist thought she'd heard someone come in, but there was no one in the hall. *Well, the visitor must be a little late.*

Sally took a left turn down the hall, disappearing around the corner. It had to be a miracle that that lady behind the counter had not seen her. Oh well. Now to find Room 105.

Good! Here was Room 103, and now Room 104, and bingo! Room 105!

She stood in the open doorway and knocked on the jamb.

Miss Brewer, the young and pretty fourth grade teacher, rose from her desk with a welcoming smile and extended her hand. "Hello. You must be Mrs. Jenson!"

Sally took her hand and replied pleasantly, "And you are Miss Brewer."

"Please come in."

I can't believe I'm doing this, Sally thought. She immediately stopped thinking such things—it could ruin her act.

Miss Brewer motioned Sally to a chair beside her desk and then continued to the bookshelf behind it. "So how are things at the Association?"

Sally sat down and kept her eyes on Miss Brewer. "Well, just wonderful so far. I'm really glad to be working for them now."

"Well," said Miss Brewer, pulling a loose-leaf binder from the shelf, "we've certainly enjoyed this curriculum, and the kids really take to it. Most of our parents are very pleased."

She set the binder on the desk in front of Sally, and Sally smiled as she picked it up. On the cover were the words, "Sexual Understanding and Family Life, Fourth Grade." At the bottom was the name of the publisher, Freeman Education Associates. She began to leaf through it.

"Could I help you find what you're looking for?"

"Oh, don't take your lunchtime to help me. I have a whole list of revisions . . . Let's see, this is the newest edition, isn't it? All right, that should make it easier, not quite as much to doublecheck."

"Just what was the problem?"

Sally had her story well rehearsed. "Well, the quotes are

accurate enough, but the sources didn't feel the attributions were clearly enough stated, so now I have to prepare a reply and . . . wouldn't you know it, I left my copy in the last town. Well, such are the hazards of being on the road."

"It must be exciting, though, servicing so many schools around the state. Has the curriculum been well received in other school districts?"

"For the most part, yes."

Miss Brewer paused to think, then chuckled, sitting on the edge of the desk. "Having trouble with the right-wing fundamentalists?"

Sally chuckled back and nodded. "That's one reason I have to review all the attributions, to make sure everybody's legally covered."

"Oh, what a world!"

Sally took a chance. "Speaking of fundamentalist problems, I understand Amber Brandon was in your class?"

Miss Brewer smiled with curiosity. "Now how did you know that?"

"Well, yours is the only fourth grade class, and the paper said that the child involved in the lawsuit was in the fourth grade, and I learned somewhere that the child was Amber, so . . ."

Amber's former teacher nodded sadly. "Isn't it awful? I'm glad they're taking this thing to court. We've just got to stop all this harassment and censorship. Enough is enough."

"Listen, don't let me keep you from lunch!"

Miss Brewer set out for the door. "Can I bring you anything?"

"Oh, no, don't worry about me. I won't be long anyway."

"Fine. Just take your time."

And with that, she was out the door and down the hall.

Sally waited just a moment, then closed the binder and placed it back on the shelf it came from. Then she looked among the other binders, books, and materials for the title she was after. The kids in the class had drawn pictures of strange faces, weird animals, gods, and bizarre cartoon characters, and the drawings were still displayed on the walls, along with several complex, mesmerizing pattern studies. The curriculum had to be here.

She found it.

Ango began to curse at Mota as his demon warriors became steadily braver. "Out! Begone, you! This is our territory, and none of your concern!"

Mota decided to push this demon a little. "Oh, is that what you think?"

He made a move toward the roof, ready to pass through it and invade their little operation.

"Attack!" Ango screamed, and every demon rushed forward, red blade flashing. "Away with him!"

Mota shot skyward, drawing a horde of spirits after him. He stopped, flipped, faced them. His sword became a continuous ribbon of light.

The first demon became two halves that passed by Mota on either side and then sank into oblivion. The second and third he swatted aside. He kicked and bowled down a cluster of eight. But they just kept coming, faster and faster, swinging and slashing with more and more strength. Mota had planned on putting on an act to keep them following him, but suddenly he found he was no longer acting. This fight was real.

The next wave of spirits surged upward. He backed away, his wings reaching higher and higher. He couldn't let this end too soon, but he was beginning to wish he could.

To the west he saw Signa involved in a similar skirmish, taking some real attacks, whipping his sword about and drawing the guards away from the school. He was backing away, about to be surrounded.

Chimon and Scion could hear the commotion all around the outside of the school. The demons sounded rather jubilant.

"YAAA!!" Suddenly four huge demonic thugs exploded through the walls on every side, their teeth bared, their talons ready to tear.

Chimon and Scion shot through the roof of the school like two rockets, retreating, totally surprised, and angry about it.

"Where did they come from?" Chimon hollered.

Scion was too busy defending himself against their swords and sharp teeth to answer. It was like being chased up a huge tree by a foaming pack of rabid dogs.

They backed away, higher and higher, trying to stay clear of those whistling red blades. What horrible situation had they walked into?

Sally's hands were shaking and she was afraid to open the three-ring binder now in her lap. The title sounded harmless enough: *Finding the Real Me—Self-Esteem and Personal Fulfillment Studies for Fourth-Graders.*

She flipped the cover open and quickly perused the title page. She didn't recognize the author's name, but the name of the publisher immediately turned her stomach: The Omega Center for Educational Studies. With great effort, she turned several more pages, skimming the contents. She found a particular index tab and skipped far forward to a later chapter.

Her heart was pounding as if she'd sprinted up a hill, and her hands were getting slick with sweat. They were shaking.

The old torments! Her mind was beginning to race again. She could hear the voices calling, mocking, cursing. There were spirits in the room!

She had to get out of there.

She carried the binder to the shelf and tried to put it back. A large atlas fell over, blocking the slot. She almost whimpered out loud as her fingers dug after the fallen atlas, trying to get a grip on it. She lifted it, it slipped out of her fingers, she lifted it again, tried to hold it in place while she jammed the binder in. The binder got hung up on a bulging manila envelope and wouldn't go in; she pressed the envelope aside with her palm.

The binder slipped back into place. As soon as her fingers let go of it, her nausea began to ease.

I've got to get out of here. Right now!

She dashed for the hallway and then ran down to the north entrance, pushing her way outside as if running from a fire.

Above and all around the school, the demons were just returning from a glorious rout. They had chased those pesky warriors of Heaven away at last, and now the territory of the glorious Ango was safe again.

Far above the school, a safe distance away, Mota, Signa, Chimon, and Scion gathered to update each other.

"What happened down there?" Chimon wondered.

"Ango and his imps were never this strong!" said Signa, still rubbing the burning sulfur out of his eyes.

Scion was checking a good-sized cut in his leg as he said, "We were all playing the fool to go into that thinking only of a diversion. They meant business!"

Far below, looking as small as an insect on the vast green terrain, Sally was running back to the Toe Springs-Claytonville Road. She would probably run to the next bus stop instead of waiting in front of the school where she might be seen. At least five taunting, torturing spirits were following her, buzzing about her head like angry hornets.

"They'll follow her to her next destination," said Signa.

"When they're clear of this place we'll take them out," said Mota. "We can't fight them here."

"Cree and Si are already at Omega. They have no idea what's in store for them!"

They all knew the problem without anyone having to say it. Mota finally did. "The prayer cover. We're losing it!"

Tom Harris pushed his grocery cart up and down the aisles of the PriceWise grocery, making his weekly rounds. He was having a little trouble with his shopping list; with Ruth and Josiah gone, he wasn't sure what items he should restock and which he should just skip for now. He crossed off the breakfast cereal—there was still plenty of that. The milk in the refrigerator was going sour. He decided he would pour it down the sink and just buy a quart today instead of the usual two half-gallons.

"Hey, Mr. Harris!"

Oh! It was Jody Jessup, the little fifth-grader. It was strange seeing her here in the store during a school day, but then, Tom wasn't usually in the store during the school day either. In any case, he was happy to see her bright smile again.

"Hi, Jody! How're you doing?"

She came running down the aisle past the cornflakes and oatmeal, her long brown hair flying. "I'm with my mom. I get to help her buy groceries."

She pressed against his side, and he gave her a little hug around the shoulders. "Well, it's great to see you."

"It feels funny not being in school anymore."

Tom agreed. "Yes, it sure does."

Then came an alarmed voice from down the aisle. "Jody! Come here!"

It was Andrea Jessup, Jody's mother, pushing her shopping cart with Jody's younger brother Brian by her side. Tom was shocked and incredulous at the coldness in her eyes.

He waved. "Hi, Andrea. Good to see you. Hi, Brian!"

Andrea ignored him. "Jody! Come here right now! I don't want you talking to Mr. Harris!" Jody hurried back to her mother. Andrea bent and barked the order directly into Jody's face. "You stay with me now, and don't talk to strangers!"

Jody started to object, "But that's Mr. Harris!"

"Don't argue with me!"

And then they were gone around the corner; Tom could hear their conversation moving down the next aisle.

"You stay away from that man," she was saying. "Don't you go anywhere near him! And that goes for you too, Brian!"

Brian started asking questions, but Andrea hushed both her children and continued down the aisle.

Tom's life came to a halt, right there next to the breakfast cereal. The Jessups used to be such good friends, and so supportive. He'd shared dinner with them on several occasions, he'd played with their kids, they'd gone together on field trips with the whole school. Jody and Brian were—used to be—two of his best students.

No more. Everything had changed. Tom tried to think of a good reason, but couldn't. He tried to think of what he had to buy next, but he couldn't think of that either.

Lord, he finally prayed silently, *I haven't done anything! Why did Andrea treat me like that?*

Then he began to wonder how many more of his own brothers and sisters in the Lord felt the same way about him.

Andrea kept pushing her cart along, grabbing pickles and relish off the shelf with hardly a glance, and moving on. She wanted to get out of the store before she saw that man again, before her children saw him again. She'd never been so upset at anyone in her life. The nerve of that man!

A small spirit, Strife, followed Andrea. He had nervous, agitated wings that never stopped quivering and a blaring mouth that more than made up for his size. He ran along the tops of the jars and boxes, hurdling the Saltine crackers and leaping over the paper towels.

He lied to you all along! he shouted to her. *And you know, Pastor Mark is lying too, trying to protect him! You don't know half of what went on in that school!*

On the other side of the aisle, rushing through the flour and sugar and somersaulting over the cooking oil, Gossip filled in all of Strife's pauses. *Sexual! He has problems with sex! It has to be sexual! You'd better ask around and see if anyone knows anything! You just never know about these people! Talk to Judy Waring! She might know!*

Andrea got more enraged, the more she thought about this whole Christian school scandal. *That Tom Harris needs prayer,* she thought.

But she hadn't done much praying.

Mulligan's ears were so red they almost glowed.

"Cole! You are just that far from being canned!"

Mulligan towered over Ben's desk like a rotting tree about to fall, and Ben felt he should stand up to keep from being crushed, except that Mulligan might interpret that move as aggressive.

Mulligan pointed his finger—it seemed a bit red too—right in Ben's face. "Were you out at the Potter place the other day?"

"Wednesday afternoon, sir," Ben replied, noting that he'd called Harold "sir." *Wow, I must be scared.*

"And just who ordered you to go out there?"

119

"The visit was voluntary, sir. I had a little free time, so I—"

"So you thought you'd snoop around without authorization, isn't that right?"

Ben drew a breath and then released it slowly before he said another word. He had to be careful now because he was upset. "I was not aware, sir, that the Potter residence was off-limits to a law officer, especially when his presence there was with the full invitation and welcome of Mrs. Potter herself."

"So how about that little visit out to the door factory? What about that?"

"They were glad enough to have me there."

"And I say you misused your badge!"

Now Ben did stand up, tall and straight. "You might be interested in what I've found out, Sergeant Mulligan, *sir*."

"If it's about Sally Roe, forget it! That case is closed because I said so!"

"The descriptions of Sally Roe that I got from Mrs. Potter and from Abby Grayson at the Bergen Door Company were consistent. Sally Roe was in her mid- to late-thirties, about five six, with long red hair."

"What of it?"

"The woman we found in the goat shed was younger, and had black hair, probably shoulder-length, but no longer."

Mulligan smiled a smile of pity. He put his big hand on Ben's shoulder and spoke condescendingly. "Cole . . . come on. It was dark in there. You only saw the body for a second. I don't know what's gotten into you."

"Harold . . . why was the house ransacked? Did you authorize that?"

"Sure I did. We were looking for evidence."

"Evidence of what? You said it was a suicide."

"Standard procedure. Isn't your shift about over?"

"I do have a message for you from Mrs. Potter. She'd like to have that mess cleaned up by whoever it was that made it."

"That's taken care of . . . Don't worry your little head about it."

"And whatever happened to Sally Roe's pickup?"

Mulligan looked at him just a little funny. "What pickup?"

"Sally Roe always drove a '65 blue Chevy pickup. I let Mrs. Potter go through our vehicle ID book yesterday, and she pointed out the make and model to me. The truck's nowhere around the property. Roe had to have driven it home from work the evening she allegedly killed herself. I was wondering if the same people who ransacked the house may have made off with her truck."

Mulligan looked a little worried. "I don't know anything about that."

"And since we're on the subject, I'm still wondering about that bloodstained shirt we found. Did the coroner ever check the blood type? That scene was full of signs of violence. And the body . . . That woman didn't hang herself!"

Mulligan turned his back on Ben, stomped into his office, and returned with some papers in his hand. He slapped them on Ben's desk. "There! The county coroner's report on the death of Sally Roe! Read it for yourself! Death by asphyxiation from hanging. Not murder, not a struggle, not anything! Now if you disagree with the coroner, why don't you come up with another body for him to examine?"

"There might be one."

Mulligan actually grabbed Ben's shirt in his fist. His eyes were wild, and he hissed the words through jaws locked shut in anger. "Stop right there! Not another word!" Ben said nothing, but he didn't back down either. Mulligan didn't like that at all. "Your shift is over for today, Officer Cole, and if I hear one more word about this from you, your *job* is going to be over, you got that?"

Mulligan let go of Ben's uniform with a feisty little shove. Ben did what he could to straighten out the wrinkles. "I'll be watching you, boy, I mean really watching you. You drop this Sally Roe thing, you hear? One more false step from you, and I'm going to have myself some real joy ripping that badge right off your chest!"

twelve

WeLL, *those guys mean business, I guess.*

Wayne Corrigan sat at his desk after-hours, drinking one last cup of coffee from his thermos and looking through several pages of notes Mark Howard, Tom Harris, and the church board had compiled in answer to the temporary injunction against the school.

All the usual arguments for corporal punishment were clearly laid out—the Scriptures from Proverbs about the rod, of course, and a definitive procedure for spanking clearly outlined in the *Student-Parent Handbook.* Lucy Brandon's signature on the enrollment agreement constituted her agreement with the handbook, so that wasn't going to be hard to argue. It was obvious the church board had done their homework many times over in this area.

As for their argument against any restraint from "further religious behavior which could prove harmful to the mental, emotional, or social welfare of the child, or any excessive religious instruction that could prove harmful," they did a pretty good study on that, with Scripture after Scripture declaring the existence, purpose, behavior, and "casting out" of demons, as well as a general apologetic for the basic gospel message. This was definitely a matter of religious belief, supposedly protected by the Constitution, sure . . .

But an exorcism perpetrated upon a ten-year-old child? A minor, with no parental consent? Where was that provided for in the handbook? When did Mrs. Brandon agree to that kind of treatment for her daughter?

He stopped cold. This case was too big and the stakes were too high. It was more than he could handle.

Yeah. Those ACFA guys found just what they were looking for; the way they would handle the case, the Constitution would be just so much toilet paper when children were involved.

Well, Corrigan, you did it again: you said yes too easily. Now the hearing's in twelve days. Better do something.

"Lord God," he prayed, "I'm in over my head again. I need Your help to bail me out . . . to bail *all of us* out."

He started scribbling out a brief for the court, trying to cover the items in the complaint. Misuse of federal funds was easy to refute, and Discrimination and Harassment were basically a walk in the park, but then came the tricky stuff, and he began to pray in earnest as he wrote every line.

On Monday morning, a week after Ruth and Josiah were first hauled from his home, Tom got a call from an unidentified lady at the Child Protection Department. Without consulting him, and with no prior notice other than this call, an appointment had been set for him to visit with his children for one hour under the supervision of a child welfare counselor. The appointment was for 11 that morning, at the courthouse in Claytonville.

He barely made it in time, pulling into a visitor parking slot at the courthouse at 10:52. He doublechecked his appearance in the visor mirror, straightening his tie, smoothing down his hair, his hands trembling and his stomach queasy from the anticipation. He grabbed a brown bag of things for the kids, locked up the car, and bounded up the concrete steps of the old stone building.

The inside hall was cold marble, tall, gray, and imposing. Every footstep echoed like a public announcement, and he felt naked in this place. Lawyers, clerks, and other just-plain folks passed him on every side, and he found it hard to look them in the eye. What if they had seen his face in the paper or on television? They probably wouldn't want his autograph.

The girl at the information desk took his name and offered him a seat on a hard wooden bench against the wall.

"I'll let them know you're here," she said.

He sat there and slowly scratched his chin, looking down at the marble floor. He felt angry, but he knew he couldn't let it show, he couldn't let it come out, or he'd only make things worse.

He prayed repeatedly, *O Lord, what can I do? I don't even know what to say . . .*

He naturally thought of Cindy, now gone for three years. Difficult times such as this reminded him of how much he always needed her, and how much he had lost. He'd recovered from the initial grief, yes, but sometimes, when life was at its darkest and the struggle was the most uphill, out of habit he would reach for her, think of her, rehearse the words to share his pain. But then would come that same, persistent reminder, the realization that she was gone, replaced by a closely following shadow of sorrow.

Cindy, he thought, *you just wouldn't believe what's happening down here. I guess it's the persecution Jesus and the apostles warned us about. I guess it always seemed like something far away, maybe in Soviet Russia, or during Roman times, but not here, not now. I never thought it would actually happen to me, and I sure didn't think it would happen to the kids.*

He pulled his handkerchief from his pocket to wipe his tears away. He couldn't let the kids see him like this—and what would the state people think?

"Mr. Harris?"

He sucked in a breath and immediately, even desperately, tried to compose himself. *Tom, whatever you do, be cordial! Don't give her anything to use against you!*

He was looking up at none other than Irene Bledsoe.

"I'm sure you remember me?" she said, sitting near him on the bench.

"Yes." He figured that would be safe.

"Before I take you upstairs to see your children, I need to remind you that this visitation is a privilege that can be revoked at any time. We expect you to remain on your best behavior and to comply with my instructions at all times. You are not to touch your children, but remain on your own side of the conference table. You cannot ask them anything about where they are staying. Any other questions that I may deem inappropriate will be disallowed, and the meeting can be terminated at any time if I find it necessary. Is all that clear to you?"

"But . . . Mrs. Bledsoe, are we going to have a chance to talk this thing out? I want to get this whole mess cleared up and get my children back home with me where they belong."

"That won't be possible at this time; our investigation is still in progress."

"What investigation? I haven't heard a thing from anyone, and I haven't even been able to get through to you."

"We have a very heavy caseload, Mr. Harris. You'll just have to be patient."

Tom felt an anger, even a hunger for revenge rising inside him, something totally un-Christian, he knew, but it was irrepressible. He just couldn't think of any words that would be civil.

Irene Bledsoe asked him again, more firmly, "Is all that I have said clear to you?"

All he could do was give her the right answer. "Yes."

"What is this package?"

Tom opened it for her to see. "I brought some things for the kids. They don't have their Bibles, so I brought them, and some pens and stationery."

"Fine." She took the bag. "Come with me."

She took off at a hurried, efficient pace, the *pock, pock, pock* of her heels telling everyone on the floor she was passing by. Tom just tried to step quietly; this kind of attention he didn't need.

She led him up the winding marble staircase to the second floor, along the balcony overlooking the front entry, and through a heavy, uninviting door with big brass hinges and a knob that had to weigh twenty pounds. They passed through a cold and bare antechamber with one tall window letting in grayish light. A security guard stood by an archway to the right, looking just a little bored, but manning his post. Tom followed Mrs. Bledsoe past the guard and through the archway.

Tom's heart leaped into his throat, and tears flooded his eyes.

There, seated on the other side of a large table, were Ruth and Josiah. They were on their feet in an instant at the sight of him, crying "Daddy," their voices shrill with excitement. They ran for him.

Irene Bledsoe stood in their way and blocked them with her arms. "Sit down! Sit down at the table!"

"I want to see my dad!" Josiah cried.

"Daddy!" was all Ruth could say, her hands outstretched.

He couldn't take them in his arms. He couldn't touch them. All he could do was cry. "Sit down now. Do like Mrs. Bledsoe says."

Ruth began sobbing, almost wailing. "Daddy . . ."

"I love you, Ruth! Daddy loves you. Go ahead. Sit down. Everything's going to be all right."

Irene Bledsoe encouraged the children to sit down with a firm hand on their arms.

"Mr. Harris, you may sit in this chair facing your children. Let me remind you of what we discussed downstairs."

We didn't "discuss" anything, Tom thought. *You gave the orders, I sat there and listened.*

He slowly slid the chair out and sat down. He couldn't waste this time crying. He tried to sober up, and pulled out his handkerchief to wipe his eyes again.

"How are you two?"

"I wanna go home, Daddy," said Ruth, still sobbing.

Josiah was trying to be brave, and wiped his eyes like his father. "We miss you."

"Is Mrs. Bledsoe taking good care of you?"

Mrs. Bledsoe answered that one. "Your children are in very good hands, Mr. Harris, and I think that should be the last of that sort of question."

Tom glared at her. He couldn't hide his anger. "Then I'd like to ask you some questions afterward."

She smiled pleasantly in the children's presence. "We can discuss that later."

Tom noticed the bump on Ruth's head the moment he saw her. Now he was ready to ask about it. "What happened to your head, Ruth?"

Bledsoe cut right in on that question, even rising a little

from her chair. "We can't discuss that! I'm sure you understand!"

"I bumped it in the car," said Ruth.

"Ruth! Don't you talk about that or I'll take you away!"

She started crying in anger now. "How come?"

"It's all right, Ruth," said Tom. "We don't have to talk about it." He turned to Josiah. "So . . . uh . . . what have you guys been doing?"

Josiah was unhappy and made no attempt to hide it. "Nothing. We sit around and watch TV."

Tom was unhappy to hear that, but he didn't show it. "Oh, does Mrs. Bledsoe let you watch TV?"

"No, Mrs. Henley does . . ."

Irene Bledsoe was right on top of that. "Josiah, we can't talk about who our foster parents are. That's a secret."

Tom tried to get the conversation back into safe territory. "So . . . how about reading? Have you read any good books?"

"No," said Ruth.

"They have some video games," Josiah volunteered. "Those are kind of fun."

"So . . . are there other kids around to play with?" Tom cringed even as he asked the question, but Irene Bledsoe let that one go.

"Yes. There's a boy named Teddy and another boy named Luke. But I don't like them."

"Oh . . ."

"They're bigger, and they pick on us."

"They pick on you?"

"Yeah, they push us around and use bad language. They're not Christians."

Ruth stuck her lower lip out and said, "Luke calls me names."

"Oh, Ruth, that's too bad. Have you tried to be friends?"

She looked at him, and her eyes flooded with tears again. "I want to go home!"

"I want you to come home too."

Tick, tick, tick. Irene Bledsoe was tapping the table with her fingernail and glaring at Tom.

Josiah must have caught that signal. He was a sharp little nine-year-old. "Ruth bumped her head on the side of the car."

"Now that's enough!" said Mrs. Bledsoe.

Tom looked at Irene Bledsoe and tried to keep his face calm. "What car, Mrs. Bledsoe?"

Mrs. Bledsoe looked at him with her eyebrows raised and her head tilted forward, so condescendingly. "Mr. Harris, we've found that children will usually concoct stories to protect their parents."

Tom caught her meaning. He had to choose—seriously, *strenuously* choose—to stay calm and cordial. "And just what story did both Ruth and Josiah concoct, Mrs. Bledsoe?"

She raised her chin and appeared to look down at him. "Mr. Harris, I can understand how you would be concerned about the injury to Ruth's head. But you should know, so are we. I'm sure that, given time to get over their fears and prior conditioning, your children will be ready to tell us the truth. For now, I think this visit is concluded." She rose from her chair. "Children, say good-bye to your father."

"We just got here!" said Josiah.

"I don't wanna go!" Ruth wailed, her face filling with fear.

"Children, we are going!" said Mrs. Bledsoe.

"Just one moment!" said Tom. The meeting was shot anyway. He dove for the opportunity. "Josiah, go ahead. Tell me how Ruth got that bump on her head."

"We almost got in a wreck . . ."

"John!" Mrs. Bledsoe yelled.

The security guard walked into the room and just let his presence be known. Tom didn't want any trouble; he made no moves.

Bledsoe grabbed both children by the arms. "Mr. Harris, I warned you to control yourself, and you can be sure that your behavior will go down in my report!"

"Which part didn't you like? When I bit the chair leg or when I broke out all the windows?"

She started hauling both kids toward the door. Tom was on his feet, ready to do something. The guard stood in his way—

just like Mulligan had stood in his way a week ago. It was happening all over again, right before Tom's eyes. Mrs. Bledsoe was pulling Ruth and Josiah by their arms, taking them away screaming. She reached the archway. He wanted to stand in her way; he wanted to reach out and stop her.

He couldn't. All he could do was watch it happen.

"What wreck, Josiah?" he asked.

"Children, come on!" Bledsoe shouted, pulling them into the antechamber.

"I hit my head," Ruth repeated. "She stopped too fast and I hit my head."

Josiah went for broke. "She went through a stop sign and almost hit a blue pickup truck! Ruth hit her head on the door of the car!"

"She? You mean Mrs. Bledsoe?"

Irene Bledsoe had Ruth through the door and jerked Josiah through before he could complete an answer. But he was nodding a firm yes as he disappeared.

"Kids, I'm proud of you! Real proud of you! I love you!"

They were gone.

"Give 'em a few minutes," said the guard, not letting Tom follow.

Tom sat at the table again. The guard went to the door to make sure Mrs. Bledsoe was in the clear.

Tom noticed the brown paper bag on the floor. Irene Bledsoe had left the package behind, and the kids had not gotten their Bibles or stationery. He couldn't touch them in this way either.

"Okay," said the guard, "you can go now."

His job completed, the guard went out the door and on to other business, leaving Tom alone in the cold, vacant room.

"O Lord . . ."

Tom broke. The tears ran down his face.

But they weren't entirely tears of grief, and they certainly were not tears of despair. He'd seen his kids, and they had shared something, despite Irene Bledsoe, despite the guard. He knew that their souls had touched, that their hearts were still together. It was not enough, of course, to see them for just those few minutes. Such a cold and regimented visit could never be enough. But for right now, it was enough to know they loved him. They loved their daddy. They wanted to be with him.

Now his doubts were gone. Amid all the pain and challenge, the smearing, the soiling of his name, he'd found himself wondering where he really stood. There were voices in his mind telling him horrible things he'd never thought about himself. He tried not to give place to such lies; but still, because the voices were so relentless, he'd wondered if there was something wrong with him, something he'd been blind to. Maybe, the voices would say, he deserved what was happening to him.

But now he knew. He still had his integrity, and before God he still had the hearts of his children. Right now, it was just so wonderful to know that for sure.

Ben and Leonard quickly ducked into Don's Wayside, trying to look casual, even though they were in full uniform, carried their nightsticks, wore their guns, and had their portable radios on their belts, hissing and squawking. Every eye in the place was instantly drawn in their direction.

It was a bust! It was something for everyone to watch and then talk about at home. The contractors sitting at the counter and the truckers sitting at the tables looked up from their lunch and wagged their stubbly jaws only enough to finish the last bite of soup and sandwich. Some kept talking only to look natural, but they were watching, all right.

The name was muttered around the room by several, and rose above the general hubbub: "Krantz. Yeah, the Krantz boy. He's still at it."

At the end of the counter, Kyle Krantz sat under the watchful eye of bald and chubby Don Murphy, the proprietor, and two blue-jeaned farmer's sons who were well-built for haybucking, steer handling, and cornering shoplifters.

"Hey, Kyle," said Ben. "What are you up to now?"

"Caught him dipping into the cash register," said Don. "Then he took off for the door trying to get away. Bub and

Jack were just coming in and held him until you could get here."

"How much did he take?" asked Leonard.

"Eighty-five dollars," said Don, indicating a wad of bills on the counter.

Leonard gave Kyle a careful visual scrutiny. The boy was only fifteen, skinny as a rail, with shaggy, unkempt black hair and pimples. His face was dull and expressionless, and his eyes were red and watery.

"You know, son," said Leonard, "I think I have cause to believe you might be carrying something illegal. I'd like you to empty your pockets for me."

Kyle hesitated.

"You heard the man," said big Jack, tilting his hat forward to emphasize his lean toward the boy.

"We can help you if you're unable," said Bub.

Kyle began emptying his pockets. First he set some change on the counter, then some cigarette papers.

"Jacket pockets," directed Leonard.

Kyle hesitated, then wilted in surrender, dug into his jacket pocket, and produced a plastic bag full of ground green leaves.

The front door opened.

"Ehh . . ." said Don, sorry to have to miss the rest of this. "Customer."

Ben glanced at the man who had come in. He was middle-aged, handsome, well-dressed. Ben recognized him: Joey Parnell, the county coroner.

Leonard was handling the Krantz boy okay. Ben said softly, "Hey, uh . . . you've got it under control; maybe I'll have a word with Parnell over there . . ."

Leonard shrugged. "Go for it."

Ben walked to the other end of the counter where Parnell had taken a stool and was perusing the simple menu.

"Excuse me," said Ben. "Joey Parnell?"

Parnell looked up and smiled. "Yes."

Ben introduced himself. "Can I join you for just a minute?"

Parnell was agreeable. Ben took the stool next to him and tried to think of where to start.

"Just off the record, unofficially . . ." he began, and felt a little sheepish even saying that. "I wanted to ask you what your findings were in that Sally Roe suicide case."

Parnell looked at the menu again, a clear signal that he wasn't interested in talking about it. "I handle a lot of cases, Officer Cole. Just what is it you want to know?"

"Well . . . now I know this may sound a little strange, but . . . were you able to make a positive identification of the body?"

Parnell looked at Ben as if he were joking. "Well, I should hope so. I wouldn't be a very good coroner if I couldn't even determine whose remains I was examining."

Ben knew he was looking foolish, but he tried to press on. "Well, what about that plaid shirt with the blood on it? Did you get that?"

Parnell didn't answer right away. He seemed to be having trouble remembering. "Uh . . . yeah, I think I got that."

"Did the blood types match?"

"What do you mean, did the blood types match?"

"Well, did the blood on the shirt match the blood of the deceased?"

Parnell broke into a grin and eyed the menu again. "Well, I don't know. I guess I never checked that. Why should I?"

"Was there a wound on the deceased that could explain where the blood on the shirt came from?"

"I . . . I don't remember that there was."

"And what was the cause of death? I think you said asphyxiation by hanging in your report?"

"Mm. That's right. I do remember that."

"I was there on the scene, Mr. Parnell, and what I saw indicated a violent death, not at all what you would expect in a suicide. Also . . . the body wasn't hanging. It was thrown violently to the floor, and there was no rope around the neck."

Parnell just looked at him, listening, without comment.

Ben pressed some more. "Could you tell me . . . just so I know for sure . . . a description of the deceased?"

Don came down the counter, and Parnell ordered a beef sandwich and some soup. Parnell took his time, and seemed to enjoy not having to talk to this young, inquisitive cop.

Ben waited politely. Finally Parnell turned to him and with a wry smile said, "No, Officer Cole, I couldn't."

That didn't sound right to Ben. "That's . . . privileged information?"

"That's right."

"Well, what about the color of the hair? I recall seeing a woman with black hair, in her twenties, medium height . . ."

"How about asking me something else?"

Ben stopped, considered, and then asked something else. "According to what I've seen around the station, and then at the Potters' rental, something's missing, perhaps something that belonged to the dead woman. Would you have any idea what everyone is looking for?"

Parnell was clearly getting impatient. "Now that question I don't understand at all."

"Well, Sergeant Mulligan sent someone to the house to search it, and I know he was asking you about something—"

"No comment, sir!" Parnell was visibly upset.

Ben figured he'd better retreat from that line of questions. But now what? "Uh . . . well, just one more question."

Parnell was emphatic. "One more."

"Is it still possible to see the body?"

Parnell chuckled at that. "Afraid not. It's been cremated. Now, is that going to do it for you?"

Ben smiled. "Sure. Thanks a lot, Mr. Parnell. Sorry to bother you."

"All right."

Parnell unfolded a copy of the *Hampton County Star* and gave it his full attention. Ben joined Leonard, who now had Kyle Krantz in custody, and they went out to the squad car.

thirteen

SALLY Roe was far from Bacon's Corner, sitting on a hard bench in a bus depot in another town, looking the part of a wayward, hitchhiking vagabond, dressed in her old jeans and blue jacket, her dyed hair braided and tucked under a wool cap, her nicer clothes hidden in a large duffel bag on the bench beside her. She was oblivious to the passing travelers and their whining children, the used sections of newspapers strewn on the benches, the gum wrappers on the linoleum floor, and the occasional squawking announcements of departures and arrivals over the public address. Her bus would be leaving in one hour. She would spend that hour writing in the spiral notebook in her lap. It would be a letter, her first, to Tom Harris.

> *Dear Mr. Harris,*

She stopped. *How do I start this? He doesn't even know me. Guess I could say that.*

> *I don't know how to start this letter; after all, you don't even know who I am. But let me introduce and explain myself, not just in this letter, but I hope in many more to follow. Perhaps by the time I have written my last letter to you, everything will be clear to both of us.*
> *My name is Sally Roe, formerly a planer-sander at the Bergen Door Company. You may have read the recent news story about my death by suicide. I assure you, I am the Sally Roe the news story talked about, and obviously, I am alive.*
> *Let me tell you what really happened . . .*

Sally could see it all happening again, even as she searched for the words to recount it.

The day had been perfectly normal and downright boring. Working at the factory always was a bore, especially working in the sanding department, operating power sanders that hummed, whirred, and vibrated until it seemed they would make a milkshake out of your brains. After a full day and a quota of twenty-five doors, she finally drove the old blue pickup down the gravel driveway to her house. She was tired, tasting sawdust, and had no other plans than to shower, grab dinner, and go to bed.

But then there were the goats, Betty the doe and her two kids, Buff and Bart. Pets, mostly. Sally inherited a buck and a doe from a lady at the factory who couldn't afford to keep them. Sally sold the buck, kept the doe, had her bred, and now had the mother and two babies who were the cutest in the world and good company, always glad to see her come home.

Sally parked the truck and headed for their pen. She would greet them first, give them some feed, have her usual one-sided conversation with them about her day, and then go inside and collapse.

The goats were excited, but not with happiness. They were glad and eager to see her again, but mostly because something was disturbing them.

"Hey . . . settle down there . . . Momma's home . . ."

She dug a pail of rolled ration from the feed bin beside the house and stepped through the gate into the goats' pen. Betty circled her, happy but upset. The kids just kept bleating and bounding back and forth along the fence.

Sally shook the pail to get their attention. "Come on, get some treats!"

She went to the shed, hoping they would just follow her and calm down. The neighbors' dog must have been around. He often got a real kick out of terrorizing her goats.

She stepped into the shed. "Come on now, it's all right—"

Shock! A rope came over her head from behind and began crushing her windpipe before she even knew what it was! The pail of feed fell and spilled on the ground. With incredible strength, an unseen assailant heaved on the loop of rope, jerking her body backward, lifting her feet off the ground. She kicked, she grabbed at the rope. No air.

Her feet found the wall, and she pushed. She and her

attacker fell back against the feeder, and it cracked. The rope went slack and she wriggled free, dropping to the floor, rolling in the straw, pulling in air.

A woman in black, eyes wild with hate, a knife! The killer pounced like a leopard, Sally ducked to one side, the knife caught Sally in the shoulder with searing pain.

Sally tried to wriggle out of the corner in which she was trapped, kicking and clawing the straw and dust. The woman's knee came down on her chest and held her there. The rope fell across her neck again. Sally kicked the woman with one free leg.

WUMP! Just that fast, like a rag doll, the woman crashed against the opposite wall of the shed, her head and limbs slapping against the boards, as if a giant had grabbed her and thrown her there. Sally had hardly made contact with her kick and felt some amazement, but at least the woman was off her. She scrambled out of the corner, her eyes on her assailant. The assassin slid down the wall to her feet and stumbled forward, her eyes blank and wandering, her jaw hanging.

OOF!! Something struck the woman with such force, it lifted her off her feet. She flopped into the straw, her arms limp and flailing, her head crooked, her body lifeless, the rope still in her hand.

> *I didn't take any time to look. I just got out of there, still trying to breathe, totally occupied with just staying alive. I remember getting through the gate and then falling to the ground and retching. I can't blame Betty and the kids for running away. Maybe it was a good thing they did.*

Sally leaned back from her writing and absentmindedly tapped the pen on the notebook, just thinking. It was a pretty bizarre way to open a letter. Maybe if she just kept writing, she would seem more credible as her story progressed. Well, all she could do was try.

> *What can I say, Tom? How can I qualify myself as a reliable witness? If you were to ask me who I am, I would have to*

reply that I don't know. For years I have asked myself the same question and now I wonder if, in the writing of these letters, I might be reaching out for an answer.

You see, Tom, I want to help you. In my own way, and drawing from my own experience, I can relate to your situation and I know how you must feel. As one lost entity without source and without destination in a universe that is ultimately meaningless, I can't tell you where my concept of "wrong" ever came from. Call it sentiment, call it "the way I was raised," figure I'm just taking a desperate stab at meaning through antiquated morality, I still feel it—what is happening to you is wrong, and I'm sorry for your pain.

She looked up at the big clock above the depot door. Her bus was scheduled to leave in half an hour. Soon the public address would be squawking out the announcement.

If you would indulge me, I would like to at least act as if something matters. I would like to do one "right" thing. I might be concocting my own concept of "good deeds" in an effort to run from despair, to convince myself that life isn't futile after all, but I have nothing to lose. If despair is the final truth we all face, then let me hide from it, just this once. If hope is a mere fiction of our own making, then let me live in a fantasy. Who knows? Maybe there will be some meaning in it somewhere, some purpose, some reward.

At any rate, I'm going to retrace some old steps and find some things out, for your sake and for mine. I hope to share some useful information with you before long—information sufficient to get you out of trouble and, most of all, bring your children back to you.

Please keep this letter, even if it sounds strange to you, even if you don't believe it. I'll write again soon.

I remain sincerely yours,

Sally signed her full name, "Sally Beth Roe," carefully took the pages from the spiral notebook, and folded them. She had a box of envelopes in her travel bag. While in Bacon's

Corner, she'd looked up Tom Harris's home address and written it in the front of her notebook. She now copied that address onto the envelope and stuffed the letter inside. She didn't seal it yet, but rose from the bench and walked over to the small depot cafeteria to get some dimes. If she hurried, she could get this letter mailed before she left for the next town.

Chimon and Scion walked beside her, wings unfurled, swords drawn. For now, the demons were hiding.

Chimon looked down at the letter in Sally's hand. "'The word of her testimony,'" he said.

"That's one," said Scion.

Terga, Prince of Bacon's Corner, was glad for some good news, and was ready to share a rare smile with Ango, the little Prince of the Bacon's Corner Elementary School.

"Chased them away, eh?" said Terga, strutting up and down the school's tar roof with Ango at his side.

Ango was ecstatic with this great honor. To think that all his underlings were now seeing him in the company of the Prince of Bacon's Corner! Before this, Terga had never even known his name.

Ango was rising to the occasion and giving his report like a real commander-in-the-field. "It was a brazen onslaught, my Ba-al. An incredibly large heavenly warrior challenged me on the roof, and another challenged my guards at the front door. Two warriors were caught inside, but were immediately chased away."

"But you overcame them all?"

"Not without a deadly struggle. I am most proud of my warriors, who showed themselves brave, fierce, and daring!"

"And I am proud of you, Ango, for proving to me that Bacon's Corner is still secure for our operations."

"Thank you, Ba-al."

"With my commendations to you and your warriors, I leave you now . . ."

Terga stopped in midsentence. Both demons heard a familiar sound, and began searching the eastern horizon. From

139

somewhere beyond the treetops, a low, droning rumble reached their ears, growing steadily louder, closer.

"Now who could that be?" Ango wondered.

The deceivers and guards in and around the school heard the sound as well and paused in their duties, buzzing and flitting out into the school yard for a look, or popping up through the roof for a better view.

Terga's wings billowed and lifted him from the roof. He drew his sword as he peered toward the east. Then he tensed just a little and called down to Ango and his troops, "They are ours!"

"But who?"

Terga looked grim, and shook his head in dismay. "I believe it is Destroyer, with fresh forces from the Strongman."

That word brought a mutter of fear from all the ranks below.

Then the visitors appeared, still a mile away, approaching like a low-flying squadron of bombers. There were at least a hundred, flying in an arrowhead formation and coming closer, closer, closer. Now the red glow of their swords appeared against the dark shadowy blurs of their wings.

Terga set down on the roof again. "Ango, prepare your forces to greet some honored guests!"

"Forces!" Ango yelled. They fluttered up out of the school and school yard. He ordered them to assemble in orderly ranks on the front lawn. They formed the ranks immediately, a motley, sleazy crew of some three hundred—tiny spirits of anger, hatred, rebellion; huge, lumbering giants of violence, vandalism, destruction; clever deceivers with their wily ways and shifty eyes. They looked sharp, all lined up in neat rows, the tallest in the back, the shortest in the front, and every demon's sword held across his chest.

Destroyer's squadron came over the town, casting a spiritual shadow upon the entire length of Front Street and putting a chill in the air that the humans down there could feel. The shadow passed over the fire station and then the row of homes along the Strawberry Loop, and dogs all over the neighborhood began to howl.

Terga, Ango, and all the assembly of demons could now see the squadron's leader well in front, at the tip of the arrowhead. They could see the yellow glint of his eyes and the red glimmer of his sword. They all bowed low.

Destroyer and a terrifying battalion of the Strongman's handpicked best descended on the school like a cloud of monster locusts, their wings producing a roar that could be felt and stirring up such a wind that some of the smaller demons on the front lawn blew over and rolled like leaves across the grass.

Destroyer alighted on the roof of the school with twelve hideous captains surrounding him. The rest of the battalion took positions all around the perimeter of the school grounds. The wings settled, the roar subsided. Now Terga and Ango found themselves in the presence of a spirit so evil that neither of them could look up for stark fear.

Destroyer took a moment to look all around. He gazed with narrow, fiery eyes at the troops gathered on the lawn. He wasn't impressed. He walked slowly toward the two bowing princes of this place, his toes settling into the tar, his talons gripping tightly with each step. He stood in front of them, his captains standing on either side like tree trunks.

"So, Terga," he asked in a voice as cold as ice, "it seems you have reason to be giddy?"

Terga straightened, said, "I have, my Ba-al," and then bowed again.

With numbing fear, Terga suddenly felt the hot edge of the Ba-al's blade under his chin. He followed the blade's prompting and raised his head.

"Who is this beside you?"

"This is Ango, the prince of this school, a brave leader."

The burning sword raised Ango's chin. "You are prince of this place?"

Ango tried to speak in a strong voice, but couldn't keep it from quivering. "Yes, my Ba-al."

Destroyer leaned close to Ango's face. "I have received word that you had a confrontation here with the Host of Heaven."

Ango smiled faintly. "It was my duty and joy to please such as you, and drive the heavenly warriors away."

"How many heavenly warriors?"

"Four, my Ba-al. One assailed me on the roof, one attacked our guards at the front, and two launched an attack from inside. We chased them all away immediately."

Destroyer pondered that for just a moment. He had no immediate compliments for Ango's actions. "What else happened that day?"

Ango wasn't at all prepared for the question. "What else?"

"Did you have any unexpected human visitors to the school?"

Destroyer was staring, waiting for an answer, and now Ango could feel a stare from Terga. But he couldn't come up with an answer. "I . . . I know of none."

"Can you give me any good reason why four—only four—of the enemy's hosts would suddenly appear here, only to allow themselves to be chased away by spirits as petty and weak as you?"

Ango shuddered. This conversation was taking a bad turn. "They . . . they came to spy on us, to invade the school . . ."

"That is your explanation?"

"That is . . . Yes, that is what I know."

Destroyer sheathed his sword, and everyone breathed a little easier. "Go back to your duties, Ango the Terrible, you and your warriors. Do your worst with these little children. Terga, I'll have a word with you."

Terga followed Destroyer to the other end of the roof, while Ango dismissed his demons to return to their duties. When Destroyer came to a stop, satisfied with the place, the twelve captains surrounded him and Terga like a castle wall.

Terga was worried.

Destroyer glared down at him—angry, but calculatingly controlled. "She was here."

Terga, of course, did not want to believe it. "How do you know, my Ba-al?"

"Where did she go from the motel in Claytonville?"

"I . . ."

"Did your petty pranksters follow her? Did they have her under their careful watch at all times?"

Terga felt he would melt right through the roof. "The . . . the Host of Heaven . . . We were confounded . . . They got in our way . . . We couldn't see her anymore . . ."

"You lost track of her! She eluded you!"

Terga knew full well that Destroyer's own ravagers were following the woman too, but now did not seem an appropriate time to remind him. "Uh . . . yes. But . . . she wouldn't come back *here*, to the place of greatest danger—"

"Danger?" Destroyer's voice was as sharp as his blade. "What danger, when you and such as this Ango are responsible for it?"

"But why would she come here?"

Terga didn't even see Destroyer's huge hand before it struck him, dashing him to the roof. Terga made no move of retaliation; he never had any intention to do so, and besides, twelve huge swords were only inches from his throat. All he could do was look up at the furious face of Destroyer as the wicked spirit unloaded his venom.

"You fool!" Destroyer shouted. "Why wouldn't she come here? This is where our Plan began, or don't you recall all our years of development, our infiltration of this place? You were here, you were a part of it. Did you think we carried it all out with no object in mind?"

"I'm sorry, my Ba-al."

Destroyer's foot caught Terga under the ribs and kicked him several feet in the air. Terga's body struck the immovable chest of one of the captains and then tumbled down to the roof again.

"You're sorry . . ." muttered Destroyer mockingly. "You let her elude you in Claytonville, you let her sneak into this school under your very nose, you let her escape again, to disappear until she pops up again to do more damage, to uncover more of our Plan, we know not where, and all you have to say is, 'I'm sorry'!"

Terga wanted to say he was sorry again, but knew that would not be accepted. Now he had no words left to say.

"Go!" said Destroyer. "Take care of your little town. Leave Sally Roe to me."

One of the captains, built like a bull, took Terga by one wing and flung him into the sky. Terga tumbled and fluttered skyward until he could recover control of his wings, then shot away in shame.

Destroyer watched until Terga was gone, then spoke in low tones to the twelve demons with him. "The Strongman does have all his players in place and a strong network ready to be used, but we have seen ourselves how vulnerable the Plan can be, especially when the Host of Heaven are interested in our enterprise, and most certainly interested in Sally Roe. They are trying to set up a hedge around her, screen her from our eyes, accompany her. They have a plan too."

One hulking spirit reminded Destroyer, "But the Strongman will not turn away from his Plan; he is committed to it."

"An easy position for him to take," Destroyer hissed spitefully, fingering the handle of his sword. "If the Plan should fail, it will not be his head that rolls, but ours. He will see to that. We must succeed."

He stopped to think for a moment, his black talons pulling like hooks at the stiff hairs on his neck.

"I am learning more and more about this Tal; he is quite the strategist, a master of subtlety. Thus far the Host of Heaven have been effective and yet largely invisible. Tal is waiting, maneuvering. He is a layer of traps, a setter of snares."

Another spirit, scarred and grotesque, growled, "I was there in Ashton. I saw the ambush."

Destroyer spit sulfur and let his anger rise. "So you know that Tal waited until our forces could wait no longer and flew headlong into his patient trap, brash and unaware. We had only our confidence, but Tal was *ready*. We will not make that mistake again."

Destroyer scanned the town from this rooftop perch. "If Tal is so subtle, we will be even more so. If he depends on the prayers of God's people, then we will work all the harder to keep God's people from praying." He chuckled a sulfurous chuckle. "You don't know about the little imps I requested from the Strongman: Strife, Division, Gossip, and a host of others flooding this town at this very moment! These humans are only of flesh, of mud, and I suggest there is one force stronger than their zeal for God: their own self-righteousness! We will make them proud, pure in their own eyes, vindictive, unjust judges over each other, and stir up such a noise among them that the simplest prayer will not be uttered!"

The warriors were impressed and muttered their awe and approval.

"In the meantime," Destroyer continued, "let us not forget that *our* people are praying as well, devoting much time and worship to our lord, and he is responding with great favor toward us, sending more and more forces to bolster our ranks and confound our enemies! Time is on our side!" Then he stopped and grinned. "So, if Tal is a master of waiting, we will be the same! Though Tal may dangle Sally Roe like a carrot before our noses, we will not assault her too soon. We will not fly into another ambush." Destroyer's eyes narrowed with cunning. "We will wait, as Tal does. We will watch, we will follow, until our moment is right, until this mighty Captain of the Host is not so mighty, but is confounded, stripped of his power by the saints of God themselves!

"And then sometime, somewhere, Sally Roe will have her Gethsemane. She will be alone. Her escorts will be unaware, unready, small in numbers. The moment will be ours to take her."

"But how will we know?" asked a fourth demon.

"We will know, just as before, because a Judas will tell us. All we have to do is find him." Destroyer hacked a hideous chuckle. "Such a marvelous thing, betrayal!"

fourteen

BEN would be getting out of the station and out on patrol a little earlier this morning. He had plans to sit behind the trees at the west end of the Snyder River Bridge and nab speeders for a while, maybe get his citation quota up a bit.

But first . . . if he could do it quietly enough, he thought he'd use the police teletype to request a crime check on Sally Roe. It just might turn something up.

"Cole . . ."

It was Mulligan, and there was something strange about the tone in his voice.

"Yes, sir."

Mulligan came out of his office and over to Ben's desk. He leaned on it with his big fist and cut into Ben with his eyes.

Ben was ready to talk, but not to be stared at. "Something wrong, Harold?"

Mulligan was almost smiling. "You been snooping around again?"

"Snooping?"

"Leonard tells me you were bothering Joey Parnell, the coroner."

Ben was a little stunned to hear that such a report had come from Leonard, of all people. "If Leonard told you I was *bothering* Mr. Parnell, I would have to disagree with his terms. I don't think I was bothering Mr. Parnell at all. I sat next to him over at Don's and just asked a few questions. It was all very casual."

"Didn't I tell you to drop this Sally Roe thing? What's wrong with your memory, Cole?"

Ben had been a wimp long enough. He stood to his feet and faced Mulligan eye to eye. "There is nothing wrong with my memory, Harold, Mr. Sergeant, sir! I have never been able to forget what I've seen pertaining to this case and the way it's been handled. I've been bothered by it, I've lost sleep over it, and quite frankly I've been very disappointed by the incompetence I've seen on the part of some duly elected public servants who should know better. If we must discuss memories, I found that Mr. Parnell's memory is no better than your eyesight in regard to the dead woman we found and her true identity. Forgive me for speaking so freely, sir."

Mulligan leaned toward Ben so that their faces were only an inch apart. "I thought you and Leonard were supposed to be doing a drug bust at Don's. I don't see any contraband, Cole. Where is it?"

"Leonard took care of that, sir."

Mulligan called, "Leonard?"

Leonard was doing something in the back. "Yeah?"

"Did you bring any contraband back from that drug bust?"

"Yeah. About a quarter kilo of marijuana. Ben took care of it."

Ben made a face and smiled a bit at the mixup. "Leonard, you handled that whole case, remember? I was over talking to Parnell."

Leonard came into the room, his face filled with astonishment. "Ben, have you slipped a gear? I gave that pot to you to file as evidence."

Ben was incredulous. "No way!"

Mulligan looked back and forth at the two men. "Guys, we are missing some pot. Now where is it?"

"I gave it to Ben to file as evidence," said Leonard.

"No," said Ben. "Absolutely not!"

Mulligan smiled cunningly. "How's about we just take a look in your locker, Cole?"

"Sure thing."

But even as Ben said that, it occurred to him what might be happening. As they went down the hall to the lockers, he knew he wouldn't be surprised if . . .

Mulligan threw open the locker. The plastic bag of marijuana fell out and landed on the floor.

Mulligan raised an eyebrow. It was no secret that he was getting a kick out of this. "Looks like you filed it in the wrong place, Cole."

Ben nodded with full knowledge of what was happening.

"Yeah, right, right." He looked at Leonard. "Next time I'll have to get a lock on my locker instead of trusting the people I work with."

Leonard countered quickly, "Careful what you say, Ben. This could be serious."

"Serious? Guys, this is *pitiful!*" Ben reached for his chest. "Hey, how about it, Harold? I'll bet you have a spicy report written up already. Don't worry. You won't need it. Guys, the game stops here. I'm not playing." He removed his badge and held it out for Mulligan to take.

Mulligan took it. "Turn in your uniform by tomorrow."

"You got it."

Ben went quietly to his desk, removed his gun, radio, and other gear, and set them down. He opened the drawer, removed a New Testament and some other personal items, then slid it shut.

As he put on his jacket, he realized he had mixed feelings about what had happened—he felt sorrow and anxiety over losing his job, but at the same time elated and relieved. At least he was losing his job for the right reasons. Hopefully the Lord would bless him for that.

Mulligan and Leonard stood in the hall together, watching him go. He examined their faces for just a moment, and then went out the door.

The two weeks were up. The hearing convened on schedule, at nine o'clock in the morning, in the department of the Honorable Emily R. Fletcher of the Federal District Court, Room 412, the Federal Courthouse, in the city of Westhaven, some sixty miles south of Bacon's Corner.

Tom and Ben rode with Mark and Cathy. They challenged the freeway, waited for the lights, made the correct turns, and arrived in Westhaven with just enough time to park in a multistoried concrete parking lot, get their parking stub, dash across the street to the courthouse, and catch a crowded elevator up to the fourth floor where they finally found Room 412.

Right away, they knew the whole experience was going to be imposing, foreign, frightening, and inscrutable. It was bad enough being in this vast building with heavy marble walls that seemed to close in on you. It was worse to know next to nothing about what was going to happen and how your fate was going to be decided by so many three-piece-suited professionals you'd never seen before. It was even worse than that to find no less than a hundred people crammed into the hall outside the courtroom trying to get in. Who *were* they, anyway?

Tom cringed. Many were reporters. They weren't allowed to bring their cameras in, praise the Lord, but they were certainly gawking at him and muttering, swapping information, scribbling in their notepads. Some artists were there, easels and chalk ready to sketch a quick portrait of these strange Christians from an obscure little town.

Where was Wayne Corrigan? He said he would meet them here. Oh, there was his hand, waving in the air above a tight circle of reporters. He elbowed his way out of the circle and hurried up to meet them, the reporters following him as if connected to his body with string.

"Let's get inside," he said, sounding desperate. "It's a zoo out here."

They pressed forward into the crowd, and somehow, one step at a time, they made it to the big wooden doors and pushed through.

Now they were in a cavernous courtroom, with deeply stained woodwork, a thick green carpet, tall, draped windows, and a bench that rose like a mountain in front. The gallery was almost full.

Corrigan showed Tom and Mark to the defendant's table; Ben sat with Cathy in the front row of the gallery. Mrs. Fields was already seated there and doing some cross-stitch. Three board members, Jack and Doug Parmenter and Bob Heely, were ready to testify as well.

Corrigan spoke to Tom and Mark in muffled tones. "The judge may not take any oral testimony, but it's good to be ready in case. It's a real circus, let me tell you. The ACFA is here in full force, and the press, and I think some people from the National Coalition on Education. We're in the hot seat. It's—"

Lucy Brandon entered the courtroom, wearing a blue dress and looking very formal. She was flanked by the blonde Claire Johanson and a tall, youthful-looking man, obviously her attorney.

"That's Gordon Jefferson, Brandon's attorney. He's ACFA."

In came an older attorney, his chin high, holding a black briefcase in front of his stomach.

"Wendell Ames, Brandon's other attorney, senior partner at Ames, Jefferson, and Morris. His father was the state founder of the ACFA back in the thirties."

The four sat at the plaintiff's table without looking their way.

"*Two* attorneys?" Tom asked.

"They're out to win. What can I say? I did the best I could with the brief. It only came to twelve pages. The affidavits— the sworn statements of yourselves and Mrs. Fields—seem effective enough, but our Scriptural arguments are going to have trouble standing up against psychological reports. They've hired a shrink, you know, some child psychologist named Mandanhi. That's him sitting in the second row over there."

They looked and saw a balding, dark-skinned man of apparent East Indian descent.

"What did he have to say?" asked Mark.

"What do you think? He has Amber diagnosed as a sick and traumatized little girl, and it's all your fault, naturally."

"Naturally," muttered Tom.

"We'll see how we do, guys. Just remember, it's only the first battle, not the entire war."

A door to the left of the bench swung open.

The bailiff stood to her feet and declared, "All rise."

They all rose.

"Court is now in session, the Honorable Emily R. Fletcher presiding."

Judge Fletcher was a dignified woman in her fifties with close-cropped blonde hair and a pleasant facial expression.

She took her place behind the bench and spoke in clear tones "Thank you. Please be seated."

They sat.

"The case is *Brandon v. The Good Shepherd Academy*. Today is a hearing on a temporary injunction issued by this court two weeks ago restraining The Good Shepherd Academy from . . ." She perched her reading glasses on her nose and referred to the documents before her. "'Outrageous Religious Behavior Against a Child, Physical Abuse by Spanking, Excessive Religious Instruction Harmful to the Child, Harassment, Discrimination, and Religious Indoctrination Using Federal Funds.' Are counsel ready to proceed?"

She looked toward Lucy Brandon and her two attorneys. Ames stood to his feet. "Yes, Your Honor."

She looked toward Tom, Mark, and Wayne Corrigan. "And the defendants . . . are you ready?"

Corrigan rose and replied in the affirmative.

She looked over her reading glasses at the crowded courtroom. "This case is obviously one of great public importance and intense public interest. If there are no objections from counsel, the court is prepared to grant permission for the use of cameras and recording devices by the press."

Gordon Jefferson stood up immediately. "No objections, Your Honor."

Corrigan noticed the immediate headshake from Tom and Mark. He stood. "Your Honor, the defendants would request that no cameras be allowed."

Jefferson countered, "Your Honor, as you have observed, this case does reflect matters of great public interest. I think the public would be well served through firsthand information that television can provide."

Corrigan whispered to Tom, "The ACFA loves to try cases in the press. They're going for this one."

Judge Fletcher didn't take long to ponder the issue. "Mr. Corrigan, the court sees no harm in such camera coverage, certainly not so much harm that the importance of public awareness does not outweigh it. Cameras will be allowed."

Several reporters bolted from the courtroom to grab their gear.

The judge flipped to the next page before her. "I have read the briefs and affidavits presented by both sides in this case. Well done, excellent on both sides, and as one might expect, in sharp dispute. In light of the short time frame, and in the interest of expediency, we will avoid oral testimony if counsel agrees, and hear this case on the basis of the affidavits and oral argument of counsel."

Wayne Corrigan whispered to Tom, "It's okay. It's to our advantage. They have to meet a higher standard of proof if there's no oral testimony." He spoke to the judge. "We have no objection, Your Honor."

Ames and Jefferson were still whispering to each other. They didn't seem too happy about the court's suggestion. Finally Ames answered, "Uh . . . no objections, Your Honor."

The judge seemed pleased with the progress they were all making. "Well then . . . if counsel are ready, Mr. Ames or Mr. Jefferson, you may proceed with your argument."

Jefferson rose, buttoning his jacket. "Thank you, Your Honor."

He walked forward and began to form his argument, wandering back and forth, studying the carpet, waving one hand in the air as if leading a choir. "Your Honor, this is not a difficult case; as the court has seen in the brief and affidavits, the complaints against the Good Shepherd Academy are well-founded. We do believe in religious freedom, of course, and far be it from us to suppose we can infringe on that sacred right. But how, Your Honor, does a child of ten have the power to decide freely in such matters when surrounded by a coercive and repressive environment such as we have found at the Good Shepherd Academy?"

Tom listened raptly to Jefferson's speech. The guy was being slanderous, he thought, but selling it all very well. The press was going to eat this up for sure.

"You have seen the report by Dr. Mandanhi, a distinguished psychologist well-acquainted with emotional trauma in children. He has clearly stated that young Amber has been severely traumatized by the outrageous religious behavior of these people, and has demonstrated such symptoms as illness, headaches, loss of appetite, and bed-wetting, not to mention severe religious delusions and even . . . uh . . . personality disorders which can be attributed to the curriculum taught and example set by the leadership at the Good Shepherd Academy. I must also inform the court that Mr. Harris is currently under investigation by the CPD for possible child abuse, and that his own children have been removed from his home pending that investigation."

Corrigan bolted out of his chair. "Objection!"

"Sustained," said the judge. "Mr. Jefferson, Child Protection Department matters are strictly confidential and are not to be discussed in open court. You will restrain from any further mention of it."

"And in light of just such tactics as this," said Corrigan, "may I again request that cameras and recording devices be barred from the courtroom?"

"The request is denied," said the judge, but then she looked toward the members of the press. "But the press is ordered not to publish anything about that revelation."

Corrigan said, "Thank you, Your Honor," and sat down. He whispered to Tom, "Jefferson knew what he was doing."

Jefferson continued, unruffled. "As for the 'outrageous religious behavior,' the details are clear in the court file, of course, and I hardly need to comment on the behavior described, that of attempting to cast a demon out of Amber, and even suggesting to an impressionable child that she is possessed by a spirit. Your Honor, this is a most unusual twist, a new and obviously bizarre form of child abuse; this must fall outside the protective umbrella of religious freedom, and we would ask the court to so rule.

"The physical abuse by spanking is clear enough as well, and even the defendants admit that the spanking did occur. As the court well knows, this practice is already forbidden by the state in any foster homes and in the public schools, and we would suggest that the precedents in law and in society are clear on this issue. This is not proper behavior toward a child, but is another form of abuse, and should also be extricated from under the umbrella of religious freedom."

Tom and Mark could see the case forming; this clever lawyer was whittling away at something he repeatedly termed "the umbrella of religious freedom." It was clear to them that umbrellas had little to do with it—religious freedom itself was the object of his attacks. But Jefferson was good at what he did, they had to admit that. His oratory was forceful, well choreographed, and persuasive. The disturbing thought now was, *Is Corrigan going to be able to top it?*

"As for excessive religious instruction," Jefferson continued, "who can object to teaching basic virtues such as honesty, self-esteem, the Golden Rule? Our difficulty is in the pervasive fundamentalist idea that we are all feeble, despicable, worthless sinners, incapable of any good in ourselves, but dependent on some outside 'savior' to lift us out of our personal morass, and without whom we have no hope at all . . . an idea we must suggest is destructive to the mental health and well-being of any child, and Dr. Mandanhi's report reflects this.

"To quickly close the matter, and not take any more of the court's time, the above-mentioned offenses do necessarily constitute a form of harassment and discrimination because no opposing view of these fundamental beliefs is allowed; this is intolerance, of course, and the seedbed of bigotry.

"But, of course, an even greater legal issue here is that these teachings and indoctrinations are being supported and paid for by federal funds, since Mrs. Brandon is a federal employee and is receiving a child care subsidy under the Federal Daycare and Private Primary School Assistance Act, part of which she has used to pay her daughter's tuition."

Judge Fletcher interrupted. "Counselor, it is the court's understanding that Amber has now been removed from the school."

"Yes, Your Honor, for her own well-being, of course. But we submit that the issue of separation of church and state is still viable since federal funds were used in the religious indoctrination of Amber while attending the school, which would bring the school into accountability to the state. This is covered in detail in our brief on the applicability of the Munson-Ross Civil Rights Act and the Federal Day-care and Private Primary School Assistance Act. While Congress intended to assist working parents with child care, no one in their right mind would argue that federal funds should be used for religious instruction. Our brief shows how legislative history and prior case law make this abundantly clear.

"Finally, we would ask that the court consider not only Amber, who was fortunate enough to be removed from the school and therefore saved any further harm; we would ask the court to also consider the children still there, still subject to this excessive behavior and instruction, still very much in harm's way. We don't know who the other children in the school are and whether or not federal funds are being used to supplement their tuition as well. That is why we are asking the court to order that the defendants produce the name of each child and any financial information concerning the child's enrollment in the school, in addition to continuing the restraint.

"Your decision here today will affect the future well-being of the other children also, and therefore we are sure the court will rule in their favor."

Jefferson sat down as every television camera in the room followed him to his chair and cameras clicked away.

Tom and Mark looked at Corrigan. He was hurriedly going over his scribbled notes, apparently hoping for an inspiration. It didn't seem to be coming to him.

"Mr. Corrigan?" said the judge.

Tom gave Corrigan an encouraging pat on the shoulder. "Godspeed, brother."

Corrigan rose to his feet. This was his moment. He buttoned his jacket as well, not to signal his determination to do battle, but because his nervous hands needed something to do. It also gave him a moment to pray.

"Your Honor, counsel for the plaintiff has taken great pains to paint a bleak and gruesome picture of the Good

Shepherd Academy. We can assure you that things at the school are much different than they've been made out to be.

"First of all, we haven't had a chance to meet with Dr. Mandanhi and discuss his findings, and therefore we can't be certain that Amber's problems are entirely due to her attending the school. As we've tried to show in the affidavits, she came to the Good Shepherd Academy with some problems already, and I suggest it would not be fair or accurate to attribute all her problems to the environment at the school. We should have the opportunity to have our own expert examine Amber, as I'm sure another expert could balance the report of Dr. Mandanhi.

"As for corporal punishment, this is certainly not the anachronism that the plaintiff is trying to make it out to be, and we are not going to resolve that issue in this case. Spanking, when administered by loving parents, or by a Christian school headmaster following agreed-upon procedure, is not abuse at all, but proper discipline, and as we have shown in our court file, a matter of Biblical doctrine, a matter of deep religious conviction.

"Also, I would remind the court that the guidelines for corporal discipline are clearly spelled out in the Academy handbook, and that Mrs. Brandon signed a letter of agreement to those guidelines. Both items are included in our brief, and speak for themselves.

"So I think this issue of spanking is not at all settled, especially when there can be no doubt that Amber's punishment was properly and lovingly administered. It would not be fair or accurate to label it as child abuse. To do so would invade the privacy and convictions of millions of parents across this country who still believe in spanking, and yes, there is the matter of religious conviction and religious freedom. These must be protected and should not be infringed upon.

"We must also object to the plaintiff's accusation of 'excessive religious instruction.' What the plaintiff refers to is a fundamental part of the gospel, but I must remind the court that the gospel is the Good News, not Bad News. The message of the gospel does not leave us all condemned . . . or as counsel for the plaintiff stated, 'feeble, despicable sinners.' We believe . . . that is, the doctrinal position of the Good Shepherd Academy is . . . that yes, man is a sinner. He is separated from God because he has transgressed God's righteous law, and, by himself, has no salvation from his predicament. But this message is never forced or imposed on any child without the positive side of the message, that God sent His Son to pay the price of our sins with His own life, and thereby save us and reconcile us to God.

"Now, I realize I may sound like a preacher here, but this is, after all, one point of contention raised by the plaintiff, and I must answer it." Corrigan brightened a bit as a thought hit him. "But maybe it would be appropriate for me to point out right here that clearly this is a religious matter. Your Honor, we are discussing religious *doctrine*, and in a court of law! Yes, Your Honor, we do challenge the plaintiff's contention that any excessive religious instruction has occurred that would be harmful to Amber. But also, we remind the court that through this complaint, the plaintiff has asked the state to rule on the propriety of a particular religious belief, and this is something the state is constitutionally barred from doing."

You got them there, thought Tom.

"We also deny any harassment or discrimination, and as the court file shows, even though the plaintiff has obtained the professional opinion of Dr. Mandanhi regarding alleged trauma to the child, the plaintiff has failed to prove any specific allegations of excessive or outrageous behavior."

The judge looked up from her notes with a quizzical expression. "Counselor, your brief included at least a cursory reference to the alleged 'outrageous religious behavior' cited by the plaintiff. Do you now deny the plaintiff's allegation that Mr. Harris attempted to cast a demon out of the child?"

Tom and Mark were certain that Corrigan would be cornered on this one, but he didn't seem to balk at the question. Apparently he'd done a lot of thinking about it. "The allegation is open to challenge, Your Honor, inasmuch as there could be many different interpretations, many different definitions of the word 'demon.'"

The judge leaned forward, lowering her chin to just inches above the bench. "Would it be fair to suppose a Judeo-Christian or Biblical interpretation of the word 'demon' in this case?"

Tom could feel his heart pounding and his stomach turning into knots.

Corrigan drew a breath and came back with his answer. "I suppose it would, Your Honor, but then, even within the parameters of a Biblical interpretation, you would have to decide between . . . uh . . . whether it would be a liberal, allegorical interpretation of the word, or the more fundamentalist, literal interpretation . . ."

The judge smiled just a little. Someone in the courtroom snickered. "I suppose we could belabor that point, counselor, and indeed enter into a theological argument. Please proceed."

Tom looked at Mark. Was that a good or bad sign? They couldn't help trying to guess what the judge was thinking.

Corrigan tried to cap off his argument. "We are here today, Your Honor, to show just cause why we should not be restrained from certain activities. Well, first of all, I would argue that these allegations of activities are spurious and unfounded at best, and that the plaintiff in this case has fallen sadly short of proving the truth of any of them. This being the case, a restraining order against the school is simply uncalled for, and I would suggest entails a violation of the separation of church and state, in that the state is encroaching on the free exercise of religion by the Good Shepherd Academy by placing itself in a position to decide for the Academy what is acceptable religion and what is not. I hope that we will not find that kind of a situation developing here, and that this restraining order will be removed. It is appropriate here for the court to remove the restraint because the plaintiff is no longer affected by the school's policies, and no other student is a plaintiff and therefore this case is moot. Thank you very much."

With that, Corrigan sat down.

"Thank you, Mr. Corrigan," said Judge Fletcher.

Then came the long, second-by-second wait. Judge Emily R. Fletcher leafed through her notes, scribbled some notes next to her notes, and then stared at her notes as a tense silence fell over the great chamber.

fifteen

FINALLY Judge Fletcher set down her pen and spoke, alternately looking through her reading glasses at the papers in front of her and then looking over them at the lawyers, litigants, observers, and television cameras.

"I doubt that either side will be entirely pleased with my decision, but contrary to Mr. Jefferson's opening assertion, this *is* a difficult case, and it puts me in an even more difficult position, where I'm called upon to balance, as it were, the Constitution and the best interests of a ten-year-old child. In trying to achieve that kind of balance, it's inevitable that both sides in this dispute are going to lose something and find their respective desires not totally satisfied.

"I've read the file and heard the arguments of counsel. I believe this is a case where some injunctive relief is warranted. However, there are some strong and some weak arguments on both sides, and some issues that seem to me to be, at least at this point, unarguable. I'll address the separate complaints one by one.

"To go down the list . . . pertaining to 'Outrageous Religious Behavior Against a Child,' I agree with the Constitution that there is a place for individual religious persuasion and practice. But I hold that there is certainly a place for proper restraint, and no place at all for any violation of the laws of the state. The complaint of the plaintiff is clear and direct, that Amber was harassed and effectively branded as someone possessed by a spirit, a demon, whatever the definition of that word might be. I do believe the propriety of such behavior should be called into question; I think this protection should remain. Therefore, the restraining order against such behavior shall issue until the matter is resolved in trial.

"I will say the same for any further spanking of any child at the Academy. The state has an interest in protecting its children, and there have been many cases where corporal punishment has been found to be inappropriate. While religious

161

conviction has its rightful place in our society, the possibility of child abuse still exists, and therefore I think it is appropriate that a restraining order should issue along the lines requested by Mrs. Brandon, and that the matter proceed to trial.

"As for the next three complaints, 'Excessive Religious Instruction Harmful to the Child,' 'Harassment,' and 'Discrimination,' I would agree with Mr. Corrigan that these are rather vague complaints that have not been established to the satisfaction of the court as harmful to the children. The court agrees that these are religious matters, and it is clear that the religious position of the Academy was well-advertised and clearly stated so that Mrs. Brandon was aware of the religious nature of the Academy before enrolling her child. If the plaintiff argues that such beliefs and teaching are inappropriate for any child, then let counsel build a case and present it in trial.

"As for the final complaint, 'Religious Indoctrination Using Federal Funds,' Mrs. Brandon has removed her daughter from the school, and as long as no further tuition is paid to the school out of Mrs. Brandon's salary, there is, in my opinion, no further violation of the law, and no further harm done until this matter can be decided in trial. The restraint is moot, then, and therefore removed.

"I will sign the appropriate written order when completed by counsel. Counsel should discuss the appropriate bond to be placed in the order. If you cannot agree, call my clerk.

"I am withholding a ruling at this time on the production order plaintiffs seek. I'm concerned about that. Further argument may be needed, or it may be moot, but it is an important issue.

"By this order I'm not saying the plaintiff's claims are unfounded, just that all the restraint requested pending trial is not warranted. The whole matter will proceed to trial in due course." She picked up the gavel and rapped it sharply. "This court is in recess."

"All rise," said the bailiff, and they all rose, and the muttering and mumbling started as Judge Fletcher left the room.

"Now what?" Tom asked.

"Now we dodge the reporters and get out of here," said Corrigan.

"How did we do?" asked Mark as Cathy took his arm and listened.

"Well, we still have a long battle ahead of us. To review, your school can stay open and you can keep teaching your normal curriculum, but spanking is out and casting out demons is taboo. The judge says you don't have to produce the names and financial records of any of the other kids, so that's one hassle avoided. I would say we did pretty well, considering how it could have gone. Let's get out of here."

Mrs. Fields and the Parmenters were full of questions too.

"Can the school stay open?" Mrs. Fields asked.

"Yes, it's all right," said Tom.

Cathy gave her a hug and said, "We're going to have a meeting with everyone and explain it all."

Jack Parmenter was still itching for a fight. "We've got to get that . . . that Jefferson punk. We don't have to stand for that kind of talk!"

"Let's talk about all that somewhere else," said Corrigan.

He led the way, and the others followed in a single file through the courtroom doors.

The camera lights were blinding; it was like daylight in the hall outside.

"Mr. Harris!" came the first reporter. "What is your reaction to the judge's ruling?"

"No comment," said Wayne Corrigan.

"What about your children?" asked another reporter. "How long have they been removed from your home?"

So much for the judge's order, Tom thought.

"Is it true that you tried to exorcise a demon from the child?" said a lady, shoving a microphone in Tom's face.

Corrigan grabbed the microphone. "We intend to try our case in a court of law, not in the press. Thank you."

More questions.

"Let's go," Corrigan said to Tom and the others.

They kept moving, even slinking, through the crowd.

They passed a cluster of reporters and cameras gathered

around Lucy Brandon and her two lawyers. Jefferson was holding forth with quite a comment for the press. ". . . The judge's decision was just what we expected. While we can't believe that anyone would allow their children to be subjected to this kind of curriculum and the harsh treatment it requires, I can understand why the judge was reluctant to rule on the abbreviated evidence that one can produce for a short-notice hearing such as this. We are, however, pleased that the judge chose to protect the children of Bacon's Corner from further physical abuse at the hands of Tom Harris and his staff . . . these fundamentalists."

Tom heard all that and turned. He had to say something. He couldn't let that get into the press.

"Come on, let's just go," said Corrigan, tugging at his arm.

They hurried from the courthouse.

The Wednesday night prayer meeting at Mark and Cathy's house was packed. Attendance wasn't that bad on any normal Wednesday night, but this night was not normal at all, and there weren't enough chairs for everyone.

All the board members were there along with their wives, as were some of the people on the prayer chain: Donna Hemphile, Lester and Dolly Sutter, Tim and Becky Farmer, Brent and Amy Ryan, and the widow Alice Buckmeier. Ben Cole was there with his wife Bev; Mrs. Fields was there, even though she regularly attended the local Baptist church on Wednesday nights. Wayne Corrigan was there as well and would probably be the center of attention.

The one person noticeably absent was Tom Harris. He'd taken his leave of absence, and felt compelled to keep his distance. Besides, Mark felt the evening's discussion would be freer and any grievances could be more easily voiced if he was not there, and Tom agreed with that.

Some other absences were a little unsettling to Mark, who, being the pastor, was more prone to notice. Andrea and Wes Jessup, who usually attended the midweek meeting, were absent, as were the Wingers. Mark knew why they were gone. There were still some disgruntled people out there who needed to have their fears and false information cleared up, and naturally, being the ones who needed most to be here, they were not. Dealing with them was going to be a tough and unpleasant project.

In all, the house had to be holding no less than fifty people. This had to be a crisis indeed.

But the house was also filled with other visitors, no less than fifty, almost an even match in attendance. Tal was there, along with Guilo, recently returned from his surveillance near the mountain town of Summit; Nathan and Armoth were ready at Tal's side, and at their command was a formidable troop of warriors. Mota and Signa, having completed their assignment at the elementary school, were in attendance and overseeing the hedge of guards now surrounding the house. This would be one meeting uninvaded by any marauding spirits.

"Messengers are ready," Nathan reported. "All they need is a word from you."

Tal looked around the room and managed a grim smile. "Maybe we'll get a better idea where the trouble is, and where our prayer cover went. May the Lord grant His people a special portion of His wisdom tonight." He took one more look around the room and then said, "The messengers will wait for my word."

"Done."

"What of Sally Roe?"

Chimon stepped forward. "Scion and I have just delivered her into Cree and Si's care. They're escorting her to the Omega Center."

"Good. Go immediately to Bentmore and prepare the way for her there."

"Done."

Chimon and Scion vanished to their next assignment.

Wayne Corrigan stood to address the group and field their questions.

"I would say it was about a fifty percent victory," he said, "which is a positive way of looking at it. The Academy should be able to run smoothly without too much interruption—"

"Until some of those kids find out you can't paddle 'em," said Tim Farmer, who *was* a farmer, showed a missing tooth whenever he grinned, and had his boy in the Academy's fifth grade. "Whatever you do, don't tell Jesse about this!"

They all laughed. They were glad it was Jesse's father who'd said it.

"You will be under a handicap, certainly," said Corrigan. "You'll have to come up with some other means to deal with discipline problems."

Judy Waring, always the hearer and bearer of bad tidings, was bursting to say her piece. "Well, I want to know what got us into all this trouble to begin with! Just what is Tom Harris doing with our kids?"

"Judy!" Mark cut in. "We're here to cover that to everyone's satisfaction, don't worry."

Amy Ryan asked a simple question. "Mark, could we hear it from you? Did Tom try to cast a demon out of this little Brandon girl?"

Mark knew he was going to have trouble as soon as he said it. "Yes, he did. She was—"

"Now there was a dumb move," piped Brent, Amy's husband. He was a muscular public utilities contractor who considered his areas of competence to be natural gas, the Word of God, and dumb moves. "How did he know if it was a demon or not?"

Judy Waring was more than ready to whip that horse. "He didn't have any idea what he was doing, and now he's gotten our school into hot water it'll never get out of!"

Mark tried to restore order, and had to speak in firm tones. "All right, everybody. Now before we all run off in a hundred different directions, let's just be quiet and first hear what Wayne has to say. Direct your questions to him, one at a time!"

"We've done something wrong," Judy insisted. "We wouldn't be in court if we didn't do something wrong."

"Judy!"

She closed her lips, but with a defiant expression.

"Come on, saints," said Tal, "you can do better than that!"

Guilo muttered, "You were wondering where our prayer cover went?"

Wayne Corrigan tried to start again. "I want to give you an accurate picture, but also I don't want to sound too negative. We *are* in the middle of a lawsuit, but it's not the end of the world . . . or of the school. It's possible we can pull through this thing and come out unscathed with the help of the Lord and everyone who can pitch in. For right now, the school is under a restraining order forbidding the use of spanking or of any religious behavior that could be construed as harmful to children."

"Casting out demons . . ." Brent muttered under his breath. Everyone heard him.

"No, now let me comment on that right now. You have to realize how the system works, and how the ACFA works. Casting out demons isn't the ultimate point of all this. It's just the issue that keeps moving to the forefront because it's sensational in nature and mostly because it involves a child. The ACFA knows that and they're playing it for all it's worth, making it the rallying point.

"But it would be better to follow and watch the phrase, 'outrageous religious behavior.' You see, what could happen in this case is that the courts—for the sake of a child—will have to rule that some particular action by a religious group constitutes outrageous religious behavior; once that legal precedent is set, it can be used in future cases to widen the original definition of just what kind of religious behavior is outrageous and can be legally challenged, whether a child is involved or not. We would ultimately open the gate for the courts to establish what kind of religious belief is acceptable and what is not, to put it bluntly."

"But what about religious freedom?" asked Lester Sutter, one of the senior citizens of the congregation. "Since when does the government tell us how to live our lives and how to raise our children?"

"Exactly. That is the real issue here, and I want all of you to understand that. This lawsuit is not about spanking or demons or anything else. The ACFA is behind this whole thing, and you can be sure they are working to set some legal precedents that will give the federal government the power to control religion and religious schools."

"They can't do that!" said Amy Ryan.

"They're doing it," said Brent.

"But what about the Constitution?"

Brent shrugged. "What about it?"

Corrigan stepped in. "Brent's aware of my point. The popular notion these days is that the Constitution is a 'living document' that can be reinterpreted by the courts as society continues to evolve morally."

"Or *decay* morally," said Frank Parmenter.

"Or *spiritually*," said Mark. "Listen, people, this isn't just some kind of legal battle. This is a spiritual battle, don't forget that."

"Yeah," said Brent, showing a slight turn-around in his attitude. "What if it *was* a demon? Pretty soon it's going to be against the law to cast one out."

"But who says we have to do what the government says?" asked Tim Farmer. "What about the apostles? They didn't obey the Jewish rulers when they were told not to preach about Jesus."

Corrigan replied, "That's an important point, and something you all need to consider seriously: you may choose to be civilly disobedient as the apostles were, and to obey the Law of God rather than the law of man . . ."

"Let's do it!" said Frank Parmenter.

"But," Corrigan was quick to add, "remember that the apostles went to prison, were beaten, tortured, and martyred for their stand. And as I've said before, Paul and Silas cast out a demon in Philippi and ended up in prison for it. Civil disobedience is not without a price." Now the room was quiet. Corrigan continued, "And that price could also mean extreme damage to your credibility in this lawsuit. Your arguments on appeal will be harder to sustain. Now of course you must follow your conscience before God, and there is Scriptural precedent for civil disobedience—the Hebrew midwives who violated Pharaoh's orders to kill the male Hebrew children, Rahab who hid the spies, the apostles who preached in the name of Jesus when ordered not to. But my advice to you is to work through the system first, the old Romans 13 approach. It will go better for you in the trial."

"What if we lose?" asked Brent.

"Then . . ." Corrigan hesitated and considered his answer. "Then you'll just have to do what you have to do." He hurriedly added, "But please remember, the legal process takes time. You must be patient and not do anything rash that could hurt your chances of winning in court. Remember, the ACFA plans to go national with this case, as far as it can go, with national media attention and as much negative publicity as they can generate. They're using the Day-care Act to get into the federal courts as well, so this case could easily have damaging precedents that could affect every other church, every other Christian school in the country. You're not just making choices for yourselves tonight, but for your brothers and sisters everywhere. You're the first domino. Remember that."

"The first domino," Brent said quietly, and then shook his head at the thought. "Looks like the persecution's started, folks."

Mark stepped in. "So what's coming up next, Wayne?"

"The hardest part of all, I suppose. We'll have to send inter-rogatories to the other side, take depositions from them, and build a defense. For those of you who don't know what those words mean, an interrogatory is simply a list of questions, things we want to find out from them. We want to know what their grievances are and what they know, so we can counter whatever their argument is going to be. The deposi-tions are similar. We will meet with the witnesses who will be testifying against us, and they will answer our questions under oath with a court reporter there to take down a verba-tim record of what they say. The other side is going to do the same with our witnesses, and supposedly both sides will know what testimony and evidence are going to be presented so they can prepare their arguments for the courtroom."

"So what can we do to help?" asked Jack Parmenter, and every face in the room agreed with the question.

"Well . . ." Corrigan looked at the ceiling for an answer. "Any lawyer is only as good as his information, and as I've already discussed with your pastor and with Tom Harris, I'm hard-pressed as far as the availability of my time to do all the homework. I . . ." He wasn't sure if he should say his next thought. "Well, with some reservation let me just say this: obviously we're up against some aggressive people, very organized, highly motivated, with contacts and assistance all over the country as near as their phone. They mean business, they mean to win, and their methods are not always above board . . ."

"They're a bunch of crooks, in other words," said Brent.

"Well . . ." Corrigan tossed up his hands. "I guess I won't debate that opinion. What I'm trying to say is, you need an investigator; someone who can dig after the facts that our opponents are going to do their best to hide. I've dealt with the ACFA before, and they do not cooperate when it comes to supplying any information in answer to interrogatories. They're sneaky, conniving, stealthy, and ruthless. Within Christian propriety, of course, you need someone who can be just as ruthless and find out what you need to know even if the ACFA is trying to hide it. That takes time, skill, and experience; you need someone who can help you with that."

"So who do we call?" asked Jack Parmenter.

"I don't know of anyone nearby who'll do it for any price you can afford."

Suddenly Ben Cole spoke up. "Well, maybe I can work on that. I'm out of a job right now; I have the time, for a while anyway."

Amy Ryan leaned forward to see Ben around several other heads. "Ben, I didn't know you were out of work. What happened?"

Ben shrugged. "It's a long story."

Bev looked at him for just a moment. "You gonna tell 'em?" Ben hesitated, so Bev jumped in. "You wanna talk about shady dealings goin' on, I think Ben got caught stickin' his nose where certain people didn't want it. He was onto somethin', I know."

Ben was apologetic. "Well, that's off the subject."

But Bev didn't drop it. Tall, lean, and athletic, she was no weakling and could be very persistent when it came to fighting for the truth. "It might be right on the subject. You know that suicide that happened a couple weeks ago?"

Some did, some didn't. Few could see what it had to do with anything.

"Ben thinks it was a murder, but the cops are covering it up. I think he was getting too close to finding something out and that's why they fired him."

Ben held up his hands and smiled apologetically. "Hey, it's a great story. I'll tell it to everybody later."

Mark said sincerely, "Ben, we'll pray about all that tonight."

Ben nodded. "Thanks. Anyway, all I wanted to say was that I'll be happy to do what I can. I'll do some of the hoofing; just tell me what to do."

Mark thanked Wayne Corrigan and then stepped to the center of the room. "Let's go to prayer. I think we're going to have a real mountain of things to do, and all kinds of battles to fight on the natural level; we'll be fighting against the schemes of men, against all the curveballs hiding in the law courts, against the financial challenge this is going to be. But none of the battle is going to succeed if we don't fight first of all where the real battle is taking place, and that's in the spiritual realm."

"Pastor," said Donna Hemphile, "may I just say something?"

"Go ahead."

Donna Hemphile stood to her feet and addressed the group. "I feel a real spirit of defeat in the group tonight, and I just want all of us to know that we don't have to accept any of this! God is our Victory, and He's already won for us! All we have to do is move in and take that victory, just pick it like ripe fruit!"

"Right on," someone said.

"Amen," said Jack Parmenter.

Donna kept talking along those lines. An address from her to the congregation usually took longer than was necessary, but her words were always encouraging, so they all learned to bear with it.

Tal could feel the Spirit of God speaking, and noticed Cathy Howard hearing the Lord's gentle voice.

Cathy leaned over and whispered in Mark's ear, "Honey, I feel a check. I don't trust her."

He squeezed her hand to acknowledge her words.

Donna kept going. "We have the right to speak what we want and see it happen. We need to search our own hearts for the strength that's ours!"

Okay, that was enough. Mark quickly, very courteously got the floor back from Donna and continued, "Let's call upon the Lord tonight, and ask Him to help us and guide us through this thing. Like Jonathan said, the Lord is not constrained to win by many or by few. If God is on our side, He'll bring things around just the way He wants them. Let's pray."

The saints joined together in prayer, a genuine concert of praise and petition. They agreed from their hearts, and as a body they were one in purpose. They asked for the Lord's special guidance for Wayne Corrigan as he worked on the case, and cried out to the Lord for the sake of the school. Jack Parmenter prayed for the kids still in the school, that their education and spiritual training would continue with strength and clarity; Mrs. Fields prayed for Tom, that the Lord would give him strength and reunite him with his children; Brent Ryan prayed for Lucy Brandon and the others who were suing them; Mark prayed for Ben and his job situation.

Tal could feel a good concert of prayer here—but he was also distracted by a bad presence in the group. Somewhere, somehow, Destroyer had planted an invisible, insidious infection, and Tal could feel it growing. Destroyer had done well; on the surface, the infection was almost impossible to notice; it was going to be hard to expose, and even if the Heavenly

Host could reveal it, the hearts of the people themselves would have to change before the germ could be rooted out.

But in the usual way, unaware of the undercurrents, the saints continued to pray, and for now it was enough.

Ben prayed for help, any help, that the Lord could bring their way—someone who would know what to do, where to look, how to fight.

And Tal got his order from Heaven.

"Go!" he said.

Nathan passed the command to two messengers waiting just outside the house: "Go!"

The two messengers instantly exploded into brilliant figures of light and shot into the sky with a rushing of jeweled wings. They soared higher and higher, the town of Bacon's Corner shrinking to a cluster of tiny lights below them, lost in the center of a vast, flat table of patchwork farmlands. Then they streaked toward the east, passing over green hills and forested mountains as if with one instantaneous leap, the winding rivers, rural roads, and gray interstates appearing ahead and vanishing behind in an eye's twinkling.

And then they arrived at their destination, another cluster of lights, though much larger than Bacon's Corner, in the middle of farmlands and countryside. They dove headlong for that cluster and it grew before them, becoming a distinguishable grid of streets, alleys, neighborhoods, a new mall, and a quaint college campus. Automobiles were still moving steadily up and down Main Street, dark little bugs with red lights on their tails and headlights peering into the pools of light they formed on the street ahead of them. The streetlights glowed in warm, welcoming amber. Up the hill above Main Street, porch lights glimmered on all the houses where families were tucked away for the evening with homework, after-dinner dishes, perhaps a football game on television.

The two messengers pulled out of their dive and shot up Main Street, etching two brilliant trails between the streetlights. Then they slowed to a hover above a small storefront office between the new bakery and a bicycle shop. They dropped through the roof and landed in the front office area.

The place was deserted; it was after-hours. They paused a moment to look around. This humble little home of the town's newspaper hadn't changed much since they were here the last time. The three old desks were still there, but now one of the two typewriters was replaced with a word processor, and the telephone system had been upgraded from one line to two.

The glass-enclosed office of the editor was still the same— still out of place in this cluttered, cramped building, and still a bit messy. On the wall above the desk was a small calendar indicating all the games in the upcoming season of the editor's favorite football team, and on the desk, in a special corner undisturbed by any papers, galleys, photographs, or scribbled notes, were framed photographs of a lovely redheaded woman and what had to be her daughter, also lovely and also redheaded.

Just behind this enclosure was the teletype room. The messengers checked the recent news releases. They found just the right one, separated it neatly from the other wire copy, then carried it into the editor's office and set it squarely in the center of his desk.

Then they waited. He was going to see it. They were there to make sure he did.

At precisely eight o'clock, a key worked in the front lock, the door opened, the little bell at the top of the door *ding-a-linged*, and the editor came in, switching on the lights, raising the thermostat, hanging up his coat, and heading for the coffeemaker. He poured in the grounds, filled it with water, and plugged it in, then stepped into his office.

The two messengers were there, watching his every move. He wasn't looking at his desk yet, but instead started fumbling with some scribbled notes on the bulletin board above the filing cabinets, muttering some unintelligible words of frustration against someone who didn't do what they were supposed to do when they said they were going to do it. He dropped some of the bulletin board pins, so he had to pick them up; and then, having removed some of the items from the bulletin board, he found he finally had enough pins to hold each item up there without doubling up the items, and that pleased him.

Then he went to the phone on his desk and picked up the receiver. His eyes fell on the wire copy the messengers had placed there, but he didn't take much notice of it.

The Lord spoke.

The messengers heard His voice clearly and wondered if the big, red-haired fellow had also. He wasn't dialing the phone yet, but was holding the receiver next to his head and not moving. He stayed that way for just a moment.

He jerked his head a little—his way of shrugging that was smaller than a shrug—and then started to dial the phone.

The Lord spoke again.

He stopped in mid-dial and hung up the receiver. The messengers drew closer for a better look.

Yes, he was reading the news item. It was about the recent hearing in the city of Westhaven, and about the Christian school scandal that was rocking a tiny, obscure farming town called Bacon's Corner.

The Lord spoke. The big man sat down at the desk and listened, holding the news item in his hand, reading it again slowly.

Finally, with a low, husky morning-voice, he said, "Well, Lord . . . what do You want me to do?"

sixteen

Near the East Coast, up in the green hills above a picturesque river, people from all over the world had found a special place to gather; with devotion, vision, and sweat they had worked to convert an old YMCA camp into a special campus, a center for learning, personal enrichment, and community. The Omega Center for Educational Studies was now in its fourteenth year of existence and growing steadily every year, supported and enhanced by teachers, professionals, scholars, artists, intellectuals, and spiritual pilgrims from all walks of life and many nations of the world. Their binding, motivating spirit: a vision and hope for world peace and community; oneness with the rhythms of nature and the eternal expansiveness of the universe; the accepting of the impulse to change; the challenging of the unknown.

Among its neighbors, the Omega Center was described in many terms of varying shades, from such labels as "a real vanguard in human potential" to such accusations as "a Satanic cult." The people who worked, lived, and studied at the Center took it all in stride. They knew not everyone would understand their mission and purpose right away, but they clung to the dream that, given time, the unity of all mankind would manifest itself. They were dedicated to seeing that happen.

It was early on a Friday morning. Cree, his wings spread and motionless like the wings of a gull, dropped over the tops of the bordering maples and glided just above the glass-smooth surface of Pauline's Lake, silently passing the small summer cottages, diving rafts, floating docks, and beached canoes. He would come up behind the Center, hopefully avoiding any spirits that might be on watch near the main Administration Building.

He slowed, rose from the lake, and drifted to a silent, stalled landing on the swimming beach. The sand was wet with dew, and a mist rose from the lake. Rowboats lay on

177

racks belly-up; the roped swimming area reflected the boat dock like a flawless mirror. To one side, back among some trees, was the equipment shack. He ducked through its walls and found a hiding-place among the canoe paddles, volleyballs, and tennis rackets.

Then he listened. There was no sound. The timing was right; the Center was almost deserted now. It was a short time between two educational retreats. The weekday group had finished, packed up, and left Thursday night; the weekend group was due this evening.

Most importantly, the prince over this place was away, feeling lax and confident during the lull, probably on some errand of mischief along with the bulk of his demonic hordes. The prayers of those faithful few saints in faraway Bacon's Corner were having their effect; the prayer cover was slight, still decaying, but enough for now, provided Cree and his warriors timed things just right.

The heavenly troops were here to find one particular resident faculty member, a lady who lived in the faculty dorm.

Cree, in appearance a Native American, with powerful bronze arms and long, ebony hair down to his shoulders, had all the stealth and cunning of a skilled hunter. His sharp eyes peered through the window and out across the lake. He drew his sword and let just the tip shine through the window.

From trees nearby, from boats on the lake, from cottages and boathouses, from the thick woods across the lake, tiny points of light answered, the tips of hundreds of angelic blades.

All warriors were in place. They were ready.

Cree waved a quick little signal with his blade. A warrior appeared from behind a rowboat, skimmed across the water, zigzagged through the trees, and joined Cree in the shack. Another warrior emerged from a boathouse, shot across the water, ducked behind the swimming dock, then made it to the shack as well. Two more, darting from tree to tree and flying low, completed the number Cree wanted. They remained for a moment in the shack, tight against the walls, listening, watching.

"She'll be awakening soon," said Cree. "She'll have four guarding her. They aren't strong, but they do have big mouths. Don't let them cry out."

They drew their swords and set out across the campus, working their way from building to building, tree to tree, smoothly, steadily.

"'Course now, the drones aren't much good for anything after they've gone flying with the queen, so they just get thrown out of the hive with the garbage. Heh! I know a lot of men who are just like that, only good for eating and mating."

Mr. Pomeroy, a jolly retiree in jeans, flannel shirt, and workboots, was talking about bees, his hobby and obsession, and Sally just let him talk; the more he talked, the less she would have to, and the less questions she would have to answer about herself.

They were riding in Mr. Pomeroy's old Chevy pickup with the rack over the bed and the dented right side—he'd run over a stump trying to pull out another one and he told her all about it. He was just on his way up to a fellow-beekeeper's house to check his hives when he spotted this lone, wandering gal out on the highway, dressed in jeans and an old blue jacket, a blue stocking cap on her head, and a large duffel bag over her shoulder. He was a neighborly sort and didn't like to see a woman hitchhiking alone; so he pulled over, picked her up, gave her a short lecture about the dangers of hitchhiking, and then asked her where she was going.

"The Omega Center," she said.

She almost expected a negative reaction from this local, traditional thinker, but apparently he'd grown used to the Center being around and had no hard feelings, just curiosity.

"Must be an interesting place up there," he said.

"I don't know. I haven't been there in years."

"Well . . . we're all searching, aren't we?"

Sally didn't want to get into any deep discussions, but she answered anyway. "Yeah, we sure are."

"You know, I've found the God of the Bible to be a terrific answer to my questions. You ever thought about that?"

Sally noticed the bee helmet and veil behind the seat and used that to change the subject. "Hey, you take care of bees?"

And that was what got Mr. Pomeroy started about workers, drones, queens, hives, honey, extractors, and on and on. Sally was glad. It got them off the uncomfortable subjects and excused her from having to talk.

"That Center's just up the road here a few more miles. I can drop you off right at the front gate . . . How about that?"

The faculty dorm was a new structure, two-storied, with twenty units. The dark-stained, grooved plywood siding and shake roof matched the general motif of the campus—rustic, woodsy, but functional. Cree and his warriors found plenty of places to hide in the thick shrubbery just beneath the rear windows.

At one end of the building, a dark, slick-hided arm hung through a closed window pane and dangled outside, the silver talons walking absentmindedly, playfully back and forth along the wall. Yes, there were enemy spirits about. This one must belong to another resident faculty member. That was his room.

The opposite end of the building was a blank wall, void of windows and flanked by some large trees. Cree appointed a sentry, and then, as the sentry watched from the bushes, the other four warriors ducked around that end of the building, floated up the wall, and disappeared into the attic space. Then the sentry followed.

They crouched just under the rafters, their feet in the pink fiberglass. Now they could hear a faint, whining sound, not unlike a violin in the hands of a beginner. It was coming from one of the rooms not too far from them. They moved forward, the roof bracing passing right through their chests as they walked. Now they were above the sound.

Cree pitched forward, sinking slowly through the fiberglass and ceiling joists until he could look into the room.

Yes. They'd found the room of Sybil Denning, a kind and matronly educator of many years, just dozing in her bed, not quite awake. She was apparently enjoying some half-dreams still playing in her head, and was not ready to open her eyes just yet.

Sitting beside her on the bed, a playful, elfin spirit moved his finger about in her brain as if stirring a bowl of soup, singing quietly to himself, giggling a little between his singsong, scratchy phrases as he painted pictures in her mind.

"You will enjoy this one," it teased in a crow's voice. "Go ahead . . . leave your body and touch the moon . . ."

There were three other spirits in the room, one hanging from the wall like a bat, one flat on his back on the rug with his clawed feet in the air, and one lying on the end of the bed as if asleep. They reminded Cree of young delinquent boys hiding in some forbidden hangout, gleefully committing sin in secret.

"Oh, don't give her *that* one again," said the spirit hanging from the wall.

"Why not?" said the dreampainter. "She always believes it."

"I can do one better."

"Tonight will be your turn."

Cree looked up at the warriors. They were ready.

The dreampainter's yellow eyes danced with delight at his own cleverness. "Oooo, remember this place? You've been here before. It is a part of you!"

A blinding flash! Four angels, four demons! Flashing swords, red smoke!

Mrs. Denning awoke with a start.

Oh. It was morning. What had she been dreaming? Walking on the moon, touching it, knowing it as if she'd made it. Yes. How beautiful. Maybe it was true, just buried behind a veil of forgetfulness. Someday she must analyze what it could mean.

She sat up. She felt rested, but not energetic. Somehow her usual inspiration wasn't with her. Maybe the previous week's work had drained her power.

Cree and his warriors regrouped in the attic to watch her. The room was empty now except for her.

She got up, got dressed, and went down the stairs. Perhaps a short walk on this crisp, clear morning would reawaken her inner potential and get the creative juices flowing. It always worked before.

"Yeah, here it is," said Mr. Pomeroy, pulling over next to a wide, gravel drive that wound back into the woods. Just next to the road was an attractive, sand-blasted sign: OMEGA CENTER FOR EDUCATIONAL STUDIES.

Sally swung the door open and hopped out. "Thanks a lot."

"God bless you now," said the kind man.

More traditional thinking, Sally thought. "Sure. Take care of yourself."

He nodded and smiled. She closed the cab door and pulled her duffel bag from the truck's bed. She gave him a wave, and off he went, apparently with bees and hives on his mind.

The sound of the old pickup faded away, and then there was only the quiet of this mountain morning. Sally stood motionless for a moment, just looking at that sign. She figured they had probably repainted it at some point, but apart from that, it was still the same. The gravel drive looked the same as well. How many years had it been? At least ten.

She was afraid, but she just had to take the chance. She started walking up that gravel drive, watching carefully on all sides. She tried to remember what it was like, where everything was. She was hoping nothing would escape her notice and surprise her.

Mr. Pomeroy's old pickup roared up the mountain road and around a long, steady curve. When the road passed behind a thick grove of trees the sound of the truck faded quickly, replaced by a whispered rushing of silken wings.

Where the road reappeared, Si, a dark East Indian, was aloft, his wings unfurled and his sword in his hand. With a burst of power he went into a steep climb and circled back toward the Center.

Mrs. Denning felt a little better out in the fresh air, walking on the smooth, asphalt path between the classrooms and meeting halls. Soon the campus would be full of people again and this restful solitude would be ended. It was certainly pleasant now; there went a chipmunk up that tree, and how the birds were chattering!

Oh, what was this, an early arrival? Just beyond the sports field, a young lady was coming up the main road into the complex. Their eyes met.

Cree touched Mrs. Denning's eyes. *Easy now . . . don't see too well.* Then he darted into the trees and out of sight. Somewhere the other warriors were present, ready and invisible.

Sally looked carefully at this woman she was approaching. She wasn't sure who she might be. She was afraid they may have known each other before. She kept walking.

Finally the two women came face to face in front of the quaint Log Cabin Cafe.

"Hello," said Mrs. Denning. "And who might you be?"

Sally smiled, but her mind was instantly far away, more than eighteen years away.

I know this woman.

The woman before her, dressed in gray pants and a casual Omega Center sweatshirt, was eighteen years older, grayer, with more lines in her face. But the gray eyes still had that same sparkle, the head still had that same playful tilt when she spoke. This was Sybil Denning!

Sally found her tongue and the name she'd decided to use. "Um . . . I'm Bethany Farrell. I was just passing through the area, and someone told me I might find a place to stay up here."

Mrs. Denning smiled. "Oh, you just might. We have overnight camping here, and some nice cabins. We're expecting people to arrive for a weekend retreat this afternoon, but they're a small group. I'm sure we'll still have some rooms empty. What did you have in mind?"

"Oh . . . just a warm place out of the rain, some blankets, maybe a mattress."

Mrs. Denning laughed. "Oh, we can do better than that! Listen, the office doesn't open for a few more hours. I think the Galvins are up by now; maybe they'll open the cafe and we can get a cup of coffee, all right?"

"All right."

Mrs. Denning turned toward the Log Cabin Cafe, and Sally followed her.

"By the way, I'm Sybil Denning."

"Pleased to meet you."

"Excuse me. What was your name again?"

"Bethany Farrell."

Mrs. Denning paused on the large patio in front of the cafe. "Bethany Farrell . . ." She stared at Sally for a moment. "Don't know why you seem so familiar to me. How do you spell your last name?"

"F-a-r-r-e-l-l."

Mrs. Denning shook her head just a little. "No . . . that doesn't sound familiar. Tell me, have we ever met before?"

Sergeant Mulligan drove over to the Post Office the moment he got the call. He parked the car quietly, went up the steps quietly, and quietly found Postmaster Lucy Brandon, then just about broke a blood vessel containing himself.

"Hi, Lucy," he said, probably too loudly.

"Oh hi, Harold," she replied from behind the counter. She was helping a patron decide whether to send something first or fourth class, and the little lady couldn't seem to make up her mind. She turned to Debbie, who was just handing a giddy junior-higher a box of baby chicks. "Debbie, could you finish helping Mrs. Barcino?"

Debbie stepped over and began checking the weight of the package on the scale. "Fourth class?"

Mrs. Barcino still wasn't happy. "Well, I don't know . . . That's kind of slow, isn't it?"

Lucy hurried to the back room and opened the Employees Only door for Mulligan. He stepped inside, his hand on his hip and his feet shuffling nervously. Lucy said nothing, but quickly stepped behind a partition for privacy. Mulligan followed her, and when they were both safe from any watching eyes, she showed him a letter, still in a sealed envelope.

He took it in his big fingers, read the address and the

return address—actually just a name, and said nothing. He couldn't think of what to say.

It was a letter addressed to Tom Harris. The name in the upper-left corner was Sally Roe.

"When did this come in?" Mulligan asked.

"Today. And look at the postmark: just three days ago."

Again Mulligan couldn't think of what to say.

Lucy was quite troubled. "I don't understand. I guess it could have gotten lost somewhere, or rerouted, I don't know, but . . . there's only one postmark, and that's . . . that's half-way across the country."

Mulligan murmured, "Somebody's being a real sicko. It's a joke."

"Well, there's no address to return it to. I just don't know . . ."

"Can we open this thing?"

"No, we can't tamper with the mail . . ."

"Mmm."

"It's kind of scary, though. The postmark is after Sally Roe's suicide. What if Sally Roe is still alive somewhere?"

Mulligan didn't handle that question very well. "She isn't! That's crazy!"

She put her finger to her lips to shush him.

Debbie's attention was caught, however, by that outburst. She was finished with Mrs. Barcino and could see just a little of what was going on behind the partition.

He struggled for an answer. "Well . . . listen, I don't know what this is all about, but let me take this with me and check into it."

"But . . . it's mail!"

He held his hand up. "Hey, we're only delaying it, that's all. We need to check into this."

"But—"

"If Tom Harris ever got this letter . . . You never know, it might hurt your lawsuit."

Lucy hesitated when he said that. "But I'm concerned about the law . . ."

"Don't worry about it. We'll cover for you. I'll just have some friends check this out, and we'll get it back to you."

"You're not going to open it . . ."

"Don't worry. Just don't worry."

He put the letter in his pocket and got out of there, leaving Lucy troubled, curious, nervous, and yes, worried.

When he put the letter in his pocket, Debbie saw him do it. She didn't know what it all meant; she just thought it might be something worth remembering.

Debbie wasn't the only one who saw it. Two little spirits were following Mulligan, flitting about his shoulders like oversized mosquitoes, carefully eyeing that letter, snuffing and hissing in a frantic, secret conversation.

Mulligan climbed into his car and cranked the engine to life. He would have some phone calls to make when he got back to the station.

The two spirits had seen enough.

"Destroyer!" hissed one.

"He will reward us for this!" slobbered the other.

They shot up the street, careening over the tops of the trucks and cars, dodging the utility poles, darting this way and that between and through the stores and businesses. Destroyer must still be nearby; they would find him.

Just beneath them, unnoticed, a brown Buick eased down Front Street. The big man driving the Buick was taking it easy going through town, just getting a feel of the place. It wasn't much of a place. On the one side was the only gas station in town, boasting cheap prices and fixing flats for ladies free. Next to it was the Bacon's Corner Mercantile, a sagging old veteran of many a hard season, just like the old rusted tractor parked alongside in grass as high as the hubs.

On the other side of the street was the Myers Feed and Farm Store. That place seemed to be getting a lot of business—there were a lot of weathered pickup trucks parked around it and a lot of John Deere hats around. Then came the grain elevators, the towering sentinels that were visible for miles and bore the name of the town for anyone who might be wondering what all these little buildings were doing out in the middle of nowhere. The PriceWise grocery seemed out of place—it needed a mall around it to look right.

"So where now?" the big man asked his wife.

She sat next to him, at least as radiant in real life as she was in that picture he always kept on his desk. "What was that church we passed back there?"

"Methodist, I think."

"Oh, here's a Lutheran."

"Yeah. Very nice."

"So where do you put a Community Church?"

"We're running out of community, Kate. We'll have to turn around."

"Guess we'd better ask somebody."

He pulled over in front of Max's Barber Shop, much to the interest of the two easygoing retirees sitting in their wooden chairs on the front porch.

"Hello there," he said, and they both stood and came closer.

"Well, hi," said Ed.

"Yeh," said Mose.

"I'm looking for the Good Shepherd Community Church."

The two grayheads looked at each other and exchanged a silent, inside joke with their eyes.

Ed leaned against the car and just about put his head through the window. "You another reporter?"

Well . . . in a way, he was. "Uh, not exactly."

Mose stood behind Ed to ask his question, even while Ed just stayed there, his nose almost through the window, looking this big fellow over. "Don't think anyone's there now. The school's in session, though, and maybe the pastor's there, but he and that other lady . . ."

"Mrs. Fields," said Ed.

"Yeah, they'd be up to their gizzards in kids right now. But Tom Harris is the real hot item. If you want to see *him* . . ."

The man looked at his wife. She already had one eyebrow raised. This thing *was* big news around this town. He turned to Mose—and Ed, who was unavoidable. "Okay. Where can I find Tom Harris?"

"You're almost there. Head on up to the bank there, turn right. That's Pond Road. You go about half a mile, and you'll see the church first, on the left, and then Tom Harris's place is just the other side of the pond, on the right, a little white house with a glassed-in south side."

"Where you from?" asked Ed.

"You've never heard of the place."

"Just wondering."

Ed stood away from the car and gave a little wave as the Buick drove away. Mose just watched with a smile on his face.

Ed nodded with great conviction. "He's a reporter, Mose. I can tell."

Tom was reading through some notes he'd made for some upcoming interrogatories. Wayne Corrigan said the ACFA probably would skirt having to answer most of them, but he was going to ask them anyway. He had a lot of questions to ask those characters, and it was going to start right here.

There was a knock on the door. He closed the folder and tucked it away on the bookshelf.

Then he opened the door. His first thought was that he was facing another set of reporters, but these two were probably married, the way they stood next to each other. The man was tall and strong-looking, about middle-aged, dressed casually. His wife was attractive, also dressed casually, but exuding a quiet dignity.

"Tom Harris?" the big man asked.

"Yes," he answered, and made no effort to hide his wariness of these two strangers. "And just who are you?"

"The name is Marshall Hogan, and this is my wife Kate. We've come a long way, and we'd like to talk to you."

seventeen

TOM made a lunch of it. He invited Mark and Cathy, Ben and Bev, and Wayne Corrigan. Corrigan was in court and couldn't make it, but the others got right over there. They pooled their sandwiches, chips, salad, and soft drinks and met with the two out-of-towners in Tom's backyard for a meeting of the minds, a serious checking-out of this Marshall Hogan. Sure, he was a Christian, and sure, he'd been through an interesting spiritual battle himself, but he was also a member of the press, and by now the press was not considered friendly or trustworthy.

They sat in a circle of chairs in the yard, munching on sandwiches and talking seriously. Marshall recounted in crisp, newscopy fashion the adventure he'd had in the town of Ashton. They were amazed. Naturally, the occult-based conspiracy to take over Ashton and the thwarting of that conspiracy went unreported in the national media. No one sitting in the yard that day had ever heard of the place or what happened there.

"And I never would have heard of you people either," he said, "if the whole thing didn't have such scandal potential. Hey, this kind of stuff the press calls news. It sells papers, and that's how it got to me, over the news wire. From what I read in the wire copy—reading between the lines, of course—you folks are up against the same thing we were facing, only worse."

Mark asked, "So you weren't disillusioned by the reports of our 'outrageous religious behavior'?"

"Maybe you *are* outrageous. Maybe you're like too many Christians who see a demon under every doily. Maybe you deserve the lawsuit and the press you're getting." Marshall looked every one of them in the eye as he spoke. "Or maybe this whole thing is legit. If it is, then I might stick around and do what I can to help you out. I've got a young gal who can run that paper while I'm away; I can take care of my own expenses up to a point. I'm a good snoop, I know how to dig things up, and I know how to fight. If this thing is what it looks like, then I'm ready to make myself available, and so is Kate."

Could this be an answer to prayer? Mark was willing to explore it further, and the others agreed. They decided to tell Marshall the details of the lawsuit and the strange incident with Amber Brandon that started the whole thing. Marshall listened intently to the whole story, and he appeared to believe it.

Then Marshall asked, "So did Amethyst ever show up again?"

Tom thought about that question. "Not in the same way. Amber stayed quiet, but she was still really strange— depressed, edgy, inattentive. She couldn't sit still during our morning devotions, and she couldn't stand hearing the Word of God. Now we know why. Amethyst wouldn't manifest at the school anymore, but she never really left."

"A tougher case than you figured on, I suppose?"

Tom turned to Cathy Howard. "Why don't you tell him about what Alice Buckmeier told you?"

"Alice Buckmeier's a widow who attends our church. She's a dear," Cathy explained. "It wasn't too long ago, just about the same time this lawsuit began, that Alice was in the Post Office mailing a package when she heard this big commotion and saw Amber screaming at a woman patron. Lucy Brandon—the postmaster—came out of the back room and tried to quiet Amber down, but she just kept screaming, and Alice says Amber was prancing like a horse again, just running circles around the woman and screaming at her and scaring her to death. The woman ran away really frightened, and Alice was just . . . she just stood there, just blown away."

"Who was the woman?"

Cathy shrugged. "Alice didn't know; she never saw her before. Anyway, Lucy Brandon chased Amber around the Post Office lobby for a long time, and I guess Amber finally calmed down and acted like nothing happened, like a total personality switch. Now that sounds . . . well . . ."

Marshall whistled at the story. "This is getting more convincing all the time."

Tom shook his head sadly. "Just try convincing the rest of the world."

"Right." Marshall pulled some news clippings from his attaché case. "The *Hampton County Star* seems to have you all figured out."

"And most of the big papers too," said Mark. "It's gone out over UPI and AP. I imagine the whole country's buzzing about it now."

"Oh sure. I see they're cashing in on the child abuse angle: 'Child Victims of Bizarre Fundamentalist Behavior.' Nice. Or how about this one from the East Coast: 'Religion as Abuse: Behind the Doors of a Private School.' Oh, I was going to ask you about this one: 'Christian School Responds to Court Order.' It says here that you still hadn't decided if you would obey the court order or not. Where's that quote? Oh. '"We must obey the laws of God rather than the laws of men," said Pastor Mark Howard.'"

Mark nodded and had to laugh. "Yes, I did say those words, but I think my entire statement was that we had heard from both sides of the question, and that some said we should obey God's appointed authorities, and some said we must obey the laws of God rather than the laws of men. I guess they caught the last part of my statement but not the first."

"So what did you decide?"

"For now, we'll submit to the court order. We figure it would be in our best interests until this lawsuit is settled. Then we'll just have to look at the question again."

Bev piped up, "Just goes to show how people with the power can decide what we know and what we don't know. It's just like what happened to Ben."

"That's nothing . . ." Ben started to say.

Bev was indignant. "Nothin'? It's got you out of a job, babe, and I don't call that nothin'!"

Cathy was in Bev's camp. "There's some other hanky-panky going on right in the Police Department. A lady was killed a few weeks ago, and they're calling it a suicide, but Ben thinks it was a murder, and now they're just covering it all up."

"And the *Star*'s coverin' it up too," said Bev. "Did you see that little puny article calling the whole thing a suicide?" Marshall only began to shake his head. "Well there. See, you didn't see it either. They didn't want anyone to see it."

Marshall got a question in. "Ben, what happened to your job?"

"They canned him," said Bev. "He knew too much."

Ben laughed and put his arm around Bev. "That's the way I see it, yes."

Marshall considered that. "Okay. Maybe we'll talk some more about that later. But let's get back to the core of this problem, and that's Amber. Tom, you said something about her claiming to have learned all this stuff in her class at the elementary school . . ."

"Right. Miss Brewer's class. I can believe it. The schools have been experimenting with a lot of new curricula. It could be that some kind of thinly cloaked occultism got in."

"What do you know about Miss Brewer?"

"Zilch. I think she's new this year."

Cathy confirmed that. "Yes, she's new. I have some friends who know her."

"All right, we'll have to talk to them and see what they know. Miss Brewer may have brought a curriculum in with her, or maybe the school board's trying out something new. In any case, it would be nice to know how Amber got the way she is, and to be able to prove it. How about it, Kate? Feel like paying Miss Brewer a visit?"

She looked up from her notes and smiled at the thought of the adventure. "Looking forward to it."

"Now . . . people of like interests tend to clump together, just like we're doing right now, and that's called networking. Once they get networked, they start working together, and that gives them a lot of clout they didn't have before. I'd like to know how much this town is networked by any occult or cosmic-type groups. They might already be in the schools. Maybe they've infiltrated into other areas of power as well."

"There's LifeCircle," Mark said.

"Some kind of occult fellowship?"

"Oh yes. You hear a lot about them around town, and they sell herbs and mystical, holistic literature down at the Mercantile. They call themselves something like, 'a supportive circle of friends devoted to personal growth and evolvement.'"

"Who belongs to this bunch?"

They all started looking at each other. No one knew for sure who was involved in it.

"I don't know anyone right offhand," Mark explained. "They don't function much in public; they're not very visible."

"What about Miss Brewer?"

No one knew.

"How about Lucy Brandon?"

No answer.

"Well, we'd better find out then. We can't see anything yet, and it may not be just this LifeCircle outfit, but what we're looking for is some kind of connection, some kind of link-up between these ACFA guys, Claire Johanson, Lucy Brandon, Miss Brewer, and ultimately Amber. We've got to know the enemy before we can deal with him." Marshall finished the last few drops of root beer. "And I guess you know this is a spiritual battle. How are things in that department? Do you have some good prayer warriors?"

The reaction wasn't immediately affirmative. There was doubt all around, on every face.

Mark tried to explain. "It's been tough because of the lawsuit, because of the accusations leveled at Tom. The people here today are all praying, but the church is really struggling with this whole thing, and there are a lot of very unhappy people. I'm still trying to get a handle on all the talk going around."

"So they're talking and not praying?"

Mark nodded. "That's about it."

Marshall thought about that and nodded. "Sounds like a

smart move on Satan's part. If he can divide the church and split you into camps, his job will be a picnic."

"Well," said Mark, "we can sure pray now, just us. I know *we're* together on this thing."

"Yeah, let's do it," said Ben.

They prayed, and took quite a bit of time at it. Marshall and Kate joined them, and that meant a lot to everyone. There was definitely a unity here, a oneness of spirit. This big man from far away and his wife were not strangers at all, but fellow-combatants. This was the hand of God.

Now long after Mark said the final "Amen," Marshall popped the final question. "So how does it sound to you? You want to deal us in, and see what develops?"

By now they were ready. Mark extended his hand, and he and Marshall shook on it. "We have fellowship, brother."

"All right, then. I've got a few projects in mind already. Cathy, see what your friends can tell us about Miss Brewer, and then Kate will drop in and visit her in person. Bev, we'll need to talk to Alice Buckmeier about that incident in the Post Office and hopefully get some more details from her; maybe then we can find out where Amber got this little horse friend and what we're really dealing with. I'll see if I can check out this LifeCircle bunch and find out who's involved."

It sounded good to them all.

The group began to break up. Cathy and Bev started clearing plates from the picnic table. Mark and Tom started folding up the furniture.

"Oh, Ben . . ." said Marshall, and Ben joined him by the back fence. Marshall leaned on the fence and looked out over a wide, green pasture bordering Tom's yard. "You were a cop, huh?"

"Yes. *Was.* They let me go about two weeks ago."

"Because you were getting too close to something they were trying to cover up?"

Ben smiled apologetically. "Well . . . in retrospect, I don't know for sure. It just seemed fishy to me."

"Let's say you *were* onto something. Tell me what."

Ben looked out at some Holsteins grazing lazily in the

distance. "I've no idea, Marshall. It was simply that the deceased, a woman named Sally Roe, was killed quite violently—at least that's how the evidence looked to me. There were signs of a struggle, a shirt stained with blood, some spilled goat feed—the body was found in a goat pen, the body itself was flung on the floor as if there had been a violent struggle. The medical examiner attributed the death to asphyxiation by hanging, the same as Sergeant Mulligan's initial conclusion, but I don't think that conclusion matched the situation found at the scene. When the landlady, Mrs. Potter, found the body, it wasn't hanging from the rafters; it didn't have a rope around its neck, nor was any rope tied to the rafters. The deceased did have a rope in her hand. And the body was flung in the straw, just as we first found it. I'm also bothered by the fact that when the call first came in, Sergeant Mulligan referred to it as a suicide before we even drove out there, and I know I gave him no information at the time to that effect.

"Add to that a disturbing development that I uncovered by talking to some people who knew Roe before her death: the description they gave me of Sally Roe doesn't match the description of the woman we found in that goat shed, which raises some frightening implications. The whole thing doesn't make sense at all, and I'm still disturbed about it."

"I see you have moles in this part of the country too," said Marshall, pointing out some new molehills in the yard.

Ben was a little disappointed. Apparently his concerns were unimportant to this man who claimed to be so interested in the problems he and his friends were facing. "Well . . . yeah. They're tough to get rid of. When they come up in my yard, I just keep scooping up the hills so they don't kill the grass. It's about all you can do."

Brother, thought Ben, *what a stupid conversation this is becoming.*

"Looks like the neighbors have them too." Marshall pointed at several molehills out in the pasture.

"Yeah, they get around," said Ben, ready to end this letdown of a conversation, starting to look around.

"Two different pieces of property here," said Marshall, looking up and down the fence. "Tom has a mole, and the farmer over there has a mole." Then Marshall looked at Ben for a moment, waiting for Ben's full attention. "How much you wanna bet that the molehills in this yard and the molehills in that pasture were made by the same mole?"

Ben stopped any other thoughts and paid attention. This guy was making a point that sounded interesting.

Marshall enhanced his point. "Ben, from up here on top of the ground, we think in terms of property lines, of separate domains. Tom has his yard, the farmer has his pasture, and the two domains are separated by this fence. But what about the mole? The fence doesn't stop him; he just goes wherever he wants and pushes up his little hills, and as far as he's concerned, it's just one big piece of ground."

"Keep going," said Ben.

Marshall smiled, his eyes squinting a bit in the sun, the breeze blowing his red hair. "The Good Shepherd Academy has a problem, and you have a problem. The Academy has a mole, and you have a mole. I'm suggesting that it might be the same mole. We're talking spiritual warfare here; spirits don't care about whose yard it is, or where our fences might be."

"So what are you saying?"

"I'm saying I'll feel a whole lot better if you and I can find out all we can about this Sally Roe."

Ben felt better. "You know, I was hoping someone would see it this way."

"I think Bev already did."

Ben carefully considered that. "She sure did." Then he dug up a buried idea. "I was going to run a criminal check on Roe before I got fired. I think I could still run a check; I have a friend with the police in Westhaven who could do it for me."

Marshall looked at the molehills again. "Can't wait to see it."

eighteen

SYBIL Denning was a kind and sociable person, and she never seemed to be at a loss for words and topics. She and Sally spent the better part of the morning wandering about the grounds of the Omega Center for Educational Studies as Mrs. Denning pointed out all the buildings, their purpose, and what new projects were currently underway.

"This plaza should be ready in a few weeks," she said, pointing to a large patio the size of a basketball court, but without any markings and bordered by newly planted hedges. "The Tai Chi Chuan program has gained such popularity that we thought it fitting to create an effective space for it."

They walked further. "This is the performance theater. It seats about four hundred, and is our showcase for any performing arts such as music, movement, dance, poetry, drama, and so forth. Oh, and down here . . ." They came to a large stone-and-glass structure. "This is our healing arts center. We've had our various workshops in classrooms all over the campus, but since last year we've tried to consolidate the research in one building. We're trying new holistic approaches to the immune system, as well as nutritional therapy, and then homeopathy, crystals, vibrational healing, even Tibetan medicine—that's a course I plan to take while I'm here. Listen, are you hungry? It's almost time for lunch, and I'm sure the Galvins will have something ready."

"Lead on," said Sally, alias Bethany Farrell.

They sat down to a tasty vegetarian lunch. Sally ordered the rice and stir-fried vegetables; Mrs. Denning ordered a large green salad.

"Obviously," Mrs. Denning continued, not skipping a beat from the entire morning's lecture, "the goal of education, true education, is not simply teaching generation after generation the same amount of academic content as a preparation for life—just the same old basics, as they say. The human race is evolving too fast for that. What we are more concerned with in education is the facilitation of change. We need to change the upcoming generations to prepare them for a global community. That means a lot of stubborn old ideas about reality are going to have to be cast aside: such notions as nationalism, accountability to some Supreme Being, even the old Judeo-Christian dogma of absolute morality. In their place, we purpose to implant a new worldview, a global scheme of reality in which our children realize that all the earth, all nature, all forces, all consciousness are one huge, interconnected, and interdependent unity. And we're no longer alone in that goal; even the National Coalition on Education has taken up the cause."

She continued to munch on her salad like a happy rabbit. "So, we bring all wisdoms of the world to this place, all systems of belief, all mystical traditions, and we bar almost nothing. Through it all, the truth can be found by each person where he finds it."

"Human potential," said Sally.

"Oh, yes, that, and spiritual wholeness, universal consciousness, all of the above!" Mrs. Denning laughed with delight. "It's been such a rewarding time for me . . . well, for many years of my life, actually. I used to teach high school English until six years ago when I came on staff here."

Sally knew that. Though her memory of Mrs. Denning the English teacher went back nineteen years, she could see it as if it were just yesterday. A scene began playing in her mind. There stood a much younger Mrs. Denning, with more brown hair than gray, scowling at her, angry at being interrupted. Sally was much younger too, a junior in high school with a drab green sweater, a thigh-high skirt, and long, straight, red hair down to her waist.

"Who are you and why?" Mrs. Denning demanded. It was a stock question she always used; she must have thought it was clever. Sally thought it was rude.

Obviously, Mrs. Denning was not feeling well at the moment. She was trying to lead a remedial reading group, and most of the students were the shaggy, acid-dropping, spit-on-the-floor type who couldn't read and didn't care if they ever did. Mrs. Denning was definitely not in her element, much less in her best mood.

Sally wasn't feeling well either. Her mother, whom she hadn't seen in almost twelve years, had just died, a pitiful alcoholic. Sally felt no remorse, but the event did deepen some attitudes she'd been developing in that high school—attitudes of fatalism, cynicism, and gloom.

Now Sally was only doing her job as an office assistant during fourth period, and trying to bring Mrs. Denning a sign-up sheet on a clipboard, a typical list of participants in an upcoming volunteer whatever-it-was. She didn't ask to be snapped at. Mrs. Denning's question hit a lot of raw nerves.

Who am I and why? Good question.

She looked down at the teacher scowling up at her, and answered quite directly, "I don't know, and you teachers have convinced me that I never will."

Well, of course Mrs. Denning got irate. "Young lady, I don't like your attitude!"

At this point in her life, Sally didn't care what Mrs. Denning liked or didn't like. "Mrs. Denning, I came into this classroom because Mrs. Bakke would like to get your signature on this sign-up sheet. I'm just doing my job, and I don't deserve to be treated rudely."

Mrs. Denning stood to her feet, ready to take up the challenge. "What is your name?"

"Roe. Sally Roe. That's R-o- . . . Got a pencil?"

Mrs. Denning had a pencil.

"R-o-e. I'm sure you'll remember it."

"I'm surprised they let you work in the office. Mrs. Bakke is going to hear about this!"

Sally held the clipboard out. "Will Mrs. Bakke be able to count on you as a volunteer?"

Mrs. Denning grabbed the clipboard and hurriedly signed it. "Now get out of here!"

"Thank you for your time."

Sally was just reaching the door when Mrs. Denning had

some parting words for her. "This *will* be counted against you, young lady!"

She stopped and looked back at this teacher, this figure of authority. "Well, you're the teacher; you have the power. Right and wrong are situational and law derives from power, so I guess that makes you right." Then Sally thought it best to footnote her comments. "Mr. Davis, Humanities 101, sixth period."

Mrs. Denning meant to report Sally's behavior, but never did. Something about that brief encounter stuck with her, and no, she did not forget Sally Roe's name.

Sally's mind returned to the present, and she chased a mushroom around her plate as Mrs. Denning continued to prattle. Sally had to smile at how different their conversation was compared to their first.

"Of course, I was involved here long before I actually came on staff. I'd be here almost every summer, working on continuing education credits and helping with the Young Potential program." Sally was just about to ask, but didn't need to; Mrs. Denning went on to explain what that was. "Several of the teachers acquainted with Omega regularly took part in a program to recruit young people from the various high schools we represented around the country, young people who showed real potential for future leadership, who displayed special ability. I recruited several young people myself from the high school where I taught. These Young Potentials, as we called them, would be a part of our summer program here at the Center, and several came back for intensive training over several summers, even after they started college."

Sally smiled. She could remember the Mrs. Denning of nineteen years ago, sitting at her desk in her empty classroom during the lunch recess, strangely pleasant.

Sally, still the skinny and stone-faced upstart, had paused outside the classroom door to get her nerves good and steely before she stepped inside. When Mrs. Denning smiled and offered her a chair, she was quite surprised and a little suspicious.

"As you have probably figured out," she said, "I didn't report that confrontation we had a few weeks ago."

Sally said nothing. She was here because Mrs. Denning had asked her to come; let Mrs. Denning carry the conversation.

Mrs. Denning rested her elbows on the desk and folded her hands just under her chin. "I apologize for being so crabby. I considered what you said, and yes, I believe I was rude to you."

Sally wasn't feeling talkative yet. "Okay."

"Sally, I've talked to Mr. Davis, and also to Mrs. Bakke and Mr. Pangborn, and we've all come to agree that you show great promise; you've risen above some real obstacles in your life and excelled academically and intellectually. Now the other teachers tell me you're asking some incisive questions and digging into the material much more deeply than the courses require."

"I want it to be *about* something," Sally said.

Mrs. Denning was impressed and nodded with a smile. "Yes. The meaning behind it all, isn't that right?"

Sally was in no mood to waste words. "I've excelled. I've learned. I've kept a consistent 4.0 average. But if I'm nothing more than a cosmic accident, then I don't see any point in all that I've done, and to be honest, I'm getting quite bored with it."

Mrs. Denning reached for a brochure and handed it to her. "You might be interested in this."

Sally looked it over as she listened.

"It's a special summer program for exceptional students. I've been involved as a summer advisor for several years now, and I'm always looking for new Young Potentials. I think you would fit the qualifications."

"What would I learn?"

Mrs. Denning was delighted to give such an answer. "The meaning behind it all."

The meaning behind it all. Now, nineteen years later, Sally couldn't hold back a bitter smile. Fortunately, Mrs. Denning didn't notice.

"Would you like any more tea?" the teacher asked.

"Yes, please."

Mrs. Denning poured the green, herbal concoction into Sally's cup.

Sally asked, "So how have all these Young Potentials turned out?"

"Marvelous! We've had an impressive record, with our Young Potentials going on to become educators, psychologists, doctors, even statespersons. You see, the strength of Omega is in the upcoming generations we educate. When we mold them in their younger years, they then mature to be the future change agents in our culture, bringing all the masses closer and closer to the ultimate goal of world community. It starts in the classroom.

"And that's what's so exciting about the changes that have occurred in recent years. Our material and curricula are gaining a much wider acceptance now. Educators and schools all over the country are attending our seminars and signing up for our programs. I think one factor would be the dissolving of the old traditional worldview, the Christian factor, that's been such an obstacle for so many years. People are starting to wake up to themselves and the need for global community. It's the only way our race can survive, of course. Now that we're educating new generations totally free of the old traces of Judeo-Christian bigotry, our success rate is rising exponentially."

Cree was hearing it all, hiding in the attic of the little cafe. But he was getting edgy; it was getting later all the time, and before too long, more people would start showing up, more teachers, more leaders, more gurus and shamans, and with them, more demons than he or his warriors wanted to face. Worst of all, the prince of this place would be back as well, and he would be most upset to find these saboteurs lurking about.

He heard a special whistle. It was Si, signaling trouble. He shot down the length of the attic, out the end of the building, and into the concealing branches of a large maple.

There was a tiny sparkle of light coming from the trees near the front gate—Si's signal. He was alerting all the warriors.

And there was the trouble! The demons appeared first, swirling and hovering in a flock of at least a hundred, following about twenty feet above an unseen vehicle. They weren't too large, probably not front-liners, but deadly nevertheless. Cree had to cringe just looking at those flashing fangs and clicking, razor-sharp talons. Assailing that bunch would best be avoided.

Then the vehicle appeared, a large van, lumbering toward the campus, stirring up the dust. It was full of weekenders— and full of demonic warriors as well.

The window of opportunity was rapidly closing. They had to get Sally out of there!

"Say," said Sally, as if she'd just remembered something, "would it be the Omega Center that published that curriculum I saw . . . *Finding Me* . . . ?"

Mrs. Denning's eyes brightened. "*Finding the Real Me*! Yes, that's a popular curriculum for grades 1-6; we have different programs for every grade, but the easiest implementation so far has been with fourth-graders. You know, we've had that curriculum available for about ten years, but never got into the schools until just a few years ago—the old Christian roadblocks again. We're having great success with it now, however. It still works, and that says a lot for the staff that put it together."

Si whistled again, and Cree got the signal. More vehicles were coming up the road: a fifty-passenger bus, full of highschoolers, several cars, another van.

The first van was pulling up in front of the registration office, its escorting cloud of demons beginning to disperse, all cackling and chattering, some roosting in the trees, some alighting on the top of the van, some just flitting about the grounds looking for mischief.

No! Cree hadn't seen these two yet. From within the van, like huge, hulking dinosaurs, two demon warriors emerged and stood guard, their swords ready at their sides, their yellow eyes darting about with great wariness. They were searching the grounds, the trees, every possible hiding-place, looking for any intruders.

Then a man stepped out of the van and stretched a bit. He was dressed in a navy-blue jogging suit and wore dark sunglasses. He was middle-aged, but obviously a real health enthusiast. His face had a strange, stony expression; the muscles seemed tight.

Cree recognized him immediately.

Steele. The mysterious Mr. Steele, overseer of the Omega Center! No wonder there were such monstrous demon guards along!

Four other men got out of the van, each with at least four demonic escorts clinging to him. These were vicious characters indeed. There was something about these four; Cree could sense that they were something even more insidious and evil than Mr. Steele.

Mr. Steele paused by the registration office to chat with some old friends who had just arrived in the school bus. He waved at all the high schoolers still waiting to pile out.

Cree could no longer signal anyone without being seen. He and his warriors would soon be boxed in.

Both ladies had finished their lunch and now sat over their cups of tea, relaxing.

Sally figured the time was right for her next question. She began to pull the neck chain from inside her shirt.

"Say . . . in all your travels, I was just wondering . . . have you ever seen a ring like this?"

She brought the ring out into the open and let Mrs. Denning have a good look at it.

Mrs. Denning put on her reading glasses for a closer look. "Hehhh . . . what is this symbol on here?"

"I've always tried to figure that out."

"Where did you get this?"

"A friend."

Mrs. Denning turned the ring over, this way and that,

studying it. "Well . . . this face could be a gargoyle, but so triangular . . . like a combination of ghoulish face and triangle . . . Fascinating."

"But you've never seen anything like this before?"

"Oh no, not that I know of."

Steele was heading for the cafe. Cree looked across the grounds. His warriors were hiding themselves well—so well that even Cree could not see them. He wasn't sure where they were, or if they were there at all.

Oh no! Beyond the lake, just over the tops of the trees, a large detachment of demons approached like a swarm of bats, appearing as a long, thin, charcoal smudge across the sky. The Prince of Omega was returning, ready for more evildoing. Soon he and his horde would be right over the lake.

Cree ducked back into the attic of the cafe to check on Sally.

Mr. Steele went into the Log Cabin Cafe and immediately greeted Mr. Galvin, who stood behind the counter polishing a long row of drinking glasses along the back shelf with a soft white towel.

"Hey, Mr. Steele, you're back already!"

Mr. Steele didn't remove his sunglasses, but he did allow a smile to cross his tight lips. "Wanted to be here for the weekend, Joel."

"What'll you have?"

"Coffee, please."

"Got a fresh batch."

Mrs. Denning heard Mr. Steele's voice and turned in her seat. "Oh, Mr. Steele! What a surprise!"

He smiled at her and came their way.

Sally looked down at the table immediately, trying to get the horrified expression off her face. Was her heart beating? For a moment she thought it had stopped.

"So how has the week gone, Sybil?" said Mr. Steele.

"Mr. Steele, I'd like you to meet a visitor we have today.

This is Bethany Farrell, a traveler from Los Angeles just looking for a change, a little bit of a challenge."

Mr. Steele removed his sunglasses. Sally looked up at him. Their eyes met.

They knew each other.

Cree drew his sword, trying to concoct a plan. With Sally cornered in the cafe he might have to call for a full assault. In any event, they only had minutes to spare now. Demonic forces were gathering on every hand. What about Si—

ROOAARRR! Cree ducked as the blazing sword slashed right over his head! Teeth! Yellow eyes! Gaping jaws!

Cree's wings exploded into a brilliant blur. He shot through the attic toward the gable end, the demon's sword like a shrieking buzz saw at his heels.

YAUGHH! The other demon guard appeared in front of him like a bomb blast, yellow teeth bared. Cree couldn't stop in time; he whipped his sword in a fiery arc.

The demon's head and Cree went sailing through the end of the building; the head dissolved, and Cree shot skyward, letting out a desperate shout that echoed over the campus and across the lake.

The remaining demon guard, a hideous monster, grabbed at Cree's feet. Cree shot upward with another burst of speed. Another demon from above swooped down like a hawk and lunged with its sword. Cree blocked it and sent the demon spinning crazily away.

The guard's blade came at his midsection full-force. Their swords met in an explosion of fiery sparks, and Cree tumbled into the trees.

Mr. Steele's lips were even tighter now, and his eyes were piercing. He extended his hand in greeting. "I'm pleased to meet you, uh . . . Bethany."

Sally took his hand, and he gripped it so tightly it hurt. For the longest time he just wouldn't let go, but held her hand and gazed at her.

"I'm pleased to meet you," she said as soon as she could find her voice.

He hasn't changed at all! He still looks the same!

Mrs. Denning was still her jovial self. "Mr. Steele is the director of the Omega Center. He's a tremendous man." Then she told Mr. Steele, "I've been showing her around the Center, just acquainting her with what we're about . . ." She just kept going on and on.

Oh, Mrs. Denning, please shut up. You're going to get me killed.

"So you've seen everything, have you?" asked Mr. Steele.

"Well, not *everything* . . ." He was hurting her hand.

He was the same way when he taught the summer classes here at the Center years ago. Sally was afraid of him then. She was afraid of him now. There was a sinister power, a presence, about him. He could hypnotize with those eyes of his.

Si shot out of the trees along with about fifty warriors at that end of the campus, taking the demons by surprise. One cluster of them was just coming onto the grounds with another automobile full of weekenders. The heavenly warriors flooded over them before they knew what was happening and removed that complication immediately.

In answer to Cree's shout, the remaining hundred warriors swept in a fiery sheet across the lake, divided into many streams, and rushed through the campus like a flood. Demons spun about, then shot forward from the trees, buildings, and vehicles with piercing cries and vicious wails. Swords clashed, wings roared, sparks flew. The angels were engaging the demons' full attention, fiercely battling two, three, six demons at once, but they were not prevailing. The evil spirits were standing their ground.

Cree shot and zigzagged through the trees, this way, that way, in, out, up, down, feinting, darting.

CRUNCH! The guard came at him, and their swords met again. This demon couldn't be shaken!

The expansive cloud of spirits beyond the lake heard the cries and saw the battle. Out front, his fangs protruding past his chin and his head bristling with spikes, Barquit, the Prince of Omega, roared a command and drew his sword. With an echoing, ringing, flourishing of red, glowing blades, the returning warriors dove for the campus.

Mrs. Denning wasn't about to stop until she had told Mr. Steele everything. "Oh, you know what? She has a strange ring she ought to show you."

Mr. Steele let go of Sally's hand. He leaned closer. She thought she felt heat from his face. "A ring?"

Sally shook her head and tried to smile, to chuckle the whole thing aside. "Oh no, it's nothing."

He was still leaning so very close. "Oh, yes. I'd like very much to see it."

The guard came down from high in the trees like a meteor. Cree shot sideways and just barely avoided being cut in half. He gave another mighty burst of his wings and headed for the sky.

. The guard had his heel! Cree pulled with his wings, but the beast jerked him down!

ZZOOOSH! Si! God bless him!

OOF! Cree's heel was free.

In a long streak of light, Si dropped out of the sky and rammed the guard full-force. Both went tumbling in a grappling, snarling ball of fire. Cree flipped over and dropped earthward again, sword ready.

The guard had Si by the throat, his big sword raised.

Cree hurled his sword, and it went through the guard's torso like a missile. Si wriggled free and cut the thing in half. It dissolved in a choking cloud of red smoke.

Cree regained his sword. He could see the Prince of Omega descending like a storm. "Let's get her out of here!"

Sally drooped her head.

"Is something wrong?" asked Mrs. Denning.

"I think I'm going to be sick." She wasn't lying.

Mr. Steele grabbed her wrist. "Let me help you to the restroom."

He lifted her from her seat.

"No, let me go alone . . ."

Mrs. Denning was a little startled by Mr. Steele's forward behavior. "Mr. Steele, maybe she can go alone . . ."

He didn't seem to hear her. He was signaling through the window to the four men who had come with him in the van. They were watching. They saw the wave of his hand and started toward the cafe.

Cree and Si had made their chance.

"No guards," shouted Cree. "He's open!"

Barquit and his demons were diving across the lake, heading for the campus, swords ready.

Sally could see four men hurrying to the cafe. They could see her through the window, and the sight quickened their step. Mr. Steele was making no effort to get to the restroom. He wouldn't let go of her.

This wasn't a man. This was . . . something else.

"I'm going to throw up!" Sally threatened.

Cree banked sharply, made a tight turn, and dropped like a missile toward the end of the cafe, his wings roaring. The wall of the cafe filled his vision, slapped past him. He was inside, careening over the tables, along the counter, sword extended.

Joel Galvin ducked, his arms over his head, and Mrs. Denning shrieked as the entire row of drinking glasses shattered from one end to the other.

Mr. Steele ducked too, pulling Sally down with him.

Cree was out the other end of the cafe, pulling up into the sky just as Si shot like a bullet through the front of the cafe and right through Steele.

"Ahhh!!" Mr. Steele's hand went to his eyes.

"Mr. Steele!" shouted Galvin.

Sally was free. She ran for the door.

Si's sword had been there. The four men didn't see her, and neither did the spirits attached to them. The spirits were fluttering about, looking for their attacker; the four men stood there squinting, shading their eyes, trying to figure out which direction the sun was coming from.

The Prince of Omega and his hordes descended on the campus, flushing out a blizzard of brilliant warriors who scattered in all directions, fleeing like frightened birds. The demons shrieked and gave chase. This was the kind of sport they were hoping for. Barquit kept looking for the leader of this marauding host, but did not see him.

Retreat! Retreat! The angels fled, leading the demonic hordes further into the sky, further from the campus, further from the trouble below.

"Good!" said Cree, following Sally.

Sally ran down the gravel road, passing more cars arriving with more people.

"Hey," somebody called, "which way to registration?"

"Just keep going," she replied. "You'll find it."

They kept going. So did she.

The Prince of Omega and his demons cheered and wailed as they chased countless angelic warriors across the sky. They had the power and they had the numbers. They would purge their territory of these brilliant troublemakers, and that would be that.

Cree and Si just kept close to Sally, trying to force her under trees and out of sight. She seemed to know what to do, where to run, how to hide. They flew headlong just above her, swords drawn, rolling steadily to look skyward, earthward, skyward . . .

They didn't know how many they'd lost in this battle. But they still had Sally Roe . . . for now.

Good. Run, girl, just run.

nineteen

Mr. Steele stood, but his hands were still covering his eyes. Mr. Galvin and Mrs. Denning hurried to his aid.

"Hey, easy now! Get glass in your eye?" Galvin asked.

"Must be, must be."

The four men hurried inside, still seeing spots in front of their eyes. One stayed by the door. Another checked the back door.

The third took hold of Mrs. Denning's arm. She protested, "Ouch! I beg your pardon!"

"That's Mrs. Denning!" Mr. Steele snapped.

The man let go of her. "What happened?"

The fourth man helped Mr. Steele to his feet. "Man, look at the mess!"

"Mr. Steele, you all right?" Galvin asked.

His eyes cleared. Galvin looked at them closely.

"I don't see anything, Mr. Steele. You feel anything?"

Mr. Steele was concerned about something else. "Did you see her?"

The fourth man answered, "Not clearly, just through the window."

"Did you see her *leave*?" he demanded.

"No."

"We didn't see a thing," said the third man. "The sun was right in our eyes."

Mr. Steele sat in anger and disgust. "The sun . . . !"

Galvin was curious. "Who was that woman, Mr. Steele?"

Mr. Steele suddenly smiled as if she were a pleasant subject. "An old friend, Joel. I hadn't seen her in years."

Mrs. Denning's eyebrows shot up in surprise. "You *know* Bethany Farrell?"

He looked at Mrs. Denning quite flustered and didn't answer.

"How are your eyes?" she asked.

"They're fine, thank you."

Mr. Galvin got a broom to sweep up the broken glass. Steele got up and motioned his four men outside.

As soon as they stepped onto the porch, Steele cautioned his men, "Nobody hears about this."

"Right," they answered, "you got it."

He spoke rapidly and quietly. "She's got a dye job now, her hair's black, and she's wearing tinted glasses. She has the ring, all right."

"She can't get very far," said the first man.

Steele whispered to the fourth man, "I'll give you some work right away if you wish."

The fourth man understood. He whispered some quick orders to the other three. "Check up and down the road right away, and then check around Fairwood."

Mr. Steele suggested, "They might check at the Schrader Motor Inn in Fairwood. She used to stay there."

The fourth man nodded and gave one final order. "If you find her, take care of her cleanly and quietly."

The three other men snapped into action.

Mr. Steele looked back toward the cafe. "Mrs. Denning will have to be interviewed. Goring will be coming from Summit on Monday, and Santinelli said he'd be here by Monday evening. We'll talk to Mrs. Denning as soon as Goring gets here. I think you should be at the interview as well."

The fourth man nodded. He was dark and lean, dressed all in black, with a sharp nose, deep brown eyes, and strange, pointy eyebrows.

"Looks like your energies hit a critical mass in there," he said. "That was quite a disturbance."

"Maybe." Mr. Steele was unwilling to admit it. "Roe might be into some new kind of power . . . She *might* be." Then his voice took on a strange, sinister tone. "But she's dealing with *us* now, so she won't last forever. The real power is ours, and it's going to stay that way!"

"No," said Ted Walroth, starting to raise his voice. "June and I have talked about it, we've prayed about it, and we just can't go on with this. Listen, Mark, we've gone astray from the will of the Lord having this school. I've always thought that, and now we're just finding it out the hard way. The Lord just isn't blessing this thing!"

Mark and Ted were in the little school office; Mark had gathered all the records for the two Walroth children, Mary and Jonathan, and had them ready to hand over to Ted, but he was still hoping against hope that he could talk Ted into keeping his children in the school.

"But, Ted . . . if you'll be honest with yourself, with June, with Mary and Jonathan, you'll have to admit that the school's done them a world of good. Their scores are up, they're close to the Lord, their self-esteem is great, they're happy . . ."

"Oh, are they?" Ted challenged. "For how long? How long is it going to be, Mark, before something happens to them too?"

Mark had heard that kind of talk too many times before, and he was getting tired of it. "Ted, I don't know who you've been talking to, but there are a lot of outright lies going around, and I hope—"

"I don't care about the lies or the gossip, I know about all that nonsense. But I believe that behind all the talk and the fear there is a definite element of risk—"

"There is no element of risk!"

Now Ted was openly angry. He pointed his finger at Mark and looked down that finger with cold blue eyes. "Now that right there is a problem in itself! You've lost your objectivity in this thing, Mark, totally and completely! If there was a problem, even a serious problem, I don't think you'd admit it! You've taken Tom's side in this thing, and I think that's unacceptable for the pastor! You don't know what kind of person Tom is when you're not around! None of us do! And if you're going to be his advocate in these matters, then I don't think we can trust you either, and I don't think we can remain under your pastorship!"

Mark took a moment to be quiet and break the momentum of this building confrontation. He spoke softly. "Ted . . . Satan is busily at work among us, trying to split us up, trying to cause division . . ."

Ted agreed. "I'll say! You can't see the Lord's will anymore, Mark, even when it's as plain as day, right in front of you! This school is a colossal mistake, a wrong step we never should have taken, and now we're paying for it, and you're just refusing to see that."

Mark tried to clarify what he meant. "I meant . . ."

"I know what you meant! And I'm saying you're wrong, dead wrong. You've been stubborn, you've been blind, you've come to the defense of a man that we simply can't trust, and now we're all under a lawsuit and push has come to shove. June and I want no part of it, and we certainly don't want our kids dragged through it." He grabbed the knob and opened the door. "I've got to go."

Mark handed him the records.

"Thanks."

Ted walked hurriedly, angrily, to the main door.

"See you Sunday?" Mark asked.

"No," Ted replied, not turning around. "Don't expect that. I don't think the Lord is happy with this church right now."

And with that, he was gone.

Tal, Nathan, and Armoth stood just outside, watching him go.

"It's spreading," said Nathan. "First in the school, and now in the church. They're at each other's throats."

Tal fell back and leaned against the school building. "Destroyer! With no change in direction, the saints here won't have a school left to defend."

"And we won't have the prayer backup to succeed in . . . in *anything!*"

"But what about the spirits responsible?" demanded Armoth. "Surely we can root them out!"

"No," said Tal, and he was quite angry and frustrated. "They have a right to be there. They were invited. The saints have given themselves over to this fight, and until their hearts break, until they repent, this cancer will never slow its spread."

"So what now?" asked Nathan.

"Mota and Signa are working to find a breach in the enemy's ranks, some weak spot in Destroyer's plan that we can expose for the saints to find. In the meantime, all we can do is keep the core group praying, fighting. The Lord will move according to his purposes. He'll—"

They drew their swords.

No, it was no demonic army, not even a formidable spirit, only a small, ugly messenger, brazen enough to fly right over their heads, waving its empty hands to show it was not an aggressor.

"Ha haaaa!!!" it called. "Are you Captain Tal?"

"I am," said Tal.

"Destroyer has a message for you!" The little imp hovered high above them, calling out its message with a high, grating voice. "He says, 'I have cut you down, great captain! Omega is mine, and ever shall be, and your army is routed and scattered! Send some more! My warriors are hungry!'"

The imp darted away like a little fly.

Tal did not smile as he said, "Sally Roe is safe. Had they destroyed her, that would have been Destroyer's message." He sheathed his sword. "We'll find Cree and Si, and make sure of their welfare. I've sent Guilo ahead to aid Chimon and Scion at Bentmore. We three will take charge of Sally's next stop. We must keep her alive."

"We are weakened, captain," said Nathan.

Tal nodded. "Gather all the forces you can spare, Nathan. We'll do our best."

Sally remembered a side road when she came to it, but couldn't remember exactly where it went. She took it anyway, just to get off the main highway. There was a red farmhouse not too far down on the right, with a gully in front and a classic-looking red barn. That registered. She'd seen it before, perhaps while bicycling. This road should eventually lead her back to Fairwood.

She heard a vehicle approaching and ducked into the woods. It was just a farmer in his pickup.

She decided to wait for just a while. She pulled out her

spiral notebook and added some quick notes to another letter, first recounting her recent narrow escape, then trying to summarize her troubled, churning memories.

I'm remembering, Tom, piece by piece. The Omega Center has grown a lot and is double the size it was when I was last there. But the spiritual forces are the same, as are the philosophies and the goals of those people.

It all seemed so utopian eighteen years ago. I can recall the classes in Eastern philosophy and the long sessions in the meadows, sitting for hours in meditation, feeling such a unity with all life, with all that is. What bliss that was. I can remember the special spirit-guides who came to me during my last summer. They opened my consciousness to realize my own divinity, and revealed worlds of experience and awareness I'd never known before. It was like an endless carnival ride through a world of enticing secrets, and my guides promised to remain with me forever.

But the joy of those days eventually soured like warm, aging milk. The bliss of meditation became more and more a form of insanity and escape; the spirit-guides did not remain with me as they promised, but decayed into illusions, ghostly images, tormentors. I had gone to Omega to find, as Mrs. Denning put it, "the meaning behind it all," but found instead a world of mindless credulity and wishful thinking, a floating, aimless quest for experience in place of rationality. Meaning? No, only self-aggrandizement. And whether a person is a small cosmic accident or a god who fills all that is, that person is still alone.

So it was futile. I can see that now, but of course "now" is too late. I am so much older, and so many fruitless years have passed. Looking back, I find it so very sad to count the years I devoted to that place and what it stands for. I find it even sadder to think that it is still there, still drawing more and more Sally Roes into its nets. I wonder, someday will those bright-eyed and optimistic teens look back across the years and find the futility that I find now? From a better vantage point, will they assess their lives and find as little value?

Those were, as I have said, days of madness. But I must REMEMBER, whatever it takes. There is still more to the story, and I must remember who these people are, where they are, and what they intend. I must remember who I am, and what I am—or was—to them.

I'll keep writing as often as I can.

"Yeah, and some very hot places are going to freeze over before I'll believe that! You heard me!"

Wayne Corrigan slammed down the phone and fumed, "They won't answer my interrogatories! They're stalling, playing games!"

"Surprise, surprise," said Marshall.

Corrigan, Marshall, Ben, and Tom were sitting in Corrigan's office comparing notes and going over the case.

"How many interrogatories did you send out?" asked Marshall, sitting on the other side of Corrigan's desk, looking through a stack of copies.

"Just the preliminaries, the basics," said Corrigan. "But they won't even answer those, they won't return my phone calls, and even if I do get through, they stonewall it. You may have noticed the response I got from Brandon's lawyer just now, that Jefferson character."

"I noticed the response he got from *you.*"

"Well, I was upset."

Ben was leaning against the windowsill, just listening to the conversation. "You did just fine. They had it coming."

Marshall concurred. "They're just looking out for their own behinds. It won't hurt to go after them a bit, keep them off-balance."

Corrigan tried to explain his frustration. "But they keep saying their records are too personal and confidential, and then Jefferson told me they haven't even assembled their discovery materials yet, and I think that's baloney. On top of that, I think they're stalling on taking depositions from our side. They want us to go first so they'll have more ammunition. I can't stall like that; we just don't have the time."

"Looks like they aren't going to give you anything without a court order."

"Yeah, tell me all about it."

"Hey, listen. Kate's asking around about this Miss Brewer at the elementary school, and she's already made an appointment to visit the class on Monday. Maybe when she gets back she'll have some goods on this Miss Brewer, and you can use that in some depositions."

"Well, that's what I need: more leads, more players in this thing. So far I'm in the dark about what the other side is up to."

Marshall tossed the interrogatories back on Corrigan's desk. "Well, it's bigger than it looks, I know that."

"Moles," said Ben.

"Huh?" said Tom.

"Get Marshall to explain it to you sometime. It's a great parallel."

Corrigan was ready for another topic. "So how about your kids, Tom? Are you going to be able to see them again?"

Tom wasn't happy about his answer. "Pretty soon, but I'm not sure when. It's all up to this Irene Bledsoe lady, and she's . . . well, she's quite ruthless. I try not to think about it too much."

Corrigan shook his head and leaned back in his chair, making the springs squeak. For him, leaning back and examining the ceiling was a typical expression of frustration. "She's feeling her oats, if you know what I mean. Tom, if you were rich and powerful, you'd probably have your kids back by now. But Bledsoe knows she has all the power she needs, and without some real pressure from people in important places, she can do whatever she wants. The laws are just vague enough to allow a lot of leeway from case to case."

"But she's so unreasonable!" Tom moaned. "She's guarding my kids like . . . like she's afraid to let them out of her sight, like she wants to control them."

"She is and she does," said Marshall.

"But you heard about that bump on Ruth's head, didn't you?"

Marshall was sitting in a swivel chair. With a simple kick he swiveled around to face Tom. "No. Tell me."

"Last time I visited the kids, Ruth had a big bump on her head, and both of them said she got it when Bledsoe just about got into a wreck driving them away from our house! Bledsoe's trying to blame that bump on *me*, suggesting that *I* did it!"

Marshall was hearing some shocking news, it seemed. "A near-wreck?"

"Yes. You should have seen how Mrs. Bledsoe tried to keep the kids from saying *anything* about that, but Josiah told me about it anyway. He said she went through a stop sign and almost hit a blue pickup truck. She stopped too fast, the kids must not have been belted in, and Ruth—"

Ben interrupted. "Wait a minute! Did you say a blue pickup truck?"

"Yes, that's what Josiah said."

"When was that?" Ben started thinking back.

"I'm not sure . . ." Now Tom started recalling. "Evidently the evening when she came and took them away . . ."

Ben brightened with recollection. "The same evening when we checked out that so-called 'suicide' at the Potter place! Listen: Cecilia Potter told me that Sally Roe drove a blue pickup truck—a '65 Chevy, to be exact—and when I was there checking out the scene later on, the truck was gone. We were wondering about that."

"The truck was gone?" asked Marshall.

Ben was getting excited. "Gone. Now listen. According to Mrs. Potter, Roe always drove that truck to work and came home in it every day. So if Sally Roe did commit suicide like Mulligan and the medical examiner said, who drove her truck away?"

"Whoever Mrs. Bledsoe almost ran into, that's who!" said Tom.

Marshall was sitting up straight in his chair. "Did your kids see who was driving that truck?"

"I don't know. I suppose . . . somehow . . . I could ask them."

Marshall looked at Ben. "You ordered that criminal check, right?"

"I've got Chuck Molsby working on that. He's that friend of mine with the police in Westhaven."

"I hope we get a mug shot or something."

"I hope she's a criminal," said Tom.

"Yeah," said Marshall, "there is that little detail. But if we can get a photo of her, and if we can get it to the kids and have them identify her . . ."

"The fur would hit the fan!" said Ben. "It would prove Sally Roe is still alive, that it wasn't her suicide that we found!"

Marshall stood to his feet. "Moles."

"There's that word again," said Tom.

Corrigan straightened up in his chair and leaned over his desk. "Hey, guys, anytime you want to explain all this to me, I'd be glad to listen. I *am* supposed to be your lawyer, you know."

Marshall took a piece of scratch paper from Corrigan's desk. "Just like a mole in your yard and somebody else's yard . . . well, in three yards, actually. Three molehills, but all the same mole." He took out his pen and drew a small circle. "Here's the first molehill: the lawsuit against the Christian school, Lucy Brandon, the ACFA, that whole ball of wax." He drew another circle. "Here's the second molehill: The ACFA uses the child abuse hotline to report Tom and get the CPD into it. Irene Bledsoe gets the pickup order and takes the kids. That connects the two molehills . . . sort of." He drew a connecting line between the two circles.

"Maybe," said Corrigan. "I mean, you know it and I know it, but proving it is another thing."

"That comes later," said Marshall. "But now . . ." He drew a third circle. "Here's the third molehill: the mysterious death of Sally Roe—or somebody else. Somehow, possibly, the real live Sally Roe crossed paths with Irene Bledsoe right after the point in time when she was supposed to be dead." He drew another connecting line between the second and third circles. "Now you have two kids who might be—*might be*—witnesses to that, and so . . . possibly . . . Irene Bledsoe is withholding them, hiding them, dragging her feet all she can, to keep them quiet. Now she might just be protecting her own position, waiting for Ruth's bump to heal, or for both kids to forget what happened. Or . . ."

Ben took his own pen and connected the third circle with the first, forming a closed triangle. "Or she's helping to cover up whatever happened at the Potter farm, which means this Sally Roe thing could be in some way connected with the attack on the Christian school, which we know is connected with the taking of Tom's kids."

"None of which you can prove," Corrigan reminded them again.

"That comes later," said Marshall again. He smiled. He felt good. "But that's what's happening. We've got moles—spiritual powers and human counterparts—under all this, and they've pushed their way to the surface in these three areas."

Tom stared at the three circles. "If you want to talk about underground spiritual activity . . . how about the mileage Satan's gotten out of this whole CPD deal? They've got me branded as some kind of child abuser, and the whole church is falling apart over it. We can't win any fight of any kind in the shape we're in."

Marshall nodded. "Exactly. Now you're catching on."

Tom wanted to believe it. "But . . . I don't see any *direct* connection between what happened to Sally Roe and what's happening at the school. There's nothing there."

"There is," said Marshall.

"There isn't!" said Corrigan. "You can't prove a bit of this!"

"We will. Call me a fanatic, but I think God's showing this to us. He's giving us the outline; all we have to do is fill it in."

Ben was getting stirred up. "You've got something, Marshall!"

"But nothing *I* can use!" said Corrigan.

Marshall put his pen back in his pocket and just looked at

that little diagram. "We'll get you something, Wayne. I don't know what, but we'll get it."

The music was soft, steady, compelling, with a relaxing rhythm and tone. Miss Brewer, a young and pretty teacher with a disarming smile, read from a script in a soothing, almost hypnotic voice.

"Feel the breeze drifting through your hair, feel the warm sun on your skin, the firm, inviting earth under your body. You're just a rag doll, totally limp, filled with sawdust . . ."

Kate Hogan sat quietly in the back of the classroom, trying to surreptitiously jot down notes as she watched the twenty-three fourth-graders go through the exercise. The desks were arranged to provide floor space for an activity area at one end of the room, and now the children lay flat on their backs on the floor in that area on blankets, pillows, or coats, their eyes closed, their breathing slow and deep, their arms limp at their sides.

"First the sawdust drains from your head . . . then from your neck . . . then from your chest . . . You just start sinking, sinking, sinking toward the ground . . ."

Kate watched the clock on the wall. So far they'd been lying on the floor for ten minutes.

The music kept playing. Miss Brewer came to the end of her soothing, lilting monologue. She paused, looked around the floor at every child, and then proceeded with some softly spoken instructions.

"Do you hear a babbling?" Then she whispered, "Listen! Do you hear it?" She took a moment for the kids to listen. "It's coming closer now, isn't it? It's your new friend, your wise person; they've come to talk to you. Let your friend appear on your mental screen. What is your friend's name?"

Kate scribbled just a few words to guide her memory. Most of the details of what she was now witnessing were familiar to her.

"Pick a room for your friend; make up a room in your mind to be your new friend's house. Make it something just right for them. Now talk to your friend, your very own wise person. Remember, your friend knows all about you . . . how you feel . . . what you like . . . what you don't like . . . all your problems and hurts . . ."

The exercise lasted another fifteen minutes or so, and the silence in the room was impressive for this age group. At last, after a predetermined amount of time, Miss Brewer counted to five slowly and then snapped her fingers. The children seemed to wake up from a trance, and sat up.

"Very good! Now we'll all take our seats and the monitors will pass out some paper. We'll draw our new friends."

The children folded the blankets, put away the pillows, hung up the coats, then returned to their desks. One child from each row passed out drawing paper. Under Miss Brewer's firm but kind guidance, the children got out their crayons and began to create portraits.

Miss Brewer walked up and down the rows, surveying each child's progress. "Oh, what a nice-looking friend! What's that on his head? Stars? He must be a marvelous creature!"

Kate took a short tour herself. The children were drawing ponies, dragons, princes and princesses, and some rather frightening monsters as well. They all received praise and compliments from Miss Brewer.

One little fellow showed Kate his picture. "This is Longfoot," he said. "I'm going to keep him in my mental basement."

The picture was typical fourth-grade artwork, but recognizable as a giant, lumbering figure with large feet.

"Look at his huge feet," Kate said playfully. "What does he do with those big feet?"

"He stomps on my mom and dad and all the big kids."

"Oh my."

A little girl turned to join the conversation, holding up her drawing for Kate to see. "See my friend? He's a dragon, but he doesn't breathe fire. He spits out jawbreakers!"

"Oh, and did you meet him today?"

She shook her head a little sadly. "No. He already lives in my head; he's been there a long time, and we're friends. I couldn't see my new friend today. I heard him, but I couldn't see him."

"Look at my picture!" said another little girl.

Kate walked over to take a look. Then she took a longer look.

The child had drawn a big-eyed, chubby-cheeked pony. The drawing was exceptional.

"This is Ponderey," she said. "He's my inner guide."

"A pony . . ." said Kate in wonder. She smiled. "That's a wonderful picture, honey. You draw very well."

"Ponderey helps me. He loves to draw."

Kate took her seat again in the back of the classroom and jotted down a few more notes, even though her hand was a little unsteady. She was so upset, she feared losing her quiet, professional manner.

Before long it was time for recess; the children filed out in a neat line until they reached the door to the playground. Then they abandoned the building like sailors from a sinking ship.

Miss Brewer sank into her chair at her desk and sighed with a big smile. "Well, that much of the day is over!"

Kate approached her and found a chair nearby. "They're a wonderful group."

"Aren't they, though? This is a great year for me; the kids in this town are really special!"

"The creative exercise was something special too; it evoked a lot of response."

Miss Brewer laughed out of pleasure and pride. "It's an adventure every time. Kids can be so creative, and there's just such wisdom and insight locked up in each one of them. You never know what they'll uncover."

"And what do you call this? Isn't it like Whole Brain Learning?"

"Sure. That's part of it. But most of the concepts and exercises are from the *Finding the Real Me* curriculum. It's a tried and tested program, and it includes the best of the proven theories now in use. It's very comprehensive."

"Well, what's the underlying principle to all this?"

Miss Brewer smiled. "You're not a parent, are you?"

"No, just a curious citizen. Like I said on the phone, I've heard a lot about what you're doing here, and I thought it would be interesting to watch."

"Sure. Well, of course our perspective is that each child should be free to achieve his or her own highest potential, and that takes a certain measure of creative and intuitive freedom. Too often an educator can stifle that potential by imposing a particular rule of behavior or truth upon the learner when the learner should be experiencing his own realities, creating his own concept of the world.

"We've found that relaxation and visualization exercises are a real key to untying each child, setting him free to start his own process of becoming. Human consciousness, even in a child, carries an incredible wealth of knowledge that no traditional classroom could ever cover even in a lifetime. That knowledge is available to each child from his own inner wisdom. We don't teach the child how to feel or how to perceive truth. All we have to do is show him how to unlock his own wisdom and intuition, and the rest just happens."

"And that's what you were doing today?"

"Well sure, exactly. We only use about two percent of our brain anyway. When we teach the children how to tap into the vast resources hidden in the rest of their brain, the sky's the limit."

"So where do these 'inner guides' and 'wise persons' come into all this?"

Miss Brewer let her eyes search the heavens as she formulated an answer. "To put it simply, there is a vast storehouse of knowledge locked up in our own hidden consciousness, and one of the ways to access it is to personify it, dress it up as a person, a character familiar to us. So, say I'm a little girl with fears about big people, grown-ups, maybe my own parents. Actually, I already have within myself all the knowledge I need to cope with whatever situation I encounter. I only need to learn it from myself. So, to facilitate that, I relax, let my mind go, and imagine—visualize—a favorite image, a character, a friend. Did you notice the pictures the children

225

drew? Every one of those drawings was the child's expression of an inner friend, an inner guide, a personification of their own wisdom with which they feel free, unhampered, and comfortable. Once they create this image, it takes on a life of its own, and can talk to them and give them the advice and counsel they need for whatever they're having to deal with. In essence, they are learning from themselves, from their own buried consciousness."

"And this is all contained in this *Finding the Real Me* curriculum?"

"It's all in there, all organized, categorized, and graded. It makes the whole task a lot simpler."

"But—if I might play the Devil's advocate for a moment— what are they actually learning from this? Is there any academic achievement connected with the time you spend going through these exercises?"

Miss Brewer paused to formulate an answer. "I think what you're alluding to is the kind of argument we hear a lot, that we're not really teaching the kids anything, but are programming them, or using them for guinea pigs. But really, what is education? It's training and equipping children to live their lives, to survive in this world, to have the right attitudes and life skills to adapt to a rapidly changing social environment."

"And . . . I take it, of course, that reading, writing, mathematics, social studies, subjects like this have their place in this overall definition of education?"

Miss Brewer made a strange face. "Well . . . basic academic training is one thing, but it won't bring about the necessary change . . ."

"Change?"

"Well, reading, English, arithmetic, and those other subjects are in another category. They can't be applied in an affective, clinical sense . . ."

Kate hesitated. This young gal was enthusiastic about her job and her teaching style, but also vague with her answers.

"Okay . . ." she said, looking over her notes. "You used the word 'clinical.' So you see your role as more than just a teacher? You see yourself also as a therapist of some kind?"

Miss Brewer smiled and nodded. "That's a fair way to put it, I think. It's not a complete education to just fill their heads with the same old ideas that were taught to their parents. We need to equip them to rise above whatever knowledge came before, and to search out their own truth and personal values."

Kate was tired of generalities. "Even if it means training young children in shamanism and Eastern meditation?"

Miss Brewer laughed as if she'd been told a joke. "You make it sound like there's some kind of religion going on here. That's a common objection we hear all the time. There were some parents who came to me with that conception, but we cleared it up. This isn't religion; it's purely scientific."

"I understand those same parents withdrew their children from this school because they were convinced you were teaching religion here, something contrary to their own beliefs."

Miss Brewer nodded. She remembered it. "I guess that's how we cleared it up. Sounds like you've already talked to them."

Kate nodded back. "Yes."

Miss Brewer was still pleasant and all the more confident. "Well, I have no misgivings about what we're doing here. I think the school board and all the teachers they hire are more than qualified to judge what is helpful and constructive for the children. And the courts have stood behind the education community in that regard. If parents don't feel they can trust highly trained professionals to be competent in handling their children, then I guess withdrawing their children is their only real option. We aren't here to cater to fringe elements who insist on living in the past."

"You referred to the school board. I take it they selected and authorized the *Finding the Real Me* curriculum?"

"Yes, unanimously. You really should meet them before you draw any final conclusions. They're a wonderful group of people. I'm proud to be working with them."

"Well, I'm sure they are. But tell me . . ." Kate was ready to ask the question, but didn't know if Miss Brewer was ready to answer it. "Wasn't Amber Brandon in your class this year?"

Oh, Miss Brewer received that question like a revelation. She closed her eyes and smiled a long, showy smile as if to say, *Aha!* "So . . . is that what this visit is all about?"

Kate decided to try some education rhetoric herself. "Well, let's just remember that we all believe in freedom of thought, freedom of information, and above all freedom from censorship for those who have a right to know." Then she tried a straight answer. "For your information, I'm a friend of Tom Harris's, and I'm doing some research for him."

Miss Brewer was truly an admirable person. She remained strong and sat up straight. "I don't mind. I don't have to make apologies or hide anything I'm doing in this classroom. In answer to your question, yes, Amber Brandon was in my class, and as a matter of fact, she's back once again to finish out the year."

"Was she here today? I don't think I saw her."

"No, and it's understandable. Due to the trauma she's going through, she just isn't willing to attend this part of the class anymore. She spends this time in the library, and then returns to class after lunch."

"Then can you tell me about Amethyst the pony?"

Miss Brewer rose from her desk and pointed out a crayon picture posted high above the chalkboard. "Here she is, right here."

Kate walked closer for a better look.

It was an eerie experience, like getting the first look at a night-stalking burglar, or seeing the face of a serial rapist for the first time.

So this was Amethyst!

She was a little purple pony with shining pink mane and tail; her eyes were large and sparkling, she had a five-pointed star on her cheek, small white wings grew from her shoulders, and she stood tall and alert under a rainbow arch. She was beautiful, a remarkable drawing for a ten-year-old. In the lower-right corner, Amber had carefully printed her name in dark pencil.

"She drew this about a month before she transferred to the Christian school," Miss Brewer explained. "She was having some remarkable experiences during our exercise sessions. I've never seen such progress in a child."

Kate swallowed. Her mouth was suddenly dry.

"And you . . ." She began, but had to clear her throat. "You hold that this . . . this image . . . is a . . . uh . . ."

"A visualization of Amber's own inner wisdom."

"I see." Kate took a moment to formulate her next question. "So . . . as you probably know, the current case against Tom Harris stemmed from a confrontation between himself and . . . and Amber as Amethyst."

Miss Brewer smiled. "Well . . . all I can give you is my opinion."

"Please do."

"Whenever a child is thrust into a situation that is intolerable, such as a case of abuse, it's not unusual for the child to bury the memory of it or any thought of it to avoid the pain and trauma of the event. Many child abuse counselors have found that one way to bring things back out into the open is to allow the child to project the memory into a neutral object, such as a figure or doll or puppet.

"In Amber's case, you have a little pony who is bright, confident, and pristine, and who has the strength to deal with such problems where Amber doesn't. When it comes to what really happened at the Christian school, Amber can't talk about it, but instead lets Amethyst come forward and do the talking for her."

Kate digested that for a moment. "But would that explain why Amethyst appeared and caused a disruption even before Tom Harris confronted her?"

"Well, we don't know everything that happened, do we? There could have been some abuse before the events that Tom Harris told you about."

"What if Amber came to the school already manifesting herself as Amethyst? Would that suggest that there had been some kind of abuse before Amber ever met Tom Harris or ever spent one day in the Good Shepherd Academy?"

Miss Brewer shook her head. "I doubt it. Amber comes from a very loving home."

Kate nodded. "All right. Say, would you have a copy of that curriculum around? I'd like to look through it."

"Certainly."

Miss Brewer went to the shelves behind her desk and scanned all the titles. "Well . . . no, umm . . ." She straightened and turned. "Well, it isn't here . . ." Then she remembered. "Oh, that's right, I'm sorry. The principal, Mr. Woodard, asked to borrow it. He was supposed to bring it back, but obviously he hasn't yet. But if you care to, you can always order a copy from the publisher."

That idea intrigued Kate. "And who might that be?"

"The Omega Center for Educational Studies. I think I have the address here somewhere."

Miss Brewer combed through some binders on her desk.

Kate had another question, a stab in the dark. "Isn't there a support group of some kind in Bacon's Corner? Some group called LifeCircle?"

Miss Brewer looked up from her search. "Oh, yes. They're a wonderful group of people."

"What is it exactly?"

"Oh, just a loosely organized fellowship of people with like interests—the arts, religion, philosophy, ecology, peace, that sort of thing."

"Do you belong to that group?"

"Yes, I do."

"Then you must know Lucy Brandon personally?"

"Uh-huh." She caught herself and smiled. "That's right; you're probably finding out all about her."

Kate smiled and shrugged. "Of course."

"Oh, here's the address." She scribbled it down on a scrap of paper.

"Then that other woman, the legal assistant for Ames and Jefferson . . . ?"

"Claire Johanson."

"Yes."

"She must be involved in that as well."

"Oh yes. She's one of the leaders. But a lot of people belong to it."

"Like who?"

Miss Brewer stopped, tapped her chin as she thought a moment, and then answered, "Maybe you should ask *them.*"

twenty

Barquit stood his ground, his nostrils chugging sulfur straight down over his burly chest and his yellow eyes steadfast, unflinching. He was the mighty Prince of Omega, and had done more mischief and won more victories for his master than this pompous, swelled-headed upstart that now stood before him, spewing threats and abuse.

Destroyer was not about to be ignored. He drew his sword and flashed it about, ready for a test between the two of them. "You blind, bumbling sloth! Revere me now, or challenge! I will abide either course!"

They hovered high above the Administration Building on the Omega Center campus, surrounded by their respective guards, escorts, and aides.

The escorts on either side of Barquit began to beseech him, "No, do not assail him, Ba-al! He is sent by the Strongman!"

"He calls me a sloth!" Barquit hissed through clenched teeth.

"*And* a bumbler!" said Destroyer. "You were away from your post, and allowed that woman to roam and learn freely!"

Barquit drew his sword so fast it whistled. He held it forth to strengthen his reply. "And where was the word I never received, that this wretch would be entering my domain? If you are so intent on capturing her, why was I never told?" He continued with an added edge, "And how is it that she is still alive at all, and free to harass us? Wasn't she supposed to be destroyed in Bacon's Corner?"

The two swords almost touched.

Just then a human voice broke in. "Gentlemen, if you'll just have a seat . . ."

The spirits in the air froze. Business was calling. The humans below were starting their meeting.

Barquit sheathed his sword. "The heavenly ranks were routed, and we still hold our territory. I'll put this behind us."

Destroyer put his sword away as well. "I'll put aside past blunders . . . for now."

They dropped through the roof of the building to join the meeting, taking place in a small conference room. Mr. Steele sat at the head of the table; at his right sat the dark man dressed all in black; at his left sat two other men. At the other end of the table, looking nervous, sat Mrs. Denning.

Mr. Steele led the proceedings. "Sybil, we'd like to thank you for coming. Let me introduce everybody. Obviously, Mr. Tisen you know. Gentlemen, this is Gary Tisen, the faculty head here at Omega." Tisen was a bearded man in his thirties, a likable sort of guy. "This gentleman here on my right is Mr. Khull, a free-lance journalist and photographer. On my immediate left is Mr. Goring, from the Summit Institute." Goring was an older man with probing eyes, meticulously combed white hair, and a neatly sculpted beard. He wore several strings of beads around his neck. "Gentlemen, this is, of course, Sybil Denning, a member of our faculty for several years now."

Everyone nodded at everyone else. Mrs. Denning smiled a little, feeling like this meeting might not be as serious as she once thought.

Mr. Steele maintained a smile, but there was something cutting in his eyes. "Now, Sybil, we had some questions about this woman who came to the Center last Friday. What did she say her name was?"

Sybil was a little taken aback by that question. "Well, Mr. Steele, that was Bethany Farrell, from the Los Angeles area, remember? You said you knew her."

Mr. Steele chuckled sheepishly, and then he lied. "I thought she was someone else. What we're trying to find out now is who she really was. Did she give you any other identification, any other proof of who she might be?"

"Well . . . no."

Mr. Steele paused at that answer. "So . . . Sybil, you see what happened? A total stranger walked onto our campus, gave you nothing more than her name and the claim that she was from Los Angeles, and that was all she had to do to get a carte blanche tour of the Center." Mrs. Denning didn't know what to say. Mr. Steele just smiled. "Well, Sybil, that's what I've always liked about you: you love people, you trust them, you reach out to them, and that's what Omega is all about, isn't it?"

She brightened just a little. "Well, of course."

"Did she say anything else about herself?" Mrs. Denning tried to remember. "Is she married, for instance?"

"No, she's divorced. She said she was just hitchhiking around the country, trying to find herself. She was looking for a place to stay, as I recall."

"And so you gave her a tour of the campus."

"Yes. I took her for a walk and talked about the Center and what we do here, and what our goals are."

Mr. Steele and Mr. Goring each drew a breath and held it a moment. Then Mr. Steele spoke. "Uh . . . Sybil, that's the sort of thing I was alluding to. To put it simply, you shouldn't have done that. We don't know who this woman was, or what her intentions were, and I'm sure you realize that there are many interests out there that are hostile to us. Our goals could be severely jeopardized if we aren't careful choosing whom we give information to. What goals did you discuss with her?"

She probed her memory, and it was painful to admit anything she found. "Uh . . . our goals for change through education . . ."

That brought an audible sigh, and Mr. Tisen even tapped the table.

"What else, Sybil?"

"Our programs, our curricula, our working into the public education system . . ." Her emotions started to show. "I'm sorry. I just didn't know . . ."

"What else?"

"Umm . . . I know we talked about the Young Potentials program . . . and our quest for global community . . . and our clinical approach to education . . ."

Mr. Goring asked a brief question. "Did you discuss the *Finding the Real Me* curriculum?"

Mrs. Denning was a little surprised that Goring knew about that. "Why . . . yes, we did. But I think it was because we were already talking about getting our curricula placed in the public schools, and apparently she'd seen it somewhere, and wondered if we were really the ones who had published it."

"Mm. Now, I understand she showed you a ring?"

"Yes. She had it on a chain around her neck. She wondered if I'd ever seen a ring like it before."

"Had you?"

"No."

"What did the ring look like?"

"Oh . . ." She tried to draw little images with her hands as she described it. "It was kind of large, like a class ring . . . It was gold . . . There was a strange, mythical-looking face on it, like a gargoyle, but triangular."

The men were keeping a poker face, with obvious effort.

Mr. Steele asked, "And you're sure you've never seen her before?"

That question suggested the possibility. "Um, well, I don't know. Should I have known her?"

Goring butted in. "No, of course not."

But Mrs. Denning thought about the face again, and that first meeting, and that woman spelling her name, "F-a-r-r- . . ."

Goring decided they'd asked enough questions. "Don't worry about this, Mrs. Denning. Obviously there was no harm done. We know you'll be cautious in the future."

A memory was emerging. Spelling a name. Who was that girl who did that? She was really sassy when she did.

Mr. Steele also tried to close out the conversation. "You've done a wonderful job here, Sybil, and we're glad to have you on board. Thanks for your time."

But Mrs. Denning kept remembering. She saw the face; freckled, stone-hard, long red hair. "R-o-e . . ." said the girl.

Mrs. Denning's eyes popped open wide, as did her mouth. "Roe! It was Sally Roe!"

Mr. Goring didn't seem to hear her. "Thank you very much, Mrs. Denning. Gentlemen, I'm ready for some coffee."

Mrs. Denning was awestruck, her mind awash with the memory. "She was a student of mine years ago! She was here at the Center in the Young Potentials program! *Now* I remember her!"

Mr. Steele cut in. "Sybil . . ."

"Whatever was she *doing* here? Why didn't she tell me who she was?"

"Sybil!"

She gave him her quiet attention.

Mr. Steele looked grim. "Save your excitement. I can assure you, it wasn't Sally Roe."

Now that was hard for her to swallow. "It wasn't?"

"Sally Roe is dead. She committed suicide a few weeks ago."

That silenced her. She was shocked, confused, speechless.

Mr. Steele dismissed her. "Thank you. I think if you hurry, you can get to your first class right on time."

She stood and left the room without a word.

Destroyer was spitting sulfur, grabbing and clawing at Steele while Barquit tried to hold him back. *You fool! Haven't you done enough damage? I'll cut out your tongue!*

Goring glared at Steele. "Not exactly a prudent line of questioning."

Mr. Steele tried not to look embarrassed. "Mr. Goring, we can rehash our slip-ups or we can talk about what we're going to do."

Goring moved on, but unhappily. "Mrs. Denning is now a liability. You and I both know she's suspicious that Sally Roe is still alive—and we both know why."

"No," said Tisen, "I wouldn't worry about that. She has a marvelous and deep loyalty to the leadership here."

Mr. Steele turned away from that issue. "She's not a problem. What I'm wondering is where will Roe turn up next, and should we forewarn anyone before she can get to them and milk them for information as she did Mrs. Denning?"

Destroyer stood back and glared at Mr. Steele. *Bungler! Fool! Idiot!*

Goring rolled his eyes. "Do you actually propose that we forewarn everyone to be looking out for a woman who is supposed to be dead? Just how far down the ranks should that information go? Don't be a fool, Steele! Once such information leaves this room, it will be beyond our control. Besides that, whom would we tell? How do we choose which direction Roe will go? We don't know what she's thinking, and obviously you had no idea she would appear here!"

Barquit stood between Mr. Steele and Destroyer before the angry predator did something rash. "I remind you, great warrior, that we received no warning! You could have foreseen she would be here, and we would have been spared this difficulty and embarrassment!"

Destroyer calmed just a little. "All right. Granted. For a time, the Host of Heaven hid her from us, responding to the prayers of the saints of God. The saints in Bacon's Corner do have quite an interest in this battle. But their prayers are weakening now. They are preoccupied with other things." Just the thought of that cheered Destroyer, and he became more pleasant. "We will find her, Barquit, but by stealth and craftiness rather than force." Destroyer could see someone approaching the room. "Ah! Behold this! We've just gained another advantage the Heavenly Host have not thought to contain."

"An advantage?"

Destroyer only smirked and looked toward the door.

There was a knock.

"Who could that be?" Mr. Steele wondered.

"We weren't to be disturbed," said Tisen.

"Who is it?" Mr. Steele demanded.

The door opened a crack, and a young student assistant stuck his head in. "Excuse me, Mr. Steele. I have a special item for Mr. Goring."

"I'll take it," said Goring.

The young man entered the room with a manila envelope.

Two spirits entered as well, quite gleeful, trying not to cackle too loudly. Destroyer ordered them to stand just behind him. They obeyed instantly.

"Very punctual," he said to them.

They tittered and cackled their delight at such a compliment.

As Destroyer and Barquit watched the young man hand the envelope to Mr. Goring, Destroyer explained, "These two messengers happened upon an interesting development back at the Bacon's Corner Post Office. I decided to reward them and secure their future services."

The young man exited. Mr. Goring opened the envelope and pulled out the contents with a puzzled expression. A small letter-envelope and a three-page cover letter fell to the table.

Almost at the same time, all four men saw the name on the upper-left corner of the envelope: Sally Beth Roe.

Goring read the cover letter. "It's from Summit. This letter from Sally Roe arrived last week at the Bacon's Corner Post Office. Lucy Brandon discovered it and referred it to the peace officer Mulligan. He checked with LifeCircle and Ames and Jefferson, the lawyers on the case. They sent it on to Summit. The people at Summit opened it and thought I should see it immediately."

Goring picked up the much-traveled letter from Sally Roe, addressed to Tom Harris. All four men looked at it with shock, awe, and then a steadily increasing jubilation.

Goring spoke first. "So . . . Sally Roe is writing letters!"

Mr. Steele was almost smiling widely. "To . . . to *Tom Harris?*"

Goring was skimming the letter from Summit. "Brandon is reasonably sure that this is the first letter." He dug Sally's letter from its already opened envelope; it was a document handwritten on three-ring spiral notebook paper. He quickly perused it. "Yes. This sounds like the very first letter. She's introducing herself . . . Oh no! She's describing her encounter with Von Bauer!"

At that, they all gathered to look over Goring's shoulder.

Mr. Steele read the account, taking great interest in how Von Bauer suddenly died. He then recalled what happened in the Log Cabin Cafe. He looked at Khull. "She is into some kind of tremendous psychic power. *Something's* protecting her!"

Goring wasn't entirely impressed. "And yet she still seems lost, confused. Look at her here, going on and on about morality, meaning, despair. The woman is a mess!"

Mr. Steele read ahead. "Mm. 'I'm going to retrace some old steps and find some things out.' That's why she was here. She's hunting for information."

"And she found it," said Goring in disgust.

Another thought was sobering. "If Tom Harris had actually received this letter . . ."

Goring looked up. "Of course. It could have spelled the end of everything, including Brandon's lawsuit." But Goring's mood began to lighten. "But as it now stands . . . Sally Roe has virtually betrayed herself to us. See here? She plans to write more of these letters, and that could be the key to finding her, predicting where she'll be, finding out what she knows, and just what she has planned!"

The four men looked at each other. It just might be that.

"If we can continue to intercept these letters, observe the postmarks, derive clues from their content, I would say we would have a remarkable advantage," Goring summarized.

"But can we trust Brandon to intercept the letters?" asked Mr. Steele. "Won't she buckle under the legalities?"

Goring smiled. "No, not Brandon. She has too much to lose by not cooperating, what with the lawsuit now in progress. Besides, if we can persuade her that it would be in her best interests to cooperate with us, then . . . we will have all the more leverage for controlling her with each letter she tampers with."

The men exchanged glances and nodded. It sounded like a workable plan.

Goring concluded, "We'll consult with Santinelli when he gets here. If he's agreeable, we'll send word back to LifeCircle to persuade Brandon to continue intercepting the letters and sending them to Summit. Eventually, most certainly, Sally Roe will tell us where she is, and . . . you, Mr. Khull, will then be of value to us."

Khull smiled, relishing the thought.

The two messengers behind Destroyer cackled and slobbered in delight.

"A Judas," said Destroyer. "Someone who will betray Sally Roe into our hands: Sally Roe herself!"

Claire Johanson and her live-in boyfriend Jon Schmidt shared a large, white house on the outskirts of town. The house was once the center of a large ranch, but the ranch had been divided into several smaller farms, and now the house remained as a comfortable, manageable estate for Claire and Jon's purposes. She was, of course, a legal assistant for Ames, Jefferson, and Morris; Jon was an architect and painter.

But most of all, they were the founders and facilitators of a movement, a fellowship, a gathering known to its members as LifeCircle.

Today was a LifeCircle meeting, not too formal an occasion, but rather a time to share, to combine interests, to discuss new discoveries and insights. There were plenty of cars parked on both sides of the road that ran in front of the house, and the house was full of people, not only from the immediate Bacon's Corner area, but from other communities as well.

In the living room, the fine arts enthusiasts enjoyed a miniconcert of mind-expanding music by a popular instrumental trio consisting of flute, guitar, and string bass. The president of the local grange was there, in a strange daze as he listened; Mr. Woodard, the elementary school principal, was also there with his wife, relaxing to the lilting sounds. Some young farmers were in attendance as well, some enjoying the music, and some thinking of moving on to another activity elsewhere on the grounds.

Upstairs, in a bedroom that was totally empty except for cushions everywhere on the floor, young men and women participated in a yoga workshop, humming and droning like a beehive, sitting in the lotus position. They were everyday people—a rancher, a carpenter, a UPS truck driver, a teacher of "special needs" children, a couple who ran a day-care center, and Miss Brewer, who taught fourth grade at the Bacon's Corner Elementary School.

Outside the back door, sitting in comfortable chairs under a vast grape arbor, a discussion group of some dozen people was taking time to share ideas and hear the opinions of a visiting author regarding the application of Zen to farming.

In a corner of the backyard, not too far from a swing set, several young children cavorted on the grass, pretending to be ponies. Leading them all was Amber, now Amethyst, jumping, prancing, and spouting words of wisdom.

"It is as you see it to be," she was saying. "If you see yourself as a black horse, that is what you are. If you see before you an open prairie, that is where you are. Create your own world, and run free in it!"

So, the kids created their own world and ran free in it—as far as the back fence, anyway.

In Claire's office on the main floor, behind closed doors, a meeting of great importance was in progress. Claire sat regally behind her desk; Gordon Jefferson, the ACFA attorney, sat at one end of the desk, his briefcase at his side; opposite them sat Lucy Brandon. Next to the door, in a neutral position, sat Jon, Claire's live-in. He was blond and handsome, like a male model for running shoes, and had a quiet, confident demeanor.

Another woman was present, a short-haired, thin, female attorney from Sacramento, who'd brought a brief from another case the ACFA had finished there.

"You'll find a lot of useful parallels in this case," she said, handing it to Jefferson. "If you have any questions, Mr. James will be happy to offer his time and services."

"Splendid!" Jefferson replied, taking the materials. "I

understand Mr. James was able to uncover some persuasive case law in this one."

"And it's yours to use as well."

Claire smiled with gratitude. "Thank you, Lenore. I suppose you know the people in Chicago are watching this one?"

The woman named Lenore smiled. "Oh, of course. So if you find yourselves in any need at all, we're ready and waiting to send you more manpower, more documents, anything."

Jon chuckled and clapped his hands. "We're off and running!"

"And that reminds me," said Claire, "we've been getting a little low on news items; John Ziegler and the folks at KBZT are always open for more news if we can find it."

Jefferson responded, "Well . . . the case is pretty much in limbo until the trial."

Jon asked, "What about Harris's troubles with the child welfare people?"

Claire shook her head. "We can't go near that, not yet. The judge ordered the press to stay away from that, and if they try to dig anything up it will look too much like a violation of her order."

"Well," Jefferson thought out loud, "if we could find something outside that order, it would help. We need to keep the Christians on the run, keep them hiding."

Jon joked, "Maybe we could use the child abuse hotline again and get Harris in trouble with someone *else's* kids."

"No . . ." said Claire, though she knew Jon wasn't serious. "We don't want to start looking obvious, and Irene Bledsoe's under enough of a load as it is."

"Well, be patient," said Lenore. "It's a gradual process, one case at a time. The consolation is that once we gain the ground, we never lose it again."

"So time is on our side," said Jon.

There was a lull in the conversation. All eyes began to drift toward Lucy Brandon, who sat silently, listening to them all.

She returned their gaze, and smiled nervously. "You're asking me to do a lot."

Claire chuckled disarmingly. "Oh, it's not as serious as all that."

Jon patted her hand. "Don't worry. There's too much power represented here for you to be in any real jeopardy. Isn't that right, Gordon?"

Gordon Jefferson jumped right in. "Of course. Listen, Lucy: these letters are not legitimate mail. They're from some crank, some sick person who's been following the case in the media. It happens all the time. Letters like that shouldn't be delivered anyway."

Claire added, "But in the meantime, we never know just what or who might be behind them, and we can't afford to take any risks."

"That's right," said Jefferson. "We don't know what the letters contain, but we can be sure that your case will not be helped in any way if Tom Harris should ever receive them."

Lucy sat there thinking about it, but still seemed unconvinced.

"Well," asked Claire, "how many have there been now?"

"The second one came in just yesterday."

"What did you do with it?"

"I still have it 'on hold.' I wanted to talk to you first."

"That was smart."

Jefferson concurred. "Real smart. You see, Lucy, we could be dealing with some pretty shady people in this case. You never know what kind of stunt they might try to pull." Then he added in a slightly quieter voice, "Also, consider the stakes involved. If you should win this case, there would be quite a bundle of money in it for you."

"But money aside," Claire added, "think of all the children this case could affect in the future. If we're ever going to build a future of peace and world community, we must deal with the Christians; we must remove their influence upon the upcoming generations. It's for their own good, for the good of humanity."

"But what about Amber?" Lucy asked.

Jefferson was quick with an answer. "You know, Lucy, I don't think you even have to worry about that. Dr. Mandanhi can present reports and testimony on Amber's behalf, and she'll never have to go anywhere near the courtroom. We'll be able to insulate her from this case altogether."

"That would be nice."

"Well, we'll just play it that way."

Claire spoke with great sincerity in her voice. "Really, if we thought this was going to be harmful to Amber, we wouldn't pursue it. It's the children we're concerned about, after all."

"Right, absolutely," said Jon.

Lucy finally smiled and nodded. "All right. I just wanted to be sure, that's all."

"No problem," said Claire.

"We understand," said Jon.

Jefferson doublechecked. "You do have the address for forwarding the letters?"

Lucy thought she remembered. "The Summit Institute, right?"

"Right."

"I have it in my private files. I'll send the letters off as soon as I get them."

They all nodded their approval. "Excellent, excellent."

The music played on, the discussions continued, the humming and chanting made the windows buzz. All in all, LifeCircle was having a fruitful day.

So was Marshall Hogan. It hadn't taken him too long to drive slowly by the house and past all those parked cars, chattering into a small tape recorder in his hand. "GHJ 445, HEF 992, BBS 980, CJW 302 . . ."

In just two passes, he had them all.

twenty-one

Dear Tom,

I want to know something for sure. Right now I don't.

Blame it on pride. When I first entered high school I relished what I was taught; that I was the ultimate authority in my life, the final arbiter of all truth, the only decider of my values, and that no prior traditions, notions about God, or value systems had any authority over my will, my spirit, my behavior. "Maximum autonomy," they called it. Such ideas can be very inviting.

But there was a catch to all this freedom: I had to accept the idea that I was an accident, a mere product of time plus chance, and not only myself, but everything that exists. Once I bought that idea, it was impossible to believe that anything really mattered, for whatever I could do, or create, or change, or enhance, would be no less an accident than I was. So where was the value of anything? Of what value was my own life?

So all that "maximum autonomy" wasn't the great liberation and joy I thought it would be. I felt like a kid let loose to play in an infinitely huge yard—I started to wish there was a fence somewhere. At least then I would know where I was. I could run up against it and tell myself, "I'm in the yard," and feel right about it. Or I could climb over the fence, and tell myself, "Oh-oh, I'm outside the yard," and feel wrong about it. Whether right or wrong, and with infinite freedom to run and play, I know I would still stay near the fence.

At least then I would know where I was. I would know something for sure.

Sally was in the town of Fairwood, a small burg along a major river, a fairly busy shipping port for that part of the state. Even though the Omega Center was only a half-hour, winding drive into the hills above the town, she had lingered and hidden here for the weekend, getting to know the place

247

again, walking its streets by day and spending the cool nights in the woods down by the river.

The town had not changed much in ten years. There was a new mall at the north end of the main thoroughfare, but every town has to have a mall sooner or later. As for the city center, all the stores remained the same, and even the Stop Awhile Lunch Counter was still there, with the same jukebox and ugly blue Formica-topped counter. The menus were new, but only the prices were different; every page still carried the same logo and the same meals.

She was remembering things. She was bringing it all back. The park in the middle of town was just the way she remembered it. The wading pool was empty and dry, waiting for warmer weather, but kids were playing on the swings and monkey bars, and Sally considered how the playground was the same but the kids were different; it wouldn't be too long before the children who were there ten years ago would be sending *their* children down to the same park to play on the same swings.

> *It's really not a bad town. I can't blame it for the feelings it evokes in me, the strange conflicts I feel. In this one place are hidden my happiest and my most bitter memories, side by side. Both have been buried so long, obliterated by drugs, by delusion, by altered states of consciousness, that I've forced myself to remain here to revive them. I must remember.*

She was being followed by friends. From atop the First National Bank building across the street, Tal, Nathan, and Armoth kept watch as she sat on a bench in the park, writing another letter.

"She hasn't found it yet," said Nathan. "I don't think she wants to. She's been down every street but the right one."

"She wants to find it, but at the same time she doesn't, and I don't blame her," said Tal. "But we'll have to help her. With our present tactics, we can only hold that motel room open for today."

"She's moving again," said Armoth.

Sally was putting her notebook back in her duffel bag and preparing to move on.

Nathan surveyed the skies over the town. "Destroyer's scouts are still around. They must know we're here."

Tal agreed. "They simply aren't afraid of us. But I consider that an advantage. I would prefer them to be very confident." Then he saw Sally turning to the right on Schrader Avenue. "Oops! No, Sally, not that way."

They unfurled their wings and leaped from the building, floating down over the tops of passing cars, banking silently around the corner, and settling to the sidewalk on either side of this singular, weary traveler. She seemed a little perplexed, not knowing which way to go.

Nathan spoke to her, *No, Sally, you've already been this way. Turn around.*

She stopped. *Oh, brother, I've already been down this street, and it was a bore.*

She turned around and followed Schrader the other way, crossing several streets, passing other pedestrians, always looking over her shoulder.

The three warriors walked with her, staying close.

Sally looked around as she walked. No, she hadn't been this way yet. Some of the storefronts looked kind of familiar. *Oh! That flower shop! I remember that!*

Then, finally her eyes caught a sight she hadn't seen—or wanted to see—in ten years. Up ahead, on her side of the street, was a large, rectangular sign, SCHRADER MOTOR INN, and below that a smaller sign, KITCHENS, DAILY, WEEKLY, MONTHLY RATES. She stopped dead in her tracks and gazed at that sign, spellbound.

It hadn't changed. That motel was still there!

Tal came up close behind her. *Steady, Sally. Don't run.*

She wanted to run, but she couldn't. She didn't want to face this memory, but still she knew she had to.

If you want to know the truth, said Tal, *you must face it even if it's painful. You've run long enough.*

She stood still in the middle of the sidewalk as if her shoes were glued to the pavement. She began to remember more and more of this place. She'd walked down this sidewalk before, many, many times. She'd visited that flower shop. There was a True Value Hardware on the corner, but now she remembered it used to be a variety store.

She started walking again, slowly, drinking in every sight. These planters were new; it used to be just a bare curb here. That parking lot across the street had undergone a change in management, but it was still a parking lot.

The Schrader Motor Inn was the same, a large, sixty-unit motel of three stories, L-shaped, with parking in front and around the back. It wasn't a high-priced place, nothing fancy, no swimming pool. The motel may have been painted; she wasn't sure about that. The entrance to the office looked the same as she remembered, and still had the large breezeway jutting out across the entrance.

She looked up at the third story, and scanned all the blue doors facing the iron-railed balcony. Yes. She could see Room 302 down near the end.

It had been her home for almost ten months. Such a short period of time, and so long ago!

Even as she passed under that breezeway and stepped up to the office door, she felt she was being a bit irrational. What purpose could such an action serve? Why dig up the past? None of this was necessary.

She was going through with it. She had to see it all again; she hadn't paid attention the first time.

She pulled the door open.

It was meant to be, came a memory from somewhere in her mind. It was her own voice. Now she remembered saying it. *My higher self ordained it.*

"Hello," said the nice lady behind the counter. "Can I help you?"

Sally could still hear her own voice echoing from the past: *After all, there is no death; there is only change.*

She knew she'd been asked a question. "Uh . . . yes. I was wondering if you had a kitchen unit available."

The lady checked her register. "Hm. You're in luck. Yes,

that fellow moved out just this weekend. It's on the third floor . . . Is that all right?"

"It's fine. Uh . . . would it happen to be 302?"

The lady's eyebrows went up. "Why, yes, as a matter of fact. Have you stayed there before?"

Sally was looking this lady over carefully. No, they'd never met, she was sure. She must be a new owner, or employee, or something. "On occasion."

The lady slid the application across the counter to her, and Sally filled it out. She gave her name as "Maria Bissell," put down a totally fictional address in Hawthorne, California, then claimed to be driving a '79 Ford Mustang with a California license plate, and she made up the license plate number as well. All she could hope was that this lady would appreciate the color of her money and not question her credentials.

The lady did appreciate the color of Sally's money, receiving a week's rent and damage deposit in cash. She handed Sally the key.

The stairway had new green carpet now. Sally could remember the worn, brown carpet it used to have.

She reached the third floor and walked along the balcony overlooking the parking lot and beyond that, the Nelson Printing and Bookbinding Shop, still there, the offset presses still rumbling inside.

She placed her hand on the railing and noticed her wrist was unhampered. The last time she ever saw this railing, she was handcuffed, and she was not free.

Out of her buried memory came the image of squad cars parked in the lot below, their lights flashing. Then she recalled the other tenants watching through their windows, peeking around the drapes, curious and anonymous. She could feel the pain of big hands holding her arms, pushing her along this balcony.

There was an aid car down there too, and some medical personnel running around. She could just barely remember them.

She came to the door. With held breath and a turn of the

key, she opened it. The chain-lock was repaired now, and apparently the doorjamb had been replaced.

Some things were different. The couch was new, but still sat in the same place. The picture on the wall just above it used to be a sailboat, and now it was a surrealistic vase of flowers. She liked the sailboat better.

The kitchen looked the same, and the cabinets hadn't changed a bit. The sink still had that brown crack. The pots and pans were in the same cupboard just to the left of the sink.

Through an archway at the back of the room was the bedroom. She knew where the bed would be, and she knew the room had a large closet. She didn't bother going in to look.

Next to the bedroom was the bathroom. She didn't want to go in there at all.

Ben was almost beside himself when Marshall came pulling into the driveway. He ran out to the car to meet him.

"Man, where have you been?"

Marshall was feeling pretty good himself. "Got some license numbers from the cars belonging to our local LifeCirclers. That'll give your friend in Westhaven some more to do, running some Motor Vehicle Reports."

"Chuck's already done a *lot*," Ben exclaimed, fidgeting on the sidewalk. "Come on in!"

Marshall hurried inside and followed Ben into the dining room. Bev was there, her eyes gawking, studying some documents spread out on the table.

"*Oh, Lord . . .*" she said.

Ben wasted no time, but pointed to a grainy, black-and-white, front- and left-profile mug shot. "That's the lady. That's Sally Roe!"

Marshall picked up the photo and studied it carefully. "Man, she's wasted!"

Indeed she was. The tired, gaunt, and dazed woman in the photographs looked every bit the part of a half-drunk or half-drugged tramp. Mug shots never were very complimentary, but even so . . .

Ben grabbed Marshall's shoulder in his excitement and started jabbing his finger at the photographs. "Marshall, that is *not* the dead woman we found at the Potter farm! But it's Sally Roe, all right! I've already been by the Potters' and the Bergen factory to talk to Abby Grayson. Both of them confirm that this is Roe."

"They must not have been too happy . . ."

"They were shocked. Yes, very shocked." Ben went on to explain. "Chuck requested a Records Check from the National Crime Information Center and the State Information Section. Sally Roe was only arrested once, ten years ago. He got the rap sheet on that, then followed that up with the local police in the town where the arrest occurred."

"Fairwood, Massachusetts . . ."

"Right. They supplied the photographs."

Marshall hesitated. He was bothered about something. "Fairwood, Massachusetts . . . Fairwood . . . I'd better check with Kate about that." He took another look at the photographs. "And we'd better get some copies of these pictures."

Bev piped up, "I'm gonna do that right now; I'm goin' down to use the church's copier."

"Great. Kate's going to need one, I know." He looked over the other documents. "Okay, now what did she do?"

Ben pointed out the crime record. Marshall stopped short. He turned the paper toward him, so he could read it better.

"Isn't that a kicker?" said Ben.

"This thing is getting juicier all the time! Any details?"

Ben pointed out a short police bulletin. "It's bizarre; nothing like I expected."

Marshall read the bulletin as his face filled with horror and disbelief. All he could say was, "Why? This is crazy."

"We've got to find out more, Marshall."

Marshall stared at the photograph again. "I've got a friend in New York, name's Al Lemley. That guy's a real friend, and he can produce. Maybe he can get us something more on this."

253

Ben had a thought. "You might want to stop in at Judy's Secretarial Service. It's in that little storefront at the four-way stop. She has a fax machine, and you could get the stuff right away."

"Yeah. For sure." Marshall looked at the crime record again and shook his head. "First-degree murder!"

"You're nothing but bloodthirsty killers, as far as I'm concerned," said Mr. Santinelli, warming himself in front of the fire in Mr. Steele's private lodge. He'd put his full and hectic schedule on hold and caught an afternoon flight from Chicago to get here. Now he was tired and cranky, and not at all happy with some of the company he was keeping.

His statement was addressed to the dark and mysterious Mr. Khull, who sat comfortably on the couch, swirling a gin and tonic about in a glass, making the ice cubes tinkle. Mr. Khull was not in the least ruffled by Santinelli's blunt statement.

"We are all that way, Mr. Santinelli—if not in deed, at least in heart. You did, after all, hire me."

Mr. Goring, relaxing in an overstuffed chair before the fire, quipped, "A decision we have all regretted, Mr. Khull."

Santinelli took an indignant puff from his cigar. He didn't like the tone of Goring's comment. "I should like to remind you, as I'm sure Mr. Khull will be happy to boast, that he already had a controlling interest in our organization, thanks to the romantic adventures of the man he eventually eliminated, our boyish upstart, Mr. James Bardine."

"James Bardine . . ." Mr. Khull seemed to have a lapse of memory. Then it came to him. "Oh yes! He died in that tragic automobile accident! I believe he fell asleep at the wheel . . ."

"Everyone believes that," said Santinelli. "My compliments."

"Thank you. We try to be thorough."

Santinelli sat down in a chair opposite Khull, making no effort to hide his disdain. "All you Satanists are thorough, I'm sure. You worship on the run, don't you, always looking over your shoulder?"

Khull leaned forward, his drink in his hands, his head drooped between his shoulders, his eyes piercing. "No. Actually, we have yet to be chased."

Mr. Steele, listening to it all from his own chair directly facing the fire, intervened. "Gentlemen—and Mr. Khull—we know how we feel about each other, so that matter is settled. We don't trust each other, and that's the way we want it."

Santinelli added, "What is also settled is that a liability has been removed—namely, Alicia Von Bauer and James Bardine and their little love nest. Such relationships can be an extreme embarrassment, and from this point forward I hope we've made a clear enough example to our subordinates that any more relationships with these Broken Birch people will not be tolerated."

Khull took a sip from his drink and leaned back into the soft couch. "Especially by those who know as much as Mr. Bardine did."

Santinelli fumed. "As much, I'm sure, as you do now, thanks to the lecherous Ms. Von Bauer!"

Khull laughed. "Such are the politics of power."

Goring responded, "And the reason you are even allowed in our company!"

Mr. Steele was eager to finish their unsavory business. "All right, whether we like it or not, Broken Birch is now part of the Plan. Let's get the ledger balanced, so Mr. Khull can go away satisfied and be about his business."

Santinelli produced a check and handed it to Khull. "There. While in our employ, and admittedly due to our negligence, Ms. Von Bauer was killed. We gave you freedom to kill our own Mr. Bardine, and here are your damages as you have required."

Khull examined the amount on the check and nodded his approval. He folded it and slipped it into his pocket. "That's settled."

"Good," said Mr. Steele. "Now get that ring back."

Mr. Khull sipped from his drink again. "Your credit is good with us, of course, but . . ."

This time Mr. Goring produced a check. "As we discussed,

here is your first half to commence the job. The second half is payable upon recovery of the ring and the elimination of Sally Roe."

Khull took that check and pocketed it. "As you know, this Roe has been very elusive."

"And we are paying you to make her vanish altogether."

Khull swirled his ice cubes. "And, naturally, her blood would be on *our* hands. How convenient for you."

Mr. Steele objected, "Your hands are already bloody."

"And yours aren't?" Khull laughed at them. "Ah, don't worry. I understand. We kill regularly, as a form of worship; it's a sacrament to us. If you kill . . . well, it's only through hirelings like us. It keeps your hands clean. You don't plunge the knife, so you don't feel the pang of conscience." He laughed again. "Maybe you are still too Christian!"

Mr. Santinelli hated this man's taunts. "If I may remind you, Mr. Khull, you are serving your own interests in this as well, perhaps more so than we. If Sally Roe should ever be found alive, if she should ever tell her story, you and your followers could easily be implicated with murder. And unlike human sacrifices that vanish without a trace, this victim is alive, walking, and talking. At least our suicide cover story has bought us all some time. I would say you owe us something for that."

Khull was only mildly impressed. "Yes, we both have something to lose if she remains alive. But how much we have to lose depends on how much we've invested, doesn't it? What is Broken Birch, compared to you and your Plan?"

"Not much," said Mr. Steele, supposedly admitting something, but actually using it as a taunt.

Khull ventured a sneer. "You're no better. Someday you'll realize that. What we are now, you are rapidly becoming. If you hate us so much, perhaps it's because you see yourselves in us!"

Santinelli barked, "I will see *you* to the *door!*"

Alice Buckmeier was a marvelous hostess, of course, and loved to have company. So what Kate had planned as a short interview turned out to be a delightful visit over tea and pastries in the widow's dining room, surrounded by knick-knacks, doilies, crystal, and pictures of sons, daughters, and grandchildren.

"You must be everybody's grandma," Kate said.

Alice laughed. "A title I wear proudly. I don't just have my own grandchildren, you know, but I'm Grandma Alice to all the kids at church, too!"

"That's wonderful."

"I love children, I really do. Sometimes it's hard to understand how people treat their children. I know it breaks the Lord's heart." She warmed up Kate's cup of tea and continued, "I've wondered about that little Amber ever since I saw what I saw at the Post Office. What must she be going through at home?"

Kate got her notebook ready. "Bev Cole says you have quite a story."

"Oh, yes. It was very disturbing. I was mailing a package off to my son—well, actually, to my grandson, Jeff. I knitted a sweater for him, and I was trying to get it there in time for his birthday. Well, I was just standing there at the counter, and that other young lady, Debbie, was weighing my package and stamping it and all that . . ."

Judy Balcom stuck her head into Don's Wayside and called, "Mr. Hogan! Al Lemley's on the phone!"

Marshall got up from the counter, paid for his coffee, and hurried next door.

Judy Balcom ran a tight little secretarial service, typing letters, making and answering calls, making copies, doing word processing, and relaying messages—to name just a few tasks—for many of the local businesses around the town. For a reasonable fee, she let Marshall call Al Lemley in New York, and now Lemley, true to his style, had wasted no time in finding what Marshall needed.

"Hello from New York," came that same East Coast voice.

"Al, are you going to make me happy?"

"No, buddy. I'm going to make you sick. Got the fax ready?"

Judy was ready.

Marshall gave Al the go-ahead.

Alice continued her story. "Now, I didn't even notice who was over in the lobby where all the mailboxes are. I never pay attention to that unless it's someone I know. But all of a sudden I heard this commotion out there like some child was getting rowdy—you know, misbehaving, and I remember thinking, Now where are that child's parents? They shouldn't let her carry on so!

"Well, Debbie was all finished with my package, so I went out into the lobby, and then I could see the whole thing. Here was this woman, just standing there in the middle of the lobby . . . She had some mail in her hand, so I guess she'd come to get her mail . . . And then, here was this little girl, this Amber, just screaming and shouting and . . . and prancing like she was a little horse, and that poor woman was just terrified!"

The fax machine started to hum and roll out some documents. Marshall picked each page up as it dropped into the bin. There were police reports similar to what he already had, and then there were some news articles from the local newspapers. One article carried another photo of Sally Roe, this time in handcuffs, in the custody of two uniformed officers.

"And what that child said!" Alice exclaimed.

"What did she say?" asked Kate.

"She pranced, then she hit the woman, and she screamed, and just kept hitting the woman, and she was saying, 'I know who you are! You killed your baby! You killed your baby!' The poor woman was just terrified; you'd think she was being attacked by a vicious dog or something.

"Well, finally the woman broke free and ran out the door like a scared rabbit. Amber ran after her as far as the door, still shouting at her, 'You killed your baby! I know you! You killed your baby!' Then Mrs. Brandon came out of the back room and grabbed her daughter and tried to pull her back inside, but she wouldn't go with her mother, she wouldn't go at all, and so they had a big tugging match right there in the lobby, right in front of me, and Mrs. Brandon was shouting, 'Stop it, Amber! Stop that right now! No more of this!'"

Kate asked, "Did Mrs. Brandon ever use the name Amethyst?"

A light bulb went on in Alice's head. "Why, yes! I do remember that! She was calling Amber Amber one minute, and Amethyst the next. She was saying, 'Amethyst, Amethyst you stop that now! You stop screaming and calm down!' I didn't understand what she meant; I thought it was just a nickname or something."

Another news article dropped out of the fax machine. Marshall skimmed it. Sally Roe had been arrested after police broke down the door of her motel room in Fairwood. Inside, they found Roe in the bathroom in a seemingly drugged stupor, and her infant daughter, less than two months old, drowned in the bathtub. Roe was subsequently charged with first-degree murder in the drowning death of her child.

Kate could hardly wait to ask her next question. The incident in the Post Office could have been coincidence, but in a small town like this, that was unlikely. She dug in her briefcase and brought out the mug shots of Sally Roe, placing them before Alice. "Is this the woman you saw that day?"

Alice's eyes grew wide, and then she gave a slow, awestruck nod. "She looks so awful in this picture . . . but this is her. Sally Roe, huh?"

"That's right."

"Is she a criminal?"

"Yes."

"What did she do?"

"Well . . . she did kill someone."

Marshall walked slowly to his car, got behind the wheel, and then just sat there for a long while, reading through the news articles and police reports Al Lemley had sent. It was fascinating stuff, full of potential leads, but also very, very tragic.

"Tramp," the prosecutors had called her. "Diabolical witch, self-centered, self-seeking, contemptible, child-killer."

The police report said that Sally Roe was soaking wet when she was found on the floor in the bathroom. The tub was overflowing. The child was in the tub, dead. She'd told the police at the time that she'd killed her baby, but when questioned later, claimed she had no recollection of what had happened.

During the trial—and Marshall found this interesting—Sally seemed detached and unremorseful. "It was meant to be," she said. "My higher self ordained this should happen. Rachel's higher self wished to die at this time, and Jonas was there to carry it out. We all determine our own fates, our lot in life, when we are to die, and what destiny we are born into the next time. There is no death; there is only change."

Jonas. A spirit-guide, according to Sally. She admitted drowning the child at first, but later seemed to change her testimony by blaming her spirit-guide. "He took control," she said, "and he did the drowning."

The jury didn't buy it. They found her guilty, and Sally was later sentenced to thirty years in prison.

As for the father of the child, he never came forward and was never found. Sally never identified him. She was simply portrayed as a tramp and her child as illegitimate.

It all happened ten years ago.

twenty-two

Drip. *Drip. Drip.*

The faucet seemed to mark off segments of time, announcing the passing of a moment, and another moment, and another moment, and another moment, like a clock, never stopping, never slowing—steady dripping, moments passing.

Traffic flowed by outside the bathroom window, but Sally didn't hear it. A siren wailed once, but she did not stir or take notice. She had no strength, no will to rise from her place there on the bathroom floor—her back against the pale blue wall, her hands limp upon her lap, her head resting against the hard plaster, but not turning away from the discomfort.

She just sat there, staring vacantly at that tub, listening to the faucet drip, watching each drop build on the tip of the spout and then, stretching with weight, break free and disappear.

Drip. Drip. Drip.

"Ms. Roe, did you think there was no law higher than yourself?"

"There is no higher reality, sir, than what I myself have created."

Drip. Drip. Drip.

"You honestly don't recall picking up your child, holding her under the water, and drowning her?"

"I told you before, I wasn't there; it was Jonas."

"But you admitted drowning your daughter!"

"Jonas performed the act. My higher self willed it, he carried it out . . ."

Drip. Drip. Drip.

"We found the defendant in the bathroom . . . She seemed dazed . . ."

"And what did she say to you?"

"She said, 'Oh no! I've killed my baby.'"

Drip. Drip. Drip.

". . . ladies and gentlemen of the jury, you have heard an

261

account of the unthinkable . . . This vile creature, void of conscience, without remorse . . ."

Void of conscience, without remorse. Void of conscience, without remorse. Void of conscience, without remorse.

A child in an infinite yard with no fence. The creator and arbiter of all reality. The center of her own universe. No right, no wrong. Only self. *I* am all that matters.

At least, that's how it used to be.

Sally shifted just a little. The hard linoleum floor reminded her of where she was: her glorious universe. Yes. A small, cold, echoing bathroom with a dripping bathtub faucet, inhabited by a murderer, a vagabond, a tramp, a failure, an empty jar drained steadily over ten years of pointless, aimless existence, a discarded piece of flesh nobody wanted.

Now she sat on the linoleum, her head against the wall, her elbow resting on the toilet, beside the bathtub where she'd taken the life of her daughter.

Her universe. Her destiny. Her truth.

She had no tears. She was too empty to cry; there was no soul within her. She continued to breathe, but not because she wanted to. It just happened. Life just happened. She just happened, and she didn't know why.

The spirits had found her: Despair, Death, Insanity, and now Suicide. They dug at her, whispered to her, scratched away her soul one layer at a time. *Murderer*, they said. *Worthless, guilty murderer! You can never do good! There's nothing good in you! You can't help anyone! Why don't you give it all up?*

It's lonely in this universe, she thought. *It's supposed to be my creation, but now I'm lost in it. I wish I could know something for sure. I wish I could find a fence at the end of this yard.*

Ah, but it is too late for that now.

Her hand fell from her lap and thumped gently against the side of the tub.

A fence.

No, it wasn't a big thought; it wasn't a stirring idea, and it didn't cause the slightest change in her breathing or pulse. It was just a notion, an inkling of a possibility, a simple proposition to toss around: this tub could be a fence.

She looked at the tub; she touched the cold, blue-green porcelain. *I could pretend,* she thought. *Just for the sake of discussion, I could pretend that this is a fence, a limitation, a boundary.*

A boundary I crossed over, and shouldn't have.

She let her thoughts continue on their own and just enjoyed listening to them huddle together and confer in her head.

What if what happened here was wrong?

Ah, come on, according to whom? There are no absolutes; you can't know anything for sure.

What if there are, and what if I can?

But how?

Later, later. Just answer the first question.

What if it was wrong?

Yeah.

Then I'm guilty. I made a wrong choice, I jumped the boundary, I did wrong.

But I thought boundaries exist only in your mind!

I did wrong. I want to think that, just once.

Why?

Because I need a fence. Even if I'm on the wrong side of it, I need a fence. I need to be wrong. I need to be guilty.

What for?

Because . . .

Sally stirred. She pressed her hand firmly against the side of the tub where her child had died. She mouthed the words, then she whispered them, then she said them out loud, "Because at least then I'd know where I am!"

Apparently she'd awakened a dormant emotion; pain came upon her suddenly, an aching deep in her soul, and with gritted teeth and a stifled whimper, she pounded the side of the tub. *"Oh, God!"*

She rested against the hard plaster wall again, panting in hurt, anger, and despair. "O God, help me!"

Despair slipped and fell. His talons had lost their grip.

There. She'd said it. She'd followed the proposition through to its conclusion, had her little fit, and now she was finished. She didn't know if she felt better. She felt a little foolish for talking out loud to herself—or to God, whatever the case may be. It didn't matter.

For some reason she felt a weight around her neck, against her chest. Her hand went to the ring hanging there. She pulled it out and looked at it again. The ugly little gargoyle bared its teeth at her.

And then a memory hit her. It hit her so hard and so suddenly that she was amazed it had stayed hidden so long.

"The ring! *Owen's* ring!"

Irene Bledsoe was visibly uncomfortable. "Mr. Harris, your friends will have to remain here."

Under the circumstances, Tom never felt better. He was sitting on the same hard wooden bench in the same cold, echoing, marble hallway in the courthouse in Claytonville; he was here for another prearranged visit with his children, and once again Irene Bledsoe was in charge.

But this time he was flanked by . . .

"Mrs. Bledsoe, this is my pastor, Mark Howard, and my attorney, Wayne Corrigan."

Both men offered their hands, and she shook them out of necessity, but she was not entirely cordial. "Hello. As I said, Mr. Harris will only be allowed to see his children alone."

Corrigan was in great form. "We are here upon Mr. Harris's invitation, and we will accompany him during his visitation. If you refuse to allow it, you'll be required to appear in court to show just cause." Then he smiled.

Bledsoe was indignant and actually had to search for her words. "You . . . This is . . . this is a private meeting! Mr. Harris must see his children alone!"

"Then I'm sure you'll be happy to remain here with us while he does so?"

"That's not what I meant and you know it! The visitation is to be between Mr. Harris and his children with a social worker in attendance."

"Meaning yourself?"

"Of course!"

Corrigan got out his notepad. "By whose order?"

She stalled. "I'd . . . I'd have to look it up."

"If it's all the same to you," said Tom, "I'd like to see my kids. They're waiting for me, aren't they?"

"One moment," she said with a raise of her hand. "Have you brought the questionnaires I sent you?"

Corrigan had something to say about that as well. "In light of the pending civil suit, I've advised my client to defer filling out any psychological surveys or other tests for the time being."

Her answer was cold and threatening. "You do realize, of course, that this will delay our releasing the children back to Mr. Harris's custody?"

"According to CPD records, you've never released any children back to their parents without first having a trial anyway, so at the moment we're resigned to that. Now, if we could proceed with the visitation?"

She gave in. "All right. Won't you follow me?"

She started walking toward the big marble staircase again, the *pock, pock, pock* of her heels echoing through the hall as an announcement of her authority, and perhaps an expression of her indignity as well. They reached the second floor, went through the big, uninviting door and into the antechamber where John the guard was stationed once again. He seemed a little surprised to see three men instead of just one, but since they came in with Bledsoe, he figured it must be okay.

"Hi, kids!"

With cries of delight, Ruth and Josiah ran to their father. Tom dropped to one knee to embrace them, and for some reason Irene Bledsoe did not come between them. Josiah was really tickled to see his dad again; Ruth just started crying and wouldn't let go of him. All the hugs went on for quite some time.

"Poor, abused kids," Corrigan whispered to Mark.

Bledsoe took her seat at the end of the table and offered chairs to Mark and Corrigan. They sat down quietly on Tom's side of the table.

"Okay, kids," Tom said finally. "Go ahead and sit down."

They went to their chairs on the other side of the table, and just then noticed Mark. "Hi, Pastor Howard."

"Hi. How are you?"

"Okay."

"We have forty minutes," Bledsoe said, mostly to remind everyone that she was still in charge.

For the next thirty minutes Tom visited with his kids, getting caught up on mostly trivial matters. The kids were trying to read more, and seemed to be getting along better with the other kids in the foster home, although Tom couldn't be sure if it was the same foster home as last time. They weren't doing any schoolwork, though, which meant they would have some catching up to do during the summer, if that happened at all. Ruth's bump had healed well and was barely visible.

But as the time grew shorter, there was one thing Tom knew he must do before leaving, while he still had the chance. Above all else, he knew he must pray with his kids.

"Hey, Daddy has to go pretty soon, so let's pray together."

He reached across the table and took their hands. They were a family again, just for that moment, and he was the spiritual head, the leader and example he was meant to be.

"Dear Lord, I just pray now for my children, and I ask You to place a hedge of protection around them. Protect their hearts and their minds, and may they never doubt that You love them and that they are in Your hands. Help them to always be good kids and live the way You want them to. I pray, dear Father, that we will all be together again."

Mark and Corrigan joined in the prayer, and listened as little Ruth prayed for her daddy and her brother, and even for Mrs. Bledsoe. Then Josiah prayed, declaring his love for Jesus and his desire to be a good child of God.

None of this was an accident. They were doing battle in this room, for even though the state might erect insurmountable walls of red tape around these children, the prayer of each child, offered in simple faith, would be enough to tear the walls down. This was where the victory would begin. They all knew it, and as the kids prayed, they could feel it.

"Amen," said Josiah.

"Amen," they all said—all except for Irene Bledsoe.

It was almost time to go. Tom opened a paper sack. "Here. I meant to give these to you last time."

"Hey, all right!" said Josiah, receiving his Bible.

"Thank you, Daddy!" said Ruth, hugging hers to her chest.

Tom also brought them some of their favorite books and the stationery they didn't receive the last time. He could see Irene Bledsoe eyeing everything he brought out of the sack, but he proceeded slowly and openly, having nothing to hide.

Well, almost nothing. Josiah was thumbing through his new book about whales when he found some photos inserted between the pages.

Tom, Mark, and Corrigan tried not to look at him too directly, lest they draw Bledsoe's attention.

"Like your book, Ruth?" Tom said, reaching across the table to help her find his little note to her on the title page. That physical gesture helped; Bledsoe watched him closely. "See what I wrote? It says, 'To my darling daughter Ruth. Jesus thinks you're precious, and so do I!'"

"Hey!" said Josiah. He was looking at the photos. "The lady in the pickup truck!"

That got Bledsoe's attention immediately. She saw Josiah holding the pictures, studying them with wide-eyed recognition. Her face went visibly pale.

Corrigan asked, "What do you mean, son? Have you seen that woman before?"

Bledsoe jumped to her feet. "Mr. Harris!"

Tom responded calmly. "Hm?"

"How dare you! How *dare* you!"

Corrigan pressed Josiah for an answer. "Do you recognize her?"

"Sure," said Josiah. "She's the lady that was driving that truck we almost hit. She always looks kind of sick, doesn't she?"

Bledsoe stomped around to where Josiah sat and grabbed the pictures from him. She took only a moment to look at them in outrage, and then defiantly she tore them in half, in quarters, in eighths, and then crumpled them up and pitched them into a wastebasket.

Then she stood there, shaking, glaring at Tom. "Just what are you trying to prove here?"

Mark spoke gently. "Mrs. Bledsoe, you're upsetting the children."

She pointed her finger in Tom's face, and her voice trembled with rage. "You have committed a serious offense! I can make things very hard for you! Don't think I can't have your children taken away permanently!"

Tom replied calmly—mostly for the children's benefit, "Then what are you so afraid of?"

She fought back. "Oh, I am not afraid, Mr. Harris. You don't scare me!"

Tom gave her a statement he'd rehearsed in his mind for quite some time. "Mrs. Bledsoe, it's been quite clear to me that you are not as concerned with the interests of my children as with your own interests. In any case, I think you're abusing your power—and my children, and me—and I intend to find out just whom you're trying to protect."

She tried to keep her voice down; after all, shouting was unprofessional. "Why, you—!" With great effort, she relaxed, assumed a professional demeanor, and announced, "This visitation is over. I think your betrayal of my trust was deplorable, and I will keep it in mind when I consider the date for our next meeting."

"It'll be sooner than you think," said Corrigan. He walked around the table, took her hand, and slapped a subpoena into it. "Try not to tear this up. Good day."

Dear Tom,

I feel different today, and I don't know if I can explain it. Undoubtedly it stems from my fanciful proposition of the morning, the possibility of my guilt. Being guilty, or even feeling guilty, is not pleasant, of course, but the mere suggestion of it seems to have weakened another nagging emotional companion of mine: despair. It makes me think of a clown hitting his thumb with a hammer to get his mind off his head-ache: now that I feel guilty, I don't feel as much despair.

But—and this is purely for the sake of discussion—it could be said that the reasons go deeper than that. As I've said before, an all-out plunge into humanism and its total lack of absolutes can leave you groping for fences, wondering where you are, wishing you could know something for sure. Now that's despair.

Then suddenly, guilt—well, the possibility of guilt—has come upon the scene, and I find myself playing with the thought that I might be standing in the wrong, which means I could have violated a standard somewhere, which means there might be a standard to be violated, which means there might be something out there somewhere that I can know for sure.

So, I guess I said all that to say this: If I really can be guilty, if I really am guilty, then at least I know where I stand. Suddenly, after all this time, I've found a fence, a boundary, and just the thought of that dispels that old cloud of despair, so much that I've noticed it.

Just consider, Tom, what great lengths I've gone to all through my life to quell despair. The Young Potentials program at the Omega Center presented a possible escape; I dove into everything they offered: yoga, TM, diet, folk medicine, altered states, drugs, and a lot of mental trips about my own divinity and ability to create my own reality. It was a long excursion into insanity, I admit it. What good did it do to make up my own truth? I was lost and drifting to begin with, and any reality born in my head could be no better off. I and the universe I created were lost and drifting together.

And then there was Jonas, my "consummate friend." He was a marvelous salesman with a lot of good lines, remark-ably skilled in flattery. We took many long walks together during my yogic trances, and he did have me convinced that all reality—including death—was an illusion to be manipu-lated, and that I, being God, could form reality to be what-ever I wanted it to be.

And for a crucial season, I believed that. I believed I had formed a reality to serve me and supply what I wanted. I believed I had formed a man who gave me pleasure without guilt. I believed I had formed a child that asked me to send her on to her next life, leaving me free to continue where I left off.

But did I form the prison bars too? I was talking about fences, wasn't I?

I lived behind that fence for seven years, and Jonas never came to visit me. I did resent that. I did blame him for Rachel's death. It was, in my thinking, his idea. He was the one who took control of my body and snuffed out her life. He committed the act. He was to blame.

But I don't think that now. I changed my mind at some point; maybe it was this morning.

"Amethyst" was right; I killed my baby.

Sally put away her notebook and went out, her mind full of thoughts, turning things over, sorting things out. She felt a change coming, though she had no idea what it could be or which direction it would go. But this walk of hers right now was going to be part of it; she was going to track down a memory and find another missing piece to the puzzle of her life.

As near as she could remember, it was an old red brick building not far from the motel, and there was an alley, an old, cobblestoned alley with a stream of water running down its center and a grate over a drain. Oh, where was that?

Tal followed right behind her. Nathan and Armoth hovered just above, swords drawn, eyes looking warily about. Destroyer was getting close. Time was short.

Keep going, Sally, said Tal. *You're getting warmer.*

She turned down a side street. This sidewalk looked familiar; these potted elms seemed to match the memory, though they were much bigger now.

A noisy garbage truck roared and rumbled out of an alley behind an old brewery, nosed its way into traffic, and then growled through its gears, heading down the street.

Sally headed for the alley.

This had to be it! The same, narrow, cobblestoned alley, the same, towering, red brick walls of the old brewery! She was walking into the past. The drain was still there, the moss on the brick walls was still the same, the smell of garbage was right out of her memory. She quickened her pace. It was somewhere along here, a loose brick in a windowsill . . . She was remembering more and more as she ran along, looking carefully at each window, hoping for any detail that would trigger a memory.

Tal could see the angelic sentries ahead, guarding the spot. There were four of them, bold and brilliant, all grim with dedication, their swords ready. They'd been at this post, watching it, preserving it for ten years. At the sight of Sally Roe approaching, they raised their swords and let out a cautious, muffled cheer.

She approached the rear corner of the building. It had to be here somewhere; she seemed to remember it being near the corner.

There was one last window, and the brick sill was at eye-level. She stopped and looked around. She was alone in the alley. She touched the sill, ran her fingers along it. It had to be the same one. Was that loose brick on the right side or the left? She put her thumb under the brick on the left end and gently pressed upward.

It budged. For the first time in ten years, it budged. The light of day flooded the cavity underneath it.

Sally's heart leaped. She could see a faint glint of gold. She lifted the brick further.

There lay the ring. It was like a miracle. Sally's emotions rose to such a pitch that a faint cry escaped from her. She reached into the niche and grabbed the ring between her thumb and forefinger. She pulled it out into the light, and let the brick sink back into place.

Ten years later, the ring was still remarkably clean except for some gray spiderwebs. She rubbed it against her shirttail, and the shine returned. She pulled the first ring out of her shirt and held the two together.

Yes, they were the same. Now there were two little gargoyles, snarling at her with identical expressions.

Tal dismissed the sentries.

Sally leaned against the brick wall and thought about the day when she planted the ring in this hiding-place. She was desperate, afraid she would be betrayed. Perhaps it was a stealthy, conniving act to steal that man's ring and hide it here, but as it turned out, she *was* betrayed, and now, ten years later, this ring could be a key to reopen the past, to view it all again, to find out what went wrong.

She thought of Tom Harris and those Christians at that little school in Bacon's Corner.

Have I done wrong? If so, then let me do something right, *just this once.*

She unclasped the chain around her neck and placed the second ring beside the first.

Back at the Schrader Motor Inn, the office door swung open; the electric eye beeped that someone had come in.

The lady behind the counter looked up. "Hello. May I help you?"

Mr. Khull smiled most pleasantly. "Good morning. I'm looking for my wife. She said she'd rented a room here . . . uh, number 302?"

"Oh!" She pulled out the registration. "Are you Mr. Rogers?"

Khull broke into a wide grin. "Yes, yes! All right, I finally found her!"

She was curious. "Well, how did you know where to look?"

"Oh, we've rented the room before. We love it. We stay here every time we come through. I was detained at home for a few days, but she called me and said she'd found the same room. I was hoping it was the one I was thinking of."

"Well . . ." She found a problem. "Uh, she only rented it to herself. I guess she misunderstood."

Khull got out his wallet. "Yeah, that's a mistake. Let me make up the balance. Is she up there right now? I think I might surprise her."

"Well, no, I think she went out. But I can give you a key."

"Great."

"Why don't you fill out another form here so I can get my records straight?"

"Sure."

He filled out another form and gave their names: Mr. and Mrs. Jack Rogers. He had a good size wad of bills as well, and paid her the balance still owed.

She looked at the address he gave. "So how are things in Las Vegas? Is it as wild as they say?"

"No . . ." He laughed. "Well, in certain places it is, I suppose. But it's not a bad place to live."

"Well, here's your key . . . Oh dear. I guess she has the only duplicate. Well, come on, I'll just go up and let you in."

"Thanks. Hey, don't tell her I'm here. She isn't expecting me until tomorrow!"

Across the street, crouching atop the hardware store, and across the motel parking lot, hiding on the roof of Nelson Printing and Bookbinding, squads of filthy warriors puffed a cloud of sulfur when they saw Khull follow the lady up to Room 302.

Destroyer watched from his vantage point above the flower shop. "They guessed right," he hissed. "She's here!"

twenty-three

"Praise God," said Tom, so excited he couldn't sit still. "I can't believe it! Progress!"

"Well, a hundred different pieces maybe," said Marshall. "But give it time—it'll fall together."

Tom, Marshall, Kate, and Ben were having another powwow with Wayne Corrigan in his office, not too long after that rather explosive meeting with Irene Bledsoe.

Ben had gotten over his excitement. Now he was pensive, probing. "She's alive. Sally Roe is alive, and Mulligan knows it."

"And Parnell too," said Marshall. "I've got him on my list."

"But what are they trying to pull, and why?" asked Kate.

"That's what I'm still waiting to hear," said Corrigan. "I love all this stuff, guys—I'm really enjoying it, but sooner or later—and let's hope sooner—it's got to add up to something. We need a case we can present in court, and so far I don't see anything that directly applies to the lawsuit."

"Right," said Marshall, looking through some notes. "So far it's all indirect, peripheral stuff. But we're getting closer. Here are the names of the people I got from that Motor Vehicle Report on the license plates. The following people are possibly involved in this LifeCircle outfit, and some of them fit right into this: Mr. Bruce Woodard, the elementary school principal, and, no surprise, our plucky Miss Brewer."

Kate inserted, "And as for Mr. Bruce Woodard, I talked to him on the phone again today, and he still assures me he'll find that curriculum so I can look at it. But if you ask me, he's stalling."

"If he is, try these names: Jerry Mason, Betty Hanover, and John Kendall, three members of the Bacon's Corner school board, all three most likely connected with LifeCircle."

"Hence the *Finding the Real Me* curriculum at the elementary school," said Tom. "It fits right into their worldview."

"And their agenda," said Marshall. "These people are just

as evangelistic about their religion as we are, and they're wasting no time." He raised an eyebrow at the next set of names. "Jon Schmidt and Claire Johanson. Schmidt doesn't impress me yet, but Johanson is big stuff, a direct connection with the ACFA. Oh, and who was that other guy? Oh yeah. Gordon Jefferson was there too, so now we have a link-up with the ACFA for sure, not to mention . . ." He scanned down the page. "Lenore Hofspring, from California. Check the ACFA California roster, Kate. I'll bet she's on it. They're bringing in some bigger guns from out of state."

"It isn't fair!" said Tom.

"Have faith. We've caught so many fish today our nets are breaking. Here's another fish right here . . . Surprise, surprise. Lucy Brandon. What a recipe. Take a mother involved in this cosmic mystic group, add the cosmic mystic group controlling the school board and pumping cosmic mystic curricula into the local school, then get a well-meaning, crusading teacher fresh out of . . . what was that teacher's college?"

Kate answered, "Bentmore."

"Right, one of America's finest, they say. Miss Brewer learned everything she knows from them, and now she's cramming it into the kids. These people have the whole system sewn up from the top down.

"Anyway, throw it all into the pot, stir it all up, and what do you get? A little girl channeling a spirit just like all the moms and pops and uncles and aunts out there at the big white house.

"We're talking about a lot of moles, a lot of demons connecting this whole thing: Lucy Brandon, LifeCircle, the school board, the school, the ACFA, and even the little girl."

Ben was puzzled. "But . . . are you saying they purposely enrolled Amber in our school just to force a confrontation?"

Marshall laid the notes on the desk and thought about that. "No. Maybe Lucy Brandon really wanted something better for her kid. Maybe the trouble that popped up was something the others—LifeCircle, the ACFA—saw as an opportunity. What do you think, Tom?"

Tom was intrigued with the notion. "When she first

enrolled Amber, she seemed concerned about the changes Amber had gone through since being in Miss Brewer's class. At the time, I honestly thought that Lucy Brandon wanted a more basic, 'traditional' education for her daughter."

"That's the feeling I get," said Marshall. "It'll be interesting to talk to her and find out what she's really thinking, and if she's doing her own thinking at all."

Kate reported, "Alice Buckmeier told me about Debbie, the girl who works with Lucy at the Post Office. Debbie was there that day and saw the confrontation between Amber and Sally Roe. She might be able to tell us something more about Lucy."

"Sounds good. And now . . ." Marshall spread some sheets of paper out on Corrigan's desk as the attorney watched. "Here's the best part, I think. It could make this case bigger than just Bacon's Corner . . . and it could blow it wide open. We don't know yet."

The others gathered around.

"That address bothered me, the location of the Omega Center that published that curriculum. That was in Fairwood, Massachusetts, right?"

Kate had that information. "Right. I got the address from Miss Brewer."

"Ben, where did you get that arrest record, the one that included the mug shots of Sally Roe?"

Ben was stunned as he doublechecked the document. "Fairwood, Massachusetts!"

"So . . . a lady gets arrested for murder clear across the country, but then shows up in this little place for no apparent reason. In the meantime, a curriculum is published in the same town where she was arrested and finds its way here . . . Maybe it's just a coincidence, except for some more molehills: a little girl who ends up demonized, most likely because of that curriculum, later confronts Roe in the Post Office, and the little mole sticks its head up out of the ground and says, 'I know you, you killed your baby!'" Marshall smiled and shook his head at his own conclusion. "That demon was in Fairwood; it knew about Sally Roe."

"And then . . ." said Ben; he was figuring it out.

Marshall verified his thought. "And then somebody comes along and tries to kill Sally Roe . . ."

"The very same day my kids were taken!" said Tom.

"*And* the very day before you got your summons."

"I love it," said Corrigan. "But what does it really mean?"

Marshall looked over all the notes one more time and answered, "I don't know. We have molehills all over the place, and demons tunneling everywhere, maybe even across the country, but . . ." He sighed. "No case. We can theorize that Sally Roe's so-called suicide has something to do with the lawsuit against the school, but . . . what? And so what? There just isn't any visible connection—yet."

Ben turned away, frustrated. "We've got to find out who that woman was, the one we found dead in the goat shed!"

"Parnell's the one to talk to."

"Well, he wouldn't talk to me! He and Mulligan are in this together, that's obvious, and they're looking out for each other."

"And I'll guess somebody higher up is watching them closely, if you get my drift."

Corrigan piped right up. "I don't get your drift."

"Humor an old reporter," said Marshall. "I'm guessing they both belong to some kind of secret group, maybe a lodge, maybe something occult, who knows, something like LifeCircle, something tied closely to it, maybe even a part of it, but not nearly as nice. Hidden. Powerful. Something has a really short leash on those two."

"But you're guessing," said Corrigan.

"Keep on guessing," said Tom. "You're a good guesser."

Marshall ran his fingers through his hair. "I'm in your camp, Wayne; a guess is only good if it pays off. We'll just have to find some levers to pull, some way to squeeze these people. Oh, Kate, speaking of levers, forget waiting for Woodard to get you the curriculum. Go to the school board, those three people . . ." He checked his list again. "Uh . . . Jerry Mason, Betty Hanover, and John Kendall. Just see what they say, but don't wait for them either. If they stall, write to Omega for it. I want to see that curriculum."

Corrigan rested his chin on his knuckles and stared at all the notes. "Man, where is Sally Roe?"

Marshall said grimly, "I imagine somebody else is wondering that too."

A rustling went through the demonic ranks surrounding the motel; black wings began to quiver, and red glowing blades appeared.

Sally Roe was returning to the motel, walking briskly up the street, alone and unprotected.

"Remain in place," said Destroyer. "Don't move."

Immediately there was a hissing and an agitation among the ranks. The officers on either side of Destroyer got fidgety.

"She is ours!" said one.

"Alone!" said another.

"Remain in place," said Destroyer.

Sally felt no anxiety, no fear. If she felt anything, it was a new kind of exhilaration. She still couldn't believe the incredible recovery of that second ring. She considered herself extremely lucky, or fortunate . . . She wasn't ready to say "blessed."

She rounded the corner, passed under the breezeway, and started up the stairs to Room 302.

"We should saturate the building!" said the monster at Destroyer's right. "Khull and his men need our power!"

"You must reinforce the demons of Broken Birch!" said the beast at Destroyer's left.

Destroyer watched, still silent, as his warriors fussed and hissed all around him, itching to get in on the kill.

Sally reached the first landing and was starting up the second flight of stairs.

Khull was in the room, waiting. One of his men, dressed as a repairman, remained near the soft drink machine at the other stairway, ready to block any escape that way. Another man, looking like a casual vacationer, took his post at the bottom of the stairs Sally had just taken.

A third man, dressed in dark clothes and smoking a cigarette, started up the stairs after her, quietly, surreptitiously.

Sally was just on the second flight of stairs when she didn't feel right about something.

Tal was beside her. *Stop*, he said. *Wait*.

She stopped. She'd seen that one man standing near the office door when she came around the corner, and now she was sure he was coming up the flight of stairs below her. When she stopped, he hesitated. Now it was ominously quiet.

Tal remained beside her; Nathan stood at the top of the stairs, Armoth at the bottom. They were making themselves clearly visible.

Tal drew his sword slowly and let its light flicker against the wall of the building for all to see. Nathan and Armoth did the same. Now they could see the demonic response: from rooftops all around the motel, the sky lit up with the red glow of enemy swords, and the air was filled with the clatter and rustling of black wings.

There was a standoff.

A taloned hand grabbed Destroyer's arm.

"Will you not attack? There are only three guarding her!" said the warrior. The demons all around squawked their eager agreement.

"Only three?" Destroyer replied. "You mean you *see* only three." He pointed his crooked finger at the warrior that had grabbed him, then at another whiner, and then at one more overly anxious fighter. "Very well. You, you, and you, attack! Do your worst!"

They shrieked, raised their swords, and shot from the roof like skyrockets, swooping down toward the motel. They would give Broken Birch all the power they needed, and Sally Roe was as good as dead!

Tal shot from the stairway in a brilliant explosion of wings, and met the three attackers over the parking lot. Two were instantly shredded; the third went careening and fluttering over the print shop, trailing red smoke from what was left of him. Back on the stairs, Nathan and Armoth closed in on Sally Roe, their wings outspread, their swords ready.

KAWOOOM! Bursting instantly out of hiding, at least a dozen warriors appeared all around the motel, their wings spreading to form an impenetrable wall.

"Oh, Mrs. Bissell!"

It was the office lady. Sally was relieved to hear her voice. "Yes, I'm up here!"

"Could I see you for a minute?"

The man on the flight below dropped his cigarette and crushed it out with his toe. Then he hurried back down and ran across the parking lot. Sally went to the balcony railing and saw him ducking around the corner.

"Hmm," said Destroyer. "How many more warriors do you suppose he has hidden in there?"

No demon would venture a guess.

"Maybe none at all . . . maybe thousands! Would anyone like to find out?"

The lady in the office brought Sally's travel bag out from behind the counter.

"I hope you won't think me too forward for doing this," she said, "but before you go up to your room, you'd better know that there's a man up there waiting for you. He said he was your husband."

Sally was horrified. "What?"

"Is he?"

Sally backed toward the door. "I don't have a husband."

"Don't go out there, not yet."

Sally stopped.

"What about that other man, the one following you up the stairs?"

Sally was amazed. She looked out the windows. "He's . . . I saw him running away." Then she backed away from the window, afraid of being seen.

"I don't know who you are, or who he is, but I ran a check and there's no such thing as a '79 Mustang with the license number you gave, and no such thing as a Buick Regal with the license number he gave. Maybe two people can be married and have different last names, but when you say you're from Hawthorne, California, and he says you're both from Las Vegas, I just don't like the looks of it."

Sally didn't know what to say. "I'm sorry."

"I got your bag out of the room when I let him in; I told him the previous tenant left it there. Is there some kind of trouble? I don't want anything weird going on in my motel."

Sally took the bag. "Thank you."

"Should I call the police?"

"Uh, no. No, I'll just leave. Keep the rent money—it's okay."

"What about 'Mr. Rogers' upstairs?"

Sally was backing toward the door. She looked out the window to make sure he wasn't lurking about. "Uh . . . yes, call the police."

Destroyer and his army could see Sally slip quickly out the front door and run down the street, completely surrounded by the angelic guards.

A demon hissed and pointed. There went Khull, sneaking out of Room 302, hurrying down the back stairs with the "repairman." The casual vacationer had also disappeared. Somehow they knew the jig was up. Perhaps it was that timely interruption by the lady in the office; maybe they'd felt Sally Roe's great "psychic power" in the place. Perhaps they could feel their demonic escorts being stalled by the angelic guard. Whatever the case, things did not feel right, and they were calling it quits.

Destroyer blew a stream of sulfur from his nostrils. "Remember," he said to his warriors, "this Tal is a layer of traps, a setter of snares. No little human as dangerous to us as Sally Roe is going to walk down the street uncovered and alone. He was there. His warriors were ready." He laughed. "But that will change."

He looked down the street in time to see Sally Roe disappear around a corner, still heavily guarded. "No, Captain of the Host! Not this time. You are still too strong, but time is on my side! I have your saints in *my* hands. This game will be *ours*. *We* will set the rules, *we* will pick the time."

Judy Waring wasn't spending as much time home schooling her son Charlie as she promised herself and everyone else she would. At the moment, her plucky little third-grader was doing whatever he wanted out in the yard while she tended to some pressing matters on the telephone.

"Well, that's what I heard," she said. "He's had sexual problems ever since Cindy passed away, and I think they were even having trouble in their marriage because of it. Did you ever notice the way he'd always stand so close to Cathy Howard? Maybe she was next on his list, I don't know."

Then the other party talked for a while, and Judy kept busy snipping coupons out of the shopping news.

Judy's turn came again. "Well, that's what I think too. I mean, how can we be sure what really went on in that classroom? Mrs. Fields is busy enough with all the kids in her class; she can't possibly be watching Tom all the time."

Gossip sat on her shoulders, dangling his skinny fingers in her brain while Strife sat on the table and watched.

"A marvelous idea!" said Strife.

"You know," said Gossip, "this woman will believe anything!"

twenty-four

"He was harsh, belligerent, and frightened the children on many occasions," said Irene Bledsoe, her face defiant, her spine straight as a rod.

She was flanked by the two ACFA attorneys, Jefferson and Ames, sitting in a conference room adjacent to Wayne Corrigan's office. Across the conference table from her sat Wayne Corrigan, Tom Harris, and Mark Howard. At the end of the table was the court reporter, taking down everything spoken.

Wayne Corrigan scanned his notes. This lady was a tiger for sure, and he was wishing he had more to go on. With the little information he had so far, it was going to be a short deposition.

"But this is based solely on the word of Amber Brandon, is it not?" he finally asked.

"Yes, and she is a bright, truthful, and responsible little girl."

"But you yourself never saw Mr. Harris displaying any of this behavior?"

"I certainly did: the first time he came to visit his children. He violated the rules we had agreed upon, he was rude, and he was belligerent."

"Belligerent. You've used that word twice. Now, is that your word or Amber's?"

Jefferson spoke up. "What kind of a question is that?"

Corrigan didn't have to tell him, but he did. "I'm trying to figure out what Amber Brandon said and get around any embellishments from Miss Bledsoe." He went to the next question. "So what about Amber's testimony to you? What specifically did she say Mr. Harris did?"

Bledsoe leaned forward just a little, but kept her spine straight. "Amber told me that Mr. Harris and the other children made fun of her, harassed her, and tried to impose their religious views on her."

"Could you be more specific? How did they make fun of her?"

Bledsoe hesitated. "Well, they . . ."

"Did they call her names?"

"I suppose so."

"Well, did they or didn't they?"

"Amber wouldn't cite any specific names, but I'm sure if we asked her, she could tell us exactly."

"All right, we'll do that." Corrigan moved on. "Now what about harassment? How did Mr. Harris harass Amber?"

Bledsoe laughed at that question. "Oh, how indeed! I suppose you consider it normal to be branded as demon-possessed, to be forbidden to play with the other children . . ."

"Mr. Harris forbade Amber to play with the other children?"

"Oh yes. She was forced to stay inside at recess and write a page from the Bible."

Corrigan made a note of it. "And did Amber say just what the reason was for that?"

Bledsoe shrugged just a little. "Oh, apparently Mr. Harris wasn't happy with her views in a particular matter, and so he decided she needed some more intense indoctrination."

"Are those the words Amber used?"

"No . . ."

"That's just your interpretation?"

"Well, yes."

"What exactly did Amber say?"

"She said that Mr. Harris wouldn't let her go out for recess, but made her stay inside and copy from the Bible."

"Did she suggest that she was being punished for an infraction of the school rules?"

"I didn't gather that from what she said."

"Did it happen once, for one recess, or was it a constant, daily practice?"

"I'm not sure."

"And again, you were not a direct witness to any of this?"

"No, of course not."

"Was anyone?"

"Well, Mr. Harris, but . . ."

"Mm-hm." Corrigan flipped to another page of notes. "Let's talk about Amethyst the pony. Is that the correct name of this . . . uh . . . alter ego?"

"I don't know. She does identify herself as Amethyst, and I understand she is a pony, a mythical character."

"So you've met Amethyst yourself?"

Ames jumped in on that one. "Excuse me, Mr. Corrigan—I don't think that question is very clear."

Corrigan asked Bledsoe, "Is the question clear to you?"

"No."

"Have you ever dealt with Amber when she was acting like Amethyst?"

She shrugged, unruffled. "Of course."

"And nothing about it seemed strange to you?"

"No, of course not. Children have been known to dissociate into alternate personalities, or make up imaginary friends in dealing with severe trauma. It's very common."

"And what severe trauma are we talking about?"

Miss Bledsoe tried to compose a clear answer. "There was severe trauma all through Amber's experience at the Christian school: harassment, discrimination, stress, imposing of Christian dogma . . . It all led to Amber resorting to a false personality to cope with it. Mr. Harris could have responded properly and dealt with the real source of Amber's trouble, but instead he compounded the trauma by branding Amber as demon-possessed, which I think is just horrendous."

"But you were not a direct witness to any of this?"

"No."

"This is all according to what you learned from Amber?"

"Yes."

Corrigan jotted some notes and went to a fresh page. "Let's talk about the Harris kids. What first brought the situation in the Harris home to your attention?"

She hesitated. "I believe . . . we received a complaint."

"You mean a hotline complaint?"

"Yes."

"So you don't know from whom?"

"No."

"It was not from the attorneys for Mrs. Brandon?"

Jefferson was right on top of that. "Objection!"

Corrigan pointed his finger at Jefferson. "This isn't a court-room, and you aren't the judge, Mr. Jefferson!"

"I resent the question!"

"Do *you* want to answer it?"

"Don't be impertinent!"

Corrigan turned back to Miss Bledsoe. "Miss Bledsoe, to the best of your knowledge, did you receive the complaint from anyone connected with this lawsuit?"

"Absolutely not!" she said with great indignity.

"Not from any of the attorneys for Mrs. Brandon?"

"No!"

"How about Mrs. Brandon herself?"

"No!"

"All right. Now, I'm sure you've had abundant opportunity to talk to Ruth and Josiah?"

"Oh yes."

"Have they reported any abuse of any kind from their father?"

"Yes, they have."

Tom looked up at that remark.

Corrigan pressed it. "Okay. What abuse?"

"Frequent spankings with a wooden spoon."

"I take it you had reason to believe that these spankings were not administered in a loving and controlled manner?"

"They were administered, Mr. Corrigan, and that to me is abuse."

"All right. Any other abuse toward the children?"

"He doesn't let them watch television."

Corrigan remained deadpan, and scribbled that down. "Were you aware that Mr. Harris doesn't even own a televi-sion set?"

"Yes. His children told me."

"Were they complaining about it?"

"I think they were. I took it that way. They're captivated by the simplest programs as if they've never seen anything like it before. They know so little about what's going on in our culture. Their lives are far too sheltered for their proper social development."

"And that is your professional opinion?"

"Yes, of course."

"And what about direct evidence of any physical abuse? Did anyone see any bruises on the children, any signs that something was amiss?"

"Well, of course! Ruth had a large bump on her head!"

It was all Tom could do to remain quiet.

Corrigan asked, "I take it the anonymous hotline caller reported that bump?"

"Of course."

"Did Ruth ever say where she got that bump?"

Miss Bledsoe assumed an even stiffer posture and answered, "We're still investigating, and until that investigation is complete, the matter is strictly confidential."

"I would think the bump is a matter of public record," said Corrigan. "You realize, of course, that the children have told their father, in your presence, where that bump came from."

"But remember, Mr. Corrigan, that it was their father they were talking to. Out of fear, a child can tell a tale to avoid further abuse."

Corrigan indulged in a quick sigh of frustration. "Ms. Bledsoe, why do I get the impression that you don't really have a concrete reason for holding the children in custody in a strange home and environment, away from their own home and father?"

Miss Bledsoe made a visible effort to keep her cool. "We have suspicions, Mr. Corrigan, and suspicions are enough reason. We are still working with the children. We have ways of drawing out the truth eventually. The children do want to tell us everything, but are often afraid."

"So you do believe that Ruth and Josiah mean to be truthful?"

"Yes."

"And yet you won't accept Ruth and Josiah's account of your near-collision with a blue pickup truck, and their claim that it was in that near-mishap that Ruth sustained the bump on her head?"

She grimaced in disgust at the question. "That's an entirely different matter! You can't trust children to be reliable witnesses in such things."

"So they are reliable witnesses only when their testimony confirms your prior suspicions?" Jefferson started getting ruffled. Corrigan spoke first. "You don't have to answer that."

Corrigan pulled out a photograph and placed it in front of her. "Have you ever seen this woman?"

Bledsoe looked at the picture of Sally Roe and did her best to draw a blank. "No, I don't think so."

"Any chance that she was the driver of that pickup?"

"Objection!" said Ames. "You haven't established that there even was a pickup."

"Miss Bledsoe, did you have a near-miss encounter with a blue pickup while driving the Harris children away from the Harris home?"

"No, I did not!"

"With any vehicle of any color?"

"No!"

Corrigan pointed at the picture of Sally Roe. "You said you've never seen this woman before. Have you ever seen this picture before?"

She hesitated. "I may have."

"Where?"

"I don't recall."

"Do you recall tearing up some photographs that were in Josiah Harris's possession during the children's last visit with their father?"

She was clearly uncomfortable. "Oh . . . I tore something up, I'm not sure what it was."

Corrigan took back the picture. "Let's talk about your driving record. Any moving violations in the past three years?"

Now she hesitated. "What do you mean?"

"Traffic tickets. Citations."

"I believe so."

"According to the Department of Motor Vehicles, you've

had five speeding violations in the past three years. Is that true?"

"If that's what they say."

"You've also been cited twice for failing to stop at a stop sign, correct?"

"I don't see what this has to do with anything!"

Corrigan insisted, "Correct?"

She sighed. "Yes."

"You've had to change insurance companies three times?"

"I don't know."

Jefferson blurted, "I think you're badgering the witness, Mr. Corrigan."

"I am through with this witness, Mr. Jefferson." Corrigan folded up his notes, relaxed, and smiled. "Thank you very much for coming, Miss Bledsoe. Thanks to all of you."

Bledsoe and the two lawyers felt no need to hang around socially, and the court reporter had another appointment. In no time at all, Corrigan, Mark, and Tom were alone in the conference room.

"Well?" asked Tom.

Corrigan wanted to be sure Bledsoe and the others were gone. He leaned over to look out through the door. The coast was clear. He sat down and thought for a moment, looking through his notes.

"Well, she's lying like a rug, and it shouldn't be too hard to trap her on the witness stand."

Mark asked, "What about Marshall's theory? She's connected to this whole thing, isn't she? She's working for them."

Corrigan thought for just a moment, and then nodded. "The evidence is still circumstantial, but there's a connection, all right, and she's working hard to cover it up. That's one reason she's being so stiff-necked with your kids, Tom. They're witnesses. If you want to hear my latest theory, I'd say she was brought in just to discredit you, but then crossed paths with Sally Roe with the children as witnesses, which complicated everything. Now she not only has to keep the kids quiet about seeing Sally Roe, she also has to keep them quiet about having that near-accident in the first place, and Ruth's bump isn't going to make that easy."

"My children are like hostages!" said Tom angrily.

Mark was fuming as well. "She's connected with Mulligan, then; she's helping him protect that whole suicide story."

Corrigan leafed through his notes. "The more we get into this, I think the more we're going to find that everybody's connected with everybody else. And don't forget Parnell, the coroner. In order to get the whole thing dismissed as a suicide, he'd have to be a part of this too."

Mark looked at his watch. "We'd better pray for Marshall and Ben. They're talking to him right now."

Joey Parnell was not happy at all when he opened his front door to find Marshall Hogan and the recently jobless Ben Cole standing there.

"Hi," said Marshall. "Sorry to bother you at home. Apparently you forgot our appointment."

He had trouble looking them in the eye. "I'm sorry. My secretary was supposed to call you. I'm sick today."

"She did tell us that," said Ben, "but only after we sat there and waited for half an hour."

"Oh, I am sorry. Well, perhaps some other time . . ."

"You'd better have your secretary call the Westhaven Medical Association too," said Marshall. "I saw the ad in the paper, and I just talked to them. They're still expecting you to speak at their conference in an hour."

"Is that why you're wearing your dress shoes and slacks?" asked Ben. "Looks like you're getting dressed to go somewhere."

Parnell became angry. "What business do you have snooping into my daily affairs?"

Marshall reached into a manila envelope. "This might help to answer that." He produced a photograph and showed it to Parnell. "Mr. Parnell, to the best of your knowledge and expertise, is this the woman who committed suicide at the Potter farm several weeks ago?"

He didn't want to look at the picture. "Listen, guys, I do

have some other things to do and I have to get ready. Now if you'll excuse me—"

"Just give us a minute," said Ben. "Please."

Marshall showed him the picture again. "Take a good look. We've checked around with several witnesses who have positively identified her; we have fingerprints, a rap sheet, the whole thing. Is this Sally Roe?"

He looked at the picture for a moment. "Yeah, sure it is. I remember her. Death by strangulation. She hung herself."

"Just checking," said Marshall.

Parnell turned away from the door. "Now if that's all . . ."

"Mr. Parnell," said Marshall, "that was a picture of my sister."

Parnell's face went blank and suddenly pale. His hands were starting to shake.

Marshall continued, "I figured since you live here in Westhaven you probably wouldn't know what the real Sally Roe looked like, and now it's obvious you've never seen her dead either."

Parnell was speechless. He kept looking down, then at the door, then inside the house, then at Marshall and Ben. The poor guy was acting like a cornered animal.

Ben asked, "Can you tell us who the dead woman really was?"

"I can't tell you anything!" he finally blurted. "Just go away—get out of here!"

He slammed the door.

Marshall and Ben walked back toward their car.

"Did you see that?" asked Marshall.

"That guy is *scared!*" said Ben.

Kate's afternoon had been, in a way, informative; at least she was being informed in a most frustrating way how difficult it was to ever see a bona fide copy of the *Finding the Real Me* curriculum for fourth-graders.

She stopped by the office at the elementary school to meet with Mr. Woodard, the principal, and look at the curriculum. Mr. Woodard wasn't there. She found him down the hall, whereupon he had a sudden recollection of their appointment.

Then the curriculum was nowhere to be found, and he couldn't understand whatever happened to it. He told her to talk to Miss Brewer. Miss Brewer was with her class and could not be disturbed, but would call her. Miss Brewer never called.

Then Kate called Jerry Mason, a member of the school board and most likely a member of LifeCircle.

"Well, I think the teacher should have a copy," he said.

Kate was getting tired of that line. "No, she doesn't. I've already checked with her and she referred me to Mr. Woodard, who then referred me back to Miss Brewer."

"Well, I don't have a copy."

"I was just wondering if you might, since you did approve the curriculum for the elementary grades."

"But do you have a child taking that curriculum?"

"No, I'm just trying to see a copy of it."

"Well, there aren't that many around, and I don't think anyone who wants to can just drop in anytime and see it. We prefer to work with only the parents. You probably should make an appointment."

Kate ran around the mulberry bush a few more times with Jerry Mason, and then called Betty Hanover, another school board member.

"Say, listen," Betty said, "we've been through all this before with the . . . the religious fringe. The community has decided they like the curriculum, and we'd just as soon have some peace now, all right?"

John Kendall was no better. "Did you ask Miss Brewer? It's the teachers who are supposed to be in charge of it. They ought to be able to help you out."

Kate put down the phone and checked off another name. Then she let out a mock scream.

If for no other reason, that curriculum had to be worth seeing simply because so many people were going to such great lengths to keep it hidden.

Another letter! It was just like the other ones—same envelope, same handwriting, same thick letter inside on lined notebook paper! Lucy grabbed it out of the pile of incoming mail and slipped it quickly into her pocket. Where were all these letters coming from? If this was a joke, it was certainly a long-lived joke, and not at all funny.

If it wasn't a joke, and these letters really were from Sally Roe . . .

She didn't want to think about that; it was easier not to consider it at all, and go on trusting all the people she now trusted.

Debbie was nearby, sorting through the mail in another mailbag. She'd stopped working, and seemed to be looking carefully at a mailing label on a magazine, but. . . . To Lucy, it seemed like Debbie was watching her, but trying not to look like it.

"Something wrong?" Lucy asked.

"Oh, no . . . nothing," Debbie answered, turning away and shoving the magazine into one of the mailboxes.

They went on sorting the mail, and nothing more was said. But Debbie had seen the whole thing.

twenty-five

wayne Corrigan had read Dr. Mandanhi's detailed report on Amber Brandon's condition. Most of it was so technical it would take another expert to refute it, if it was refutable. One thing was clear to even a lay reader of the document: Mandanhi held the Good Shepherd Academy responsible for Amber's troubles, and had a low opinion of Christianity. This deposition would not be easy.

Mandanhi was a gentle man, however, and not unpleasant to deal with. He was in his forties, of East Indian descent, well-dressed, well-mannered, professional. Attorneys Ames and Jefferson sat on either side of him, as they did Irene Bledsoe, but didn't seem quite as edgy for his sake as for Bledsoe's. Apparently they were sure Mandanhi could take care of himself.

Corrigan started with some basics. "So could you review for the record Amber's basic symptoms of trauma?"

Mandanhi brought a few notes, but didn't seem to need them. "Amber's behavior is typical of any child her age who has undergone extensive emotional trauma: bed-wetting, moodiness, occasional nausea, and frequent escapes into fantasy . . . a loss of reality, paranoia, the fear of unseen enemies—spooks, bogeymen, that sort of thing."

"And you attribute all this to the environment at the Christian school?"

He smiled. "Not entirely. There could well be other factors, but the pervasive religious overtones of the school's curriculum would be, in my opinion, sufficient to exacerbate Amber's preexistent emotional turmoils. The Christian doctrines of sin and of a God of wrath and judgment, as well as Christianity's imposition of guilt and accountability, would immediately assimilate into the child's preestablished identity structure, producing a whole new set of reasons for her to be insecure and fearful of her world."

"Have you discussed any of this with the pastor of the

Good Shepherd Church, or with the headmaster of the school?"

"No, sir, I have not."

"So do you know for a fact that the school was imposing any kind of guilt or fear upon the child?"

"I have examined the child, and I know she went to the school. A clear connection is not hard to draw."

Corrigan made a few marks in the margin of his copy of Mandanhi's report. "Now . . . about this Amethyst, this little pony that Amber becomes . . . What was that term you used?"

"Dissociative disorder, or hysterical neurosis, dissociative type."

"Uh . . . right. Could you explain just what that is?"

"Basically, it is a disturbance or alteration in the normally integrative functions of identity, memory, or consciousness."

"I'm going to need that in simpler terms, doctor."

He smiled, thought for a moment, and then tried again. "What Amber is displaying is what we call Multiple Personality Disorder; it's a condition in which two or more distinct personalities exist within one person. This disorder is almost always brought on by some form of abuse, usually sexual, or severe emotional trauma. The onset is almost invariably during childhood, but often is not discovered until later in life. Statistically, it occurs from three to nine times more often in females than males."

"I wanted to ask you about some of these complications you listed."

Mandanhi consulted his own copy of his report. "Yes. Complications, difficulties that can arise when this disorder manifests itself."

Corrigan scanned the list. "External violence?"

"Yes. A total break with social norms of behavior, social inhibitions. Blind rage, injury to others . . ."

"How about screaming, kicking, resisting authority?"

"Oh yes."

"Suicide attempts?"

"Very common."

"How about Amber?"

Mandanhi thought for a moment, then shook his head. "Her case seems rather mild in that area."

Corrigan found another new word. "What is coprolalia?"

"Violent, obscene language, usually involuntary."

Corrigan stopped on that one. "Involuntary?"

"The victim has no control over what he or she says; the utterance is spontaneous and can include animal noises, growls, barking, hissing, and so forth."

"Uh . . . how about blasphemy?" Corrigan felt a need to explain that. "Uh . . . railings, obscenities, slanderous statements against a Deity?"

"Yes. Quite frequent."

"And then there are . . . altered states of consciousness?"

"Yes, trance states."

"And according to your experience, this sort of thing is usually—or almost always—brought on by severe emotional trauma or sexual abuse?"

"That is correct."

"And this is your assumption regarding the Good Shepherd Academy?"

"It is."

"But you haven't talked to the school personnel about this?"

"No."

"I see." Corrigan jotted some notes and read a few more notes. "The press seems to have some firm opinions about what went on at the school, and they've said some pretty rough things about Tom Harris. Have they gotten any of their information from you, doctor?"

"I have not spoken to them personally, no."

Corrigan raised an eyebrow. "But it's reasonable to think that your opinions, in some form or another, have gotten into the hands of the press?"

He didn't seem too happy to have to answer. "I believe so."

"How about the Child Protection Department?"

Mandanhi looked at the lawyers. They didn't seem too

distressed. "The CPD received a complete copy of my report, and I have consulted with them on a regular basis."

To Corrigan that was not a complete surprise, but he could still feel a tinge of anger. "So . . . they must think the Academy's quite a dangerous place for children."

"You would have to ask them."

Corrigan's voice rose just a little. "What did you tell them?"

Mandanhi balked at the question. "What did I tell them?"

"You've regularly consulted with them. Have you led them to believe the school is a dangerous place for children?"

"I can't tell you what they believe."

Corrigan let the question go. "Then I suppose by the same token you can't explain why there hasn't been an all-out investigation of the school and its personnel, and of every parent who has their child enrolled there?"

Mandanhi only shrugged. "That is not my responsibility to know. I don't make the decisions."

"Would the CPD representative you've regularly consulted with happen to be Irene Bledsoe?"

"Yes."

Corrigan said nothing in response to that; he just wrote it down. "Have you ever heard of a Miss Nancy Brewer, fourth grade teacher at the Bacon's Corner Elementary School?"

"No, sir."

"Have you ever heard of the *Finding the Real Me* curriculum that Miss Brewer teaches to her fourth-grade class?"

"No, sir."

"Then you are not aware, doctor, that Miss Brewer regularly teaches the children to relax, achieve susceptible states of consciousness, and contact inner guides?"

The question grabbed Mandanhi's interest, but he still had to reply, "No."

"Were you aware that, prior to Amber's enrollment at the Christian school, she was a student in Miss Brewer's class and went through that curriculum?"

That grabbed Mandanhi's interest even more. His expression became a little grim. "I was not aware of that."

"Are you familiar with a local organization called LifeCircle?"

"Yes."

"Are you aware that they regularly practice consciousness-altering techniques such as yoga, meditation, and . . ." Corrigan paused and then hit the term with emphasis." . . . trance channeling?"

"I am aware of that."

"Are you aware that Lucy Brandon and her daughter Amber are both closely involved with that group and its practices?"

"Yes."

Corrigan wasn't expecting all these affirmative answers; he was a little shocked. "Then can you please explain to me, doctor, just how you can be so sure that only the Good Shepherd Academy is to be blamed for Amber's abnormal behavior?"

He smiled. "I do not blame the Academy for Amber's behavior; I blame it for the trauma that precipitated the behavior."

Corrigan had to get a grip on himself. This man was starting to bother him. "But in light of what is happening at the elementary school and at LifeCircle, can you agree that such behavior as Amber's can be taught and conditioned in a young child *without* severe trauma?"

Mandanhi laughed. "Since you are asking me, I will tell you that I do not recognize the validity of anything that may be happening at the elementary school or at LifeCircle. I look upon these things as highly subjective, even religious matters, something I prefer not to approach clinically."

"So Amber's behavior, in your opinion, must indicate severe emotional trauma as its only cause?"

"That is what I have written, and that is my opinion."

Corrigan stopped for a moment. He was frustrated, but tried not to show it. He went back to some other notes he'd jotted on the report. "So, doctor, between the Christians, the LifeCirclers, Miss Brewer, and even Amber, it looks like we have a lot of different opinions as to what this Amethyst really is."

"I am not responsible for any opinion other than my own," the doctor interjected.

"Would you agree that Amber is able to communicate with this . . . whatever it is?"

"That is not untypical for a dissociative. The different personalities are often aware of each other, will often converse, and sometimes even disagree and argue."

"And it's normal for Amber to blink out and not remember the passing of time when Amethyst is manifesting herself?"

"That is quite typical."

"How about special knowledge? Is it possible for Amethyst to know information that Amber could not possibly know or have prior opportunity to learn?"

Mandanhi hesitated. "I'm not sure I can answer that. The disorder does present a lot of questions at times . . ."

"Such as?"

"Oh . . . My colleagues and I have always been mystified by that one trait you mentioned, special knowledge—some would call it clairvoyance or ESP. But another phenomenon we often find in this disorder is an actual physiological change in the person affected. The normal personality may not need eyeglasses at all, while the alternate personality does; or both may wear glasses, but the prescription will be quite different. The blood pressures can be different, or the reaction to certain medications; the bleeding and clotting rates can be different, and we've even noted a clear and measurable change in the blood composition."

Corrigan wrote it all down. "Any explanations, doctor?"

Mandanhi shook his head and smiled. "There is still much we do not know about ourselves, Mr. Corrigan."

Corrigan had heard enough. He was ready for the next witness. "How would you feel if I talked to Amber about all this? Would she be willing to talk about it?"

Mandanhi considered that. "I don't see that it would do any harm, provided you limit yourself to reasonable questions and behavior toward the child."

"Well, I was thinking I'd like to have our own psychologist examine Amber as well."

Suddenly Jefferson jumped on that. "No, Corrigan. Forget it. That isn't going to happen."

Corrigan knew he'd hit a nerve somewhere. "Hey, come on. Dr. Mandanhi doesn't seem to think it'll hurt."

Ames was really hot about it. "You're not going anywhere near that child! She's suffered enough!"

Corrigan turned to Dr. Mandanhi. "How about it, doctor? Think it'd be okay?"

Mandanhi looked at the attorneys and caught the meaning in their eyes. "Well . . . I suppose not, Mr. Corrigan. I suppose it would be harmful."

"You suppose?"

"It *would* be harmful."

"Forget it!" said Jefferson.

Fat chance, thought Corrigan.

twenty-six

Before Sally noticed, she was writing by the light of the overhead lamp above her seat, and not by the daylight coming in through the window. It was getting late. The hazy red twilight was giving way to the deepening gray of night, and now the farms and fields rushing by outside were beginning to hide behind the reflection of her own face. The rhythmic rocking of the railcar and *click-click-clacking* of the tracks had a lulling effect, a dulling effect, and she was feeling sleepy.

It would be another day or so before she would reach her destination and revisit old Bentmore University. Her stomach turned with fear at every thought of it. These would be the powerful people, the influential ones, the molders of education and educators. If the people at Omega remembered her, undoubtedly she would be remembered at Bentmore. But still she had to go. She had to see that place again.

> *So, my stay in Room 302 in Fairwood was suddenly ended, and I am on the road—riding the rails, actually—once again, with only my duffel bag and my life as possessions. I don't mean to sound flippant, but running for my life is a whole new experience for me. First of all, I've never done it, and secondly, I never thought I would be running from the people I once trusted and admired so deeply. One of the hardest lessons I have had to learn is that the utopian dream of a new world order is not without its dark side, its power-mongers, schemers, manipulators, and killers. Behind all the Mrs. Dennings and Miss Brewers who dream of refining and guiding mankind, there are the Mr. Steeles who dream of subjugating and controlling mankind. The Dennings and Brewers work hard to prepare all mankind for a global community; the Steeles look forward to running it.*
>
> *And then there are the Sally Roes who get caught in the middle, disillusioned by the idyllic dreams of the Dennings*

and Brewers and trying to stay out from under the crushing boot of the Steeles. Perhaps they are the ones the Steeles fear the most: they know all the tenets, but no longer believe in the faith. They can get in the way more effectively than anyone.

She paused, and looked at her reflection in the window, a tired face with the blackness of night behind it, and it occurred to her what sorts of allegories she would have drawn from such a picture only a few days ago, or even yesterday. She could have written about the blackness of her soul, or the great void that lay beyond the visible Sally Roe, or the transience of her life, nothing more than a fleeting reflection on a thin pane of glass—here during the night, but gone by morning.

Oh, it was great stuff, but for some reason she just didn't feel that way. Something deep inside her was still changing, like a gradual and steady clearing of the weather.

Tom, remember my last letter, when I talked about guilt? I haven't forgotten any of those thoughts; as a matter of fact, they are still churning in my head, and I don't know where they will eventually carry me.

Since I last wrote, I did come up with one challenging proposition about guilt: that it could be a fact, and not just a feeling.

I'm sure you know how much the rest of us despise that one aspect of Christianity: the classic "guilt trip." If I recall the jargon correctly, we are all "sinners," we are all guilty. Religion has always been, in my perception, one big guilt trip, and no one wants to feel guilty. That is why my friends and I spent so much time and energy concocting a universe in which right and wrong did not exist—if there is no right or wrong, there is no need to feel guilty about anything.

Now for the wrench in the works, first thrown in this morning: the possibility of guilt as a fact and not just a feeling. If—and I emphasize the word if—there is a fixed standard of right and wrong—a fence, as I've said—then it is possible to be guilty of an offense, all feelings of guilt aside. I can be on the wrong side of the fence and be in the wrong regardless of how I feel about it.

Please bear with me if I state the obvious; I have the distinct fear that you got all this clear in your own mind when you were a child and are getting bored, but please bear with me. I have to think it through, and it helps to do it on paper.

Let's say I rob a bank. That makes me guilty of robbery. Let's say I don't feel guilty about it. If robbery can be established as wrong, then I'm still guilty of robbery, regardless of how I feel.

The feeling—or lack of feeling—does not change the fact.

So, reflecting on what I've learned through the years in the humanist and mystic camps, I see that much of it was an attempt to escape from guilt through philosophy, meditation, drugs, etc., etc. But now I have to ask, what exactly have I been trying to escape: the feelings or the fact? I have been able to escape the feelings—for a season. The feelings you can bury, suppress, deny, or talk yourself out of.

But what can change or erase the fact? So far I haven't thought of a thing.

Wayne Corrigan had mixed feelings about Thursday's deposition; he felt prepared in some ways, and in other ways he was sure he and his volunteer crew of investigators had not yet scratched the surface of what Lucy Brandon and her lawsuit were really all about. But here she sat, the plaintiff herself, dressed up in a gray pantsuit, flanked by Ames and Jefferson, ready to hold forth and looking nervous.

Mark and Tom were present again, and Corrigan had plenty of notes for reference.

They went over old ground first, rehashing the offenses against Amber at the Christian school. Lucy seemed to have a much better grasp of the details than Irene Bledsoe displayed.

"He would often grab Amber by her shoulders and shake her until she produced the answer he wanted," she said.

"Can you give us an example?" Corrigan asked.

"Well . . . she told me once about Mr. Harris trying to get Amber 'saved,' and he was quite forceful about it, shaking her, insisting that she say that Jesus was her Savior. She just wanted to say that He was her example, or her friend, or her guide, but that wasn't good enough for him. He shook her, yelled at her, and really upset her. Then he made her stay in during recess until she changed her attitude. It was horrible; she cried about it all that evening. It was all I could do to get her to go back to the school the next day."

Tom jotted a note to himself. This testimony was a blatant lie, but it was not surprising. He'd heard Amber use the same truth-stretching whenever she tattled.

"This is, of course, Amber's account?" asked Corrigan.

"Yes, it's what she told me."

"And you were not a witness to this?"

"No, but I believe my daughter."

"Did you ever discuss this with Mr. Harris?"

"No, I didn't."

"Why not?"

She had to search for an answer. "Oh, I guess my mind was on other matters, and it didn't seem important at the time."

"But it seems important now?"

"Why, yes."

Corrigan showed her a document. "This is your signature on this Parental Agreement Form, correct?"

She looked at it. "Yes."

"And if you'll notice paragraph nine on this form, it states that you have read the Student/Parent Handbook and agree to all it contains. Did you read the handbook, and did you agree to all it contained?"

Lucy was quite reluctant to answer. "Yes."

Corrigan checked some records. "Is it true that Amber was paddled on . . . March 25th, and that Mr. Harris informed you about it that evening by telephone?"

"Yes."

"And is it true that at that time you approved of the spanking?"

"Yes."

"To the best of your knowledge, has Amber ever been spanked since then?"

"No."

"So, just to make sure I have this straight, you are suing the school for physical abuse by spanking, but as far as you know there was only one incident of spanking, and you approved of it beforehand when you signed the Parental Agreement, and also at the time the spanking was administered? Do I have that right?"

She was unhappy, but answered truthfully, "Yes, that's right."

"Were you aware of the infraction for which Amber was spanked?"

Lucy thought for a moment. "I think she was being disruptive in class."

Corrigan didn't want to go into the next subject, but he had to. "Do you recall the nature of the disruption? Do you remember Mr. Harris describing it to you?"

Lucy stumbled with an answer. "She was . . . being noisy, um, playing at her desk . . ."

Corrigan dove in. "Well, let's just go ahead and talk about Amethyst."

Lucy brightened with recollection. "Oh . . ."

"Do you recall now that Amber was spanked because she was portraying Amethyst in the classroom and disturbing the class, and not heeding Mr. Harris's orders to stop that behavior?"

"Yes."

"Mrs. Brandon, we've heard a lot of opinions about who or what Amethyst really is. Who or what is Amethyst in your opinion?"

Lucy looked down at the table, thought about the question, even laughed just a little, and then shook her head. "I'm not sure. I guess she's just a character that Amber made up, but . . . Well, Dr. Mandanhi said it's possibly an alternate personality, but I don't know . . ."

"Are you affiliated in any way with a fellowship group in the Bacon's Corner area called LifeCircle?"

"Uh . . . yes."

"Isn't it true that that group holds to a belief in channeling and spirit-guides?"

She laughed, but it was a nervous laugh. "Well, we embrace a lot of different beliefs; we all have our opinions about channeling. I guess ultimately we don't question it, we just experience it."

"Would you say that Amber was channeling Amethyst?"

"Oh, she could be channeling, or she could be pretending she's channeling, or . . . I don't know. There are many different views. It's really something to be experienced for what good can be derived from it; it's not to be questioned."

"Have you ever considered that Amethyst could be a spirit?"

The term seemed to shock her. "A spirit?"

"Yes, a spirit-guide, or an ascended master, or a disembodied entity from the astral plane. Those are familiar terms to you, aren't they?"

She smiled, impressed. "You know a lot about this sort of thing, don't you?"

Corrigan smiled back pleasantly. "Well, I try to do my homework. But do you think Amethyst could be a spirit-guide? Is that possible?"

She furrowed her brow and looked down at the table, struggling with such a thought. "Some believe that. I still don't know what to think."

Corrigan scribbled in his notepad. "At any rate, on March 28th, Mr. Harris and Amethyst had a confrontation. Do you recall hearing about that?"

"Yes. Mr. Harris called me at the Post Office. It sounded serious, so I came over."

"Did he tell you what happened?"

"Yes. He said that Amber had been . . . Oh, I can't remember how he put it, but he basically told me that they thought she had a demon and tried to cast it out of her. I was outraged. I'd never heard of such a thing."

"You've never heard of casting out demons?"

She answered bitterly, "That's strictly a Christian idea, an invention of organized religion, and I resent that it was imposed upon my daughter! Channeling is a gift, a special ability; it has nothing to do with religion!"

"But you do understand that the Bible teaches otherwise?"

Lucy was angry and hurt. "Mr. Corrigan, she's just a *child*, a child with a special gift! She doesn't have to explain her gift to me, or defend what she's experiencing. I've never singled her out or harassed her; I've just loved her, accepted her, and just let her have her gift for whatever good it can do for her and for the rest of us. She's just a child, not a theologian or a scholar or a priest or a lawyer, and what power does a ten-year-old child have to stand up against—" she hesitated, but then spewed out the words— "against hard-nosed, prejudiced, religious adults in that school who abuse their power and their size, who have no tolerance and no understanding, who just . . . attack her, pounce on her, scream at her, and accuse her of being possessed . . ."

She buried her face in her hands for a moment. Corrigan was just about to call for a recess, but then she recovered and finished her statement. "They just had no right to treat my daughter that way, to single her out and persecute her just for being different."

Corrigan figured it was time to go on to the next question. "When you came to the school, what did you find? How was Amber?"

Lucy thought for a while, recalling it. "She was . . . she was sitting in the school office, and she looked awful. She was very tired, and I remember she was wet with perspiration and her hair was all uncombed. She was upset . . . moody. When I took her home, I found that her body was bruised in several places like she'd been in a terrible wrestling match. I was just shocked." Lucy's emotions began to rise. "I couldn't believe such a thing could happen to my daughter, and at a Christian school where . . . Well, I once believed that a Christian school, of all places, would be a good place for Amber, a safe place. I didn't think that Christians would stoop to such behavior. But they did."

Corrigan spoke gently to her. "Mrs. Brandon, was it Amber

as Amber who remembered the incident? Could she tell you what happened?"

Lucy was still composing herself. "I don't think she's ever been able to talk to me directly about it. She has to be Amethyst to talk about it."

"So it was Amethyst who told you what happened?"

"Amber pretending to be Amethyst, or channeling Amethyst, yes."

Corrigan thought for a moment. "Mrs. Brandon, whenever Amber becomes Amethyst, after she stops being Amethyst, does she remember anything that Amethyst said or did?"

Lucy smiled a little sheepishly. "Well . . . she says she doesn't."

"All right. At any rate, that incident occurred on March 28th, but you didn't take Amber out of the school until April 20th. Can you explain why, after such an outrageous incident, and such selective, prejudicial behavior toward Amber, you still kept your child enrolled at the school?"

"I . . ."

"Obviously you consulted a lawyer during the interim?"

"Yes."

Corrigan produced a photocopied, handwritten record. "Part of the discovery materials included this photocopy of a journal you kept. Do you recognize it?"

"Yes."

"So, between March 28th and April 20th, you kept detailed records on the school . . ." Corrigan leafed through the many photocopied pages. "You kept track of all the lessons, the Bible verses for each day, the discipline problems, the Bible projects . . . quite a detailed account."

"Yes."

"So isn't it true that you kept this record all this time, with Amber still enrolled, because you fully intended to bring this lawsuit against the school?"

Jefferson jumped on that. "I object, counselor. That's a matter of speculation and conjecture; there's a total lack of foundation."

"So let's get some foundation. Mrs. Brandon, some time

after March 28th, didn't you consult a friend at LifeCircle for legal advice regarding these matters?"

Lucy even shrugged a little. "Yes."

"Was it Claire Johanson, legal assistant to Mr. Ames and Mr. Jefferson?"

"Yes."

"And what was the result of that conversation?"

"The result?"

"Didn't you decide at that time to pursue a lawsuit against the school?"

"I think so."

"You think so?"

"Well, yes, I did."

"And in preparation for the lawsuit, you began keeping this detailed record of everything happening at the school, correct?"

Lucy was chagrined. "Yes."

"All right. Now, having established that, let me ask this question: Since you kept Amber enrolled at the school despite the outrageous behavior demonstrated against her, is it possible that gaining more material for your lawsuit was more important to you than your own daughter's well-being?"

"I'll definitely object to that!" said Jefferson.

"And I'll drop the question," said Corrigan, unruffled. He looked at his notes. "Does Amber still become Amethyst from time to time?"

Lucy smiled as she reluctantly admitted, "Yes, she still does."

"Was she displaying this kind of behavior even before she enrolled at the Christian school?"

"Yes."

"Is it true that she learned to . . . create or visualize Amethyst in her fourth-grade class at the Bacon's Corner Elementary School, a class taught by a Miss Brewer?"

"Yes. Miss Brewer is a wonderful teacher."

Corrigan paused. "Then why did you transfer Amber to the Christian school?"

Lucy seemed a little embarrassed. "Oh . . . I thought her

313

time in the elementary school had served its purpose. Amber was fulfilling her potential and discovering herself, yes, but . . . she wasn't learning much else."

"A little weak in academics?"

"A little. I thought some balance would be good for her; a wider realm of experience."

"I understand." Corrigan went to another matter. "Do you recall an incident at the Post Office several weeks ago when Amber, as Amethyst, had a confrontation with a patron in the lobby?"

Lucy was visibly disturbed by that question. "How did you find out about that?"

"Do you recall it?"

"Yes."

"Does Amber recall it?"

"No. She was . . . Well, she was Amethyst at the time, and now she doesn't remember any of it."

"She doesn't remember it?"

"No."

"Is it true that Amber, as Amethyst, became very aggressive toward the patron?"

Lucy was sickened by the memory, and perhaps by the question. "Yes."

"She circled the patron, struck her several times?"

"I . . . I did see her hit the lady, yes."

"Did Amber, as Amethyst, make loud, screaming accusations against the lady?"

"Yes."

"Would you say that Amber's behavior was violent, uncontrolled?"

She didn't want to admit it. "Yes."

"So violent that the lady was forced to flee from the lobby?"

Lucy was getting upset; the memory was a painful, perplexing wound. "That's what happened. I couldn't get Amber to stop. I was just so embarrassed."

"Did Amber know this woman?"

"No. I just don't know how she could have."

"And as far as you know, the woman did nothing to provoke this attack?"

"No."

"Do you recall what Amethyst was screaming?"

Lucy's eyes dropped to the table; she rested her forehead on her fingers. "She was saying . . . something about the woman's baby . . . saying, 'You killed your baby.'"

"Do you know who the woman was?"

"I don't know . . . I think so."

Corrigan took out a photograph and showed it to her. "Is this the woman?"

Jefferson jumped in. "Really, I don't see what this has to do with anything!"

Corrigan just gave him a correcting look, and he remained quiet.

"Is this the woman?"

Lucy stared at the grainy photograph. Her face answered the question before she said it. "Yes."

"Do you know who this woman is?"

She seemed to give in. "Her name is Sally Roe. She was a patron at the Post Office. But that's all I know about her."

"And she committed suicide just a few weeks ago, isn't that true?"

Lucy lashed back, "That wasn't Amber's fault!"

Corrigan paused just a little at that outburst, then said, "We're not saying it was. Now, you heard Amethyst—Amber, whatever—accuse Sally Roe of killing her baby, correct?"

"Asked and answered," said Jefferson.

"Just trying to be sure," said Corrigan.

"Yes, I did," said Lucy.

"Were you aware that Sally Roe had a criminal record?"

It was obviously news to Lucy Brandon. "No."

Corrigan produced some documents. "This is a copy of her criminal record, and here are some news clippings. You'll notice the highlighted areas: she was convicted of first-degree murder ten years ago. As you can see here, and here, and on this news story here, she was found guilty of the drowning death of her baby daughter."

He waited for it all to sink in, and watched the blood drain from Lucy Brandon's face.

"Obviously your daughter, as Amethyst, was correct in her accusations against Sally Roe in the lobby of the Post Office. To the best of your knowledge, was there any way that Amber could have known about Sally Roe's past?"

Lucy could hardly speak. "No. *I* didn't even know about it."

"Can you explain, then, how *Amethyst* knew about it?"

Lucy took time to answer only because it was difficult. "No." She tried to do better. "Psychic ability, maybe."

"On whose part, Amber's or Amethyst's?"

Lucy shook her head, quite flustered. "I don't know. I don't understand these things. But it can happen in channeling."

"So Amber was channeling?"

"Yes, I guess she was."

"And apparently this special gift of hers has a rather violent side to it?"

"I don't know . . ."

"You did have quite a wrestling match with Amethyst, didn't you? It was several minutes before you could get your daughter under control?"

"Yes."

"And when the incident was finally over, would you say your daughter was wet with perspiration, probably disheveled, tired, moody, maybe even bruised a little?"

Lucy was reluctant to answer that.

Corrigan pressed it. "Wasn't that her general condition?"

"I suppose so."

"And during the scuffle, didn't you refer to your daughter as Amethyst?"

She looked puzzled.

Corrigan asked it another way. "Didn't you wrestle with your daughter, and say words to the effect, 'Amethyst, you stop this . . . Amethyst, calm down'?"

Lucy's voice was barely audible. "I suppose I did."

"Just who were you talking to?"

Lucy didn't appreciate that question. "My daughter!"

"Which one?" Lucy hesitated, so Corrigan built on the question. "You've already stated that Amber has no recollection of the incident, and normally does not remember anything that Amethyst says or does. You have admitted that Amber was channeling. Would it be correct to say that it was Amethyst, and not Amber, who was displaying all this aggressive behavior?"

"But it was my daughter . . ."

"But a different and separate personality, correct?"

Lucy stared at him. She was thinking about it. Corrigan could sense Ames and Jefferson getting more and more tense.

"Correct?" Corrigan asked again.

"Yes," she said finally. "I think that's correct."

"So . . . if someone—even yourself—should ever confront Amethyst, they would actually be confronting a personality other than your daughter?"

"I guess so. Maybe."

Ames and Jefferson did not like that answer. No doubt they would have quite a conference with Lucy Brandon when this was over.

Corrigan decided it was time for a provocative benediction. "So, does it seem so strange to you now that Mr. Harris might also have had a similar encounter, not with your daughter Amber, but with Amethyst, a separate personality: a violent struggle, a wrestling match, a demonstrative confrontation? Can you imagine what it must have been like for him to have Amethyst behave in the classroom as she behaved in the Post Office lobby, screaming, hitting, and producing information that Amber—as Amber—could not possibly know? Can you understand now what conclusion a Biblical Christian would come to when confronted with a violent, uncontrollable, alternate personality in a young, innocent child?" He didn't need an answer, and he didn't wait for one. "Thank you, Mrs. Brandon. I know this has been difficult for you. That's all for now."

twenty-seven

Bentmore University was nestled—almost hidden—within the tight, red-brick grid of a major metropolis. In every direction, it was just across the street from the noise, litter, traffic, and growing pains of the city. It had outlived the rise and fall of a low-income housing project on its north flank; on the west side, the delicatessens, tailors, and cleaners were now owned by third generations; on the east, the tugs still pulled their barges up and down the murky river, the rumble of their engines audible across the campus when the wind was right; on the south, several new apartments had become the only view in that direction, and now the streets down there were filled with big old cars driven by retired folks who drove slowly.

In the center of it all, Bentmore lived on, standing firm and steadfast in red brick and white stone, its halls, dormitories, libraries, and labs evenly dispersed on the lawned terrain, its patterned brick sidewalks radiating like spokes from every entryway, crisscrossing and networking like trade routes to every point on the campus.

To the human eye, Bentmore seemed an oasis of peace, reflection, and learning amid the hubbub of its surroundings; in the spiritual realm, the real trouble was within its borders, not outside them.

Guilo met with Tal and his top warriors on the roof of the old North American Can Company, located just across the river from the campus. Beneath their feet, soup cans, juice cans, fruit cans, and sardine cans took shape and clattered by the windows in an endless, rolling parade; across the river, still veiled by the morning mist, old Bentmore was ominously quiet.

Guilo stood beside Tal to give his report. He was nervous, agitated, ready for a fight, his hand resting on the handle of his sword. "Some of their best are there. The great deceivers,

the great builders of the Enemy's coming kingdom, all super-
vised by a behemoth who calls himself Corrupter."

"I've heard of him," said Tal. "He has power and great
deceptive ability, but not much speed or wit in battle."

"An advantage, to be sure. If we remain stealthy, there is a
lot we could do before he becomes aware of it."

Nathan peered through the mist and thought he saw some
hulking spirits gliding occasionally between the structures,
but most of them were unseen. "They remain hidden, tucked
away inside the buildings."

"Very occupied," said Armoth. "Classes are in session."

"Corrupter is a bit comfortable at the moment, and off-
guard," said Guilo, "but Destroyer is going to be another
problem. He is on his way now, with all his forces. Then old
Bentmore will be like a hive of hornets at rest. Merely shake
the tree, and . . ."

"They will overrun us," said Tal. "Destroyer's troublemakers
in Bacon's Corner are doing well at this point; our prayer cover
is as weak as it's ever been, and we're left with seriously
depleted numbers. Direct confrontations are going to be risky.
We'll have to lean heavily on stealth and strategy . . ."

Guilo allowed himself a quick, stifled chuckle as he eyed
the campus. "I remind you all: they could eat us alive."

The benches here and there on the campus were still wet
with dew and mist, but Sally found a comfortable desk
hidden away in the stacks of the Research Library. So far she
hadn't seen library staff that she recognized, and that set her
a little more at ease. Thanks to a small cleaning shop on the
west side of the campus, her better clothes—slacks, blouse,
dress jacket—were cleaned and pressed; she'd replaced her
wayfaring-stranger ensemble with a more presentable outfit,
and stashed her duffel bag, replacing it with a less obtrusive
carry bag. She could recall looking sharp and professional
twelve years ago, with carefully coordinated outfits and her
hair tightly pinned. Today the best she could look was
casual and twelve years older, with tinted glasses and dye-
blackened hair pinned up as best as she could arrange it.

She just had to hope she looked different enough from the Sally Roe people would remember.

> *Oh, I must have been so proud of my calling as an educator! As I sit here and observe the graduate students around this place, working toward their Master's degrees just like I did, I can see the same pride in their faces, I can sense the same highbrow demeanor. To be honest, I see myself as I was back then. The old Bentmore mold has not broken. I can guess what they're thinking: they are world conquerors, missionaries for a bold message of global change.*
>
> *And I would say they are correct. Bentmore is still turning out great educators, great agents of change. They will be the teachers, the administrators, the principals, the authors, the lobbyists. A nation will follow them; they will restructure an entire culture.*

Sally checked her watch. It was after 9 in the morning; someone should be in Professor Lynch's office by now, either his secretary or Lynch himself. This would be the greatest risk of all, but she must contact him. Of all people, he should have some of the answers she needed.

She'd checked for his name and number in the campus directory, and surprising as it was, after twelve years Samuel W. Lynch was still head of the School of Education. As she remembered him, he was definitely fit for the position, always an imposing man of great knowledge, stature, and strength.

A tall, athletic undergrad had just finished using the pay phone on the wall behind her. She grabbed the opportunity. She would try to get an appointment with Lynch, perhaps during his office hours. All she could hope was that the man was not as brilliant as she remembered him to be; perhaps he wouldn't recall who she was.

Wayne Corrigan and Gordon Jefferson, the ACFA attorney, were never going to be good friends, that was readily apparent.

"Mr. Jefferson, I'm simply saying that we have the right to confront our accuser!" Corrigan was feeling very forceful, and had his mouth so close to the receiver that Jefferson heard a roar every time Corrigan pronounced an *s* or an *f*.

Jefferson came back just as firm, and even a little snide. "Your accuser, Mr. Corrigan, is Lucy Brandon, not Amber, and you have already deposed Mrs. Brandon in such a harsh manner as to cause her terrible distress! We wouldn't think of putting Amber in the same situation."

"We do not wish to cause Amber any grief—none at all! We'll work within restrictions, we'll be gentle. But so far everything we've heard, all the testimony, all the grievances, have come through either Lucy Brandon or Dr. Mandanhi. The real complainant in this case is neither of these people, but Amber herself."

"Amber is not going to testify or be forced to go through a deposition. We will fight that, sir!"

"We must have Amber's direct testimony concerning the complaints brought against my clients."

"It would be too traumatic for her. She's already so deeply wounded by these unfortunate events, we simply cannot allow her to be traumatized further by being put through the stress and pain of a deposition and a trial!"

"Then we want our psychologist to examine her. At least then we would have our own expert testimony to balance the testimony of Dr. Mandanhi."

"Absolutely not! Amber is not to be involved in this case in any way. She must be kept separate from it; she must be protected from any further abuse and intimidation!"

Corrigan sighed and looked across his desk at Marshall, who was closely listening and watching Corrigan's side of the conversation. Marshall made a wringing motion with his hands as if twisting an invisible arm and whispered, "You stick it to 'em!"

"I'm afraid we can't back down in this matter," Corrigan told Jefferson. "If you won't change your mind, then we'll ask the court to compel her availability and testimony."

"We're prepared for that," said Jefferson.

"Very well, then."

Corrigan hung up, and then he thought for a moment. "Maybe I pushed Lucy Brandon too hard. Now they're hiding Amber under a bushel."

Marshall nodded an emphatic nod. "Sure. Irene Bledsoe, and Lucy Brandon, and this Dr. Mandanhi character can say all they want, but Amber's the key to this whole thing. As long as Amethyst is doing her—its—stuff, Amber's going to be a real risk."

"Sure, if we can just get her on that stand, or get our own expert to examine her. I mean, if we can just get Amethyst to manifest once, we could build an argument that Tom's behavior in confronting Amethyst was justified." He smiled. "Wouldn't it be great if we could get Amethyst to tear up the courtroom? We could *win* this case!"

"They know that."

"Well, we *do* know what happened in the Post Office, and that has them scared. We need to beef up that defense; we have Alice Buckmeier's eyewitness account, but another witness would sure be nice, especially if Lucy decides to squirrel out of her deposed testimony somehow."

Marshall answered, "Well, there's still that other gal, Debbie, who works at the Post Office with Brandon. Alice says she was there, but I'm wondering where her loyalties might lie."

"We'll just hand her a subpoena and find out."

"And then there's the victim of Amethyst's attack."

Corrigan nodded. "Our greatest unsolved mystery. She's like a ghost, you know? We have pictures of her, eyewitness accounts of her, facts and information about her, but as far as what she has to do with this case, she's like a mirage, she simply isn't there."

"So push this Amber thing. Go ahead and ask for a hearing. The ACFA could use a dose of their own medicine. If it doesn't do anything else for us, it'll buy us time. You never know when something big will break."

Corrigan was captivated by the thought. "Amber, we've got to get you on that stand!"

323

Claire Johanson got Dr. Mandanhi on the phone only minutes after Jefferson had hung up on Wayne Corrigan.

"Doctor, your report is too weak."

Dr. Mandanhi was nonplussed, and also a little impatient. "Now . . . which report is that, the first one or the second one, or the second version of the first one?"

Claire made a disgusted face only because Dr. Mandanhi would not see it over the phone. "The first version of the second report, the one establishing that Amber is in too delicate a mental condition to be deposed or to testify."

"And what do you mean when you say it is too weak?"

"It just doesn't have enough persuasiveness; it would be too easy for the defense to play down. Corrigan is going to ask for a hearing to decide whether or not Amber should be made to testify, and we need something stronger to present to the court."

Mandanhi paused a moment. He was clearly unhappy. "Ms. Johanson, we've been down this path before. You didn't think my first report was strong enough either!"

"Well, it's the way things go—"

"Ms. Johanson, when you first brought me into this, I gave my fairest, most objective opinion regarding Amber's condition. I agreed with you and with the child's mother that the child had suffered harm. Why wasn't that enough?"

Claire was feeling the pressure from above and now from this doctor below. "Because, Dr. Mandanhi, in a court of law an argument has to be forceful, it has to have overwhelming power to persuade. Your first version was too . . . too . . ."

"Too factual?" Mandanhi suggested. "You would rather I lied and fabricated additional trauma just to win a court ruling?"

"Not fabricate, doctor. Enhance maybe, just make your opinions more forceful."

"Well, I feel I did that with my first report. I gave you what you wanted, and I think more than the facts warranted. Now you want me to do that again?"

Claire hesitated. Then she snapped, "With the facts at hand your second report could be enhanced. Make it stronger, make it persuasive! It shouldn't be too hard to show how the stress on Amber would cause her permanent psychological harm."

"Are you asking me to lie?"

"I'm asking you to use the facts, be an advocate, and protect Amber. She must not testify!"

Sally got her appointment with Professor Samuel W. Lynch, and made it to his office on time at 6 in the evening. It was an odd hour, but he was usually in his office at this time anyway and would be happy to see her.

He had a new office now, on the second floor of Whitcombe Hall, the main hub of the Bentmore School of Education. Whitcombe Hall was a newer structure of steel, marble, and glass and towered ten stories over the rest of the campus. Apparently Bentmore was proud of its contributions to education and wanted to display that pride in a big way.

Room 210 was more than just a room; it was the whole north end of the floor, divided off by a wall of glass with impressive double doors. The secretary was working late as well, and could look through that glass wall from where she sat and see anyone coming down the hall. She saw Sally the moment Sally got off the elevator, but she didn't seem to linger on the sight too long. That was comforting.

Sally pushed through the doors and tried to address the secretary from a distance. "April Freeman to see Professor Lynch."

The lady smiled and nodded. "Yes, the woman from the *Register*?"

"That's me."

"All right, fine." She picked up her telephone and pressed a button. "The lady from the *Register* is here to see you." She looked at Sally. "He'll be right with you. Go ahead and have a seat."

Sally stood near the couch in the waiting area, but did not sit in it. She was too uncomfortable to sit, and apt to run. The fib about being a reporter from the campus newspaper was working so far, but if anyone should think to call the *Bentmore Register* office to check on any of this, her disguise was history. Besides that, a man was already sitting there, and she'd caught him looking at her once, even though he was supposedly reading a magazine. Maybe he was reading that magazine, but maybe he wasn't. What was he doing here at 6 in the evening? The way she felt right now, every person in that place was a potential killer.

Her heart was pounding; if her hands shook much more, it would show. She tried to take some deep breaths to steady herself.

"Miss Freeman!"

That voice! After twelve years she still remembered it. She turned.

There stood Professor Samuel W. Lynch. Oh! That tremble was so great, it had to show! She stiffened her body to remain steady, forced a smile, and extended her hand. "Hello."

He shook her hand. "A pleasure. Come this way."

He turned, and she followed him back toward his office.

This wasn't right. It wasn't twelve years later. It had to be twelve years *ago*. He hadn't changed. He was still the same, distinguished, overweight, gray-haired gentleman, the same articulate pedagogue she'd admired. She would have recognized him anywhere.

Was she as familiar to him? Hundreds of students must have passed through his life since she was last here; surely her face would be lost behind all the others.

He led her into his office and offered her a comfortable, padded chair. She sat immediately and found herself looking up at just about everything. The book-lined walls in this room towered so high overhead that she felt she was sitting in the bottom of a deep well. The room was dead silent, like a crypt.

Lynch took a seat behind his desk and relaxed for a moment, studying her face, his hands clasped in front of his chest.

She looked back at him and tried to smile. She was beginning to feel the silence. This wasn't right. Someone should be saying something by now.

"So you're with the *Register*?" he asked, still relaxed, leaning back in his chair.

"Yes, I just started this quarter."

"And what is your major?"

"Um . . . economics."

He smiled. "Good enough. What do you think of Professor Parker?"

Oh-oh. Was this a test? Who was Professor Parker? Was it a he or a she? Was Parker even alive?

Sally fumbled. "Oh . . . I still get the profs mixed up. I just transferred in . . ."

He laughed. "No matter. You'll get to know them, and I'm sure they'll get to know you. You'll find we're a cordial institution, one big family. Where are you from, anyway?"

She was using a phony accent. "Oh, uh, Knoxville, Tennessee."

Sally opened her notebook just for something to do, something to fill the awkward, empty time. Her mind had suddenly gone blank as if a dark cloud had entered it. One moment she knew what she was going to say, and the next moment she felt that part of her brain had died.

And Professor Lynch was just sitting there, not saying a word. Silence filled the room like deep water; the warm, stuffy air pressed in on all sides.

"Uh . . . I just wanted to ask you some questions . . ." Sally said, pulling a notebook from her carry bag and leafing through it. Where were the questions? She'd written several down, but now . . . "I'm just trying to find my questions; I had them here somewhere."

"Don't be nervous," said Lynch. "I won't bite you."

She laughed. So he'd noticed! "Thank you. I'm still a bit new at this." She found the questions. "Oh! Here we go. I thought it would be interesting to track down a Bentmore success story and do an article about Owen Bennett."

He smiled. "Ahhh . . . That would make an interesting story. Owen Bennett is a fascinating man."

"He was a professor here for many years, I understand."

"Oh, yes! But say, would you excuse me for just a moment?"

"Certainly."

He rose from his chair and hurried from the room, leaving her alone in the bottom of this dark, oppressive well.

The silence closed in again, heavier than ever. She had trouble breathing, as if her chest were collapsing, as if the air were too thick to inhale. It had to be her imagination, the stress, the nervousness.

She closed her eyes and opened them again. The room still seemed dark. Maybe darker.

High above her, the walls holding hundreds of books on all those shelves looked like they were leaning more and more toward the center of the room. It was a wonder all the books—and some of them were massive—weren't sliding off the shelves and crashing down on her. At the same time, the ceiling, distant as it was, seemed to be receding even further away, making this well, this pit, this trap all the more deep.

Sally closed her eyes. She did not want to believe that her old tormentors were lurking about. She could not accept that she might be trapped in this pit with them, with no escape, helpless, with no choice but to wait for the first clap of their invisible jaws.

But try as she could, she could not shake this . . . this *presence*. No, it wasn't the walls and the books that were closing in. These illusions were only born out of a devouring, inner terror. There was something else oozing into this room, something from her childhood nightmares—that steady, unrelenting, slowly advancing *thing* of terror, that bogeyman, that monster, that unseen, voracious, undefeatable enemy she could never run fast enough to escape from. It was here somewhere, hiding behind the books, maybe wriggling through them, staring at her, watching her shrink into the chair, watching her tremble and sweat.

Her palms were leaving wet patches on the arms of the chair. Her skin was crawling.

She had to get out of here. She'd made a mistake; she'd

walked into a death trap. This room was alive with evil, about to crush her.

She saw it! A cry escaped from her throat before she could stop it. Just behind the desk, directly opposite from where she sat, a row of angry, golden eyes glared at her from the bookshelf. Her own eyes blinked shut. She thought better of that, and opened them again.

They were still there, not moving. But . . . no. They were not eyes. She exhaled slowly and tried with all her might to steady her emotions and her thoughts. She looked at them deliberately; she gazed at them, even challenged them.

They were four golden symbols on the spines of four ornately bound volumes. They still seemed to be staring at her. She tried to stifle her imagination. She had to be objective about this.

She leaned toward them. They were faces. Ghastly, triangular faces, all staring, all seemingly snarling at her. Little gargoyles. Deep, vacant eyes, almost like sockets. Bared teeth. High, shining foreheads.

Her heart began to race. Her mouth dropped open, and she stared transfixed. With fingers numbed and fumbling, she pulled at the chain around her neck. The two rings emerged from hiding and she held them side by side in front of her face, looking at them and then beyond them at the faces on the four volumes.

Identical.

twenty-eight

when Lynch returned to his office, he found his guest looking quite wilted and noticeably white.

"Are you feeling all right?" he asked.

She smiled weakly. "Oh, to be honest, I think I'm battling a little bit of flu or something."

"Oh, I'm very sorry. Let's try to proceed with this interview as quickly as possible, then."

Sally didn't feel like proceeding, but she did. She got out her pen, and prepared to take some notes.

Lynch started talking without any questions. "As you must know, Owen Bennett was a law professor here for several years, and a good friend to all of us. He was adventuresome, innovative, intelligent . . ."

This moving tribute to Owen Bennett continued for several minutes. Sally wrote it all down as best she could, hoping desperately to find some point where she could just cut it off, thank Professor Lynch, and get out of there.

Professor Lynch had been sitting in his chair, turned slightly away from Sally, looking at the books on the wall and speaking in fluid sentences, his fingers spread and his hands bouncing against each other, fingertip to fingertip. Now, with hardly any pause at all, but with a strange, ominous change in his tone, he turned his chair toward Sally and continued his comments. "Now, it was in that particular year that Owen, having completed the initial structuring of the Law Advisement Council and having entrusted its administration to capable hands, took up another, even more pioneering challenge, that of serving on the advisory board for a new visionary effort: The Omega Center for Educational Studies, located in Fairwood, Massachusetts."

Sally wrote it down. She noticed that he stopped to watch her write it down.

"This came as a surprise to some people. They asked, 'What interest could you possibly have in that place?' For a man of

Owen's professional stature, such a role on the advisory board of an obscure, metaphysical institution seemed a condescension.

"But they didn't know Owen as his closer friends did. Those who knew Owen well knew that he was a master of the politics of power; he understood that power can be a commodity to be sold in exchange for favors and more power, a bribe that can be slipped to the right people to accomplish a certain agenda, and even a lever to control the wills and purposes of underlings or professional enemies. He was already welcome in the company of legislators and judges, corporate executives and politicians, all the *right* people who could make the right things happen in the right places for anyone who had enough influence with which to bargain. Owen had influence, but taking this position gave him even more.

"The Omega Center, you understand, is a center for the facilitation of change in our society. As a man thinks, so is he. Change the way he thinks, and you change the man. Change the way a society thinks, and you change the society. The Omega Center is dedicated to changing the way our society thinks, and hence changing our society, beginning with its most vulnerable and moldable segment: its children.

"That, Ms. Freeman, was the kind of thing that could attract Owen as honey attracts bees. If such an institution as the Omega Center can actually play a part in controlling what our society will become, then it would be most beneficial to be one of the people who control the Omega Center. Owen Bennett became one of those controllers, a controller of a controller! Now he had something others would want."

Lynch turned his chair so that he was facing Sally directly. "But of course you know all that. It's one of the simplest principles of survival in this world: if you want to get ahead, have friends in high places." His eyes narrowed, and a grin—it looked malicious—slowly spread on his face. "As an example, I can recall a student I had some time ago, an extremely bright young lady who actually spent several summers at the Omega Center before she started her studies here at Bentmore. She came here with a high recommendation from the Omega Center, and we were happy to give her special attention. She remained here until she earned her Master's degree in education and then, wouldn't you know it, she desired to return to the Omega Center and be a part of that dream.

"Fortunately, she and Owen Bennett were the closest of friends, and by that time he was on the Omega advisory board, so her position with the Omega Center was an instant reality." He laughed and leaned on his elbows. "So you see, even as I have taught my students, it does help to have friends with influence to offer, especially in a field where you may be changing a society against its will."

Sally smiled and jotted down some notes. He just kept staring at her.

She was finished. *Very* finished. All she wanted was to get out of there. "Thank you so much for your insights. I'd like to take this home now and organize it. Perhaps I can call you again?"

"Oh, just one more thing!" he insisted, gesturing for her to remain seated. "Yes, friends in the right places are important, and power is definitely a tool, but you must remember never to be too close to your friends, because any weapon, any lever you may use to gain power over others, can also be used to gain power over *you* unless you take necessary precautions. I know of one man, a skilled, upcoming young attorney, who allowed a lady friend of questionable background to know him just a little too well, and she later attempted to use that knowledge as a lever against him. It created a most ticklish situation! Do you understand?"

She was on the edge of her seat, ready to stand and walk out of there. "Well, yes, like blackmail, I suppose."

He brightened at her correct answer. "Yes, that's it exactly! In gaining power over others, you never want to rule out blackmail as one lever to get what you want or to protect yourself!" He suddenly reached into his pocket and brought out a small jewelry box. "This is why I stepped out of the office momentarily. I knew you'd be interested in this."

He flipped it open and showed her the contents.

It was a gold ring. The same gargoyle.

Professor Lynch's voice grew quiet and somber. "This young lawyer hired his lady friend to kill someone. Yes, that's right, *kill* someone, and he paid her a large sum of money to do it. But she was subtle and clever; she stole a very personal item of his, his sacred ring, knowing that forever afterward she would be able, should she have the need, to prove that she had had an alliance with him. She wore the ring on her person when she tried to carry out the grisly deed, and we have good reason to believe she carried the money on her person as well so that, should something go wrong, she would be found with it and a connection could be made to the one who hired her. At any rate, the ring was identical to this one and, with the money, was a perfect lever to blackmail and manipulate him."

He let her view it for just a moment, and then abandoned all cordiality when he demanded, "You do have the ring in your possession, don't you?"

She rose to her feet but wobbled there, feeling faint, light-headed with terror. Words wouldn't come. There weren't any words.

"I . . . Thank you, sir," she said, nausea washing over her. "I need to go now."

She hurried to the door and threw it open.

The man from the waiting area! He was no longer reading a magazine—now he filled the doorway, blocking her escape!

Lynch spoke to her coldly. "This is Mr. Khull, a highly motivated individual now in our employ. We knew there was a probability you would be here next, and so we invited Mr. Khull to be on hand should it happen. Why don't you have a seat again so we can complete this interview . . . Sally Beth Roe?"

Khull leaned toward her. She backed away until she bumped into her chair, then sank into it.

Lynch sat down and glared at her for several moments.

"So what do you hear from Jonas these days?" he finally asked.

She looked at him for the first time since she sat down. There seemed to be no reason to carry on her act. The Tennessee accent vanished. "He's gone. I haven't channeled him since I went to prison."

Lynch smiled. "I imagine he felt there were more respectable people to work with, not vile, pitiful baby-killers."

She looked down in shame and defeat. She no longer knew how to defend herself.

"Yours is a pitiful story," said Lynch. "I had such great hopes for you. I groomed you, I honed you myself, I made you what you are—excuse me, *were*. You were a born leader, Sally. We were counting on you. Owen was counting on you. Such marvelous potential, such incredible spiritual connections!" He paused just to look at her forlorn frame. "But oh, how you toppled! Oh, how you fell!"

Perhaps it was hate that gave her the strength to say, "I didn't fall far enough, I guess. That woman you were talking about, who stole the man's ring—I take it she's the one who tried to kill me?"

He was not at all disturbed about it. "So I've heard. But that brings us back to my original question: What did you do with the ring you took from your attacker's finger?"

She couldn't think of a good enough lie, so she said nothing.

He nodded in response. "Of course. You're not going to tell me. As we've already discussed, you took it for insurance, for . . ." He couldn't help laughing. "For leverage! Oh, Sally, as your teacher I feel condemned!" He reached over and picked up the little jewelry box, eyeing the ring inside it. "Fine, fine. You don't have to tell me. Now that we have you, the ring doesn't matter. But really . . ." He looked at her and laughed as if he'd seen a joke. "Why do you want to help that pitiful little teacher in Bacon's Corner? What good could you possibly do?"

Now he circled his desk and stood above her, making her feel even smaller. "Do you feel guilty perhaps? Now, that would be so unlike you, Sally." His voice went down in tone, and every word cut like a knife. "Since when does guilt mean

335

anything to you, a murderous wench bereft of conscience? As for Tom Harris, you will never find a more insignificant nothing! He is garbage, like you! And what can garbage offer to garbage? Who would believe a word you said? Who would give you the time of day?" He laughed, genuinely amused. "But I can understand your infatuation with the man; you make a perfect pair: a child killer and a pedophile!"

He was trying to cut her down, and even through her weakness and torment she was beginning to resent it. "What happens now?"

He circled back around to his chair and sat down, letting her wait for an answer. "First, some advice which will probably go unheeded, but maybe not. I strongly suggest, Sally, that you abandon this escapade of yours, whatever your intentions. Find another little farm somewhere near another obscure little town, and disappear—forever."

He seemed so relaxed. A moment passed, and nothing happened. Nothing was said.

Sally looked at him, then at the sinister Khull, and then back at Lynch again. She felt too weak to get out of the chair; she was helpless regardless of the answer to her question. "Are you going to kill me?"

He smiled. "You are one scared little waif. Well, it will be good for you. It will provide incentive for you to seriously consider your options. There are only two: Find a deep, deep hole somewhere, Sally, and disappear into it. Let us not see your face again in this life. Or, consider your life ended altogether, perhaps today, perhaps tomorrow, but most certainly."

He nodded to Khull, who stepped away from the door. With a glance back at Sally, he released her to go.

She reached down and picked up her carry bag. Then she pushed her way out of the chair, found strength for the first step, then the next, then enough strength to get to the door.

"Sally!" Lynch called.

She wasn't about to stop. Khull made sure she did.

"Don't ever blame Jonas for what happened. *You* did it, Sally. *You* are the one to blame!"

"I know that, sir," she replied.

"Disappear, Sally. Disappear!"

She went through the door, then found new strength to quicken her step down the hall to the big glass doors. She got through them.

Then she ran. Tears started to blur her eyes. With her renewing strength she realized how terrified she was. She could never wait for the elevator. She took the stairs.

Tal had some special warriors busy at a dairy far away. He needed to shake things up in a home near the Bentmore campus.

Marv and Claudia Simpson were just starting to enjoy this short stay with their daughter and son-in-law when the phone rang.

"It's Mack, at the dairy," his daughter Jessica said.

Marv scowled and took the phone. "Okay, Mack, break it to me gently."

"Marv," said Mack, "you'd better get back here. Lizzy's getting ready to drop that calf now!"

"Now? She's a week early!"

"And the milking machine is on the fritz too. I don't know what's wrong with it!"

Marv grimaced. "Oh, great!"

"And that stupid tractor won't start for anything!"

"Doggone! Ed and I were planning to go to the ball game tonight!"

"Well, it's your dairy. Do what you want."

"Oh, right, sure, some choice I've got!" He looked at Claudia, who only shook her head in sad resignation. "All right, we'll get going right away, but we're going to have to drive all night."

"Well, I'll try to hold down the fort until you get here. Sorry to interrupt your visit."

"Yeah . . ."

Marv hung up, questioning why God would allow such things to happen at such inopportune times.

Mota stood in the room, making sure things happened. *Come, Marv, be quick about it!*

Khull took a moment to relax in the same chair where Sally had sat, and listened to Professor Lynch's side of a long-distance conversation.

"Mr. Goring, I was disappointed. She was hardly the formidable foe she seems to be in her letters. A breeze would have knocked her over. That's right." He listened for a moment, then forwarded a question to Khull. "How many men do you have tailing her?"

Khull answered quickly. "Five around the building, five more on the main campus walks."

Lynch brought back an answer. "Well covered. After today, the saga of Sally Roe will be over. Yes. I'll bring you word as soon as I know. Oh, and will you want the ring back?" He chuckled. "I guess I can always flush it down the toilet. Then Bardine and his ring will be together!" He took some time to laugh at that wisecrack, and apparently Goring was laughing at it too.

Khull laughed for about half the time, then stopped abruptly.

Lynch started his good-bye. "Very well, then. Happy to be of service. Yes. Give my regards to everyone at Summit. Yes, I'll see you all at the conference. All right. Good-bye." He hung up the phone and leaned back in his chair. "Oh, such a nasty business!" He looked at Khull. "But I suppose you Satanists take it all in stride?"

"We are *all* killers at heart, Professor Lynch."

"Well, I hope you just do it quickly, and spare me the details!"

"It's too bad you let her go."

"Don't be silly. I don't want it happening anywhere near here. I can't let anyone in this office suspect I had anything to do with it."

"Well, maybe you thought she was weak and helpless, but it looks like she was still clever enough to rip you off."

338

Lynch looked toward Khull, then followed his gaze to the bookshelf behind the desk.

Khull announced even as Lynch noticed it, "Looks like she took your rosters."

The four volumes that bore the strange symbol of the snarling gargoyle were gone, leaving a distressing gap.

"Destroyer!" said Tal, and all the warriors looked. Yes, there he was, swooping over the campus like a huge, black hawk. "He'll take her this time!"

Guilo pointed with his sword to a huge, black shape rising from the Administration Building. "Corrupter! He's slow, but he sees well!"

"Keep him busy and out of our business!" Then Tal started barking orders as warriors shot into the sky in all directions. "Scion, decoys! Chimon, stay with her. Signa, back him up! Nathan, Armoth, block the bus stop! Cree and Si, set screens!"

Lynch grabbed Khull's arm. He was desperate. "Khull, make sure your men succeed! They must succeed!"

Khull looked at Lynch, then at the gap in the bookshelf, and smiled a wicked smile. "Hm. You must be pretty scared."

Destroyer could see a tiny, frightened figure bursting out of Whitcombe Hall. "Hmm. So how strong are you now, Captain Tal? We will make you show us." He called to his captains, "Take her!"

"There she is!" said one thug to his partner. He'd spotted Sally running from Whitcombe Hall, heading south toward the nearest bus stop. It was dark. They could take her into any of the gardens, alleyways, or groves and finish her instantly.

They were large, burly men, heavily tattooed; one had a deep scar on his left cheek; both wore a large earring in one ear. Beneath their dark leather coats, they carried the shining silver tools of ritual death.

The second one put a portable radio to his jaw and muttered, "She's—".

He was about to say which direction she was going, but suddenly she was gone.

Both men bolted from their hiding-place and stood in the middle of the walkway. Sally Roe had vanished.

Cree and Si stood directly in front of them, wings outstretched. Behind them, Sally continued to run south.

A shriek from the sky! The two warriors shot a glance south. Sally was dashing down some steps, dropping out of sight. Above them, four demon warriors dropped like falcons. Cree and Si bolted, one this way, one that, disappearing in a flash of light into the buildings on either side of the walkway. The demons went after them.

"The woman!" screamed Destroyer from the sky. "Get the woman!"

The demons spun in tight circles, their red blades streaming fire, and kicked the two men in their backs. *Move! This way!* Then they shot down the campus, the walls, windows, and walkways a blur on either side, their black wings screaming.

The two thugs ran after them.

"She was heading south," the man barked into his radio.

Corrupter rose above the campus with the agility of a hot air balloon, watching the incredible spectacle on every side. He spotted Sally and pointed. "There! There—do you see her?"

A bolt of light came from somewhere, delivering such a blow to his head that he tumbled backward, end over end, like a helpless, spinning beach ball, wailing and howling.

Guilo knew he'd be out of the way for a while. He darted away with other things to do.

Sally took only a few seconds to duck into some shrubs and retrieve her hidden duffel bag. She jammed her carry bag into it and continued running.

She rounded a corner near the Psych Library, saw the bus

stop illuminated by an amber street lamp, dashed that way, slipped and stumbled to a stop, and dashed back the other way.

The bus stop was covered. Somehow she knew who those two men were.

Run! said Nathan. *The other way!*

Armoth took the blows from the two demons guarding the bus stop just long enough to slow them down. They didn't want him—they wanted Sally Roe.

Two more normal-looking killers were at their post by the Memorial Fountain. One saw through the vertical jets of water and spotted the woman running north toward the Sculpture Garden.

"Heading north!" he barked into his radio. "The Sculpture Garden!"

Sally was heading west—not north—toward the Physical Sciences Building when she ducked behind a tree to hide from four fierce-looking characters running north toward the Sculpture Garden. As soon as they had passed, she headed west again.

"Where'd she go?" a killer asked, looking this way and that.

The Sculpture Garden contained plenty of weird sculptures in stone and steel, but no fleeing woman.

Scion, looking like himself again, took wing and swooped out of the Sculpture Garden with four black bats hot on his tail. As soon as he cleared the roofs, still trailing a stream of light, Si crossed that stream with a searing trail of his own and drew aside two of the demons. At least these buzzards would be busy for a while.

Sally ran past the Physical Sciences Building, over a plaza, and then down a long flight of concrete stairs to the busy street below. A taxi was approaching. She waved furiously. "Taxi! Taxi!"

Two men, looking like any other university students, spotted her and started her way.

The cab driver thought he saw someone trying to flag him.

Two demons dropped through the roof and clawed through his brain.

Huh? Eh, she isn't there . . . Now where was I going, anyway?

The taxi drove by, swerving from lane to lane, not slowing. Sally bolted into an alley.

It was a blind alley—sheer concrete walls and no escape.

The two men closed in behind her, silent, skillful. If they moved quickly enough, they could finish her before she had a chance to scream. One had a long scarf in his hands, the other held a gleaming knife.

Filthy spirits were there too, whooping and frothing, bouncing off the walls like golf balls down a gutter. This was it!

Mota rode on the roof of Marv Simpson's ranch wagon as it rolled lazily down Hannan Boulevard on the south end of the Bentmore campus. When it came to a corner, Mota's wings burst forth like fireworks and the next thing Marv knew, he was in a right-turn-only lane and had to turn right, heading up the campus's west side.

"Doggone," he muttered.

"Weren't we supposed to go the other way?" Claudia asked.

But he was looking this way and that and trying to change lanes, getting more and more frustrated. "Now how do we get out of *here?*"

Sally backed away until she came up against the sheer, featureless concrete at the end of the alley. So much for flight. Now for fight. She raised her duffel bag to shield herself.

No sound, only shadows blurring in the street lights. The scarf hit her face, her head hit the wall, one eye was covered, she couldn't see.

A knife flashed!

Chimon was there and parried.

The knife deflected and lodged in the duffel bag.

A blow to her neck! She pitched forward, grabbing the knife man. He pulled the blade free and plunged it at her again.

The knife ripped through her coat. Her scream was muffled inside the scarf.

A searing blade opened Chimon's shoulder. Two demons caught his backhanded sword and dissolved.

The knife slashed Sally's coat open, but missed her flesh.

Scion came in low, ducked under a cluster of lashing, hacking spirits, and rolled into the knife man's legs. He fell backward. The knife clinked on the concrete. Scion had rolled into the middle of a death trap. Twisting and spinning, he was able to fend off most of the demons' blows, but one wild blade caught his leg, cutting it deep.

Chimon had a screaming, flopping, slobbering demon by the feet. He batted Scion's attackers away in one powerful swing, then whipped the flailing body over his head and smacked the scarf man in the face.

The scarf slipped away. Sally could see again. She lunged forward and broke free.

The knife man grabbed her coat sleeve.

Signa dropped out of the sky, tracing an exclamation point of light. His sword caught the seam at Sally's shoulder and the sleeve tore away.

She ran. Alive!

The knife man was looking for his knife. The scarf man couldn't tell where he was in the dark.

Chimon, Scion, and Signa were cut, bruised, and limping, but they grabbed hold of Sally and got her out of that alley.

Destroyer saw it all, and screamed for his hordes. The spirits gathered from every corner of the campus, swords burning, wings roaring, ready for a kill. With Destroyer at the point of a massive arrowhead formation, they dove toward the street.

In Bacon's Corner, Lucy ran into Amber's bedroom expecting blood, bruises, an accident, something horrible.

It was nothing of the kind. The child was beside herself, screaming, cursing, pounding the walls.

343

"Amber, what's wrong?" her mother cried, trying to embrace her.

She spun around like a vicious animal and stood apart from her mother, her fingers curved like claws, her eyes wild and glaring, darting about the room as if watching distant events. "Cut her up! Grab her, take her, cut her up!"

Lucy backed into the wall and remained there, speechless. There was no stopping Amethyst when she was like this. She'd tried before.

Destroyer and his hordes were screaming out their war cry, their sulfurous breath forming yellow streamers that etched the sky like comb's teeth.

Marv Simpson was looking for a place to turn around and getting more and more frustrated. He hardly noticed that woman running out of the alley.

"Oh my," said Claudia, "what's going on here?"

Tal dropped through the roof and filled the whole backseat with his massive frame. *Stop and pick her up!*

Marv saw her again. She was actually running into the street.

"Oh!" Claudia exclaimed, "she's coming toward us!"

"Oh, man, a nut case! We've got to get out of here—"

Tal grabbed Marv's head in his two huge hands and forced him to look toward the woman. *PICK HER UP!*

"Let's pick her up," said Claudia.

He pulled over.

Guilo shot into the sky, flanked by Nathan, Armoth, Cree, and Si. They intercepted Destroyer and his henchmen like a clap of thunder over the campus. The demons were like an irresistible wall, and the angelic warriors went tumbling and spinning aside. Destroyer and his horde resumed their course, dropping toward that station wagon; the five warriors recovered, circled, and dove down on the demons' backs like falcons. The vile spirits fought them off, but they had to take precious time to do it.

344

"Need a ride?"

Sally pulled the door open and clambered into the backseat. "Please. Get me away from here!"

Four men appeared on the sidewalk, two with radios. They saw her get into the car and quickly disappeared.

Marv was still lost. "How do I get out of here?"

"Left, up at the corner," said Sally, "and then go under the tunnel."

"Tunnel?"

Destroyer and his warriors skimmed over the top of the Physical Sciences Building and dropped toward the street, closing in on the station wagon. Tal and Mota clung to the car's roof, swords ready, wings covering the passengers inside. Then Guilo shot out from a side street, Nathan and Armoth whipped around a bank building, Scion dropped from an overpass, Chimon and Signa weaved among the cars only inches above the pavement, Si came up through a manhole, and they all pounced on the car, covering every square inch of it, their drawn swords making it look like a glowing porcupine.

This would be it, a direct, power-for-power battle!

But suddenly, surprisingly, Destroyer pulled out of his dive and followed only twenty feet above them, passing through the traffic lights, telephone lines, and street signs, keeping an eye on them, sizing them up. The sight of the small band of warriors clinging to the vehicle, swords drawn for a last stand, made him laugh. It made his henchmen laugh.

Finally he shouted to them, "Call it a victory, captain! *I* call it progress! You are weaker than ever now, and the next time will be ours. The fruit will be ripe, and we will pluck it down with ease! And don't concern yourself with hiding her. We will always know where she is!"

They climbed into the night sky and were just disappearing into the darkness when the car went into the tunnel.

"What now?" Chimon asked, holding his wounded shoulder.

"Name it, cap," said Scion, holding his useless leg. "We'll do it."

"We are spent," said Tal. "Even though we confused Khull's men, Destroyer could have taken us, and it's only by the hand of the Lord that he didn't know it. It's time we hid her in Ashton."

"And let her hear of the Cross!" said Nathan.

"We'll get her there and let the Spirit speak to her." Then he added with an unabashed anger, "While we get back to Bacon's Corner and root out this prayer blockage once and for all!"

"Uh," asked Marv, "where you headed?"

Sally was gasping for breath, sick with terror, and dripping with sweat. She was not entirely rational. "I don't care. Anywhere. Anywhere away from here."

Claudia looked over her shoulder at the pitiful creature slumped over in the backseat, weeping, panting, dripping with sweat. "You poor dear!"

Marv looked at her through the rearview mirror and could see the fear in her eyes. The Lord spoke to his heart. Yep, it was no accident that he'd picked her up. "Well, you just take it easy and try to rest. We'll get you far away from here. I know just the place."

twenty-nine

LUCY Brandon was feeling weak and ill, but trying not to show it, even as she scribbled a forwarding address on still another letter from Sally Roe and slipped the letter into the bag of outgoing mail. She didn't want to do it, but she could see no alternative. Her lawyers were pressuring her, her friends at LifeCircle were smiling and encouraging her, Sergeant Mulligan was watching her, the lawsuit was moving full speed ahead, and the momentum was overpowering, carrying her along like a runaway train.

But after no less than twenty of these letters, she'd seen enough. She was afraid, she was ignorant of legal strategy, and perhaps she was a little too trusting and gullible, but she wasn't stupid. There was no question in her mind that Sally Roe was alive.

The more she thought about that, the more devastating it became. Gradually, just one small idea at a time, she was allowing herself to think the unthinkable: something more than a lawsuit was in progress and she was being lied to by someone, maybe everyone. If she was being lied to, she was probably breaking the law for all her friends and not for herself. If all that were true, then—she'd tried to bury this thought for weeks—she was being used.

She had no question that her daughter Amber was being used, if not by these legal eagles, then certainly by that once-cute little pony Amber had befriended in Miss Brewer's fourth-grade class. The laughter, the fun and games, the cartoon-character charm were all things of the past. Amethyst was no friend of any kind.

But now Lucy was in so deep, how could she back out? What direction could she turn? How—

The bell rang at the front desk. Debbie was on her break, so Lucy hurried to the front.

This big man looked familiar. She'd seen him around

town, but he wasn't from around here. She immediately felt uncomfortable.

"Can I help you?"

"Hi. I'm Marshall Hogan. I'm a friend of Tom Harris, and I just got a letter here from the Omega Center for Educational Studies in Fairwood, Massachusetts . . ."

He acted like he was giving her a cue, but she didn't catch whatever it was. "Yes? Is there a problem?"

"Well . . . I suppose you know that they're the publishers of the *Finding the Real Me* curriculum that Miss Brewer uses at the elementary school?"

"I still don't see your point."

"Well, I wrote to the Omega Center to order a copy of the *Finding the Real Me* curriculum, and they tell me here in this letter that they only make that curriculum available to educational institutions, and not to the general public. Don't you think that's a little strange?"

Lucy knew she didn't want to talk about this. "I'm not the Omega Center, sir, and I'm not responsible for their policies. Now unless you have some business with the Post Office . . ."

Marshall looked behind him. No one else was standing in line. "I'll just be a second. Let's talk about that local group, uh, LifeCircle. I understand that LifeCircle is a major force in education around here: three of the school board belong to it, the principal of the elementary school—Mr. Woodard— belongs to it, Miss Brewer belongs to it, and you belong to it. The school board adopted the Omega Center curriculum, Mr. Woodard implemented it, Miss Brewer's teaching it, and your daughter Amber contacted her inner guide, Amethyst, because of it."

Only a week ago Lucy would have felt invaded, and very angry. Today was different. "What about it?" She really wanted to know.

She was trying to look strong and unshakable, but Marshall caught the curiosity in her eyes. "Let me ask you this: Why do you suppose Miss Brewer couldn't produce the curriculum when we asked to see it, and neither could Mr. Woodard, and neither could the school board, and now the

Omega Center itself won't allow me to order a copy of it? When I consider how all you people are connected, it sure makes me wonder if your lawsuit against the Good Shepherd Academy might have something to do with it. Do you suppose there's something in that curriculum your friends don't want us to see?"

Lucy didn't answer for a long moment. She'd never thought about the question before. She wanted an answer herself. "I don't know, Mr. . . ."

"Hogan. Marshall Hogan."

"What are you, an investigator or something?"

"Sure, something like that. Mostly just a friend of your opponents in this lawsuit."

"Well, obviously I can't talk about any of this."

"I understand. Thank you very much for your time."

"You're welcome."

He left the building, and Lucy returned to her work, or at least tried to return to it. If she was pensive and troubled before her visit with this Mr. Hogan, now she was totally distracted. What else did that man know, and why didn't she know it?

Marshall got back to Ben and Bev's, and placed a collect long-distance call.

Back at his newspaper, a young, pretty, bespectacled brunette answered the phone from inside Marshall's glass-enclosed office. "*Ashton Clarion*, Bernice Krueger speaking."

"Hey, Bernice, this is Marshall."

"Well, well!" She closed the office door against the outside clamor and plopped down at his desk, ready for the latest. "Can any good news come out of Bacon's Corner?"

"Well . . . the walls of the fort are getting thin, but no breakthroughs yet."

"Keep digging."

"That's why I called. You remember I told you about that curriculum at the elementary school?"

"Right. The kids getting into alpha mind control and spirit-guides. Did you ever get a copy of it?"

349

"No dice. They're stonewalling it, as far up the ladder as Omega itself. Are you still in touch with that guy in Washington, what's-his-name . . . ?"

"Cliff Bingham. Sure. He got me some inside stuff on the last election."

"I'm wondering if he couldn't check with the Library of Congress and find an original copy of this thing."

Bernice grabbed a pen and started writing herself a note. "I'll call him. What exactly do you want?"

"*Finding the Real Me*, a curriculum for fourth-graders."

She wrote it down. "Published by Omega Center . . ."

"Uh . . . Omega Center for Educational Studies, Fairwood, Massachusetts."

"Any idea what year?"

"Beats me."

"Okay. We will see what we will see."

"Okay, now let's talk about the Tuesday edition. Pull that malt shop story; John likes it, but his wife will have a fit . . ."

They talked business. Bernice took notes, pulled files, read copy over the phone, and got orders from her boss.

Outside, the midweek, midday business in the town of Ashton was in full swing; people, grocery carts, and vehicles were circulating through the parking lot at Carlucci's Market; the fire fighters were hosing down the apron at Station Fifteen and shining up the pumper; Clyde Sodeberg and his sons were beating the still-green concrete off some forms over at the new Midwest Savings and Loan project.

Driving past it all, and then stopping at the second of four lights along Main Street, Marv and Claudia Simpson introduced Sally Beth Roe—they thought her name was Betty Smith—to their town.

"It's a great place to live and do business," said Marv. "At least it is now. We've had our share of trouble, but things have settled down quite a bit, and I think we're having a turn for the better."

The light turned green and Marv piloted the big station

wagon further down the street, past the small stores, the True Value Hardware, the local newspaper . . .

"That's the *Ashton Clarion*," said Marv. "It comes out on Tuesdays and Fridays, and the editor's a saint. I think he's been out of town for a while; I don't know what he's been doing."

They drove past the high school. It was new this year, because enrollment was up.

Marv turned left at the third light and drove up a gradually graded street into a quiet neighborhood with massive oak trees lining the street, small, garishly painted bicycles leaning against the oaks, and orange basketball hoops on every other garage. The lawns were neat, the sidewalks were clean, and the cars all seemed to know their proper parking places.

Marv turned left again and came to a row of large, turn-of-the-century homes with white, beveled siding, large chimneys, massive roofs, cozy dormers, and wide, roomy front porches. He pulled over and parked in front of the third house on the right, probably the most inviting house of all, with a perfectly manicured lawn, colorful planted borders, a pillared front porch, and an inviting porch swing. In front, just beside the walkway, was a small, unpretentious sign: Sara Barker's Boarding House.

"Here's the place I told you about," said Marv.

"It'll be just right, I think," said Claudia. "You'll have time to think things through and get your head clear."

Sally took their hands and held them tightly. "You've done me a wonderful kindness. Thank you very much."

"You're welcome," said Marv. "We'll have you out to the dairy sometime."

"I'd love that."

"Oh, here's Sara now," said Claudia.

"Sara's a good gal; you'll like her."

Sara was, and Sally did. The house actually belonged to Sara and her husband Floyd, but they thought using just her name on the sign would be more charming. Floyd was a tall, thin man of few words who had recently retired from the grain business and was now trying his hand at being a writer when he wasn't serving as the handyman for the boarding house—which he was at the moment. He was glad to meet her and shook her hand warmly. As for Sara, she impressed Sally as everyone's idea of the perfect grandma, a short little woman with close-cropped gray hair, little round glasses, and a cute story about most everything.

"We used to have eight kids, and now they're gone, so we have all these rooms empty and ready for the right people," she explained, showing Sally through the big house. "We've had mostly single women here; some have troubles at home and need to stay away, some are on their way somewhere else—you know, between things—and the two that are here right now are here for keeps until they get married, I suppose."

The living room was old, classic, with a high ceiling, finely milled wainscoting, inviting, comfortable, antique furniture, and even an old pump organ from Ashton's first pioneer church. The dining room was large and well-suited for a big family, or for a houseful of boarders.

"Now, we have a downstairs bathroom, but it's being worked on . . ."

They were in the central hallway just below the big staircase, and they could see a toolbox jutting into the hall through the bathroom door and hear the clunking and tinkering of work going on.

Sara stepped around the toolbox and then out of the way, so Sally could look in. "When we get the plumbing fixed, things should be back to normal."

Sally looked into the bathroom. It was large, and during normal times it was probably very nice. Right now it was a mess; the carpet was rolled back, there were tools and pipe fittings on the floor, a glaring work light hanging from the vanity mirror, and, strangest of all, a young man in coveralls on his knees in front of the toilet—he seemed to be hollering down into the bowl.

"No," he shouted, "come back up! You're going the wrong way!"

A muffled voice—it was Floyd's—came from below somewhere. "Who put all this stuff down here, anyway?"

"You put it in, Floyd; don't blame me!"

Then the young man noticed Sally watching him. "Oh, hi there."

"Hi."

Sara leaned in. "Hank, this is Betty Smith, a new boarder. Betty, this is Hank Busche, our pastor."

He waved a wrench at her. "Pleased to meet you. I'll be happy to shake your hand later." It was clear to see that his hands were quite dirty at the moment.

Sally was fascinated. This was a pastor? "Why are you yelling down the toilet?"

He thought that was funny. "Well . . . that's Floyd down there. Have you met Floyd?"

Floyd's voice came from under the floor. "Yeah. That's Betty, right?"

Hank hollered back. "Yeah."

"We've met."

"She's here to inspect your bolting job."

"Oh, I'm in trouble now!"

Hank explained, "Floyd used the wrong bolts to put this toilet in fifteen years ago, and now we can't get the nuts loose underneath."

Sally's smile was a weary smile, but it felt good.

Sara said, "You're tired. Come on upstairs and I'll show you your room."

But Sally hesitated just a moment. "You don't look like a pastor."

Hank smiled, brushing some hair away from his forehead with his forearm. "Thanks."

Why not go straight to the horse? Sally thought. "I suppose you know God?"

"Sure, I know Him."

He was so matter-of-fact about it. He didn't even hesitate with that answer. Sally tried a tougher question. "Can you prove He exists?"

Hank sat back from the toilet and just looked at her for a moment. "Got a Bible?"

Sally was about to say no, but Sara said, "There's one up in her room."

Hank was thinking. He almost looked like he was listening. "Tell you what. Read Psalm 119, and just ask God to speak to your heart while you read it. See what happens."

"Psalm 119," Sally repeated.

"Right."

"Good luck with the toilet."

"Thanks. And nice to meet you."

Hank sat there a moment after Sally and Sara were gone. The Lord had spoken to him about this woman named Betty.

Floyd's voice came from below, "Psalm 119? What kind of Scripture is that for getting somebody saved?"

Hank was puzzled himself. "I don't know. It's the Scripture the Lord told me to give her."

"The longest chapter in the Bible . . ." Floyd muttered.

Hank prayed, right there. "Lord God, please make Yourself real to Betty Smith. Show her how much You love her."

"Amen," said the voice under the toilet. "Now can you flush me a smaller wrench?"

Atop the house, Tal consulted with the two angelic princes of Ashton, Krioni and Triskal.

"We are honored to see you again, captain," said Krioni. "We'll always remember the victory achieved here."

Tal scanned the horizon and could see the thick hedge of angelic warriors that surrounded the town, sealing it off from demonic invasion. They were there to serve the saints within, responding to their prayers, widening doors of opportunity to minister. The town was not perfect, not without problems; it still had its taverns and turmoils, its scrapes and its sins. But the Lord was working in Ashton, its saints were praying, and for Sally Beth Roe it was safe.

"I leave her in your hands, Krioni. I see Hank is planting the right seeds already."

Triskal smiled. "The Spirit of God is continuing to draw her."

"Care for her in the meantime. Make sure she meets Bernice, but don't let Bernice know who she is until the right time."

Krioni gave Tal a knowing look. "Once again you have a plan. How is it unfolding?"

Tal looked grim. "Steadily, but miserably."

Krioni nodded. "You and the others are going to need some time to heal up, I see."

"Destroyer learned from what we did here. He got to the saints first. He and his demons are wreaking strife and division that church hasn't seen in years, and every day our situation grows more precarious. I'm going back to Bacon's Corner to stop that campaign. Nothing else can proceed until I do."

Triskal's face wrinkled with concern. "But is there time, captain?"

Tal answered simply, "No. We'll just have to do what we can. If you can use this crisis to arouse specific prayer from the saints here, so much the better."

Triskal smiled. "Count on it. They will pray."

Krioni added, "But it sounds like Sally Roe is headed for even greater jeopardy."

Tal nodded, with regret. "We cannot bring the plan up short, or spare her every last step. We will win all . . . or we will lose all."

Krioni and Triskal embraced him. "Godspeed."

Tal drew his sword to rally his warriors, and they shot into the sky, bound for Bacon's Corner.

"Lost?" Destroyer roared. "You dare to tell me you lost her?"

Six loathsome spirits stood before him on the roof of Whitcombe Hall at Bentmore University. They'd locked their eyes on the thick, rolled roofing and refused to look up. They were silent, with no fitting words of explanation. Destroyer and Corrupter were not too far from shredding them this very moment.

Destroyer wanted an explanation, and right now. He grabbed one demon by the hair and jerked his head upward so their eyes would meet. "I knew *you* would never lose her, but follow her to the ends of the earth so we could choose our time, taunt the Host of Heaven, pick the fruit when it was ripe, and now . . . you have lost her? Tell me how!"

"We followed her," the thing said.

"And?"

"She went west with the dairy farmer."

"*And?*"

The spirit looked at his comrades. They wouldn't even return his gaze, lest Destroyer think they knew something. "The farmer took her to Ashton."

Destroyer gave the demon's hair a painful yank, twisting his neck backward. "*Ashton?*"

The demon winced with pain. "We followed as long as we could, but we were turned back."

Destroyer's eyes burned with fury. "The Host of Heaven?"

The warrior was almost falling over, squirming in Destroyer's iron grip. "They hold that territory, they and the saints of God!"

Destroyer released the demon's hair and the warrior dropped to the roof, rotating the kinks out of his neck.

Destroyer and Corrupter moved away to consult privately.

Destroyer was turning the air yellow with his frantic, anxious panting. "That slimy, slippery, subtle Captain of the Host! I should have anticipated this! He is hiding her in a stronghold we cannot penetrate!"

Corrupter muttered, "She is free, and alive, and now has *both* the ring and the rosters."

"The rosters are *your* fault!" Destroyer insisted.

"And her disappearance? Is that not yours?"

"If we lose track of her now . . ."

"That is not an option."

" . . . the Strongman will take both our heads from our bodies with his bare hands!" Destroyer spit sulfur in a new burst of rage. "Never! The Captain of the Host will not defeat me! I will not be humbled by these feeble saints!"

He screamed to his henchmen who stood guard nearby. They snapped to attention.

"Gather your hordes! We return to Bacon's Corner! We will finish this business and decimate the saints, silencing their prayers once and for all!"

Claire Johanson hung up the telephone in her office and then stared at it, motionless, deep in thought.

Jon knew that look on her face. "What is it?"

"That was Mr. Goring, from Summit. Sally Roe showed up at Bentmore. She was right in Samuel Lynch's office."

Jon rose from his chair, anticipating an answer he would not like. "She didn't get away?"

Claire sighed, letting her hand fall to the desk with a slap. "She did. Khull and his men chased her all over the Bentmore campus, but she managed to hitch a ride with some stranger and they lost her."

Jon threw up his hands in anger. "Great. That's just great! I'm really starting to wonder about this Khull. He's had two chances now and came up empty both times!"

Claire cautioned him, "Please keep your voice down. Some LifeCirclers are in the house."

Jon tried to calm himself, but couldn't sit down or relax at all.

"She has the rosters," Claire added.

Jon looked at her curiously. "What rosters?"

"Professor Lynch's membership rosters."

Jon stared at her blankly. He couldn't bring himself to believe it. He shook his head. "Now that has to be a mistake. Somebody's wrong. That isn't true."

"It's true."

He shook his head again, harder. "No, it is not true! It's too unthinkable to be true!"

"Lynch stepped out of the office to get his ring and contact Khull. She must have snatched them from his bookshelf while he was gone. He didn't notice until after she left."

Jon shouted at that. "She *left?*"

Claire shushed him, feeling defensive for Lynch. "He couldn't have her killed right there in his office! Khull's men were supposed to take care of her elsewhere, secretly."

Jon fumed and huffed and paced around the office. "Is Professor Lynch still alive?"

"Of course he is."

"Why?"

Claire looked away impatiently. "Jon, what would that solve?"

Jon was having trouble keeping his voice down. "That old codger is a liability! He should be eliminated, and Khull as well!"

Claire sighed and rested her chin in her hand. "Maybe they will be, I don't know. I don't control such things."

"So, when is that hearing?"

"Nine o'clock Monday morning."

Jon cursed. "We should have known by now! There are other forces working on Roe's behalf, directly opposing us. I can feel it. No doubt they're working against this lawsuit as well. We could get a wrong ruling."

Claire was about to disagree, but then decided she couldn't. "I believe that is a possibility."

Jon stopped to give Claire a good look in the eye. "If we lose in this hearing, and they can put Amber on the stand, or even depose her . . ."

Claire agreed. "I'll call the others."

"And Hemphile too. I want her in on this. We have to hit that church!"

"We already have . . ."

"I mean hit them harder! Something right up front!"

Claire stood, her finger to her lips. "Someone might hear you."

He tried to quiet himself. They could hear a LifeCircle yoga class going on upstairs, right above their heads.

Claire had another caution. "You know that with any overt action we'll be risking exposure . . ."

Jon chuckled at that. "Come on. They're old-fashioned, fringe, fanatic Christians. Who's going to believe them?"

She acquiesced. "All right."

"We'll curse the church, and we'll curse Sally Roe. Can we get anything she owns?"

"Well, I guess the rental house still has all her belongings in it."

"Anything alive?"

Claire thought for a moment. "Oh, yes. As a matter of fact, I think she did have some animals."

Jon smiled and calmed a bit. "Good. Good."

thirty

It was quiet at Floyd and Sara Barker's after dinner. Floyd and Sara were settling into the couch downstairs for some reading; Michelle, the young college girl, was in her room studying; Suzanne, a young attorney just new in town, was out meeting a prospective partner.

Sally was fed, bathed, warm, and secure in her little corner bedroom, snuggled in the soft bed under one of Sara's hand-made comforters, her back supported by an ample supply of large pillows.

For the first time in so many years Sally had trouble calculating the number—she finally figured it had to be about twenty-five—she held in her hands a volume she had blamed for the world's woes, belittled as an overrated anthology of myths, resented for its narrow views of morality, condemned as oppressive and authoritarian, and ignored as an out-moded, stagnating lead weight around the intellectual ankle of mankind.

It was one of Sara Barker's Bibles.

She found the book of Psalms immediately. It was in the middle of the Bible.

"Just open your Bibles right to the middle," came a voice from her past. "Psalms is right there in the middle."

What was that woman's name? Oh, Mrs. Gunderson, that's right. She was an older lady. She was old as long as Sally ever knew her, as if she'd hit a peak in years and just stayed there. Every Sunday morning, Sally would clump down the church stairs with all the other seven- and eight-year-olds and gather in Mrs. Gunderson's Sunday school class in that cold church basement, in that small, echoing classroom with the hard wooden chairs and the chalkboard that still bore the un-erasable traces of lessons from weeks ago.

Then Mrs. Gunderson would tell them a story, placing paper Bible characters on the same green-grass-and-blue-sky flannel background. Even now, as Sally lay in the bed with the Bible in her lap, she could remember those stories: the wee little man who climbed the sycamore tree, the fishermen who fished all night but caught no fish, the disciple—she thought it was Peter—who walked on the water to meet Jesus, the man named Lazarus whom Jesus raised from the dead, Moses, Noah, and of course Jonah who was swallowed by the fish.

Strange. She'd put those stories out of her mind as far back as junior high school, but now, at thirty-six, she remembered not only those stories, but also the deep feelings of conviction and morality she always had after every Sunday school: I want to be good. I want to do good things and love God. I want Jesus to come into my heart.

Such old memories, such long ago feelings. But the memories were pleasant, and the feelings they evoked were warm and comforting, which caused her to pause and reflect. How many pleasant memories did she really have? Not too many. Maybe these, some of her oldest, were her happiest.

Psalm 119. Hmm. It was a long chapter. She read the first verse.

"Blessed are they whose ways are blameless, who walk according to the law of the Lord."

That first verse was enough to grab her attention, and she read on.

Verse 3 said, "They do nothing wrong; they walk in his ways."

Verses 4, 5, and 6 continued the same theme: "You have laid down precepts that are to be fully obeyed. Oh, that my ways were steadfast in obeying your decrees! Then I would not be put to shame when I consider all your commands."

How did that pastor know? She'd asked him the toughest question she could think of, but he came back with the answer she needed, the one perfect for her situation, right here and now, the very next step in her musings.

She continued to read, and the words spoke to her over and over again about something she'd fled from for years, denied, fought against, and finally lost . . . but perhaps needed most of all.

Absolutes. A genuine right and a genuine wrong. A fence, a point of reference, a way to know something for sure.

She couldn't let these ideas get away from her. She hopped out of bed and hurried to the closet for her duffel bag. The few clothes she had were in the laundry at the moment, so the bag was a lot emptier, containing a still frightening amount of freshly minted cash, her notebook, which she set aside, and . . . the rosters from Professor Lynch's office.

She felt sick at the sight of them, as if there was an evil attached to them, as if an invisible, poisonous stowaway had come along to haunt her. They frightened her; they gave her the same stomach-turning fear and disgust one feels while waiting for something horrible to jump out in a late-night horror movie.

Unseen by Sally, though she could sense them, the same little quartet of demons still lurked about, watching her, looking for opportunities. They had followed her everywhere she went, and could pass through any angelic hedge because she carried them with her. Despair was enjoying his job less and less; the more Sally continued in her quest, the less of his poison he could sow in her mind. Fear had had much to do and a lot of fun doing it, and was glad to have those rosters along, but Death and Insanity were getting frustrated. Sally had found some new purpose somewhere; Death was no longer welcome in her thoughts, and her thoughts were becoming too clear and rational for Insanity to scramble.

All four reached out for her, but at the moment there was nothing to grab.

Sally closed the duffel bag, leaving the rosters hidden and confined. *Not now, rosters; I'll deal with you later. I don't want to feel sick, I don't want to struggle. Just give me a break. Let me rest awhile.*

The demons slinked away to wait.

She grabbed up her notebook and pen, and hopped into the bed again.

> *Good feelings, don't go away. Let me meet with you awhile,*
> *study you, figure you out; let me think things through.*

She began another letter to Tom Harris.

> *I'm working my way through Psalm 119, and if I under-*
> *stand the message correctly, there are at least two absolutes*
> *being presented, two things I can know for sure:*
> *1)There is a right: to obey God's laws and follow His*
> *ways.*
> *2)There is a wrong: to disobey God's laws and not follow*
> *His ways.*
> *How am I doing so far? I hope you're keeping up, because*
> *now it's going to get tougher.*
> *Psalm 119 also talks about two human conditions that*
> *are the direct result of the two absolutes:*
> *1)Do what is right, and you'll be happy and blessed.*
> *2)Do what is wrong, and you'll be put to shame.*
> *Now is that simple or what? Too simple, I suppose; too*
> *basic to be believed and accepted by people like me who*
> *insist there is no reality higher than themselves.*
> *But, Tom, I do believe I have been put to shame. Even the*
> *vicious, cutting remarks of an enemy, Professor Lynch, make*
> *that clear to me. He was trying to destroy me, I know, but*
> *there was nothing he said that wasn't true. I couldn't argue*
> *with him. The truth is, my life is in ruins.*
> *But can I accept the Bible's explanation for it? Dare I*
> *trust this Book? If the Bible is trustworthy, and if I did*
> *choose to believe it, then I could, once and for all, determine*
> *who and where I am: in the wrong, outside of God's favor,*
> *put to shame.*
> *Not a comfortable thought, but at least I would have an*
> *immovable rock under my feet.*

Despair flopped to the floor beside the bed, holding his stomach and moaning. Death and Insanity weren't feeling very well either, but took it out on Despair.

"You're losing her, leech! You're the one in charge of this mission! Do something!"

Fear volunteered, "Perhaps I could think of something to frighten her."

Despair hissed at him, "You've done that, and driven her closer to the truth!"

Sally felt sleepy at last. For now, her questions were resolved, her thoughts were recorded, and she could rest. She set the notebook on the bedside table, put all the pillows aside except one, and clicked off the lamp.

As she lay there in the dark, she noticed how peaceful she felt. This was the first night in a long time that she did not feel afraid. Instead, she felt . . . what was this? Hope? Yes! This had to be hope. It felt so foreign, so different.

Out of her distant past, she could recall once again those old feelings and thoughts from Sunday school: I want to be good. I want to do good things and love God. I want Jesus to come into my heart.

She fluffed her pillow and let her head sink into it. Hm. Jesus. Now what does He have to do with all this?

Very early on Sunday morning, Ben Cole stood in the gate to Sally Roe's goat pen, incredulous, sickened, wary of proceeding inside. This couldn't be real. Things like this just didn't happen, not around here.

He looked back toward the field between the Potter home and the rental. Mrs. Potter stood in the middle of the field, nervously wringing her hands and watching, but refusing to come any closer.

He looked back toward the goat pen. Buff and Bart, the two kids, were still alive, but disturbed and jittery. As for Betty, the doe . . .

Ben finally entered the pen, closing the gate behind him, stepping carefully through the dirt and straw, searching the ground for any clues. He approached Betty's dead and butchered carcass. She hadn't been killed too long ago. It had to have been the previous night.

He turned and shouted to Mrs. Potter, "Did you hear anything?"

"No," she replied.

Ben looked around the carcass. No clues. No footprints. The dirt did seem to be disturbed, however, probably brushed and raked to erase any clues.

Mrs. Potter came closer, but still wouldn't look.

"Have you called the police?" Ben asked.

"Well, I called you."

He smiled. "I'm no longer with the Police Department."

"I know. But I wanted you to come. I don't trust Sergeant Mulligan. I don't think he'd do anything about it."

Ben backed away from Betty's carcass and joined Mrs. Potter near the fence. He was wishing he had a camera to record this.

"Well," he said, drawing his first full breath, "I'm going to do something about it."

Betty lay in the straw, her throat cut, her body totally drained of blood, and all four legs cleanly and skillfully removed, missing without a trace.

The morning air was chilly, but Ben could feel a chill that had nothing to do with the weather. In his spirit, he could feel some real trouble approaching.

Well, maybe I should, Sally thought. *It's one thing I haven't tried yet. It could provide more information that would round out my perspective. It might clarify some of the old memories I haven't been able to fully recall. It would be an interesting glimpse into middle-class American religious culture. Perhaps it might—*

"Get your coat, then," said Sara Barker. "Floyd's warming up the car right now."

Sally answered a little late, "Well, sure, I'll go. Why not?"

And that's how she found herself standing in front of the little white Ashton Community Church, a half-mile up Morgan Hill on Poplar Street, on a warm and beautiful

Sunday morning. People were already filing inside, talking, laughing, hugging like old friends, guiding their small children by the hand and calling to the older ones to come on and hurry up, church was starting.

Sara spared no pains to make sure Sally met everyone. "Hi, Andy, this is Betty Smith. Edith, how are you? I'd like you to meet Betty Smith, our new boarder. Cecil, it's great to see you're feeling better. Have you met Betty Smith?"

Sally smiled and shook the hands extended to her, but with only half her attention. The sight of a little girl in a Sunday dress, holding her mother's hand and carrying a Bible, triggered a memory.

Thirty years ago, that was me.

Sally could remember wearing a pretty dress and a matching ribbon in her hair. She could remember carrying a Bible too, a gift from the lady who held her hand back then, her guardian, Aunt Barbara. Sally's mother, lost to alcohol, had never been much of a positive influence. Aunt Barbara, on the other hand, always took her to Sunday school. Aunt Barbara took religion seriously, and in those days Sally respected that. It was good for Aunt Barbara, and yes, it felt right for Sally too.

"Well, we'd better get in there," said Sara, her words jolting Sally from her reverie.

They went up the front steps, through the double doors, and into a small foyer where a few clusters of people—Floyd was part of one cluster—were still getting caught up on each other's week.

Oh, there was the Sunday school attendance posted on the wall. She remembered that. She remembered always bringing an offering, too; that was important in those days.

The people around her were of all kinds. Some were well-dressed, some were in blue jeans; there were older folks and many younger; there were plenty of young children about, suggesting a middle-class, Protestant baby boom.

Sally quickly had to admit to herself that, Christianity itself notwithstanding, there was little reason to be uncomfortable in this place. Her lack of acceptable attire could have been a

367

reason—she had only her slacks and blouse and could not wear the jacket because of the knife holes in it, not to mention the missing sleeve—but now she saw that attire had little to do with acceptance, and neither did ethnic background or social status.

Well . . . I guess I won't be uncomfortable.

She followed Floyd and Sara to a place in a wooden pew near the back and sat down. Her feet could touch the floor. The last time she sat in a pew, her feet dangled. That was when . . . Tommy Krebs! Yes, now she remembered him, that little snotty kid with the crewcut and the marker pen without a cap. She finally tattled on him and that brought some peace for a while, but not before he'd blackened her knee. Yes, that all happened in a pew just like this one, during the Sunday school's opening exercises. Oh! What was that song she and all those other little moppets used to sing? "Jesus loves me, this I know, for the Bible tells me so . . ." Oh, yes. That song had to be one of the oldie-goldie hits of American Protestantism; obviously *she* never forgot it.

She tried to relax, and looked around the small sanctuary at the backs of all those heads. Oh, there was the pastor, Hank What's-his-name, closing off a conversation and taking a chair on the platform. Now he looked a little more like a pastor, with a suit and tie, but she knew she'd never forget that guy wrestling with a toilet back at the boarding house.

This was becoming quite an experience. There was so much to see and remember, so many feelings to sort through, she hadn't become bored yet. Rather, she was captivated.

But . . . what am I doing here, really? she wondered. *Is it just because Sara invited me?*

No, not really. The invitation was as good an incentive as any, but not the real reason. Sally did want to be here, even though it was only now that she realized it.

Is it a matter of curiosity?

No, more than that. Curiosity was one thing, hunger was another.

Hunger? For what—fond memories? Nostalgia?

No, more than that. It was more a haunting sensation that

she had come full circle after thirty years and found, just as strong as ever, a truth, a treasure, a special matter of the heart she once held but lost. She couldn't recall her life being as shaky during her Sunday school childhood as it had been ever since. There was just something about the convictions of this culture, the solid certainty of everything.

Maybe that was part of it. Maybe those experiences of long ago were the last solid ground Sally had ever walked on.

Yes, things were so different then.

Sally, Sara, and Floyd all scooted over a little to make room for a young lady to sit next to Sally.

"Hi," she said, offering her hand. "I'm Bernice Krueger."

"Um . . . Betty Smith." She had to be sure she remembered the right name.

"She's our new boarder," said Sara.

"Oh, great," said Bernice. "You new in town?"

"Yes."

"What brings you here?"

"Oh . . . just traveling."

"So how long have you been here?"

"Uh . . . I just got here yesterday." Sally was hoping this wasn't going to be a long interview. She decided to get the subject off herself. "So what do you do?"

"I work for the local newspaper. I'm a reporter and assistant editor, and I also wash the coffee cups and empty the wastebaskets."

"Oh, that's interesting."

Bernice laughed. "Sometimes it is. Well, it's great to have you here."

"Thank you."

There was a slight pause. Bernice looked forward and Sally thought the conversation was over, but then Bernice turned to Sally again with an additional thought.

"Say, if there's anything I can do for you, please let me know."

The offer was a little abrupt and unexpected. It made Sally wonder what this Bernice Krueger was thinking. *Do I seem that pitiful?* Sally did appreciate the compassion, but knew she could never accept it. "Thanks. I'll remember that."

The service began, and it was a real study in middle-class fundamentalism. Sally decided she would be an objective observer and take mental notes.

The content of the songs was worth noting: in every case, the lyrics spoke of love, worship, adoration, and reverence for God and for Jesus Christ, and it was readily apparent, as expected, that the people believed and practiced with great conviction the sentiments expressed in the songs.

As the service progressed through the songs and then a time of sharing inspirational personal anecdotes, Sally found it easy to get caught up in the very phenomenon she was observing. She was enjoying it. These people were happy, and even though the form and process of worship seemed a little odd and foreign to an outsider, Sally knew and reminded herself that next to her own yoga techniques and trance channeling, this stuff was tame, normal, even downright bland.

The time came for prayer, and Pastor Busche opened the floor for prayer requests. An elderly man was having trouble with a pulled muscle and asked for prayer, as did a young lady concerned for her husband who "didn't know the Lord," a young father who needed a job, and a lady whose sister had had a child born prematurely.

Then the young lady who worked at the newspaper, Bernice Krueger, spoke up. "Let's remember to pray for Marshall and Kate while they're away. I guess things are getting pretty difficult, and they're encountering a lot of spiritual resistance."

"Right," said Pastor Hank, "we've all been following that. We'll be sure to pray about it."

And then the pastor led the congregation in prayer, glorifying and praising God, and then asking God to supply all the requests that the people had made.

"And we remember Marshall and Kate as well, involved in spiritual warfare . . ."

That topic caught Sally's interest. Spiritual warfare. Wow! If these people only knew what *she* was going through.

thirty-one

"'BUT he was pierced for our transgressions, he was crushed for our iniquities; the punishment that brought us peace was upon him, and by his wounds we are healed.'"

Bernice Krueger read the words in a soft voice from her Bible as Sally followed along in the Bible she'd brought from Sara Barker's. They were sharing a booth at Danny's Diner on Main Street, not far from the *Clarion*. They'd ordered their lunch, it was on the way, and now, over coffee, they were taking a second look at Hank's sermon text for the morning, some verses from Isaiah 53.

Bernice read the next verse. "'We all, like sheep, have gone astray, each of us has turned to his own way; and the Lord has laid on him the iniquity of us all.'"

"Sin and redemption," said Sally.

Bernice was impressed. "Right. So you know *something* about this."

"No, nothing really. It's a phrase I've heard in some circles, apparently a quick way to define the typical Christian view of things. We always hated the idea."

Bernice sipped from her coffee. "Who's 'we'?"

Sally brushed off the question. "Just some old friends."

"And what did you hate about it?"

Sally sipped from her coffee. It was an effective way to buy time to formulate an answer. "The notion of sin, I guess. It's hard enough for anyone to feel good about himself, and it seemed so negative and oppressive to teach that we're all miserable, no-good sinners. Christianity was the curse of mankind, enslaving us and holding us back from our true potential." She felt a need to qualify that. "Anyway, that's what we thought."

"Okay, so that's what you thought about the sin part of it." Bernice smiled, and tapped the passage from Isaiah 53 that still lay open under Sally's nose. "But did you catch the redemption part? God loves you, and He sent His Son to pay for that sin with His own death on the cross."

Now Sally remembered Aunt Barbara and Mrs. Gunderson telling her that. "So I've heard."

"But getting back to what the Bible says about sin, since when is that such a shock? Mankind has been proving for thousands of years the kind of stuff he's made of. Listen, man's problems aren't due to politics or economics or ecology or levels of consciousness; man's problems are due to his ethics—they're lousy."

Sally heard that. It sank in. That was putting it simply enough, and hadn't she demonstrated the truth of those words in her own life? "I guess I'll agree with you there. But let me just confirm something: I take it the Bible is the ethical standard by which we determine what's 'lousy'?"

Bernice gave an assertive nod. "*And* what's good, what's righteous."

Sally pondered that. "That being the case, I imagine this standard puts us all on the wrong side of the fence."

"I think you'll find that idea acceptable if you're honest with yourself. You've lived long enough to know what we as human beings are capable of."

Sally even chuckled. "Oh, yes indeed."

"And here's God's answer for it." Bernice pointed out the phrases and reviewed them. "'He carried our infirmities and our sorrows . . . he was pierced for our sins and crushed for our iniquities . . . the Lord has laid on Him all our sins.'"

"Why?"

Bernice thought for a moment. "Well, let's talk about justice. You do something wrong, you end up in prison, right?"

Sally definitely agreed. "Right."

"Now, in the ideal sense, all legal loopholes aside, there are only two ways out of there: change the rules so that what you did isn't wrong so you aren't guilty, or pay the penalty."

"I've tried changing the rules," Sally admitted.

"Well, in God's scheme of things, rules are rules, because if they weren't, they wouldn't be worth much, and right and wrong would be meaningless. So what's left? The penalty. That's where God's love comes in. He knew we could never pay the penalty ourselves, so He did it for us. He took the form of man, took all our sins upon Himself, and died on a Roman cross two thousand years ago."

Sally examined the passage again. "So tell me: did it work?"

Bernice leaned forward and said, "You be the judge. The Bible says that the penalty for sin is death, but after Jesus paid that penalty He rose from the dead on the third day, so *something* was different. He conquered sin, so He was able to conquer sin's penalty. Sure, it worked. It always works. Jesus satisfied divine justice on that Cross. He bore the punishment in full, and God never had to bend the rules. That's why we call Jesus our Savior. He shed His own blood in our place, and died, and then rose from the grave to prove He'd won over sin and could set us free." Now Bernice started getting excited. "And you know what thrills me about that? It means we're special to Him; He really does love us, and we . . . we *mean* something, we're here for a reason! And you know what else? No matter what our sins are, no matter where we are or what condition we're in, we can be forgiven, free and clear, a clean slate!"

The lunch came—two soups and two salads. Sally was thankful for the pause in the conversation. It gave her a chance to think and to wonder, Who gave this young lady the script anyway? How was it that she could say so many things that spoke directly to Sally's situation?

Well, Bernice did go to Pastor Hank Busche's church, and *he* had a way of hitting the nail on the head. His suggestion to read Psalm 119 was perfect, and his morning sermon on Isaiah 53 was just more of the same perfectly tailored message, exactly what she was ready to hear.

But there was still a snag in all this. Sally took a few bites of her salad while she considered her next question, and then she formed it as a comment. "I don't feel forgiven."

Bernice answered, "Have you ever asked God to forgive you?"

"I've never even believed in God, at least not in the traditional sense."

"Well, He's there."

"But how can I know that?"

Bernice looked at Sally and seemed to know her heart. She replied simply, "You know."

"So . . ." Sally stopped short, and ate some more salad. She couldn't ask the question she had in her mind. It would seem too silly, too childish, like a dumb question already answered. But still . . . she had to hear a direct answer, something she could carry away without any doubts. "Well, I hope you'll indulge the question . . ."

"Sure."

"It's easy to speak in comfortable, generalized, generic terms . . ."

"Be as specific as you want."

"Did . . ." She stopped again. Where was that emotion coming from? She pushed it down with another bite of salad. Now she felt all right. It seemed safe to ask. "Did Jesus die for *me*?"

Bernice did not answer lightly or flippantly. She looked Sally in the eye and gave her a firm, even reply. "Yes, He died for you."

"For me, for . . ." She had to remember her alias. "For Betty Smith? I mean, Bernice, you don't know me . . ."

"He died for Betty Smith just like He died for Bernice Krueger."

Well, she got her answer. "Okay."

That was the last item on that topic. Bernice could sense her lunch guest was getting uncomfortable, and didn't want to make things worse. Sally was afraid she'd opened up just a little too much to an innocent stranger, and dared not risk dragging this nice woman into her troubles.

Bernice resorted to purely social conversation. "So how long have you been on the road?"

Sally was even afraid of that question. "Oh . . . about a month or so, something like that."

"Where are you from originally?"

"Does it matter?"

After that, conversation was difficult, and both regretted it. Except for small talk and purely social conversation, the lunch was more important than any more words. The salads disappeared, the soup bowls went empty, the minutes slipped by.

"I enjoyed meeting you," said Bernice.

"I guess I'd better get back to Sara's," said Sally.

"But listen . . . why don't you come by the *Clarion* when you get the chance? We could have lunch again."

Sally's first impulse was to refuse, but finally she allowed herself to relax, trust just a little, and accept the invitation. "Well . . . sure, I'd like that."

Bernice smiled. "Come on. I'll drive you back to Sara's."

The old farm outside Bacon's Corner had been deserted for years, the barn empty and graying. Ever since the owner had died, no human was ever seen in this place, not a sound was heard, not a single light glowed—except for certain nights no one was supposed to know about.

On this night, the dull orange glow of candles appeared through the cracks in the clapboard siding and through the chinks in the weather-warped door of the massive old barn. Inside, human voices muttered, murmured, and rumbled through rhythmic chants and incantations.

There were about twenty people inside, all clothed in black robes except for one woman who wore white, standing around a large pentagram etched in the bare earth floor. In the center of the pentagram, two hind legs cut from a goat lay crossed in an X, and a candle burned at each of the pentagram's five points.

At the head of the circle, the woman in white led the meeting, speaking in low, clear tones, a large silver cup in her outstretched hands. "As from the beginning, the powers will be brought forth through blood, and restitution by our hand will balance the scales."

"So be it," the others chanted.

"We call forth the powers and minions of darkness to witness this night our covenant with them."

"So be it!"

Demonic wings rustled in the rafters as dark, destructive spirits began to gather, looking down with gleaming yellow eyes and toothy grins, basking in all the adoration and attention.

In the peak of the roof, clinging to the rafters and overseeing it all, Destroyer could mouth the ceremony even as he listened to it.

"May their fury be kindled against our enemies, against all who oppose. May their favor be with us as we dedicate this offering."

"So be it!"

"May the woman be found."

"So be it."

"So be it," agreed the demons, exchanging glances.

"It will be," said Destroyer. "It will be."

"May she be driven from hiding, and crushed as powder," declared the woman.

"So be it," chanted the others.

The demons nodded and cackled in agreement, their wings quivering with excitement. More spirits arrived. The rafters, the hayloft, the gables of the roof were filling with them.

"Defeat and division to the Christians, ill health, ill will."

"So be it."

Destroyer spoke quickly to the gathering demons, pointing to this one and then that one, assigning hordes to every task as the spirits murmured their acceptance.

"May they grant a court decision in our favor! We give to them the heart and mind of Judge Emily Fletcher!"

"So be it."

Destroyer looked around their group and finally settled on a larger, hulking spirit roosting on a diagonal brace. He'd handled courtrooms before; he would be in charge of that.

"And now . . ." The woman drew the silver cup to her lips. "Through blood we seal the success of the powers, the death of Sally Beth Roe, and the defeat of the Christians!"

"So be it!"

The demons all leaned forward and craned their necks, wanting to see. They giggled, they slobbered, they gave each other happy pats and pokes. Destroyer became drunk with exhilaration.

The woman pulled back her hood and took a drink from the cup. When she withdrew the cup, the stain of fresh goat's blood remained on her lips.

Claire Johanson, high priestess of the coven, passed the cup to Jon, who drank and passed it on to the next person, and every witch, male and female, drank to seal the curses.

Then, in chorus, their arms shooting upward, the witches let out an eerie wail: "So be it!"

"Go!" said Destroyer with a clap of his wings and a point of his crooked finger.

The marauding spirits shot out of the barn, pouring from the roof like black smoke from a fire, like bats from a cavern. They dispersed in all directions, howling and cackling, full of lustful, destructive mischief.

On Monday morning, the day of the hearing in Westhaven, Pastor Mark Howard was thankful he'd arrived at the church earlier than everyone else. Hopefully he would be able to clean up the mess before any of the school kids saw it.

He'd already opened the school building and turned up the heat; so the facility was ready, and he still had about forty-five minutes before the parents started dropping off their children. He hurried down into the church basement, opened his office, and grabbed the telephone.

His voice was quiet and somber as he spoke, almost afraid of being heard. "Good morning, Marshall. This is Mark. Sorry to wake you up so early. Please come to the church right away. I'm going to be calling Ben, and I hope to have him here as well. Yes, right away. Thank you."

He opened the utility closet under the stairs and grabbed a mop and bucket. He was so upset he forgot he would need a garbage can as well. With his heart racing, he ran upstairs and out onto the front porch of the church.

The blood on the front door was dry. It would take some scrubbing to get it off.

Oh! I've got to get the garbage can! No, not yet. I'd better wait until Marshall and Ben get here. I hope they get here before the children do. O Lord Jesus, we pray for the covering and protection of Your shed blood over this place!

Come on, guys, hurry up! I can't leave these things here!

At Mark's feet, crossed like an X and staining the church steps red, were two front legs from an animal, most likely a goat.

At nine o'clock that morning, representatives of the press, the ACFA, the National Coalition on Education, and even a few churches converged on Room 412 at the Federal Courthouse in Westhaven, the courtroom of the Honorable Emily R. Fletcher.

Wayne Corrigan and Tom Harris were already seated at the defendant's table; Gordon Jefferson and Wendell Ames, Lucy Brandon's attorneys, were seated and ready for combat, with Lucy seated between them. In the first row of the gallery, Dr. Mandanhi was waiting to testify.

KBZT Channel Seven News reporter Chad Davis was there, prowling about for any news tidbits or comments while Roberto Gutierrez set up the television camera.

John Ziegler was there as well, and Paula the photobug had already snapped some pictures—uninvited—of Tom and Corrigan.

The bailiff stood to her feet. "All rise."

They all rose.

"Court is now in session, the Honorable Emily R. Fletcher presiding."

The judge took her place behind the bench. "Thank you. Please be seated."

They sat. So far everything was going the same as last time, and just like last time, the judge perched her reading glasses on her nose and looked over the documents before her.

"The defendant has requested today's hearing to determine whether or not the child in this case, Amber Brandon, should be excused from any deposition or testimony. It is the court's understanding that counsel for the plaintiff strenuously opposes any deposition or testimony from the child, and so the court has been asked to rule on the question." She looked up and seemed just a little impatient with the whole matter. "Mr. Corrigan, please proceed."

Corrigan rose. "Thank you, Your Honor. Our request is simple enough, and not at all irregular. The complaint against my client includes charges of harassment, discrimination, and outrageous religious behavior. But may I remind the court that thus far, any testimony pertaining to these charges has not come from the plaintiff's key witness, Amber herself, but secondhand, through Amber's mother, Lucy Brandon, and from the plaintiff's expert witness, Dr. Mandanhi. We've made many requests to talk to Amber, to have our own psychologist visit with her so Dr. Mandanhi's opinions can be balanced with those of another expert witness. But counsel for the plaintiff has adamantly refused to cooperate, and we are concerned that my client's right to confront his accuser is being infringed. Also, with no opportunity to question Amber and hear her testimony for ourselves, we have no assurance that the indirect testimony coming through Mrs. Brandon and through Dr. Mandanhi is not in some way colored, tainted, or embellished.

"Counsel for the plaintiff has insisted that Amber is in too delicate a condition, at too fragile an age to go through a deposition or a court trial. But we can assure counsel that we would not in any way resort to harsh tactics.

"Also, the record is clear that Amber is a strong-willed child and has stated conflicting facts, even to her mother. In addition to that, Amber's mother has testified in deposition that there are other influences affecting Amber's life which she was exposed to outside the school. Only Amber herself can answer the many unanswered questions that arise in these areas.

"All we're asking is that we be allowed to hear the details from Amber herself, and that our own psychologist be allowed to examine Amber to verify or refute the findings of Dr. Mandanhi."

Corrigan took his seat, and the judge recognized Wendell Ames.

Ames wasn't quite as exciting to watch as the younger Jefferson, but he did exude a dignity of experience that was in itself persuasive. "Your Honor, this entire case is being brought to court because of severe damage done to an innocent child, the extent of which is clearly shown in the affidavits and the reports of Dr. Mandanhi. As attorneys for the plaintiff, we wish to right a wrong, to redress a grievance, and to somehow undo the harm that has been done. It was never our intention, as responsible human beings, to only increase Amber's pain by putting her through the trial process, dredging up all her old wounds, and putting her hurts on public display.

"We have presented an additional opinion from Dr. Mandanhi, detailing for the court Amber's current emotional condition and establishing that it would not be in her best interests to be made to testify or give a deposition. If the court so requires, Dr. Mandanhi is here to testify in person as to Amber's fragile state of mind and emotions at this time."

Judge Fletcher looked at Mandanhi and then at Ames. "Would the doctor have additional statements to make not included in his written opinion?"

"I'm sure he could clarify for the court any items the court may need clarified."

The judge quickly perused Mandanhi's report. "I think it's clear enough. Any further oral testimony would most likely be cumulative."

"Very well."

"Anything else?"

"Yes. Even though there are strong arguments on either side, we would hope that common sense and decency will speak more loudly and persuasively than any argument, and that the court would spare this innocent child the pain and grief of reliving her hurts, of being challenged and doubted by the defense, of being put on display, as it were, in open court.

"We understand the legal process, of course. We understand that the defendant does have a right to confront his accuser. But we remind the court that we are dealing with a case of child abuse, a fact the defendants have already admitted."

"Objection," said Corrigan. "The defense has made no such admission."

Ames responded, "Your Honor, I was simply referring to what has already been established, that spanking does occur at the school, and that the school does teach pervasive and imposing doctrines . . ."

The judge was a little impatient. "The affidavits are clear on what the school practices and teaches, Mr. Ames. If the defendants want to stand by their practices, this in no way constitutes an admission of guilt. The objection is sustained."

Ames regathered his thoughts and continued. "At any rate, Your Honor, we hold that Amber is a child of tender years who needs to be protected. That is, after all, the motivation behind this suit in the first place. Given that, we must plead that the court spare Amber any further pain and trauma by ruling that she need not be deposed and she need not testify, or go through any more grueling examination by still another psychologist."

Ames sat down.

The judge looked at Corrigan. "Anything else?"

Corrigan stood. "I suppose it might be effective to point out why I don't have anything else I can say. If, as the plaintiff argues, Amber Brandon is in such a pitiful state of mind and emotion that she simply must not be allowed to testify or participate in the trial, we are left with having to take counsel's word for it, with no way of knowing how true these claims are. Amber could actually be in this bad a condition, but we could never confirm that. The plaintiff might be conducting a clever, purposeful cover-up, but we could never know that either. Counselors for the plaintiff obviously think they know all they need to know about Amber and what she allegedly went through at the hands of the defendants, but the defendants and their counsel know virtually nothing apart from the filtered hearsay provided thus far. Without

Amber we are being restricted, expected to present a persuasive defense, but forbidden to cut through to the real heart of the matter, to the real source of these complaints. I repeat again, we do not want to hurt Amber in any way or add to her trauma—if there be any trauma. We simply want to get to the facts so we can prepare to answer the charges. You have our brief as to the law which shows that Amber must be made available."

Corrigan sat down, and the judge looked at Ames and Jefferson. "Anything else?"

"No, Your Honor," said Ames.

"Court will recess, then, and reconvene at 2 this afternoon for my ruling."

"All rise," said the bailiff, and they all rose, and out went the judge.

Tom whispered to Corrigan, "How do you think we did?"

Corrigan wasn't very happy. "I have no idea. I think that's the weakest argument I've ever presented for anything." He fretted, fumed, replayed the hearing in his mind. "I should have stressed the law more; it's supposed to be on our side . . . Did you see her reaction to Mandanhi's affidavit? She took it as gospel!"

"How about some lunch?" Tom asked.

Corrigan followed him out of the courtroom, still muttering to himself.

thirty-two

The spirits were aloft and rampant, goaded on by goat's blood and blasphemy, by rage and conspiracy, by Destroyer's reckless indignation and thirst for immediate victory over the subtle Captain of the Host and his prize, the elusive Sally Beth Roe.

Infested by lying demons, the Warings (Ed and Judy) and the Jessups (Andrea and Wes) were meeting for lunch at the Warings' home to prayerfully discuss the latest news hot off the prayer chain: June Walroth had just heard that Tom regularly beat his daughter Ruth, and always dressed her in long sleeves so no one would notice; someone else—they didn't know who, but the person had to be reliable—was concerned because Pastor Mark and Cathy were having some marital problems, most likely because Mark had been unfaithful years ago; the Christian school was actually in terrible debt because Tom and Mrs. Fields were pilfering some of the money.

Andrea was aghast. "Are you sure about that? I can't believe Mrs. Fields would do such a thing."

"Well," said Judy, "do you know how little money she makes teaching at that school? It would be a real temptation, let's face it."

"But who told you about this?"

Ed was reluctant to reveal their source. "It's . . . Well, let me just say that it's someone close to the church board, someone I've really come to respect, all right? But this is all in strict confidence!"

Wes was immediately angry. "So why hasn't the board told the rest of the church?"

"The party I spoke to is concerned about the same thing. She's in a real fix: she doesn't want to violate the confidence of the board, but at the same time she's hurt because so much of this is being kept secret."

Judy piped in, "I think we need to have a congregational meeting, that's what I think!"

Andrea concurred. "And get this stuff out in the open once and for all!"

Ed nodded. "Well, I've talked to Ted and June Walroth, and they're ready for one."

Wes just shook his head and even laughed to vent his nerves. "This is all going to come out in that trial, you know. Somehow those ACFA guys are going to dig this up, and they're going to sue the ever-loving buns off our church!"

Gossip, Slander, and Spite thought that was funny, and shrieked with laughter. What wouldn't these people believe?

At the school, Mrs. Fields and Mark had just broken up their third fight, and now eight kids—six who were fighting and two who were urging them on—were staying inside for noon recess, cleaning the blackboards, dusting the furniture, and sweeping the floor. It had been a trying day.

Mrs. Fields plopped into her chair and heaved a deep sigh. "Pastor, what's happening around here?"

Mark wanted to say they were under spiritual attack, but he steered clear of that out of concern for Mrs. Fields. She was a sensitive woman, and it would have been distressing for her to learn what he'd found on the front steps that morning.

He finally just asked her to pray with him, and that is how they spent their noon hour—in between peacekeeping missions on the playfield.

Dreaming, dreaming . . . little baby girl . . . Rachel . . . pink and fat, laughing . . .

"Come on, sweetie, time for your bath."

Water running in the tub, just the right temperature.

Let her play in the running water. "See that? Isn't that fun? Time to get all clean."

Jonas. He's calling.

Not now. I'm giving Rachel a bath!

Pulling, pulling, yanking me from my body . . . No, not now . . .

Sudden blackness, floating, no feeling, no sounds, no pain, nothing but sweet love, bliss, oneness . . . A long, long tunnel, a bright light at the end, getting closer, closer, almost there, I've got to get back! What's happening to Rachel?

SLAP! A hand across her face!

"Come on, lady, snap out of it! Get up!"

Water everywhere, all over the floor. I'm sitting in it, I'm soaked. Who's this guy?

"Can you hear me? Get up!"

He's a cop! What's wrong!

"Aw, she's stoned, man, bombed to oblivion!"

Where's Rachel? "Where's my baby?"

The tub, filled to the brim, running over, water everywhere, cops, medics, the landlady, everything a blur.

A piercing, stabbing horror slowly rising. The unthinkable invading her mind. "Oh no! I've killed my baby!"

"Ma'am, I need to advise you of your rights. You have the right to remain silent . . ."

Up off the floor, held in strong arms, her hands bound behind her. "Where's my baby?"

"Get her out of here."

"Where's my baby?"

"Your baby is dead, Sally. Come on."

The quickest image, only appearing for a second: a tiny bundle on the kitchen table, medics all around, covered in a white cloth . . . one little pink hand showing.

"Oh no! Rachel! I've killed my baby! Jonas!"

Pain from handcuffs, her arms twisting, soaking wet, shoved out the door.

"Rachel!!"

"Come on, Sally, let's go!"

AAWW! Sally jolted awake in the darkened bedroom, almost falling off the bed. Her four tormenting companions were all over her.

Forever, forever, said Despair, *you will be condemned forever. You are what you are, you can never change it.*

385

Insanity piped in with renewed vigor, *It's all in your poor twisted mind, you know. You're a very sick lady!*

Death always follows you, said Death. *Everything you touch, everything you love, will only die.*

And they'll get you for this! said Fear. *All the spirits you've ever crossed are waiting to get you!*

Sally rolled over and buried her face in the pillow. "O God, help me!"

He can't help you . . . you've offended Him, He'll never hear you . . . we have you now . . .

Sally looked toward the window. The daylight was still visible around the edges of the drawn curtain. She checked the clock beside the bed. Four P.M. She flopped onto her back and tried to calm down, steady her heart, slow her breathing.

She told herself, *Easy now, girl, it was all a dream, a nightmare. Calm down.*

Her heart was still pounding and her face was slick with sweat. *Some nap this turned out to be; I feel worse.*

She tried to sort it all out. Yes, the dream was like a videotape; that's the way it happened. She hadn't had that clear a memory of it in years. *O God, what did I do, what did I do? How could I let this happen to me, to my daughter?*

Jonas, my wonderful counselor and friend, my infinitely wise spirit-guide!

The thought of that spirit made her sick.

I trusted him! I gave him my life, my thoughts, my spirit, my mind, and now . . . now I find out how evil he was. Or is.

Evil. Well, there's another absolute. Jonas is one incredibly evil spirit, and no one's going to convince me otherwise.

What had she just been reading? She rolled slowly off the bed, planted her feet on the floor, and went to the window. She pulled back the curtain and had to squint in the daylight that flooded the room. There, on the table under the window, was Sara's Bible, still opened to the Gospel of Mark. She'd just started reading it before she got sleepy and lay down. There was something it had said, and at the time she only gave it a passing thought.

She sat at the table and looked that passage over again.

Here it was, in chapter 1: "Just then a man in their synagogue who was possessed by an evil spirit cried out, 'What do you want with us, Jesus of Nazareth? Have you come to destroy us? I know who you are—the Holy One of God!'

"'Be quiet!' said Jesus sternly. 'Come out of him!' The evil spirit shook the man violently and came out of him with a shriek. The people were all so amazed that they asked each other, 'What is this? A new teaching—and with authority! He even gives orders to evil spirits and they obey him.' . . .

"That evening after sunset the people brought to Jesus all the sick and demon-possessed. The whole town gathered at the door, and Jesus healed many who had various diseases. He also drove out many demons, but he would not let the demons speak because they knew who he was."

Demons. They're demons. Sally believed it. She'd never given this Bible much credence since her Sunday school days, but right now, sitting in that room, having awakened from as clear a lesson as she could ask for, she believed what this Book said about these spirit entities. The whole thing was a sham, a deception, a spiritual con game. These things were as evil as evil could be.

Where's that notebook? I've got to write to Tom.

> *Tom, you know this already, and that's why you're in all this trouble, but let me assure you as one who has been on the other side, you are correct. Amber Brandon has contacted a spirit-guide, and now that thing is controlling her life, her thoughts, her behavior. I had Jonas, now Amber has Amethyst, and if I haven't said it clearly enough before, let me say it clearly now, because now I know it clearly: these spirits are evil; they are out to destroy us. Just look at what Jonas did to me. I don't blame him entirely; I asked him into my life, I gave him my mind and body. But I found out too late what his real agenda was.*
>
> *And what about Amber? I suppose for her it was all fun and games to begin with. Now I'm almost sure she's into something she would rather be out of, but can't escape it. To be honest, I'm not sure that I have escaped it.*

> *But if the Gospel of Mark is correct, and this Jesus of yours can order these spirits around and rescue people from their power, then I hope you have enough faith in your Savior to get His help.*
>
> *And, Tom, while you're at it, please put in a good word for me.*

Destroyer's spirits were laughing themselves silly as they fluttered out of the courthouse.

The judge rose, everyone in the courtroom rose, and then she went out, leaving the ACFA attorneys feeling pretty cocky while Wayne and Tom could only stand there with their mouths open.

Corrigan was so upset he could hardly keep his voice down as he muttered to Tom, "We are absolutely going to appeal this one. I've never seen a more obvious, ludicrous breach of justice or denial of due process in my career!"

Tom didn't know whether to have hope, or put up a fight, or give it up, or go home and die, or what. "Okay. If you think that will work."

"I don't know if it will work or not, the way these courts are getting so stacked, but we might have better luck with a different judge. Ultimately, it has no bearing on the decision to appeal. I'd be as remiss as the judge if I didn't appeal her decision. Come on, let's get out of here."

Just outside the courtroom, Wendell Ames was basking in the floodlights and catering to the microphones as he delivered a prepared statement to the press. "We are certainly gratified that a person of the stature of Judge Fletcher acknowledges that children of tender years still need protection from admitted child abusers, even in a court of law . . ."

"That's all," said Corrigan. With a sudden, uncharacteristic anger, he forced his way right into the circle of reporters. "Gentlemen and ladies, I will have a statement for you as soon as Mr. Ames has completed his statement."

He got their attention right away. They were hungry. They flooded him with questions, many of them quite loaded.

He brushed all the questions aside and said what he

wanted to say. "First of all, to correct Mr. Ames, this case centers on constitutionally guaranteed freedom of religion and not on child abuse. No admissions of any kind have been made, and try to get that right when you run your stories. If spanking is child abuse, then let's put half the country in jail right now!

"Secondly, seeing as the attorneys for the plaintiff continually insist on trying this case in the press, let me just throw this into the mill for your consideration: a) Everything we've heard in this case has been filtered through Amber's mother and the attorney-appointed child psychologist, Dr. Mandanhi, and we insist we have the right to confront our accuser, who is Amber, and just get to the truth. b) We do not intend to be harsh toward Amber or abuse her in any way. We will accept reasonable restrictions, and we will work with the judge and with the plaintiff's attorneys accordingly.

"Now, as to this ruling of Judge Fletcher: it is clearly erroneous and absolutely contrary to the law, and we have no choice but to appeal to the Court of Appeals without delay. Now try not to edit that too much."

With that, and with more questions still being hollered at them, Corrigan and Tom hurried down the hall to the elevators.

Back in Bacon's Corner, little Amber Brandon was giddy and laughing when she got off the school bus, and had been so disruptive on the bus that the driver was only minutes from writing her a discipline slip to give to her mother. But Amber's stop came first, and so the driver was satisfied with just getting Amber and her playmates off the bus.

Her playmates were used to seeing Amber acting like a pony, and some had even played the pretend game with her. But today Amethyst was not a fun pony to play with. She pushed her friends, she teased them, she stole their books and threw them about, she jumped, pranced, somersaulted, and mocked them.

All Amber's friends went home angry at her, vowing never to play with her again.

But Amethyst just kept laughing and prancing, and she didn't care a bit.

It was definitely time to get all the team together. That evening, Mark and Cathy opened up the church and the core group gathered—the Howards, Ben and Bev Cole, Marshall and Kate Hogan, Tom Harris, and Wayne Corrigan—along with the elders, Don Heely, Vic Savan, Jack and Doug Parmenter, and their wives. Push had come to shove. God was moving in their hearts and they could all feel the threat from outside; it was time to do some serious business with the Lord.

They sat in a close circle on the pews and some pulled-up chairs at the front of the sanctuary, ready to compare notes, talk it out, pray it through.

"I figured we should meet here tonight," said Mark. "This seems to be the center of Satan's attention right now, the center of his attacks. We need to pray a hedge around this place."

"Let's meet the enemy!" said Ben.

"It's high time we did!" said Jack.

Mark smiled, encouraged. "I want to tell you, the battle is getting thick out there!"

"So how did your deposition go last week?" Doug Parmenter asked.

Mark sighed; Corrigan rolled his eyes a bit. Mark answered, "Ames and Jefferson are laying a trap of some kind, that's obvious. They were just so kind and yet . . ."

Corrigan completed the thought. "They were trying to milk Mark for anything they could find to use against him, to set him up for a fall." He looked at Mark. "I think you did all right, though, pastor. You came out squeaky clean, and they didn't like that."

"Well, praise the Lord for that. 'He who walks in integrity walks securely.'"

"Right on," said Bev.

Mark turned to Corrigan again. "Wayne, since we're on the

subject, why don't you tell all of us what's next in the legal process?"

Corrigan looked a little tired and depressed. "Well, of course, Tom and Mrs. Fields are scheduled for depositions in the next few weeks. But in the meantime, we're going to appeal today's ruling to the Court of Appeals, and then we'll have to wait and see. We may not win there either, but at least it will buy us a little more time. Mind you, this is just a minor detail in the whole lawsuit, only one little skirmish in a long and costly war." He looked at Marshall. "We'll have to hope that something else breaks in this case. It just feels like we're so close!"

"How about that curriculum?" asked Kate. "I'm convinced now that the school system isn't going to let us see it without some real legal pressure. They're stalling."

Corrigan nodded. "I wouldn't be surprised if they were hoping they can outlast the court system and hide that curriculum until we're already in court. Well, with today's ruling and the appeal process starting, that's going to be hard to do. I'll definitely issue a subpoena for that curriculum tomorrow."

"As far as something else breaking," said Marshall, "we just might have it, or a part of it, or an inkling of how we might track down a corner of a part of it. I'm talking about the curse put on the church this morning."

Bob Heely asked, "Did you go to the police about that?"

Ben replied, "Are you kidding? I'm about 90 percent sure that Mulligan's in on this thing! Those goat legs came from Sally Roe's goat, and you know how Mulligan's been covering up that attempt to murder her. He's got to be a part of this curse too, or at least helping whoever it was that did it."

Jack Parmenter had to ask, "Are you really sure about that?"

Marshall stepped in. "Not yet. But the point I'm making is that now we have concrete evidence that there's some witchcraft or Satanism in the area, some organized, heavier form of occultism like a coven, a secret society, whatever. And that means there are people—and I mean normal-looking, everyday people you'd never suspect—that belong to this group. And in a town this size, they can pull a lot of weight and intimidate a lot of people. Mulligan and Parnell the coroner might be under the control of these people, or they might belong to the group themselves.

"But don't miss this point: Whoever these people are, they've clearly spelled out that this church and Sally Roe have something in common: we are their enemies, and they mean to do us harm. They killed Sally's goat and drained its blood, probably for use in their ceremonies. Now that's a contact point for them, something that belonged to the person they want to curse. They took off the legs and left the front ones here at the church. That includes us in the curse they've leveled at Sally Roe. I'm guessing that the hind legs are still with the witches somewhere as a contact point at their end."

"Why the legs?" asked Corrigan.

Marshall guessed, "Well, you can't run far without them, and right now Sally Roe is running, I'm sure of that."

Tom's wheels were turning rapidly. "So there are your moles again, Marshall! They've tried to put Sally Roe and us under the same curse; so even though we can't see it yet, there has to be a connection: Sally Roe has something to do with our situation, with this case, and they know it."

"You've got it."

Corrigan clenched his fists and looked toward Heaven with mock drama. "Oh, if only we could prove all this! If only we knew who these weird people are!"

"I don't know about you, but I have some suspects," said Marshall. "We would do well to take some careful second looks at Sergeant Mulligan and Joey Parnell. They've been close to this whole Sally Roe thing, and we know Parnell is scared spitless right now."

Ben was more blunt. "Parnell's in it, no doubt."

"And I'll even throw in Irene Bledsoe, the CPD lady, as a suspect. She's working with the whole Brandon/ACFA camp, and she's being anything but objective."

"Oh, man, I hope not!" said Tom.

"How're the kids?"

"I saw them on Friday. They're hanging in there. The foster home sounds pretty rough, but at least they're not in Bledsoe's daily care. A witch taking care of my kids, that's all I need!"

"And there might be still another suspect," said Mark. They turned to hear who, but he fell silent and thoughtful, exchanging a look with Cathy. "How do we know that one of these witches, or Satanists, or whatever they are, hasn't come right into this church? We've been having no end of trouble, and I've never seen so much division as long as I've pastored here."

Cathy added, "I feel that we do have some kind of poison working directly among us, no question."

"It does happen," said Marshall. "They do infiltrate churches; they know all the Christian lingo, they know the Bible, they make it a serious business to pass for Christians and stir things up from the inside."

That stopped them all cold. Suddenly they found themselves looking at each other like all the suspects in a "whodunit." It was a downright creepy feeling.

Jack asked Mark and Cathy, "Any idea who?"

Mark shook his head. Cathy answered, "No . . . but listen: we have one. We have a demonic mole in this church. I just feel that from the Lord."

Marshall nodded. "That's a distinct possibility."

They pondered that for only a moment, and then, without a further word, Mark slid from his chair and sank to his knees right there. The others did the same. It was spontaneous. They knew what they had to do.

"O Lord God, have mercy," Mark prayed. "Where we have sinned, forgive us. Grant us wisdom to know what we're doing wrong, and repentance from that wrong. Have mercy on us, Lord God, and restore us."

His prayer continued, and the others prayed right along with him. Tears started to flow, unbridled weeping before the Lord.

Ben prayed, "Lord, help us to sort this whole thing out.

Protect us from our enemies, and give us a victory for what's right."

"We pray for all the children," said Cathy. "This is their battle too, maybe even more than ours. Satan wants our kids, and we just can't let him have them."

Mark declared, "We just pray now for a hedge of angelic warriors to surround this place and guard it. Surround Your people, Lord, and protect us all from any curses leveled against us. We plead the shed blood of Jesus over ourselves, our ministry, our children, the school . . ."

"Protect Ruth and Josiah," prayed Tom. "O Lord, please protect my kids."

"Bring an answer, Lord," said Marshall. "We have enough hunches and theories to fill a warehouse, but we need an answer, something solid, something positive, and we need it fast. Please break through the walls the enemy has put up; break through, Lord God, and bring us an answer."

"And, Lord," said Jack, "if there is an invader in our church, a demonic mole, we just put chains on that person right now, we bind the demons associated with him or her, and we ask, Lord, that this person be exposed."

Outside the church, Nathan and Armoth set up the hedge, a regiment of the best warriors available for the job, all standing shoulder to shoulder around the church property, swords ready, alert, ready for a fight.

Tal was pleased with this little bit of progress. "That should hold things together for a while. Now to root out that mole!"

"It looks like we'll be ready," said Nathan, regarding the prayers from the people inside the church.

"Of course," said Tal. "And it was nice of Destroyer to get so reckless. He's exposed the breach we needed!"

thirty-three

I† was Tuesday morning and the *Ashton Clarion* was out on the stands, in the grocery stores, and on the front porches all over town. That used to mean it would be a little calmer around the *Clarion* office; Cheryl the cub reporter could relax and catch up on advertising clients, Tom the paste-up man could go fishing or work at home in his yard, and George the typesetter could sleep in.

Well, this Tuesday things were a little different. The *Clarion*'s tough, whip-cracking editor was gone on an assignment—he never was clear about its exact nature—but that didn't mean there would be any vacation. Actually, because Marshall was such a hard worker, it meant more work than before, and Bernice Krueger, now filling Marshall's shoes, could be just as tough, demanding, and efficient as her boss.

So, Tuesday was rolling along at a brisk pace, everyone was there, hard at work, and Bernice never seemed to be in one room or chair for any more than two minutes at one time. With papers, galleys, or a cup of coffee in her hand, she was constantly running to the front to check a traffic revision story Cheryl was trying to get out of the county road crew, then charging to the back with more copy for George to typeset, then running into Marshall's glass-enclosed office to answer phone calls, then running up to the front desk to wait on a customer because Cheryl was busy taking an ad over the phone.

I am going to visit with Betty Smith, Bernice kept telling herself. *So help me, when my lunch comes, or before that, or during break, or sometime, I'm going to sit down and visit with her; she must think I'm so rude, inviting her here just to ignore her!*

But so far "Betty Smith" was not feeling slighted or snubbed. She was sitting in the teletype room, watching the news stories come clattering in over the news wire. For the last half-hour it had been interesting—for the last few minutes it had been riveting. She now held a particular news story in her hand, and she was devouring the news.

"WESTHAVEN—Federal District Judge Emily R. Fletcher today ruled that a ten-year-old child, key witness in the much publicized Good Shepherd Academy child abuse case, would not be required to testify or be examined by defense psychologists, agreeing with the plaintiff's attorneys that such further questioning and examining of the child could prove harmful.

"Citing expert evaluations offered by psychologist Dr. Alan Mandanhi, Judge Fletcher concluded that the mental state of the child is in such a tender and vulnerable state because of the alleged abuses that any further recounting of them would do even greater damage.

"'We are here to speak for the children,' she said, 'and protect them from abuse. We cannot justify even further abuse in the cause of preventing it.'"

Several daily newspapers from around the country lay ready on the table for Bernice's perusal when she got the chance. Sally reached for the one on the top of the stack, a large newspaper from the West Coast. She found nothing about the case on the front page, but the second page did carry a story, along with a nonflattering courtroom photograph of Tom Harris and his attorney. The description under the photograph identified them as "alleged child abuser Tom Harris and attorney Wayne Corrigan."

It was all bad news for the Good Shepherd Academy.

She found an editorial in the second newspaper. The ACFA could not have written it better.

"This will be a precedent-setting case, interpreting the Federal Day-care and Private Primary School Assistance Act, and defining whether the state may breach the wall of separation in order to protect innocent children from harm done in the name of religious freedom.

"Freedom of religion is part of our heritage, but freedom of religion does not mean freedom to abuse. It is our hope that this case will establish once and for all a binding legal and social mandate that religious practice, though free, must never violate the laws of the state, but be subject to the state for the good of all."

It sounded so virtuous, so American, so right. But the writer had never met Amber Brandon. None of the journalists across the country had ever looked into those demon eyes and heard that mocking, accusing voice. They'd never been a victim of the wrath and ruination Sally's former associates could dish out. Instead, as if on cue, they were writing, reporting, selecting, and interpreting the same ideas and opinions, as if the same instructor taught them all.

I can't stay here, Sally thought. *I have to move on. I have to finish.*

"Hey, Betty!" It was Bernice, standing in the doorway looking a bit frazzled. "I'm sorry it's such a madhouse around here, but I think I'm caught up for the time being. Are you keeping yourself occupied?"

Sally set the newspaper down. "Oh, I was reading the newspaper and the items coming in over the wire. It's been interesting."

Bernice could tell she was bothered about something. "How are you doing?"

Sally evaded the question. "I think there's a bus leaving in an hour. I need to be on it."

"Moving on so soon?"

"Could I have . . . Would it be okay if I had your address and telephone number? I'd like to be able to contact you later on."

"Sure thing." Bernice wrote it down on a slip of paper.

"Oh, and the *Clarion's* address too?"

Bernice wrote that down as well, and handed it to her. Then she looked for a moment at the trouble in Sally's eyes. "Is there anything else I can do?"

Sally thought for a moment with a timid smile on her face. "Well . . . you could pray for me. You never know, it might work."

Cheryl called from the front, "Bernice, it's Jake's Auto Repair on the phone . . ."

"I'll call them back."

"He's leaving in ten minutes. He needs to talk to you now."

Bernice was obviously frustrated, and looked at Sally apologetically. "Listen, after this call we'll just get out of here. I'll take you to lunch, all right?"

Sally smiled. That was all. "Um . . . is there a Post Office around here?"

"Sure, just two blocks up the street on the right-hand side. It's on the way to the bus station. I can drop you by there."

"Great."

"Give me a second, okay?"

Bernice hurried into Marshall's office and took the call from Jake's Auto Repair. Jake could talk and talk about the same thing over and over as if he had nothing else to do with his time and no one else did either. "Okay, sure, we'll change the ad in Saturday's issue, all right?" He went back to the beginning and started the conversation all over again, and Bernice mouthed the words, "No, listen, you already told me that. We'll take care of it for Friday." He started squawking. "Well, that issue's already out, it's history, we can't change that now." She pounded the desk with her fist. This guy was impossible! "All right, listen, Jake, you know our deadlines just like everybody else; don't give me that! You'll get the change on Friday. Yes, that's a guarantee. Hey, didn't you tell Cheryl you had to leave in ten minutes? You're late. Goodbye."

She hung up and bolted from the office, grabbing her coat. "Okay, Betty, let's get out of here! Betty?"

She went into the teletype room. Betty was gone. She stepped into the hall. "Cheryl?"

"Yo!"

"Where's Betty?"

"She left."

That stung. Bernice's first question to herself was, *What did I do? Oh brother, it's what I didn't do! That poor gal. I don't blame her. I shouldn't have invited her into this madhouse!*

She dashed out to the street, but Betty Smith was nowhere in sight. Bernice's initial thought was to run after her, or get the car and try to find her, but then that thought melted away as a more practical one took its place: *This is probably the way she wants it. It's just the way she is, poor thing. Oh well. Maybe she'll write or call sometime.*

Maybe. Bernice felt terrible.

She went back inside.

Tom came out from the back room. "Say, what about that ad for Jake? Cheryl says you talked to him."

"We're rewording it. Cheryl has the new copy, so tell George to set it right away."

"All right. But what about that aluminum can drive? Are you sure you want that on page 3?"

Bernice kept moving down the hall, her mind occupied. "Change Jake's ad first, and then I'll take a look at page 3."

"Well, I need to know—"

"Just give me a second, will you?"

Tom turned on his heels and headed toward the back again. Bernice ducked into the teletype room knowing she owed Tom an apology.

She plopped into the chair Betty Smith had sat in, and took just a moment to pray. *Lord, I could have done better. I could have given her my time. I should have done more to tell her about You . . . Doggone! What a lousy way for this to end!*

Her eye caught the wire copy lying on the table, an item from Westhaven . . .

Westhaven? She snatched up the wire copy and scanned it. Yes. It was the latest news on the Good Shepherd Academy case in Bacon's Corner!

The warrior Triskal stood in the teletype room with her, just watching. He had his orders, and now the time was right. He gently touched her eyes.

Okay, Bernice. Time for you to see.

Bernice saw the newspaper opened to the editorial page. She saw the editorial. Good Shepherd Academy. Bacon's Corner.

Betty had been reading about that case! Is this why she

seemed so troubled, so secretive? A lone woman, traveling, elusive . . .

It was like a stab through the heart. Hadn't Marshall told her about some woman they were trying to find?

She bolted from the room and dashed into Marshall's office.

Bev Cole turned off her vacuum cleaner and answered the phone. "Hello?"

Bernice was frantic. "Is this the Cole residence?"

"Yes, it is."

"Is Marshall Hogan there? This is his assistant at the *Ashton Clarion*, Bernice Krueger."

"Oh, he's out right now. I can have him call you."

"Well, who am I talking to?"

"This is Bev Cole."

"Do you know anything about the Good Shepherd Academy case?"

"Oh boy, do I!"

"What about that woman that's missing? Do you know anything about that?"

"Oh, you mean Sally Roe?"

Bernice recognized the name. "Yes! That's the one! Do you know what she looks like?"

Bev stumbled a bit on that one. "Well . . . we've never met her in person. All we have is a bunch of police and newspaper photos, and they aren't very good . . ."

"Does she have long, black hair?"

"No, I think her hair's red."

"What about her age?"

"I think she's about thirty-six now."

"Can you send me those pictures?"

"You want me to mail them to you?"

"Can you fax them? I need them right *now*."

Bev was getting flustered. "Well, the only fax machine is down at Judy's Secretarial, and Ben's gone with the car."

Bernice gave Bev the *Clarion's* fax number. "Get them to

me right away, as soon as you can, all right? Send me everything you have on her. And have Marshall call me."

"Hey, what's happening over there?"

"I've got to go. Please get that stuff to me!"

"Okay, you've got it."

Bernice hung up and then ran into the front office. "Cheryl, get your keys! We've got to find Betty!"

Cheryl half-rose from her desk, still wondering what was going on. "What . . ."

Bernice grabbed her purse and dug for her own keys. "You go down to the bus station and see if she's there. I'll check at the Post Office. If you find her, stall her and call my pager."

Cheryl got up and grabbed her coat. She had no idea what this was all about, but Bernice was so frantic, it had to be important.

Lucy Brandon unlocked her front door and stood back to make sure Amber went inside. "Go ahead, Amber." No response. "Amethyst, go inside, and quietly."

Amethyst complied, moving rather stiffly, a pout on her face. She went to the stairway in the front entry and sat down on the first step, her chin in her hands. Then she glared at Amber's mother as Lucy closed the door and hung up her coat.

"How dare you bring me home!" she said finally in a low, seething voice.

Lucy was angry enough by now to directly face this creature. "I had to, and you know it! Miss Brewer refused to have you in the class anymore."

Amethyst bared Amber's teeth in an animal-like snarl. "She knows not what she wants! First I was invited, and now I am rejected! Miss Brewer is a turncoat and a fool!"

Lucy bent low over Amethyst and spoke directly to her. "And you are a filthy, destructive, disrespectful little imp!"

Amethyst snarled at her.

Lucy slapped her soundly across the face. "Don't you snarl at me, you little monster!"

But Amethyst began to laugh a fiendish laugh. "Why are you slapping your *daughter*?"

Lucy wilted a little. She didn't know what to do. "I want you to get out of my daughter. I want you to leave her alone!"

Amethyst smiled haughtily. "Your daughter is mine. She invited me in, and now I have her. She is mine." Then she pointed her finger right in Lucy's face. "And you are mine as well! You will do as I say!"

Lucy felt a terrible rage and even raised her hand, but had to stop.

Amethyst taunted her. "Go ahead. Slap her again."

"No! You won't do this to us!" She called, "Amber! Amber, wake up! Amber, answer me!"

"She can't hear you."

A formula, a tradition from Lucy's past, came to her mind. "In the name of Jesus Christ, I command you to come out of her!"

Amethyst raised her eyebrows in mock horror. "Oh, now you're throwing that name around! Ha! What is He to you?"

Lucy didn't know why she grabbed Amber's body. It was an unthinking, desperate act. She was trying to find her daughter in that little body somewhere. "Amber!"

SMACK! Lucy stumbled backward, her hand to her face, stunned. Like a wild animal escaping from a cage, Amethyst bolted from the hallway. Blood trickled from Lucy's nose; she dug in her pocket for a handkerchief as she ran around the corner into the dining room, bumped against the table, recovered, went through the kitchen doorway. She could hear silverware rattling to her right.

Amethyst had opened the cutlery drawer. Amber was holding a knife to her own throat. "Stop or I'll—"

But this was Amber's mother, wild with rage and maternal instinct. Lucy clamped onto the arm holding that knife and jerked it away with such force that Amber's entire body came up from the floor as Amethyst screamed. Lucy slammed into the counter behind her, bruising her spine. The hand would not release the knife.

The drawer flew open; butcher knives, steak knives, utensils all shot across the kitchen and clattered against the opposite cupboard doors.

Amethyst snarled, cursed, spit in Lucy's face. Her strength was incredible.

Lucy worked the knife loose. It fell away, hung in midair, spun, came at Lucy point-first.

"Aaww, Mommy!" came Amber's voice.

Lucy spun away as the knife went past her and dug into the dining room carpet. She fell to the floor with Amber still in her arms.

Amber screamed a long, anguished scream of terror. "Mommy . . . Mommy!"

Lucy held her tightly. The blood was still dripping from Lucy's nose. She wiped it away with her hand.

"Mommy . . ."

"I love you, Amber." Lucy wept in pain and fear. "I'm right here, honey. I have you."

"Mommy, why do I do bad things?"

"It's not you, sweetheart. It's not you."

"I don't know why I'm bad!"

Lucy held her tightly. For now, she had her daughter back. "Shhh. It wasn't you. It wasn't you."

Bernice and Cheryl returned to the office two hours later with nothing to show for their frenzied efforts. Bernice had checked with the Post Office, but the clerk on duty knew nothing of any strange woman coming through; another clerk may have seen her, but was now gone for lunch. Cheryl searched the bus station and even waited for the mysterious Betty Smith to appear, but there was no sign of her. There was, however, an eastbound bus that left only moments before Cheryl got there. Both ladies had searched up and down the streets between the *Clarion* and the bus depot, but Betty Smith/Sally Roe was gone.

As soon as Bernice came in the door, Tom and George were full of questions.

Bernice talked as she hung up her coat. "Paste Jake's ad on page 4 and shove over the Insurance box; just yank those personals and put them alongside the classifieds this time. Go to twelve point instead of sixteen for that notice, and change 'howl' to 'bark,' we'll get a pun out of it."

"Yeah," said George, "I thought of that."

They were content for now. Bernice checked the fax machine, nestled against the wall in the front office, next to the photocopier. They'd received a transmission—the long ream of paper poured out of the machine and lapped upon itself several times on the floor. She carefully tore it off and then found the first page.

Cheryl was there to see it too. There, looking vacantly over her ID number in a police photo, was Betty Smith, alias Sally Beth Roe.

"I'd better call Marshall," Bernice said in a weak voice. "He's going to love me for this."

Cheryl asked, "What about Sara Barker? Sally Roe stayed in her boarding house. Maybe she knows something about Sally's plans."

"Call her."

Bernice contacted the Cole residence in Bacon's Corner. Ben Cole was there this time.

"Did you get that fax?" he asked.

"Yes, Ben, thank you very much, and thank Bev too. I need to talk to Marshall."

"Well, he's still out, hunting for information."

"Well, I have some for him. Have him call me, will you? I'll either be at the *Clarion* office or at home."

At the elementary school, Mr. Woodard was all smiles and pleasant as he handed the *Finding the Real Me* curriculum across the office counter to Kate Hogan. "There. Actually, a subpoena wasn't necessary. I know we would have found it sooner or later."

"Well, it never hurts to jog somebody's memory a little," said Kate. "Thanks a lot."

She hurried to her car, the thick binder under her arm. That she actually had possession of this document was almost beyond believing. Now the question was, would it answer any questions or confirm any hunches?

As soon as she got into her car, she flipped the curriculum open to the title page.

The publisher: Omega Center for Educational Studies, Fairwood, Massachusetts.

The title: *Finding the Real Me: Self-Esteem and Personal Fulfillment Studies for Fourth-Graders.*

The authors: Dee Danworth and Marian Newman.

She read every word on the title page, and quickly skimmed the introductory pages for any leads, anything that might tie in Sally Roe. So far, nothing.

Well . . . if it was there, she was going to find it. She started the car, and headed back to the Coles' house.

When Bernice called Hank Busche, she was close to tears. "She was right here, Hank, right under my nose, and I didn't see it; it never occurred to me! Her life is in danger, and we could've helped her, and I let her get away!"

Hank was just as shocked and dismayed. "It's incredible. I talked to her when I was over at Barkers', and I could feel a tug from the Lord then. I just knew she was here with a real need."

"We've just got to pray that we find her, that she writes to me or calls or *something!*"

"I'll get on the phone. We'll get something going."

Triskal and Krioni soared high over the town of Ashton, their wings rushing, shedding, rippling, sparkling trails of light. The prayers were beginning all over the town, and the Spirit of God was stirring up even more.

"There now," said Krioni. "This should make a difference in Bacon's Corner!"

"Let's just hope it isn't too late!" said Triskal.

All over Ashton, with one accord, the saints knelt wherever they were—beside their beds, at couches and chairs in living rooms, in a garage next to a jalopy, next to a television that had been turned off for this important moment, over a sink where dishes were soaking in suds. Some were visiting friends, and they all sought the Lord together; school kids paused in their homework to say a quick word; grandparents and relatives across the country joined the prayers by telephone.

They prayed for this woman, this unknown, mysterious, and troubled stranger named Sally Beth Roe. They prayed for her safety and that she would find whatever she was seeking.

Most of all, they prayed that she would turn to God and meet Jesus Christ.

They prayed for a place they'd never heard of before: Bacon's Corner. They sought the Lord on behalf of the believers there, and asked for a real victory in their time of siege and struggle. They bound the demonic spirits in the name of Jesus and by His authority, forbidding them to do any more mischief among those people.

Bernice skipped dinner so she could fast that night. She spent the time sitting on the couch in her apartment, praying and waiting for the phone to ring. It finally did at just about seven o'clock.

"Hello?"

"Bernice, this is Marshall."

"Marshall!" Then Bernice choked up.

"Hello?"

She blurted it out. "Marshall, she was here!"

Marshall knew immediately what Bernice meant, but he didn't want to believe it. "Are we talking about Sally Roe?"

"She was here, Marshall, right here in Ashton!"

"Where is she now?"

Bernice slumped on the couch, heartsick. "I don't know. I didn't know who she was until she left town on the bus. She was staying at Sara Barker's . . ."

Bernice told Marshall everything she knew: how she'd met Sally Roe in church, had lunch with her, and tried to visit with her at the *Clarion*, but just got too busy.

Marshall had to be the most frustrated man in the world right now. Bernice could hear him trying to hide it, trying to remain calm and civil. "We've got to find her, Bernie. We've got to find her."

"I know."

"Did she say anything about the case?"

"She's following it, Marshall. She was reading the wire copy that came in today, and some newspaper stories about it. She seemed pretty upset about that recent ruling."

Marshall paused again. Bernice could just envision him chewing up the phone book. "Well . . . was she coherent?"

"Very coherent, intelligent, articulate. And I think very hungry spiritually. We talked about Jesus and the Cross at lunch on Sunday. She didn't seem to buy into it, but she understood it." Then she added, "But she was elusive about herself. Secretive. She wouldn't talk about herself at all."

"That sounds like every other report I've heard about her. You got those mug shots from Ben?"

"Yes, over the fax. It's her."

"I finally saw the *Finding the Real Me* curriculum today."

"Oh, man, don't tell me . . ."

"I won't. There's no visible connection. But the content is solid confirmation of what Miss Brewer is doing with the kids in the class, along with all the usual humanist, cosmic stuff: collectivism, global consciousness, altered states, relativism . . ."

"All the usual 'isms' . . ."

"But no mention anywhere that Sally Roe had anything to do with it. So we still don't know what this whole attempted murder thing is about, or what Sally Roe has to do with this case, and I've used up a lot of precious time."

"She did get my phone number and address from me."

"No kidding!"

"So there's still hope."

"Yeah, and we've got a lot to hope for. Keep praying."

"Oh, we're all praying for you, Marshall, right now. The whole bunch of believers over here."

"Good! We need something to break, and real soon!"

thirty-four

The prayers reached to Heaven from Ashton, from Bacon's Corner, and everywhere in between, and it was as if the Lord God was waiting for just this moment, just this particular cry from His people. He began to move His sovereign hand.

Tal got the report from a courier in the early hours of Wednesday morning. "Guilo!"

Guilo was at his side in an instant.

Tal's voice was strained with excitement. "The Lord has spoken! She's ready!"

"Praise to the Lord!" said Guilo. "Where? When?"

"She's left Ashton and is almost to Henderson. It'll only be a matter of hours. We'll meet her there with everything we can muster! If we can get her through before Destroyer and his minions find out, we may be able to tip the scales at last!"

Guilo drew his sword with a metallic ring and a flash of light. "A turning point!"

"Mota and Signa will remain here with their warriors ready, watching that breach." Tal smiled for the first time in weeks. "They just might get some real action today!"

> *Dear Tom,*
>
> *I arrived by bus about seven o'clock this morning, and I imagine I'll get a room soon enough. For now, I'm quite comfortable just sitting in Lakeland Park near the city center. The sun is warm, the bench is dry, and the nearby pond is placid and full of ducks.*
>
> *I would not call the city of Henderson an inviting place, but it does have some major advantages: it is a large, metropolitan city, and therefore easy to hide in, and it has an immense downtown library, an excellent place for finding certain information. I'll be going there today, or tomorrow, or whenever I finish a more immediate matter demanding my attention.*

A more immediate matter. Sally was a little surprised at her detached, businesslike tone, as if she were going to type a letter or make a purchase. In reality, she was about to enter into a relationship that could potentially alter the course of her entire life, totally restructure her worldview, and bring into consideration every moral issue, every act, every decision, and every attitude of all her previous years; her deepest scars and emotions, the most personal and guarded areas of her life, would be laid bare. The relationship would be confrontational, perhaps devastating.

At least, that is what she expected from the arrangement, and for that reason she'd pondered the move all through the night, weighing the pros and cons, considering the costs, testing and eliminating the options. It became clear to her that she would have to pay an enormous price in terms of ego and self-will, and that the arrangement would carry with it staggering implications for the future. But every second thought was entertained and answered, every objection received a fair hearing, and in between the fierce and heated debates Sally conducted with herself on the floor of her own mind, she slept on it.

By the time the light of day peeked through the bus windows, she'd settled in her mind that, with all things considered, such a major commitment would be the most logical, practical, and desirable thing to do, with advantages that far outweighed the disadvantages.

It was quiet in the park, with few people around besides a matron walking her poodle and a few yuppies jogging to work. She moved to another bench closer to the pond, out in the full morning sun, and sat down, her duffel bag beside her.

Then she took a good long look at herself. Dressed in her jeans and blue jacket, with a stocking cap on her head and a duffel bag beside her, she looked like a homeless vagabond.

She was.

She looked solitary and lonely.

She was.

She also looked small and insignificant in a very large world, and that carried more weight in her mind than anything else. What must she look like to a God big enough to have created this huge globe on which she was sitting? Like a microbe on a microscope slide? How would He even find her?

Well, all she could do was make some noise, call out to Him, cause a disturbance, send up some verbal flares. Maybe she could catch His eye or His ear.

She placed her notebook in her lap and flipped to a page of notes she had prepared. Now . . . where to start?

She spoke softly, just barely forming the words on her lips. She felt self-conscious and she was willing to admit it. "Uh . . . hello." Maybe He heard her, maybe He didn't. She said it again. "Hello." That should be enough. "I imagine You know who I am, but I'll introduce myself anyway. It just seems the thing to do. My name is Sally Beth Roe, and I guess one refers to You as . . . God. Or maybe Jesus. I've heard that done. Or . . . Lord. I understand You go by several titles, and so I hope You'll indulge me if I grope a bit. It's been a long time since I've tried to pray.

"Uh . . . anyway, I would like to meet with You today, and discuss my life and what possible role You might wish to play in it. And thank You in advance for Your time and attention."

She stared at her notes. She'd gotten this far. Assuming she'd secured God's attention, she proceeded with the next item. "To quickly review what brought this meeting about, I guess You remember our last visit, approximately thirty years ago, at the . . . uh . . . Mount Zion Baptist Church in Yreka, California. I want You to know that I did enjoy our times together back then. I know I haven't said anything about it in quite a while, and I apologize. Those were precious times, and now they're favorite memories. I'm glad for them.

"So I suppose You're wondering what happened, and why I broke off our relationship. Well, I don't remember what happened exactly. I know that the courts gave me back to my mother, and she wasn't about to take me to Sunday school like Aunt Barbara did, and then I went to live in a foster home, and then . . . Well, whatever the case, our times together just didn't continue, and that's all . . . Well, I guess it's water under the bridge . . ."

Sally paused. Was there some kind of awakening happening inside her? God could hear her. She could sense it; she just knew it somehow. That was strange. It was something new.

"Well . . ." Now she lost her train of thought. "I think I do sense that You're listening to me, so I want to thank You for that." She got her thoughts back again. "Oh, anyway, I guess I was an angry young woman, and maybe I blamed You for my sorrows, but . . . at any rate, I decided that I could take care of myself, and that's basically the way it went for most of my life. I'm sure You know the story: I tried atheism, and then humanism with a strong dose of evolution thrown in, and that left me empty and made my life meaningless; so then I tried cosmic humanism and mysticism, and that was good for many years of aimless delusions and torment and, to be honest, the mess I'm in right now, including the fact that I'm a convicted felon. You know all about that."

Okay, Sally, now where do you go from here? You may as well get to the point.

"Well, anyway, I guess what I'm trying to say is that Bernice, back in Ashton, was right, at least as far as Sally Roe is concerned. I have a moral problem. I've read some of the Bible. Uh . . . it's a good book . . . it's a fine piece of work—and I've come to see that You are a God of morals, of ethics, of absolutes. I guess that's what 'holy' means. And actually I'm glad for that, because then we can know where our boundaries are; we can know where we stand . . .

"I'm beating around the bush, I know."

Sally stopped to think. How should she say it? Just what was it she wanted from God?

"I guess . . ." *Oh-oh. Emotion. Maybe this is why I can't get around to it.* "I guess I need to ask You about Your love. I do know it's there; Mrs. Gunderson always talked about it, and so did my Aunt Barbara, and now I've had a brief glimpse of it again in my talks with Bernice and that pastor, Hank the Plumber. I need to know that You'll . . ."

She stopped. Tears were forming in the corners of her eyes. She wiped them away and took some deep breaths. This was supposed to be business, not some emotional, subjective experience she might later doubt.

"Excuse me. This is difficult. There are a lot of years involved, a lot of emotion." Another deep breath. "Anyway, I was trying to say that . . . I would like very much for You to accept me." She stopped and let the tightness in her throat ease. "Because . . . I've been told that You love me, and that You've arranged for all my wrongs, my moral trespasses, to be paid for and forgiven. I've come to understand that Jesus died to pay my penalty, to satisfy Your holy justice. Um . . . I appreciate that. Thank You for that kind of love.

"But I . . . I want to enter into that kind of relationship with You. Somehow. I have wronged You, and I have ignored You, and I have tried to be a god myself, as strange as that may sound to You. I have served other spirits, and I have killed my own offspring, and I've worked so hard to lead so many astray . . ."

The tears were coming again. Oh, well. Considering the subject matter, a few tears would not be inappropriate.

"But if You will have me . . . if You will only accept me, I would be more than willing to hand over to You all that I am, and all that I have, whatever it may be worth." Words from thirty years ago came to her mind, and they captured her feelings perfectly. "Jesus . . ."

She couldn't stop the emotions this time. Her face flushed, her eyes filled, and she was afraid to go on.

But she did go on, even as her voice broke, as tears ran down her cheeks, as her body began to quake. "Jesus . . . I want You to come into my heart. I want You to forgive me. Please forgive me."

She was crying and she couldn't stop. She had to get out of there. She couldn't let anyone see her like this.

She grabbed her duffel bag and hurried away from the pond, turning off the walkway into the nearby trees. Under their sheltering, spring-fresh leaves, she found a small clearing and sank to her knees on the cool, dry ground. With a

413

new freedom that seclusion brought, the heart of stone became a heart of flesh, the deepest cries of that heart became a fountain, and she and the Lord God began to talk about things as the minutes slipped by unnoticed and the world around her became unimportant.

Above, as if another sun had just risen, the darkness opened, and pure, white rays broke through the treetops, flooding Sally Beth Roe with a heavenly light, shining through to her heart, her innermost spirit, obscuring her form with a blinding fire of holiness. Slowly, without sensation, without sound, she settled forward, her face to the ground, her spirit awash with the presence of God.

All around her, like spokes of a wondrous wheel, like beams of light emanating from a sun, angelic blades lay flat upon the ground, their tips turned toward her, their handles extending outward, held in the strong fists of hundreds of noble warriors who knelt in perfect, concentric circles of glory, light, and worship, their heads to the ground, their wings stretching skyward like a flourishing, animated garden of flames. They were silent, their hearts filled with a holy dread.

As in countless times past, in countless places, with marvelous, inscrutable wonder, the Lamb of God stood among them, the Word of God, and more: the final Word, the end of all discussion and challenge, the Creator and the Truth that holds all creation together—most wondrous of all, and most inscrutable of all, the *Savior*, a title the angels would always behold and marvel about, but which only mankind could know and understand.

He had come to be the Savior of this woman. He knew her by name; and speaking her name, He touched her.

And her sins were gone.

A rustling began in the first row of angels, then in the next, and then, like a wave rushing outward, the silken wings from row upon row of warriors caught the air, raising a roar, and lifted the angels to their feet. The warriors held their swords Heavenward, a forest of fiery blades, and began to shout in tumultuous joy, their voices rumbling and shaking the whole spiritual realm.

Guilo, as brilliantly glorified as ever he was, took his place above them all, and swept his sword about in burning arcs as he shouted, "Worthy is the Lamb!"

"Worthy is the Lamb!" the warriors thundered.

"Worthy is the Lamb!" Guilo shouted more loudly.

"Worthy is the Lamb!" they all answered.

"For He was slain!"

"For He was slain!"

Guilo pointed his sword at Sally Beth Roe, prostrate, her face to the ground, still communing with her newfound Savior. "And with His blood He has purchased for God the woman, Sally Beth Roe!"

The swords waved, and their light pierced the darkness as lightning pierces the night. "He has purchased Sally Beth Roe!"

"Worthy is the Lamb who was slain," Guilo began, and then they all sang the words together with voices that shook the earth, "to receive power and wealth and wisdom and strength and honor and glory and praise!"

Then came another roar, from voices and from wings, and another flashing of hundreds of swords. The wings took hold, and the skies filled with warriors, swirling, shouting, cheering, worshiping, their light washing over the earth for miles around.

Miles away, some of Destroyer's demons covered their eyes against the blinding light.

"Oh no!" said one. "Another soul redeemed!"

"One of our prisoners set free!" wailed another.

A quick, sharp-eyed spy returned from taking a closer look. "Who is it this time?" they asked.

The spirit answered, "You will not like the news!"

Tal and Guilo embraced, jumping, spinning, laughing.

"Saved! Sally Beth Roe is saved! Our God has her at last!"

They remained, along with their warriors, keeping the

hedge about her strong and brilliant, making sure her conference with the Lord would proceed undisturbed.

Time passed, of course, but no one seemed to notice or care.

Later—she didn't know how much later—Sally pressed her palms against the earth and slowly lifted herself to a sitting position, brushing dry leaves and humus from her clothes and using a handkerchief to wipe her face. She had been through an uncanny, perfectly marvelous experience, and the effect still lingered. A change, a deep, personal, moral restoration had taken place, not just in her subjective perceptions, but in fact. This was something new, something truly extraordinary.

"So this must be what they mean by 'getting saved,'" she said aloud.

Things were different. The Sally Roe who first ducked into these woods was not the same Sally Roe that now sat in the leaves, a trembling, awestruck, tear-stained, happy mess.

Before, she had felt lost and aimless. Now she felt secure, safe in God's hands.

Before, her life had no meaning. Now it did, with even more purpose and meaning yet to be discovered.

Before, she had been oppressed and laden with guilt. Now she was cleansed. She was free. She was forgiven.

Before, she was so alone. Now she had a Friend closer than any other.

As for her old friends, her tormentors . . .

Outside that hedge, thrown there like garbage into a dumpster, Despair, Death, Insanity, Suicide and Fear sulked in the bushes, unable to return. They looked at each other, ready to squabble should any one of them dare to say the first word.

They were out. Vanquished. Through. Just like that. Somehow, she'd no sooner become a child of God than she began to assert her rights and authority as such. She didn't say a lot, she didn't make it flowery. She simply ordered them out of her life.

"She learns fast," said Despair.

The others spit at him just for saying it.

"This is marvelous," she said to herself, chuckling in amazement and ecstasy. "Just marvelous!"

Tal and Guilo were watching, enjoying every moment.

"'The word of her testimony and the blood of the Lamb,'" said Tal.

Guilo nodded. "That's two."

"Captain Tal!" came a shout. A courier dropped from the sky like a meteor, snapping his wings open just in time to alight directly in front of Tal. "Mota sends word from Bacon's Corner! The prayers have brought a breakthrough! They've opened the breach, sir! They're ready to expose Broken Birch!"

Tal laughed with excitement. "Well enough! The kindling is stacked, and"—he looked at Sally—"we now have the match to start the brushfire! Nathan and Armoth!"

"Captain!" they replied.

"Sally's ready. Follow her from here on, and be sure Krioni and Triskal are warned to secure Ashton from invasion. When she lights the brushfire, sound the signal for Mota and Signa in Bacon's Corner."

"Done!"

"Cree and Si, establish your armies at the Omega Center. When the fire reaches there, send it on to Bentmore."

They were gone immediately.

"Chimon and Scion, prepare armies at Bentmore; be ready to send the fire on to Summit."

They soared away.

Tal turned to the courier. "Tell Mota and Signa that they have the prayer cover and can proceed closing the trap. After that, have them wait for the signal from Nathan and Armoth."

The courier flew off with the message.

Tal put a brotherly hand on Guilo's shoulder. "Guilo, the Strength of Many, it's time to position the armies at the Summit Institute!"

"YAHAAA!" Guilo roared, raising his sword for the other warriors to see. "Done!"

Tal unfurled his wings with the sound of a crashing ocean wave. He raised his sword high, and they all did the same so that Lakeland Park was flooded with the flickering light. "For the saints of God and for the Lamb!"

"For the saints of God and for the Lamb!"

Mota got the word from Tal, and not too soon. He and Signa were just then hiding in the ventilation ducts at the Bergen Door Factory, looking for an opportunity to throw a wrench into Destroyer's clever, unseen assault on the saints of Bacon's Corner.

Signa was pointing out supervisor Abby Grayson, moving among the router tables with her ever-present clipboard in hand, just keeping things running smoothly as she had done for the last twenty years. "They've never brought their intrigues and manipulations into this place, at least not so much as to be seen. Abby has no idea what's been happening."

Just then, a pimple-faced youth came down the main aisle through the plant, catching a few stares from some of the workers and looking very uncomfortable.

"All right," said Mota, "here we go. Hopefully Abby's going to have her eyes opened."

"Come on, Abby. Pay attention."

The kid walked up to Abby looking hesitant, embarrassed, but determined to have an audience with her. No voices could be heard above the roar of the machinery, but Abby's lips weren't too hard to read: "So what can I do for you, Kyle?"

Come on, said Signa. *Tell her.*

Two angels immediately stood by Kyle Krantz's side, dressed like factory workers—the people couldn't see them, but any demons might. Kyle—wayward, oft-busted, former pot-smoking Kyle—needed all the encouragement he could get. He was just plain scared.

Come on . . . Mota urged.

Kyle leaned close to Abby's ear and said what he had to say

before he lost his nerve completely. Abby seemed a little puzzled, maybe even shocked at his words.

"Let's get inside my office," she said.

The two angels looked up toward the ventilation ducts and gave strong, affirmative nods.

"Done!" said Mota.

"Better surround that office. Those two need to talk!" Signa added.

Only an hour later, Abby Grayson gave Ben Cole a call from her little office cubicle. Ben could still hear the muffled noise of the factory in the background.

"Well hi, Abby! This is a pleasant surprise."

"Oh, this crazy world's full of surprises. I heard you were fired. Is that true?"

The question seemed rather blunt, but very much like Abby. "Well, yes, it is. It's a long story . . ."

"I'm going to make it longer. I've just heard some information you ought to know."

Ben sat down on the sofa. "Go ahead."

"I just had a long talk with Kyle Krantz—remember him? You've busted him a few times for carrying pot."

"Yeah, right."

"He was working here and doing all right until he got fired yesterday. The word among the supervisors was that he was peddling drugs around the plant, and we have strict rules about any of that stuff, so out the door he went. But he got brave and came to see me today, and . . . Well, normally I wouldn't believe him, but considering everything else that's happened, maybe this time I do." She hesitated.

Ben figured he'd better make it easier for her. "Hey, don't worry. I'm with you so far."

"Well, Ben . . ." She had to build up the nerve to ask it. "What would you say if I told you that we have some witches in town, and some even working here in this plant?"

Ben sat up straight, his whole body full of attention. "I would be very interested to know about that."

"So you don't think it's crazy? I did say *witches*."

Ben's memory still carried vivid scenes of a goat dismembered and its two front legs crossed and bloody on the front steps of the church. "No, Abby. We've seen quite a few strange things lately. I don't think it's crazy at all."

"Then maybe you'd better hear what Kyle has to say. Will you be free after four o'clock?"

Does a duck swim? "You just name the place."

thirty-five

I**t** was about four-thirty, and there was a cold wind blowing across the long-neglected, weed-infested fields of the old Benson farm. The white paint on the farmhouse was turning a gritty gray and beginning to peel like a sunburn; the windows were broken out, the shakes on the roof were beginning to splinter away in the wind; the apple and pear trees in the front yard were blossoming, but now reached skyward in a wild profusion of unpruned trunks and unsightly suckers. The Benson farm had been deserted too long and was simply not surviving, but fading steadily into decay and ruin with every passing season.

A heavy chain blocked the driveway, and Marshall could drive the Buick no further. A NO TRESPASSING sign hung from the chain and swung forward and backward in the wind, right above the Buick's grill.

"Is this the place?" he asked.

Kyle Krantz, the young delinquent who couldn't seem to stay out of trouble, sat in the seat beside him, nodding his head and looking scared. In the backseat, Abby Grayson and Ben Cole looked at the dismal scene before them, and found it easy to believe what Kyle had told them about it.

Kyle pointed. "That's the barn right back there. That's where it was."

"I take it they were trespassing, just like you were?" asked Marshall.

Kyle had grown dull toward such loaded statements. "They were here, man."

Marshall looked at the others. "So, I guess we'll have to trespass too."

They got out of the car and took a moment to look the place over. As near as they could tell, they were the only living beings here. There were no sounds except for the wind and the occasional cheep of the swallows nesting under the eaves of the farmhouse.

Marshall ducked under the chain, and the others followed. The driveway wound around the farmhouse, went past a garage and toolshed, then opened into a wide, graveled area in back—a turnaround and access for farm machinery, supplies, and livestock that were no longer there. On the far side of this open area stood the old gray barn, weathered but intact, the main doors shut.

"Just what were you doing here anyway?" Marshall asked the boy.

"Billy and I were looking for a good place to have a kegger. We always do that 'cause we find good spots no one knows about."

"So this barn must have looked pretty inviting."

"Yeah, back then it did. Now it doesn't."

"How did you manage to get this close without anyone seeing you?"

"It was dark, and we snuck in around the other side of the house. They weren't watching for us anyway; they were too busy doing all their weird stuff."

They reached the doors.

"Have you ever gone inside?"

"No way. Billy and I just wanted to get out of here, and that's all."

The big door swung open with a long, aged creak. The inside of the barn was cool, dim, and expansive. No one entered. Marshall was waiting for his eyes to grow accustomed to the low light.

Finally they could all make out the dirt floor. It seemed plain enough—just smooth dirt. They saw nothing out of the ordinary. They looked at Kyle. He was immediately uneasy and defensive.

"I saw it, man. They were here."

"Okay," said Marshall, "show us what you saw."

Kyle went into the center of the floor and turned in a circle, his finger extended out and toward the floor. "They had a big circle carved in the dirt right here, and a big pentagram in the middle of it." Then he pointed to a spot toward the back wall. "There was a big bench there, like an altar, and there was blood on it, and there were about twenty people standing all around the circle with robes on and hoods over their heads, and they were all chanting and shouting, and there were candles around the circle. They had candles at all the points of the pentagram."

Marshall looked around the barn. "What cracks did you and Billy look through to see all this?"

Kyle pointed to the side of the barn. "Right over there."

The daylight was now plainly visible through two large spaces between some loose boards. Marshall went to where the cracks were, crouched down to their level, and looked back. He was satisfied—the cracks provided a wide, clear view of the area in question.

"You say they had hoods on their heads?"

"Yeah. Black robes and hoods, and they were barefoot."

"So how do you know who they were?"

"'Cause some of them were facing this way. I could see their faces turned right at me." Kyle was offended and edgy. "I don't know why you don't believe me!"

Marshall held up his hand to calm the boy. "Hey, I didn't say I didn't believe you. But listen: you've got plenty of reason to get back at Mulligan, or any cop for that matter."

"Not to mention getting your job back," said Abby.

"I'm not making it up, man! I saw Mulligan. He was standing right here, with a robe and a hood on, and chanting just like all the others."

Ben was inspecting the spot where Kyle claimed an altar had stood. "Marshall."

Marshall joined him. Ben had scratched in the dirt with his finger and uncovered some brown stains. He was able to pick up some clumps of stained dirt in his fingers. "Could be blood. I'll take a sample."

"See?" said Kyle.

Marshall asked, "Tell me about that blood you saw. What were they doing with it?"

"They were drinking it out of a big cup, a big silver cup. They were passing it around."

"How do you know it was blood?"

"The lady said it was."

"What lady?"

"Well, the leader, I guess. She was standing right there, and she said something about making some woman die and beating all the Christians. Uh . . . she said, 'Defeat to the Christians!' And she drank from the cup and passed it around, and they all drank from it." Then Kyle remembered something else. "Oh yeah, man, get this: they had some animal legs right here in the middle of the circle."

Oh-oh. Kyle could tell he'd impressed them with that. Hogan and Cole were looking at him, dead serious and ready to hear more.

"Tell me about the animal legs," said Marshall.

"They had to be goat legs. They were crossed right here, like an X." He saw something. "Hey!"

"Hold it!" said Marshall, touching Kyle to stop him from disturbing the dirt at his feet. "Ben."

Ben crouched for a close look. "Yeah. More blood. And here are some hairs."

"Goat hairs," said Kyle. "That's what they are."

"So they wanted to defeat the Christians, huh?" asked Marshall.

"Yeah, they were really hollering about it." Another memory. "Oh, and they were saying something about a courtroom, winning in a courtroom."

"And they were after some woman too?"

"Yeah."

"Did they say her name?"

The name meant nothing to Kyle, but he remembered hearing it. "Uh, Sally on Death Row, or something like that."

He was batting a thousand now. He could see it all over their faces.

Marshall dug into his jacket pocket. "Did you see any of the other people's faces?"

"Sure. The woman leader took her hood off, and I could see her."

Marshall produced some color photographs he'd taken

with much care, stealth, and a telephoto lens. He showed Kyle a picture of Claire Johanson.

"Yeah! Yeah, that was her!"

"The woman who led this whole thing?"

"Yeah."

Marshall showed Kyle a picture of Jon Schmidt.

"Yeah! He was here too."

Marshall slipped in a picture of his sister.

"No. I've never seen her before."

A photo of Irene Bledsoe.

"Uh . . . no, I don't think so."

Officer Leonard Jackson.

"No."

Bruce Woodard, the elementary school principal.

"Naw, not Mr. Woodard. Man, where'd you take all these?"

Marshall put the pictures away. "Kyle, I think you're giving it to us straight. Now listen, I'm not a cop, and whatever you tell me I'm not going to take it to the cops. I just need the information. It's important. I want you to tell me the real truth: did you have any marijuana on the job at the Bergen Door Company?"

Kyle raised his hand as if taking an oath. "None, I swear. Hey, Cole knows I've had some here and there, but not on the job. My old man would kill me, and besides, I need the work bad."

Abby cut in. "So you're saying that you were set up just to get you fired?"

"You got it. I didn't put that marijuana in my locker."

Marshall looked at Ben and could tell he was recalling a similar incident involving marijuana in a locker.

"Any idea who put it there?"

"Who do you think? I saw her here, and then opened my big mouth about it in the lunchroom, and so she must have found out about it. She gave me some pretty dirty looks after that, and then, bam! *She's* the person who says they ought to search my locker, and then they find the pot. Real handy, you know?"

Ben added sympathetically. "And considering your reputation, there wasn't much point in denying it."

"You got it."

Abby objected, "But Donna's been with Bergen almost as long as I have. I can't believe she'd pull a stunt like this."

"She was here," Kyle insisted. "She was standing right next to Mulligan. I saw her, and she knows it, and that's why I got fired." Kyle then recalled bitterly, "Then Mulligan comes down to the factory and tells me he'll let it go this time if I behave myself and 'make the right choices,' he said. I know what he was doing. He was telling me to keep my mouth shut or he'd bust me for good."

Marshall reviewed it all in his mind. "So . . . looks like we might have a real club here: Claire Johanson, Jon Schmidt, Sergeant Mulligan, and . . ."

Kyle resented Marshall's hesitation. "She was here! I swear it!"

Marshall completed the sentence. "Donna Hemphile, Kyle's supervisor at the Bergen Door Company, and a member in good standing at the Good Shepherd Community Church!"

Thursday afternoon, Officer Leonard Jackson had some unwelcome visitors. He was sitting in his squad car, cleverly hidden in the trees at the west end of the Snyder River Bridge, just watching for speeders and having a pleasant day building up his citation quota, when suddenly, without prior notification of any kind, a big brown Buick swung off the road and into the trees, pulling right up alongside him.

Now who in the world was this? Leonard felt invaded. This was a desecration of a sacred place.

A handsome black man rolled down the window on the passenger side of the Buick. "Hey, Leonard, how's it going?"

Ben Cole.

Leonard tried to be sociable. "Not bad, I suppose. What can I do for you?"

Ben looked toward the driver of the Buick. "Have you met Marshall Hogan?"

Leonard had seen him around town and never felt good about him. "No, we've never met."

Marshall called a greeting. "Hello, Officer Jackson."

"Hello."

Ben said, "We'd like to have a brief word with you."

"Well, I'm on duty . . ."

"How's your quota so far?"

Leonard realized Ben would know everything about his job, so bluffing wasn't going to be possible. "Well . . . I guess I'm doing all right. I've logged twelve so far."

Ben was impressed. "Hey, you're way ahead of the game! How about taking a short break for a little conference?"

"I promise you'll find it interesting," said Marshall.

At Summit, five demon messengers gathered just outside the dark, musty, secret chambers of the Strongman, each with an urgent message for Destroyer.

The first demon said to his fellows, "I bring word that Broken Birch has been breached!"

The second demon nodded in acknowledgment and added, "I bring word that Hogan and Cole are about to corner Officer Jackson!"

The third demon gasped at that news and growled his own. "I bring word that they will be seeing Joey Parnell again and may frighten him into talking!"

The fourth said, "I bring word that Pastor Mark Howard is rooting out the division in his church even now, and the Enemy is healing all the damage we've done!"

The fifth said, "I bring word that Sally Roe has—"

Oh. The ground suddenly quivered with a roar that came from inside the Strongman's lair. Apparently Destroyer and the Strongman already knew about that.

Destroyer dared not draw his sword—such an aggressive move would only worsen the Strongman's fury. So he dashed to and fro, grabbing the air in violent, desperate wingfuls, his arms covering his head and face, as the Strongman came after him with flying blade and swinging fist, his mouth foaming with rage, his jowls flopping, his rancid breath turning the air yellow.

"A reversal!" the Strongman screamed. "She was ours, and now you let them have her!"

"I allowed no such thing!" Destroyer countered. "I was biding my time—"

Contradicting the Strongman was a poor idea. It earned Destroyer a violent swat across his head from the flat of Strongman's blade. "Lazy, unmoving, blind idiot!"

"She is ours, my liege!" Destroyer shouted over Strongman's roaring. "Tal and his hordes grow weaker by the day!" *SMASH!* A huge fist in the neck. "Soon they will fall away from her like overripe fruit—" A clawed, scaly foot to the rump. "—from a tree, and we will take her!" *OOF!* A knee to the stomach.

"You were going to take away Tal's prayer cover!" yelled the Strongman. "What became of that?"

"As I've tried to tell you, we have been whittling it away!"

"*Whittling* when you should have been chopping, dashing, shredding, *slaughtering!*"

"You will see it!"

"I wish to see her destroyed, bumbling spirit! Live up to your boastful name! Pierce through a chink in her armor! Let her own sins rot her away!"

"Her sins are gone, my Ba-al! She has come to the Cross—"

WHAM! A folded wing against the midsection. Destroyer tumbled and fluttered sideways across the room.

"NOOO!" the Strongman screamed. "You will not mention *that!*"

"But we can still take her . . ." Destroyer insisted, although rather weakly.

"We will not . . . turn . . . back!" the Strongman roared, waving his sword in a fiery, rushing arc with each word. "I have a plan—I will see it unfold! Let the blood of the Lamb defeat the others—it will not defeat me! I will tread upon it, march around it, assail it and bury it, but I will not surrender to it!"

"I know we *will* take her!" Destroyer insisted again.

"YAAAA!" The Strongman brought his sword down with immeasurable fury, trailing a long, crimson streamer of light.

Destroyer drew his own blade in an instant and blocked the razor edge with a shower of sparks. The power of the blow slammed him into the wall, and the Strongman held him there like a ton of fallen earth.

Now they were eye to eye, the yellow, glowing orbs almost touching, their sulfurous breath mixing in a putrid cloud that obscured their faces. The Strongman's arm did not weaken; he did not lessen the weight that held Destroyer motionless.

"You will do it," he said finally, his voice a low, panting wheeze, "or I will feed you to the angels myself—in tiny pieces!"

With an explosion of arms, wings, and one blade that seemed like several, the Strongman cast Destroyer from the room, and he tumbled into the five demons still waiting for him outside. They bowed before him—as soon as they could crawl out from under him.

"We bring word, Ba-al!" they said.

"What word?" he asked.

They told him.

He cut them all to pieces.

Tom, I am free. I could just see that Cross so clearly, just as it must have looked on that bare, forlorn hill two thousand years ago, and I was flat on my face before it, so weighed down with my wrongs, my boasts, my choices, my SELF that I couldn't rise an inch. All I could do was lie there, admitting and confessing everything and reaching out to that rough-hewn piece of wood like a drowning man reaches for a lifeline, and grabbing hold for my very life.

And how can I describe it? I apologize, but the words will not capture the experience: I had nothing to offer Him, no incentive at all for Him to forgive me, not the slightest item of value with which to barter or cajole. All I had was what I was.

But He accepted me. I was so surprised, and then relieved, and then, with the steady realization of what had happened, ecstatic! My offering—nothing other than myself, Sally Beth Roe, pitiful, failing, and wayward—was accepted. I was what He always wanted in the first place, and He received me. He lifted the load from my heart, and I could feel it go; I could just sense it all drawn away from me and rushing up to that Cross. I felt so light, I thought I would be carried away by the slightest breeze.

I was able to raise my head, and then saw the closing of our transaction: a trickle of blood running down the wood and puddling on the ground. The payment. Such a gruesome sight, such a discomforting thought, but really, to be honest, quite appropriate considering what Jesus, the Son of God, had just purchased.

I am free. I am ransomed. I've never felt this way before, like a slave set free who was born a slave and never knew what freedom was like.

I want to get to know this Jesus who has ransomed me. We've only just met.

Sally laid her pen down on the small motel room desk, and wiped some tears from her eyes. She was still shaking. Just beside her notebook, a Gideon Bible lay open to the Gospel of Matthew, chapter 11:

"Come to me, all you who are weary and burdened, and I will give you rest. Take my yoke upon you and learn from me, for I am gentle and humble in heart, and you will find rest for your souls. For my yoke is easy and my burden is light."

thirty-six

That night, Marshall and Ben found County Coroner Joey Parnell at his home in Westhaven. As usual, he wasn't glad to see them, nor was he willing to chat.

"Now get out of here and don't come back!" he ordered through his barely cracked front door.

"Mulligan's controlling you, isn't he?" said Marshall. "He knows about that hit and run, and he's been hanging it over your head."

The door didn't close. "Who told you about that?"

"A source close to the Bacon's Corner Police Department. You struck a deal with Mulligan, and he's owned you ever since." The door started to close. Marshall talked fast. "You hit a high school girl named . . . uh . . . Kelly Otis, and Mulligan tracked you down, and you were just then working on a case of suspected homicide, some female transient, and Mulligan made you a deal: falsify the cause of death of this female transient, and he'd let the hit and run slip by. Am I right so far?"

The door cracked open a little more. "Just what do you want from me?"

Marshall tried to sound compassionate despite the urgency that kept making his voice tense. "How much longer do you want this to go on? You can be their puppet for the rest of your life, or you can help us put a stop to it."

Parnell was silent for a moment. Then he opened the door wide enough to pass through. "Come inside before somebody sees you."

Parnell's wife was beside him. She was dark-haired, stout, and looking as troubled as he was. "This is Carol. We can talk freely in front of her; I've told her everything."

"Would you like some coffee?" she said quite mechanically. It was clear she didn't know what else to do.

"Yes, thank you," said Marshall, and Ben accepted as well.

431

"We'll sit in the dining room," said Parnell, leading them through the house.

They sat around a large table under a dimly glowing chandelier. The low, somber lighting seemed to match Parnell's mood; he looked worn, tired, at the end of his strength.

Without cue or question, he started talking as if he'd saved this story for years. "The transient was a thirty-two-year-old woman named Louise Barnes—she was homeless, a scavenger, no family. She was found dead in the woods along the Snyder River, about six miles north of Bacon's Corner. I remember the details perfectly because I want so much to forget them." He paused to gather his thoughts and control his emotions, then continued. "Her body was found hanging by the ankles from a tree limb, the blood drained. There were abundant signs of bizarre, ritualistic murder that I won't go into. The hunters who found her had apparently startled the killers, who fled before they could dispose of the body altogether.

"I received the remains and finished the autopsy. I found the cause of death to be homicide, of course. But then . . . as you have already heard, I did get into a mishap near the high school on my way home. I didn't see the girl, Kelly Otis, until she stepped from behind a tree and into the street, and . . . and I hit her. I slowed just enough to look, to see that she was still alive though injured. Some other people were running to help her. I . . . I just couldn't let the incident damage my career. I'd just gotten the coroner's job, and you know how the political world is, how fragile a reputation can be. I fled.

"Sergeant Mulligan came to my office the next day, and we met in private. I expected him to question me about the hit and run, but he immediately asked me about the body of Louise Barnes and what my findings were. I told him, and that's when he made the offer to let the hit-and-run incident pass, just bury it, if I would alter my findings and not report the real cause of death." Parnell just stared at the table, his face etched with pain. "I accepted his offer, filed the cause of death as accidental, and it was the worst decision of my life.

"There have been three ritual murders since then that I

know of, and I'm sure many more that no one will ever know of. The three brought to me I quickly wrote off as accidental deaths. They were unknowns, possible runaways. I was hoping they would not be missed, but simply buried and forgotten, and that's what happened.

"But you see, I knew Sergeant Mulligan and his friends would be watching me. I knew I would have to perform to satisfy them, and so, with each murder I concealed, I fell deeper and deeper under their control, and that's where things stand at the present time."

Marshall asked, "Just who are these people? *What* are they?"

Parnell reached into a cabinet and pulled out a file folder, then set it before him closed, his folded hands resting on top. Carol brought the coffee and sat down beside her husband, putting her hand on his arm and saying nothing.

"If you want a name to call them, you can use the term Broken Birch. It's a secret label they share among themselves. They're a coven of witches, Satanists, occultists, whatever you wish. They're linked with hundreds of other such groups across the country. And taken together, these people wield incredible power, mostly through terror."

"And they're responsible for those ritual murders?"

Parnell looked at the telephone hanging on the wall. "You should know that right now I can pick up that telephone, call any one of six different phone numbers, and have both of you dead within twenty-four hours. The other side of that, however, is that there are other parties who can make the same call regarding me, and I could be dead just as quickly, and may very well be if they find out I've talked to you. Unknowns and transients are used for ritual sacrifices; people who are known and would be missed are . . . Well, fatal accidents are arranged for them."

"Can you tell us who belongs to this bunch?"

Parnell shook his head slowly for emphasis. "First of all, I don't know all of them. Secondly, I wouldn't tell you if I did. I can only confirm what you already know: Sergeant Mulligan is involved, and has been for years. As I understand it, he and some of the men from the local lodge checked it out and found the transition very easy. Because he holds such power in town and is head of law enforcement, they were quite willing to include him."

"Can you confirm Claire Johanson?"

Parnell hesitated, and then answered, "Yes."

"What about her boyfriend, Jon Schmidt?"

"Yes, he's part of it."

Ben wondered, "So what about all those people involved in the LifeCircle fellowship? Do they tie into this?"

Parnell shook his head emphatically. "They aren't supposed to know about it. All those well-meaning people being pulled into the LifeCircle group are simply being used and manipulated; they have no idea that Broken Birch is at the core of it, and they have no idea what their leaders are really up to."

Marshall asked, "What about Donna Hemphile? Is she a part of Broken Birch?"

"I believe so. It's hard to be sure sometimes, they hide it so well." Parnell drew a breath to change gears, then opened the file folder. "Here's what you really want to know, and all I really want to tell you."

He distributed the contents of the folder on the table in front of Marshall and Ben. With great interest, the two men examined several police mug shots and the rap sheet on a young, beautiful, black-haired woman.

"Not Sally Roe, obviously," said Parnell.

Ben recognized her. "The dead woman we found in the goat shed."

"I did some checking on my own. Her name is Alicia Von Bauer, twenty-seven, a Satanist, a member of Broken Birch. You'll note her criminal record: animal mutilations, public nudity and perverse behavior, prostitution, pornography. I might add to that list ritualistic murder, but who could ever prove it?"

Marshall asked, "So you think this Sally Roe thing was another ritual murder, or at least an attempt at one?"

"Exactly. It's clear to me that her death was arranged, and it was supposed to appear to be a suicide."

"That's how you recorded it, anyway," said Ben.

Parnell nodded. "With an unforeseen additional service: identifying the body of Alicia Von Bauer as that of Sally Roe. I do what I'm told, Mr. Cole. But obviously, something went terribly wrong, and all I can figure is that Sally Roe—or something else—overpowered Von Bauer, and Roe escaped."

"That's our theory," said Ben. He picked up the most recent photograph of Alicia Von Bauer for a closer look. The deep black eyes seemed to stare back at him from the page. It was eerie.

Marshall asked, "Where's the body now?"

"Cremated. We did that as soon as possible."

"Disposing of the evidence?"

"Exactly."

Marshall didn't know if he'd get an answer to the next question. "Mr. Parnell, we have a lot of reason to believe that this attempted killing isn't just a Broken Birch affair. What about the big people Claire Johanson and Jon Schmidt are connected with? Would they have something to gain?"

"I think you're on the right track. I'm sure the order for the murder came from someone higher up."

"How do you know?"

Parnell even smiled a little. "Because it's the first time I've seen Sergeant Mulligan afraid. Not long after I collected the body, Mulligan called me, asking if I'd found any personal effects on the body, which I hadn't. I could tell he was getting pressure from someone much higher, much more powerful than him or his Broken Birch friends. He was desperate enough to tell me what to look for, something missing that should have been there."

"Yeah," Ben recalled, "I asked you about that. Somebody even ransacked the rental house."

"So what was missing?" asked Marshall.

"A gold ring," Parnell answered. "Someone took it off Von Bauer's finger with cooking oil. I found traces of the oil still

435

on Von Bauer's finger. The other thing missing was ten thousand dollars in cash."

Marshall and Ben looked at each other. They both had the same thought.

Ben spoke it. "Somebody hired her."

"Who?" asked Marshall.

Parnell shrugged. "I'd advise looking for someone rich, influential, and very powerful."

Ben responded, "A mighty big mole, Marshall."

Marshall had no comment. Right now he was overwhelmed with a sudden, flesh-crawling fear he hadn't felt since a few years ago in Ashton, when it seemed all the evil in the world was about to crash down on him. A mole? Suddenly the analogy was inadequate. What Marshall felt was more like a dragon, a monster—dark, insidious, clever, and big enough to fill the sky, with jaws gaping just above them, dropping to the kill, closing like a vise.

Far away from Bacon's Corner, and still hidden from her enemies, Sally Roe sat among the floor-to-ceiling shelves at the downtown library in Henderson, flanked on every side by invisible angelic guards, and paging through a massive National Bar Association directory of attorneys. She had a hunch, only a guess, but in her thinking it was the strongest possibility.

At her elbow sat Volume IV of the four rosters she had stolen from Professor Samuel W. Lynch's office, its full title: *A Continuation of the History and Roster of the Royal and Sacred Order of the Nation.* Each of the four volumes contained about two hundred pages. Most of the pages were devoted to weird, esoteric, ceremonial mumbo-jumbo, secret rites and initiations, minutes of meetings, and bylaws. At least fifty pages in each volume were dedicated to the names of members. The pages of names held her attention for the time being; she'd been scanning them for hours.

She now had another volume lying across Volume IV to hold it open to page 68, *The 168th Brotherhood of Initiates.* Like the 167 pages in this and the three volumes that came before, this page listed the names of new members brought into the Order of the Nation in one particular year, and contained two columns of fifteen names each. The column on the left contained bizarre, esoteric names like Isenstar, Marochia, and Pendorrot. The column on the right contained real names, some of them even familiar. Two-thirds of the way down the left column, she'd found the name she had looked through several years' worth of pages to find: Exetor.

At first, Exetor was just a mysterious word she'd found engraved on the inside surface of the ring she'd taken from the finger of her would-be assassin. Until she stole the rosters and studied them, the engraving made no sense at all. When she finally found page 68 in Volume IV of the rosters, it made a lot more sense. Exetor was a secret name or title, ninth on the list of fifteen. Directly opposite the name Exetor, in the right column, was the real name of the man who had received the title.

"James Everett Bardine."

James Bardine. He'd been initiated into the Sacred Order of the Nation along with fourteen other men twelve years ago, and upon his initiation had been granted the secret Brotherhood name of Exetor and his Ring of Fellowship bearing his secret name.

Very impressive, even spooky, and not to be scoffed at. The Nation could have been just another lodge or fraternal organization, some secret society or club where all the good old boys could get together, have a secret meeting with its oaths, handshakes, funny hats and rituals, and afterward down some beers and be rowdy. Almost every town had a lodge or secret order of some kind.

But the Nation went beyond that. It bound a lot of familiar names together and gave them at least this society in common. She'd found the name of Samuel W. Lynch among the 129th Brotherhood of Initiates—he'd been initiated into the Nation fifty-one years ago, and as he showed her in his office, still kept his cherished Ring of Fellowship.

The second ring in her possession—the one she'd hidden for ten years under the brick windowsill in Fairwood—bore another secret name, Gawaine, but she already knew whose ring it was. She quickly found his name at position seven, opposite the name Gawaine, in the 146th Brotherhood of Initiates: Owen Jefferson Bennett, initiated thirty-four years ago when a senior at Bentmore University.

Good old Owen. There were so many things he never told her.

All this was fascinating, of course, but first and foremost in Sally's mind at this moment was the name of James Everett Bardine. The Nation was a strictly male organization, but a female assassin was wearing his ring. What was the connection? Who was Bardine in the first place?

Perhaps it was the current lawsuit causing all the stir in Bacon's Corner that made her think Bardine might be an attorney; perhaps it was the fact that the Nation seemed to have no ordinary, blue-collar people in its membership, but only bankers, businessmen, educators, attorneys, and statesmen—purveyors of power.

Whatever the case, she was now narrowing her search in the "B" section of the Bar Association directory, and getting closer.

Barcliff . . . Barclyde . . . Barden . . . Bardetti . . . Bardine. James Everett Bardine.

Bingo. This guy was an attorney. The listing was current, published this year. Bardine was working for a big law firm in Chicago: Evans, Santinelli, Farnsworth, and McCutcheon. They were members of the American Citizens' Freedom Association.

Sally had to sit back and think about that. *James Bardine is a member of the ACFA . . . The ACFA is bringing the lawsuit against the school . . . The killer was wearing Bardine's ring.*

Did this mean a connection between the ACFA and Sally's would-be killer? Sally thought so. She would be looking up more names, that was certain. She couldn't wait to write to Tom and tell him.

But who in the world was that fiendish woman in black?

Friday morning, Pastor Mark Howard found his way through the noisy, busy, bustling Bergen Door Company, protective eyewear and earplugs in place, dodging the forklift, ducking around the doors being stacked, being sanded, being moved. He engaged a clipboard-carrying foreman in a brief, shouting conversation, and got directions to the small cubicle office of Donna Hemphile, Finish Supervisor. Mark could see Donna through the glass enclosure. He stepped up and tapped on the door.

"Yeah, come in!"

Mark stepped inside.

Donna Hemphile swiveled around in her desk chair and stuck out her hand. "Hey, Mark! What a surprise! What brings you here?"

Mark had no time for sweet-and-easy, beat-around-the-bush phrases. "Some pretty serious matters, Donna."

Donna looked at the clock. "Well, you know, I have to be out of here by—"

"I already talked to Mr. Bergen. He has someone else handling that new band saw. He said I could have an hour with you."

Donna had to digest that for a moment, and then relaxed back in her chair. "Okay. Have a seat."

Mark wheeled the only other chair around and sat facing Donna. "I've been running all around town since Wednesday night trying to nail some things down, and I haven't slept much. You know the kind of trouble we've been having in the church since this lawsuit came up. I've felt like a seaman trying to patch the leaks in a sinking ship before it goes down completely."

Donna nodded. "Yeah, it's been rough."

"Anyway, I finally got three families together for a conference: the Warings, the Jessups, and the Walroths. It was a pretty good meeting, I guess. Ed and Judy Waring are still disgruntled, but the Jessups and Walroths might be coming around." Mark paused. He was going to change directions. "But I wanted to ask you about something they all told me, and you know, I never thought about it before this. You're on the prayer chain, and your name comes before the Jessups, the Walroths, and the Warings."

"Mm-hm." Donna just sat there listening.

Mark plunged in. "So, let me ask you point-blank: Did you tell June Walroth that Tom Harris beats his daughter Ruth, and that's why he puts long sleeves on her so often?"

Donna chuckled at that. "No."

"Did you tell Judy Waring that Cathy and I are having marital problems because I was unfaithful and had an affair a few years ago?"

Donna smiled and shook her head. "No."

"Did you tell Ed Waring that the school was in bad debt because Tom and Mrs. Fields were stealing the school's money?"

"No."

"Did you tell Andrea Jessup that Tom's had some real problems with sexual deviancy ever since Cindy died?"

"No."

Mark was finding Donna's extremely brief answers a bit jarring. "You don't have any other comment about all this?"

Donna smiled and shook her head in seeming incredulity. "Why should I say anything, Mark? Those people are gossip-hounds. This is the kind of thing they'd come up with."

"Why do you suppose they all came up with the same source for their information?"

She tossed up her hands. "Beats me. They must have something against me, I don't know. So what else do you have on the list?"

"Well . . . somebody who doesn't even go to our church. Kyle Krantz, the kid who got fired on Tuesday for having marijuana in his locker."

At that, Donna rolled her eyes. "Oh, brother!"

"Well, he has an interesting story to tell, and you know, a lot of what he has to say checks out. I guess you know his side of the story, right? That someone planted that bag of pot in his locker to set him up?"

"Oh yeah, I've heard it, all right. He could have come up with something more original. All the kids use that line."

"I've heard it before myself, from Ben Cole. Somebody planted some confiscated marijuana in his locker at the police station, and Mulligan fired him. Of course, it was Mulligan, according to Kyle, who came down to the plant here and struck a deal with Kyle and didn't book him for possession, isn't that right?"

"That part of it wasn't my concern. I just fired him according to company policy."

Mark slowed down a little for emphasis. "Kyle says Mulligan told him he'd let it go if Kyle kept his mouth shut about some things he knew."

Donna got just a little tense. "Well, listen, Mark, what goes on in this plant is my business, and none of your concern."

Mark didn't back off, but kept going. "Somebody killed Kyle's dog too; they cut it open and left it on the front seat of his car. Maybe they were trying to give him a little reminder to watch himself."

Donna leaned her elbow on her desk, propped her hand under her cheek, and gave every appearance of patiently humoring a childish, assuming, overimaginative minister.

Mark kept going. "That was weird enough in itself, and I don't know if I would have believed Kyle if something similar hadn't happened to us, right at the church. Monday morning, somebody splashed goat's blood on the front door and left two goat legs crossed on the porch. It was some kind of curse, or maybe it was a warning, I don't know. But just the day before, on Sunday morning, Ben Cole went out to the Potter place to investigate the killing of a goat that used to belong to Sally Roe. All the blood had been drained out, and the legs cut off.

"Then, according to Kyle, on that Sunday night he and a friend were out at the Benson farm and saw a witch coven holding a ritual in the barn, and wouldn't you know it—the witches, or Satanists, whatever they were, were drinking goat's blood and were standing in a circle around two more goat legs, calling for the defeat of the Christians and for the death of Sally Roe."

That finally evoked at least a small comment from Donna Hemphile. "Heh. Pretty bizarre."

Mark hit her squarely with the next sentence. "And Kyle

says *you* were there, that you were part of that group holding the ritual, along with Sergeant Mulligan, Claire Johanson, and Jon Schmidt—probably Tom Harris's, and our church's, worst enemies right now."

Donna said nothing. She just leaned back in her chair and kept listening, surprisingly detached.

"We also checked with Kyle's friend and gave him quite a thorough testing with some photographs Marshall had of the people Kyle claimed were there, as well as some photographs of people who were not there, and some phony information we claimed Kyle had told us. The friend checked out on every detail. I'm convinced we have two reliable witnesses."

"And a pretty wild story," Donna reminded him.

"Well . . . after all we've been through, and everything we've seen and learned, it isn't that wild. It's disgusting, it's tragic, it's bizarre, but at this point I find it incontrovertible, especially since Mulligan—and perhaps yourself—have stooped to such terror and intimidation tactics to keep the boys quiet about it." Donna didn't look like she had any comment to that, but Mark didn't wait for one. "Donna, you said that what happens here at the plant is your business and none of my concern. Well, what happens to my church is my concern, so let me just get down to the direct question: Were you there at the Benson farm on Sunday night?"

"No," she said simply.

"Are you involved in witchcraft or occultism?"

"No."

"Are you trying to destroy my church with gossip and division?"

She chuckled, and the chuckle had a note of mockery in it. "Of course not. Hey, you're going through difficult times. If you don't all stick together, you won't make it."

"What about Sally Roe?"

"Never heard of her."

An unplanned question occurred to Mark. "What about the social worker for the CPD that took Tom's kids, Irene Bledsoe? Is she purposely working against us, trying to destroy Tom's reputation?"

Donna laughed. "Hey, as far as I know, she's just doing her job. If you ask me, Tom's a sick man, and I think she can see that."

"What about that time you saw Ben Cole first visiting Abby Grayson here at the plant? Did you report that to Sergeant Mulligan?"

"You mean, did I snitch?"

"Whatever."

"I don't really know Mulligan. Why would I go out of my way to tell him about one of his own cops?"

Mark looked at Donna, and Donna returned his gaze. There was no question remaining between them.

"Donna . . . you don't lie very well."

She smiled that same subtle, mocking smile. "On the contrary, Mark—you did approve my application for church membership."

Mark nodded. "So I did. So I did." He'd heard enough. "Well, I could go through the Biblical pattern and come back with some witnesses to go through all this again with you, but . . . what do you think? That probably isn't worth the trouble, is it?"

Donna just kept smiling. "No need, really."

The phone rang. Donna picked it up. "Yeah. Okay. I'll be right there." She hung up. "Well, sorry, that was Mr. Bergen. He wants to meet with me right away."

"I know," said Mark, rising from his chair. He let himself out the door, and walked down the aisle. Donna was not far behind him.

Mr. Bergen's office was about halfway down the floor. Mark looked through the window; Abby Grayson, Kyle Krantz, Kyle's friend Billy, and Marshall Hogan had already been there quite a while. Mr. Bergen, a stern-looking man in his sixties, was pacing about the office, waiting impatiently, visibly angry.

Mark cracked the door open and stuck his head in long enough to catch Mr. Bergen's eye. Bergen looked his way immediately; he was expected.

"It's all true," said Mark.

Then he closed the door and went on his way, pausing just long enough to look back and see Donna Hemphile go into the office of her boss.

thirty-seven

LUCY Brandon could feel her scalp crawling and her stomach twisting into a knot. This was her second such phone call today, interrupting her work at the Post Office and scaring her to death.

"Don't talk to Hogan," said her once-kind friend Claire Johanson. "Don't say a word to him, or to any of those people! It could go very bad for you if you don't protect any knowledge you have!"

Lucy tried to keep her voice down so Debbie wouldn't overhear. "Claire, what's happened?"

"Nothing has happened!"

"I got a call from Gordon Jefferson just like yours. He wasn't kind at all. He kept telling me I'd be in legal trouble if anything leaked, and I didn't even know what he was talking about . . ."

Claire didn't answer right away. She was working on a reply that was safe—or downright deceiving. "The hearing before the federal Court of Appeals is coming up soon, and things are getting critical, that's all. I think it has all of us on edge."

"So why come down on me?"

"It's not just you. We're clamping down on everyone, even ourselves. Too much information is getting out, and it could ruin our case. We have to be careful. I'm sure you understand that."

"This all seems so sudden."

"Well, it just seems that way. Don't worry about it. Just keep quiet, and keep things to yourself from now on. I have to go."

Click.

I'm going to explode, Lucy thought. *I'm just going to go crazy, stark raving mad. I can't take this anymore!*

Ding!

A patron was at the counter. *No, I can't see anyone, I can't talk to anyone. I just want to get out of here. But where could I go? How would I explain my daughter? What about the trouble I've gotten myself into?*

Ding!

Oh, where's Debbie? Lucy looked at the clock. *Oh, wonderful! She's on break, probably across the street buying some sugarless gum or something.*

"Coming."

She gathered herself, trying to calm down, and stepped to the front.

The patron was Tom Harris.

Both of them immediately felt awkward and even shied back a little.

"Oh, I'm sorry," said Tom. "I mean, I don't have to—"

Lucy looked this way and that. There was no one else in the lobby. "Well, I can wait on you."

Tom stood back from the counter. He extended his arms to lay some packages in front of Lucy. "I wanted to send these to my folks."

Lucy pulled the packages toward her, turned them around, turned them around again, read the addresses, read them again, still didn't know what she'd read. She just couldn't think. Was she supposed to weigh them? She set all three on the scale at once and fumbled with the sliding weights. No, no, this wouldn't work, not all three . . .

She set the packages down and without looking up tried to say, "I'm sorry any of this ever happened," but her voice was too weak and trembling.

Tom heard her anyway. "Sure. So am I."

She tried to concentrate on the packages. "Well, I guess we aren't supposed to talk about it."

"I understand."

"Do you think Amber's possessed?"

The question didn't just slip out—Lucy pushed it out. She wanted to know.

But Tom Harris was muzzled, and acted like it. Even though he wanted to answer, he could only look at her in obvious frustration. "You know I can't talk about that."

"*I* need to know. For *me*."

He shook his head sadly, painfully. "I can't talk about it. But listen . . ."

She listened.

"Uh . . . Jesus Christ conquered the spiritual forces of evil on the Cross. The Bible says He disarmed them and made a public display of them. He has all authority over them, and He's given that authority to His people, the true believers in Him. He's the answer. That's all I can say."

"Have you ever seen someone possessed?"

Tom took back his packages. "I wish I could tell you all about it. Maybe when this lawsuit is over, huh? I'll . . . Listen, no offense, okay? I'll mail these later."

He hurried out the door, leaving Lucy with her questions unanswered.

"Evans, Santinelli, Farnsworth, and McCutcheon," said the receptionist.

"Mr. Bardine, please," said the woman's voice on the other end.

The receptionist hesitated. "Uh . . . I'm very sorry to inform you, but Mr. Bardine is deceased. Did you have any current business with him? We can arrange for someone else to complete that."

The other party was understandably shocked by the news. "Did you say Mr. Bardine was deceased?"

"Yes, I'm sorry to tell you that. He was killed in an auto accident several weeks ago. It was a real blow to all of us here at the firm."

"Well, I'm . . . I'm shocked to hear that myself."

"I'm sorry. Perhaps you'd like to talk to Mr. Mahoney, Mr. Bardine's superior. Perhaps he can help you."

"Oh, thank you, no. Let me sort things out first."

"Fine. Thank you for caring."

"Good-bye."

The receptionist hung up the phone and went back to typing a letter on a sophisticated electronic typewriter, sitting at a massive, dark oak, brass-fitted desk, in a plush carpeted office with twelve-foot-high, wood paneled walls and ornate lighting fixtures, as gray-haired senior partners, junior partners dressed for success, aggressive legal assistants, ambitious secretaries, and powerful incognito visitors moved tight-lipped and chin-high up and down the halls with their brief-cases, legal files, or yellow legal pads.

The Chicago offices of Evans, Santinelli, Farnsworth, and McCutcheon were more than a palace; they were a citadel of power and legal technocracy, where knowledge and power were synonymous and time was money—lots of money. Here the czars of case law and the architects of legal precedent groomed the future by challenging, bending, stretching, and even crossbreeding the law, turning it their way as far and as often as their money, skill, connections, and power would allow.

These were the offices of the elite: the promoters of the favored and the deposers of the dispensable, the guarantors of success and the instigators of ruin.

Atop this ivory tower, at the pinnacle of the pyramid, strode the ruthless and powerful Mr. Santinelli.

"Good afternoon, Mr. Santinelli," said the receptionist.

"Good afternoon," he replied with a faint, obligatory smile, extending his hand to receive the newly typed letter. "I'll be having a special meeting for the next half-hour; there will be no calls, no disturbances."

"Yes, sir."

Santinelli continued down the aisle to a tall and imposing mahogany door. An aide swung the door open just in time for him to pass through it, and then closed the door after him like a slab over a crypt.

Santinelli was in the private conference room adjacent to his office, a soundproof, secret, and rather gloomy place. The woodwork still seemed to absorb the light, and the floor-to-ceiling, velvet curtains were still drawn over the windows.

Three men stood in a tight cluster at one end of the room, talking in hushed voices. They nodded a greeting when Santinelli came in.

One of them was Mr. Khull, the man entrusted with the elimination of Sally Beth Roe.

Santinelli made some quick introductions. "Gentlemen, allow me to formally introduce Mr. Khull, who will be assisting us in the present pressing matters. Mr. Khull, I present to you Mr. Evans, a partner in this firm, now fully devoted to our present legal concerns, and Mr. McCutcheon, our director of administration and finance."

"A pleasure," said Khull.

"I've spoken with Mr. Goring at Summit and Mr. Steele at the Omega Center," Santinelli reported. "It's clear to all of us that Sally Roe has been tracking down the owner of that ring she slipped from Von Bauer's finger, and using Von Bauer's fee to finance her cross-country sleuthing. They agree with us that the rosters are enough to lead her to the late James Bardine, which means she'll have to come here, though we can't be sure when. Mr. Khull has secured the building for that eventuality, and of course we have your assurance, Mr. Khull, that the failure at Bentmore University will not be repeated?"

"Last time we were a little too discreet, I would say. I have twice the personnel here as I had stationed at Bentmore, and our techniques will be much more direct this time."

"The hearing in the federal Court of Appeals is on Monday," Santinelli fumed. "A ruling in our favor will not be much consolation if Roe is still at large. When she comes, you may bring her to this room and kill her right here, as far as I'm concerned."

Khull stifled a laugh.

Just across the conference table, Destroyer and the twelve grotesque warriors who flanked him did not stifle their laughter at all, but thoroughly enjoyed the thought of killing that woman.

Destroyer's laugh was a brief indulgence, however. He still bore the bruises and shame from his recent meeting with the Strongman, and now his exhilaration at the thought of Sally Roe's impending death was mixed with desperation.

You will take her this time! he growled, his wings flared in anger, his crooked finger pointing across the table. *You will take her and kill her!* Then he shouted to his warriors, "Surround this place, and post sentries over the city! She will not evade us this time!"

The warriors swooped out of the room with a thunderous war cry, almost crazy with a thirst for blood.

Destroyer glared at Khull, and muttered to himself, *Come to us, Sally Roe. Whatever your condition, Cross or no Cross, this time nothing will stop us. Nothing!*

On the outskirts of Chicago, Sally Roe sat in a dismal, musty room at a cheap motel, staring at the telephone and wondering what to do next. So James Bardine was dead! She'd spent no small amount of time preparing herself to confront him face to face, to bring it all to a head, and she had come so close, but now what could she do? Well, there was no point in visiting Evans, Santinelli, Farnsworth, and McCutcheon. The man she sought was no longer there.

But obviously Bardine wasn't the only player in this game; there were other players and strategists, from the clumsy police in Bacon's Corner to the mind-molders at Omega, to the highest levels of the educational establishment at Bentmore University, and even beyond that. They all knew about her, they all wanted that ring, and they all seemed quite determined to kill her.

With reluctance, she brought back an old thought she'd entertained several times in the past few weeks and went over it again. There was one final ploy she could try, one do-or-die way to find and identify the people who were responsible for this whole nightmare. Did she say do-or-die? It would most likely be die, if God didn't see fit to spare her.

Funny. Before she encountered the Cross, she saw no reason to live but feared death. Now she had a reason to live, but did not fear death at all. It was an odd kind of peace, a fascinating sense of rest and stillness deep in her soul. Someday she would have to analyze it and clarify just what had happened to her, *if* she lived long enough. If not . . . Well, maybe she'd lived long enough already.

She got out her notebook again, and began to compose her very last letter to Tom Harris.

Nathan and Armoth were tense with anticipation and preoccupied with strategy, but they were there by Sally's side when she started that letter.

"'The word of her testimony, the blood of the Lamb, and she does not love her life so much as to shrink from death,'" said Nathan.

"That's three," said Armoth.

Sally's pen glided over the paper.

> *Tom, this will be my last letter to you. I have told you all that I have done, and all that I know, and I've shared with you my encounter with the God and Savior you serve. What more could remain but to see you face to face and finally bring this trouble to an end?*
>
> *There is no doubt in my mind that the ACFA has pulled some big strings, or vice versa, and are connected with the attempt on my life, which must be connected with the attack against you and your school. I now have the gold ring taken from my would-be assassin as well as the four volumes of the History and Roster of the Royal and Sacred Order of the Nation, which prove the ring belonged to the now deceased James Everett Bardine, an attorney in high standing with the ACFA. I also have other information, much of which I have provided in many letters, that should prove invaluable to you in your defense against this lawsuit.*
>
> *All that remains now is for me to return to Bacon's Corner to aid your attorney in building his defense, and ultimately to testify in open court on your behalf.*
>
> *I believe it's time I heard from you. Please contact me at the Caravan Motel.*

She gave Tom the address and telephone number, then closed her notebook. If she hurried, she could get the letter photocopied and mailed.

But first, there was one more letter to write. She flipped to a fresh page in her notebook—she'd used up the pages in two notebooks by now, and was starting into her third—and began her first and last letter to Bernice Krueger, c/o the *Ashton Clarion*. She wrote hurriedly, saying only what was essential.

The young clerk at the Post Office was just bagging up the mail for the evening pickup when a lady in jeans and a blue jacket came to the counter with some more. He was in a hurry; the truck was coming any minute. He took care of her quickly, applied the necessary postage, and threw the rest of the mail into the mailbag.

There was the truck! He grabbed the bag and headed for the back door.

The lady went out the front door, glad she'd made it in time.

In the rush, one letter fell from the mailbag to the floor under the front counter and lay there facedown.

It was addressed to Bernice Krueger, c/o the *Ashton Clarion*.

thirty-eight

On Monday morning, without prior warning and totally unexpected, the fax machine in the *Ashton Clarion* office warbled its electronic ring and was barely heard over the prepublication bedlam that usually marked Monday mornings. Bernice didn't hear it at all; she was in Marshall's glassed-in office trying to convince Eddy's Bakery to buy just two more column inches so she wouldn't have to keep filling in that space with stupid one-liners.

"Hey listen," she said, "we'll make the donut bigger, and then make the coffee mug bigger, you know, show more steam coming out or something. The readers will grab right onto it. Sure they will!"

"Bernice!" Cheryl called through the glass. "You're getting a fax!"

Bernice looked up at Cheryl. "What?"

Cheryl said something back, and all Bernice could hear through the glass was the word fax. The rest was meant for lipreaders.

A fax? From who? So far she was drawing a blank.

The phone squawked in her ear. She had to give a reply. "Oh, yeah. Well, think about it, will you, Eddy? I'll give you a deal on it. Well, let *me* think about *that*. Okay, good-bye."

Cheryl knocked at the door lightly, cracked it open, and tossed the sheet of paper in, hot off the fax machine.

Bernice grabbed it before it floated to the floor and gave it a once-over.

Oh! This was from Cliff Bingham, her contact in Washington, D.C.! She'd forgotten all about him. Well, well! He'd found the *Finding the Real Me* curriculum for fourth-graders at the Library of Congress and sent her the title page with a note scribbled at the top: "Bernice, is this the one you're after?— Cliff."

She smiled. *Well, Cliff, you did all right, but Marshall's seen the curriculum already; you're too late. Thanks anyway.*

She went to her Rolodex to find Cliff's number, found it, and picked up the telephone. She punched in the number, and looked over the title page again as she waited for the ring and the answer.

Then she saw it. She slammed the phone down. She scanned the page again to make sure. She checked the publication date.

She picked up the phone and pounded out the number for the Cole residence in Bacon's Corner.

"Hello?" It was Bev Cole.

"Hello, Bev. This is Bernice Krueger in Ashton."

"Oh, hi! What do you know?"

"I've got to talk to Marshall right away!"

"Hooo, well he isn't here, and I don't know where he is."

"I've got to—oh, nuts! Did he say when he'd be back?"

"No, he runs around so much I never know where he is, he and Ben."

"Bev, listen, I'm going to fax him something. He should be able to pick it up at Judy's, right?"

"Oh yeah, if she's open."

"I'm going to fax it to Judy's Secretarial Service right now, and you tell him to get over there right away and pick it up, all right?"

"Okay, I'll tell him. Hey, you sound excited."

"Oh, I'm a little excitedseeyoulatergood-bye!"

She scrambled out of the office and made a beeline for the fax machine.

Marshall, where are you?

Lucy Brandon was going through the morning mail, sorting it, slipping it into all the Post Office boxes and assigning it to the four different carrier routes. She was ill, nervous, overwrought, and exhausted, and now she was beginning to hate her job, especially when letters came in from "S. B. Roe."

Like this one, fresh out of the bag, no sooner thought of than in her hand! How many did this make? It had to be more than thirty. Thirty-plus envelopes, all stuffed with several thicknesses of the same lined notebook paper, all written in the same, fluid handwriting just visible through the envelope, and all addressed to Tom Harris.

So I guess when I forward this one, I'll be violating federal law over thirty times. What a thought. What if I just delivered it to Tom Harris? What if I slipped it into his carrier's box, just one of these letters, just once?

"Good morning, Lucy!"

She literally jumped, dropping the letter to the floor.

Sergeant Harold Mulligan!

"Sergeant! What are you doing back here? You scared me to death!"

He stooped and picked up the letter from the floor. "Ah, another one, eh?"

She tried to take it from him. "Yes, thank you kindly—"

He wouldn't let go. "Naw, now just hold on, Lucy. I've got orders regarding any further mail from Miss You-know-who."

She didn't care. "I'll take that letter back, sergeant! It's United States mail!"

What? He actually grabbed her arm with painful force and pushed her against the wall! He hurt her, and she just couldn't believe it!

He spoke to her in a low, threatening voice she'd never heard from him before. "And just what do you think you're gonna do with it, huh, Lucy? Are you thinking you just might mail it where it's supposed to go? Huh?"

"You let go of me!"

"You listen to me, little lady! Any more mail from Roe, you put it right in my hand, right here, see? You don't mess with it, you don't even think about it, or you are gonna have one big, ugly pack of troubles!"

She was getting scared. "I'm doing what I'm told, Harold, you know that. Please let go of me!"

"Just wanna make sure we're clear on this—"

"Excuse me," came a voice from the front.

It was Marshall Hogan.

Oh man, how much of this did he see? Mulligan immediately turned his aggressive posture into a teasing one and let Lucy go. "Okay, Lucy, take care!"

He went out the back way with the letter in his pocket.

Debbie stepped up to the counter to help the big, red-haired man. Lucy hurried forward. "I'll take care of him."

Debbie backed away, but could see Lucy was in no condition to help anyone. Too late, though. They couldn't talk about such a thing in front of a customer. She went back to her sorting, but kept an eye on her boss.

"I'd like a book of stamps," said Marshall gently.

She reached into the drawer under the counter. Her hands were visibly shaking, and she couldn't look up.

"Are you in trouble?" Marshall asked.

"Please, I can't talk to you," she said on the verge of tears.

"Just sell me some stamps then," he said. "Do that first."

She finally found a book of stamps and set them on the counter.

He had something else on the counter as well. "This is County Coroner Joey Parnell's report on the woman who committed suicide, supposedly Sally Beth Roe. See the description? Black hair, in her twenties. Here . . . look at this." He set a photograph in front of her and continued to talk in quiet, gentle tones. "This is a police mug shot of her. She had a criminal record. Now I know you know what the real Sally Roe looks like; you identified a picture of her at your deposition. But this is the woman who was found dead. She was a member of a secret coven of witches who call themselves Broken Birch, and when she tried to kill Sally Roe, she was working for someone—she was carrying ten thousand dollars."

Lucy looked down at the picture, still shaking but listening.

Marshall continued, "Now that cop who just roughed you up back there has done all he can to cover this up and make it look like a suicide, and we think we know why: he belongs to that coven; he's in on the whole thing. As a matter of fact, that coven lays claim to some pretty big wheels in LifeCircle—some of your own friends, including Claire Johanson and Jon Schmidt."

Marshall waited just a moment for that to sink in, and then concluded, "As for Sally Roe, we have good evidence that she's still alive somewhere, probably hiding for her life. So the question I'd like you to consider is this: Why would the same friends who are helping you in this lawsuit want Sally Roe killed?"

Lucy didn't say a word. She could only stand there stone-still, staring at the photographs as tears filled her eyes.

Marshall got his answer from her face. He took back the coroner's report and photos and slipped a piece of paper to her. "This is where you can reach me, at Ben and Bev Cole's house. Call me anytime."

He paid for the book of stamps and walked out. Lucy still didn't move, even as Marshall's money for the stamps sat on the counter in front of her.

Debbie saw the whole thing. Now she was finished with just watching. She was going to do something.

The mail . . . I forgot the mail!

Bernice got into her Volkswagen Beetle and zipped over to the Ashton Post Office a little late this morning. In all the excitement, her daily mail pickup had slipped her mind.

She went into the lobby, said hello to Lou, the young mail clerk, and opened the *Ashton Clarion*'s Post Office box.

Krioni stood beside her, as interested in the morning mail as she was. He was looking for an important letter from Sally Roe.

Bernice flipped through the junk flyers, the bills, the letters to the editor . . . Ah, here were some checks in payment of advertising and want ads; those were always nice.

Nothing unusual, everything routine. She dropped all the mail into her large plastic shopping bag and headed out the door.

This was a horrendous development! Krioni shot through the roof of the Post Office and met Triskal high above.

"Nothing!" he said.

Triskal wasn't ready for that report. "Nothing? No letter?"

They could see Bernice getting back into her little car, far too calm and unruffled.

"It didn't get here," said Krioni, agitated, frustrated, and thinking fast. "It's lost . . . It's misplaced . . . I don't know! We'd better get word to Nathan and Armoth. If we don't get the fire started in time, Sally Roe is as good as dead!"

Sally's last letter to Tom Harris lay open on Claire Johanson's desk, and Claire was on the telephone.

"The Caravan Motel," she said. "I think our magic worked after all; this is the first time Roe has ever revealed her whereabouts. Apparently she'll be there for a while; she's waiting for Tom Harris to contact her." The party on the other end was elated. "Well, I'll breathe easier when we have her, before she writes to anyone else. And I'll breathe easiest of all when she's dead." More elated squawkings from the other end. "Yes, I'm sure Mr. Santinelli will be pleased. Give him our regards."

Claire hung up, rested her chin on her knuckles, and smiled at Sergeant Harold Mulligan. "Harold, help yourself to a drink."

Nathan shot through the roof of the Post Office near Chicago and flew over the heads of the busy staff, looking this way and that, banking and swooping over the tables, counters, and carts, then ducking under the tables, flying just inches above the linoleum, his sharp eyes scrutinizing every scrap of paper, every piece of junk mail, every—

There! Just under the front counter, facedown, lay the lost letter to Bernice Krueger. It was going to take some special measures to get it to Ashton in time. He grabbed it, arched upward, and looked around the room for the right mailbag to put it in.

Snatch! The letter was gone from his hand! He spun about in time to see a brazen little imp holding the letter in his claws, grinning a toothy grin, hovering on blurred black wings.

"Ooo," said the demon, "and what have we here?"

Nathan didn't have time for this. His sword was instantly in his hand.

OOF! A kick from a black, clawed foot! Another spirit came at him from the side, sword ready!

Nathan dashed the demon's sword aside with his own, then kicked the demon back, sending him through the wall of the building.

Another spirit dropped from above; Nathan shot sideways to dodge a plunging sword, then mowed the spirit in half.

Where was that imp? There! Hiding behind the sorting bench!

Two more spirits! They must have heard there was a fight in here. Nathan dove for the first, his sword raised, but the other spirit grabbed his ankle and jerked him backward. His sword cut through space, and that was all. The first demon was ready now with his own sword, laughing and drooling. The ankle-grabber was still pulling, his claws digging in.

Well, use what you have, Nathan figured. His wings roared with power, pulling him forward. With incredible strength and perfect timing, he swung his leg in a high, sweeping kick, giving the ankle-grabber a thrilling ride until Nathan brought him down with skull-crunching force on his partner. They were out.

There went the imp with the letter! Nathan shot sideways and caught him in the belly. The legs drifted to the floor while the imp dissolved. Nathan caught the letter, made a quick search, then slam-dunked it into the right mailbag. It would go out on the next truck.

As for the demons, Nathan knew there could be trouble—some of them had gotten away with the knowledge of this letter.

In the sealed conference room at Evans, Santinelli, Farnsworth, and McCutcheon, Santinelli hung up his private line and looked across the table at the anxious Mr. Khull.

"Mr. Khull, I've just been given some good news. You'd better gather your choice personnel."

That "good news" went out through the demonic ranks like a shock wave, and as Destroyer flew up through the roof of the law office building to gather his hordes, he suddenly found he had all the friends and yea-saying lackeys he needed to finish the job, especially the demons from Broken Birch. They were swarming in from every sector of the sky, whooping and hollering, wanting to be a part of this glorious moment.

"I knew it!" he gloated, and with no small measure of relief. "I knew it would work! Our Judas has come through at last, and now Sally Roe will have her Gethsemane! We will take her!" Then he added under his breath, "And I will throw her as a gift into the Strongman's face!"

The demons were muttering, nodding, and rumbling their approval and admiration of Destroyer's great wisdom as they came to rest on the roof, hovered overhead, buzzed in tight circles around the building, and even tripped over each other.

This motley, bloodthirsty swarm needed to be brought to order. Destroyer soared into the sky where every gleaming yellow eye could see him, and waved his glowing red sword in wide circles to get their attention. Most of them settled down and listened. The others were too busy hooting, hollering, and sparring.

"Forces!" Destroyer called.

His twelve captains converged immediately.

"We need to weed this garden and select the best! Choose warriors for our mission, and send the rabble to Summit. Let the Strongman put them to work!"

The captains soon had the spirits thoroughly sifted; the best warriors stood ready, swords gleaming. The pranksters, imps, and harassers were ordered to Summit, and left with much grumbling.

Destroyer was satisfied. He addressed the great horde. "We will prepare the way for Broken Birch! Death to the woman!"

"Death to the woman!" they shouted as one, and with an explosion of wings they rushed into the sky.

From miles away, Tal, Nathan, and Armoth saw the demons rise like a swarm of shrieking, whooping bats over Chicago, heading south. This was an armada of death for Sally Roe, a black cloud of doom.

Tal had received Nathan's news about Sally's last letter.

"Then it's going to be a day late. Our fire is delayed, and Sally will soon be in their hands!"

"Can we stop them?" asked Armoth.

Tal shook his head. "Everything is in motion now. We're committed."

"We do have warriors posted to monitor everything," Nathan assured his captain.

"But Destroyer will take her," Tal replied, his voice weakened with the pain of it. "And he will do what he wants with her . . ."

Marshall no sooner got back from his trip to the Post Office for stamps than he was out again, this time heading for Judy's Secretarial Service, quite curious and adequately baited by Bernice and her maddening flair for suspense. To hear Bev Cole tell it, the fate of the world depended on Marshall picking up whatever Bernice was going to fax to him.

Sally Roe remained in her musty little room at the Caravan Motel, sitting in the only chair, reading from a Gideon Bible.

"Who shall separate us from the love of Christ?" she read. " . . . I am convinced that neither death nor life, neither angels nor demons, neither the present nor the future, nor any powers, neither height nor depth, nor anything else in all creation, will be able to separate us from the love of God that is in Christ Jesus our Lord."

She closed her eyes, gave thanks, and kept reading, just waiting hour by hour in her little room.

Marshall pulled into the small parking area in front of Judy's Secretarial. Well, was anybody there? The lights were on inside, but there was no sign of Judy. Hm. That looked like a note taped over the OPEN sign hanging in the window. He got out to have a look.

Outside Chicago, two cars turned off the main thoroughfare, came down one block, and slowed long enough for the people inside to get a good look at the Caravan Motel.

"Hm, so this is the Caravan," said Mr. Khull, giving the old motel a quick once-over. "Roe isn't operating on much of a budget."

"What a dump," said one of Khull's three favorite killers, a young, wiry woman with long, blonde hair who could have passed for a college student.

The Caravan Motel was no joy to behold. Long ago, before the freeways diverted all the interstate traffic, this place probably did a profitable and respectable business in housing weary travelers for the night. Now times had changed, the fourteen little cabins were run down, the lawn had surrendered to weeds, and most of the business here was probably the disreputable kind.

"Which cabin is she in?" asked a tall, youthful-looking man. He'd gotten within a knife's blade of Sally Roe on the Bentmore University campus. He still had his knife, and he was looking forward to a longer, more satisfying encounter.

"Fourteen," said Khull, "right on the end near the road. We won't have to pass any of the other rooms. She's making it easy."

Khull parked the car just past the motel, and the other car pulled in behind. Altogether, eight people got out of the two cars. Khull gave the four men from the second car a slight nod, and they scattered immediately up and down the street, covering every avenue of escape from the motel.

"Okay, babe," said Khull, "check and make sure."

The young woman went ahead of them, walking into the motel office.

Khull and the other two just stood on the sidewalk, talking and looking casual.

She came out again, and pointed discreetly at Number 14.

"Let's go," said Khull.

"Oh, hi," said Judy. "Been waiting long?"

"No, not long," said Marshall. "About ten minutes, I guess." He'd seen the little note she'd taped in the window, "BACK IN TEN MINUTES."

"Had to get a new typewriter ribbon. I can hardly read my

letters anymore." She had a small sack in her hand, which meant her trip must have been successful.

"I think I have a fax waiting for me."

"Oh yeah, you do."

Judy unlocked the door and let him in. "It came in not too long ago. I think I put it . . . Let me see, where did I put it?"

The young blonde knocked on the door to Number 14.

Sally tensed, closed her eyes, and prayed a quick prayer. Then she rose from her chair and approached the door. "Yes?"

"Maid," said the woman.

Judy finally found the sheet of paper that had come out of the fax machine. "Oh, here you are."

Marshall took it and thanked her. Now this looked familiar. It was even disappointing. Hadn't he told Bernice he'd already seen the curriculum? What was the big deal? All the way over here to Judy's for this?

But what was Bernice's note at the top? She'd written it in bold marker pen.

"Okay, just a minute," Sally said, and looked around the room one last time. She was ready. She went to the door and put her hand on the knob.

"Marshall," said Bernice's note, "have you seen this? Call me."

From the note, a huge arrow drawn with a wide-tipped marker pen bled down the page to a glaring circle at the bottom.

Within that circle was the name of the curriculum's author—its *real* author.

Sally Beth Roe.

WHAM! The door burst open and almost caught Sally across the face. Khull was all over her, then two more blurred figures. Arms grappled and grabbed, the room spun around her, she fell to the floor, her face smacking the worn carpet. A sharp knee gouged into her back, pinning her down so hard she thought her ribs would crack. They grabbed her arms and twisted them behind her until she cried out in pain, then bound them with loop upon loop of tight, cutting rope.

AAW! Khull grabbed a fistful of her hair and wrenched her head up from the carpet. She couldn't breathe. He held a glimmering, silver knife to her throat. "Make a sound, and this goes in."

She closed her mouth tightly, trying to contain the cries of pain and terror she just couldn't help.

The room was full of people, searching every corner, every drawer, under the mattress, dumping out her duffel bag, going through all her possessions.

"You know what we're looking for," said Khull right into her ear. He grabbed one of her bound hands and forced her index finger open. "Tell us where the ring is and where those rosters are, or I start cutting."

"If I tell you, you'll just run off with them yourself!" said Sally. The knife came against the base of her finger. She gushed the words out. "I'll tell the people who sent you! Turn me over to them!"

The knife remained in place.

Sally blurted, "You want to get paid, don't you?"

The knife stayed where it was; Khull's grip on her finger never loosened. She could feel the edge of that knife against her skin, and she prayed while an eternity passed.

Destroyer stood in the room, not at all willing to lose the prize once he had found it.

Take her to Summit, he said to Khull.

Khull leaned over Sally, longing with every fiber of his being to run his knife through her heart. He hesitated, breathing hard.

Destroyer put his hand on his sword. *You will take her to Summit, to the Strongman, and you will do it now!*

After the longest, most agonizing moment, for no apparent reason, Khull took away the knife and let her finger go.

Sally thought she would faint. She was close to vomiting.

"Get her up!"

She was snatched from the floor in an instant by no less than four huge thugs, and held tightly, unable to move. Now she could see Khull's face leering at her, the eyes full of hate. Demon eyes.

SLAP! His hand felt like iron across her jaw, cheek, and nose. She almost blacked out. Warm blood began to trickle from her nose and down over her mouth.

Khull grabbed a fistful of her hair again and held his knife right under her nose. "We're going to take you to our friends. They are going to get the whole package right in their laps, and listen to me now: you'd better give them everything they want when they want it, because I will be right there, and if they don't get what they want, they are going to give you to me. To *me*, understand?"

"I *will* cooperate."

"Not a sound from you!"

"Not a sound."

Khull looked at her with all the lust and murderous intent of the Devil himself, and then gave the order: "Let's go."

The young blonde woman stuffed everything Sally owned into Sally's duffel bag, and a thug grabbed it up.

In broad daylight, like a gruesome parade, Khull led his band of rogues and their captive, bound with rope and her nose still bleeding, out of Number 14 and to the street. Sally could see some curtains cracked open across the courtyard, but no one dared show their face. Even the owner of the place, an ugly, chain-smoking woman in her fifties, caught just a glimpse of them and then turned away, being careful to mind her own business.

They took Sally to the first car, shoved her into the backseat between two men—one of them was the young knife-wielder she'd met at Bentmore—and drove away unhurried, un-hampered, and unchallenged.

The Caravan Motel was almost invisible under a crawling, hissing swarm of evil spirits. Every person in every building was motivated by fear, self-interest, and even self-delusion.

465

No, they didn't see anything. It wasn't what it looked like—it just seemed that way. It wasn't their problem. A lot of that kind of thing happened around places like this; so what?

Destroyer and his twelve key warriors flew just above the two automobiles, wary and braced for any angelic resistance. The resistance never came. They did see some heavenly warriors, but the warriors made no moves against them; they were intimidated by the great demonic numbers, no doubt.

"Ha!" Destroyer laughed, elbowing his closest warrior. "What did I say? Their strength is gone! Tal has no more numbers to boast in, and . . ." He was delighted with his own craftiness. " . . . I do believe we have surprised them all! Before they could muster any new strength, we have snatched their new little saint right from under their noses!"

As the two automobiles turned onto the main thoroughfare and sped away, many of Nathan's prize warriors were on hand to watch, hiding in the shadows, crouching behind trees, parked cars, and houses. They kept a close watch, but they did not intervene. The word had spread quickly and clearly among them all: This was Destroyer's moment, and Captain Tal's biggest risk ever.

Out on the interstate, a U.S. Mail truck sped along, heading southward from Chicago toward the easy rolling hills of the Midwest and the quaint little college town of Ashton.

On board, in a mailbag, just a little dirty and wrinkled by now, was that letter addressed to Bernice Krueger.

thirty-nine

Marshall was impatient, and that made him anxious, and that made him irritable. Ben Cole just kept pacing around the house trying to think of what else to do, Kate sat next to Marshall at the dining room table, flipping through all their accumulated files for any information Marshall might need, and Bev Cole just kept watching it all and praying softly, "Lord Jesus, we need You now!"

Marshall was on the phone with John Harrigan, a friend and contact with the FBI. "Oh yeah, she wrote it, all right. I got back to my reporter, and she'd already gotten back to this Cliff Bingham guy, and he verifies the edition he found was recent, published only two years ago." Marshall rolled his eyes and gritted his teeth. This conversation wasn't bringing results fast enough. "So that means the curriculum the school gave to us was doctored; Sally Roe's name was deleted and substituted by two other names, and that fits right in with the cover-up I told you about. No, I don't have a case yet. I thought you guys were the ones who are supposed to investigate these things. Well, I'm close, real close, and I do think it's something for you guys to handle. The Omega Center's in Fairwood, Massachusetts, and Sally Roe was almost murdered clear over here in Bacon's Corner, for crying out loud! Now is that across state lines or what?" More talk from the other end. "All right, listen: can you give me a number where I can reach you anytime, I mean, right in the middle of the night if I have to? I won't call unless I've got some real stuff for you, but when I do get it, time will be that much shorter for Sally Roe." He got an objection. "Come on, I'll owe you one. Just remember that lead I got you in that cocaine operation." Marshall grabbed his pen. "Good man!"

He got several numbers, said good-bye, and hung up.

Everyone in the house converged on him. "Well? What did he say?"

"He'll be on call. I've got phone numbers to reach him at

work, at home, at church, and I've also got his paging service, so he's covered. But what he's waiting for is some firm information to justify the FBI getting involved."

Ben was indignant. "What's wrong with all that stuff you gave him?"

"Eh, it was enough to make him interested, but not enough to make him stick his neck out."

"What about Wayne Corrigan?"

Kate answered, "I left a message at his office. He'll get what we have."

"O Lord Jesus, protect Sally Roe!" said Bev.

Guilo had returned to his post in the mountains above the picturesque town of Summit, and though the surroundings were as strikingly beautiful as ever, the invisible evil was even worse. Educators, statesmen, jurists, entertainers, corporate moguls, and financiers from all over the world were gathering just a mile up the valley from Summit at the Summit Institute for Humanistic Studies. Their semiannual conference was just getting underway, and as these global planners gathered, demon lords and warriors of the most conniving sort gathered with them, filling the valley with a swirling, sooty, steadily thickening cloud of spirits. The demons hovered, hooted, sparred, and jostled, more numerous, riotous, and cocky than ever before.

"They are expecting a real party," said Guilo.

Mr. Santinelli, kingpin of the law firm of Evans, Santinelli, Farnsworth, and McCutcheon, Mr. Goring, the lord and administrator of the Summit Institute for Humanistic Studies, and Mr. Steele, the ruthless ruler of the Omega Center for Educational Studies, were together again, enjoying a brandy by the fire in Mr. Goring's rustic chalet on the Summit Institute campus. This meeting brought back the memory of their last meeting at Omega, when things were not so rosy; they could recall the indignation of having to endure the very presence of that most undesirable of personalities, Mr. Khull—and, of course, at that time Sally Roe was still at large.

Now they clinked their glasses together in a toast of victory. Indeed, with the news that came in earlier today, things were definitely different.

"To the future!" said Santinelli.

"To the future!" echoed Goring and Steele.

They sipped from their drinks, smacked their lips, and even allowed themselves a chuckle or two

As they relaxed into Goring's soft couch and easy chair, Santinelli addressed the pressing matters before them. "I've sent our private jet to bring Mr. Khull and his personnel. They should arrive here with the prize in a matter of hours."

"Have you ever met her?" asked Steele.

Goring and Santinelli exchanged glances.

"Not I," said Goring, "but I'm looking forward to it."

Santinelli agreed. "An outrageous fish story can never compare to actually seeing the fish hauled in. Actually, I'm impressed that Khull was able to restrain himself and deliver her to us alive."

Goring spoke with great anticipation. "I'll be fascinated to meet her. I have many questions, to be sure."

"Oh," said Santinelli, "we'll all have questions for her—serious questions."

"Any word on the ring or the rosters?" asked Steele.

"None. But with Sally Roe in our custody, I can't imagine that will be a problem."

Goring cautioned, "But just remember, there are many delegates and visitors about. Our present business would be quite distasteful to most of them, I'm sure; so our guests must never know about it."

"Agreed. And I have instructed Khull to preserve Roe's appearance, just in case she may be seen by someone."

"Now," said Goring, "there is that other matter that we discussed . . ."

"Of course," said Santinelli, "the whole matter of Khull in particular and Broken Birch in general."

"Mm," said Steele, nodding. "I've thought about that too. Now that they're in bed with us, they won't stop until they control the bed."

"I've consulted with Mr. Evans and Mr. Farnsworth, and they have some of their best people looking into it. If we move carefully, and lay a thoroughly thought-out plan, we could accumulate some damning evidence against Broken Birch while keeping ourselves clean. Evans and Farnsworth are quite sure that the whole lot of them can be arrested for crimes totally unrelated to our enterprise."

Goring smiled and nodded. "Excellent. I've already consulted with my board, and they think such a plan would be feasible. We'll be able to call in some favors from our corporate and governmental resources, and I'm sure they'll be most willing to see what we want them to see and to look the other way when it would be . . . worthwhile."

"Then we must proceed on this without delay," said Santinelli. "Khull and Broken Birch have finally done their job, but upon delivery of Sally Roe we must erase any association with them."

Goring added, "Any *memory* of them in *any* circles, if we can help it!"

Santinelli raised his glass. "I'll drink to that!"

And so they did.

The van had been driving along the winding, climbing, meandering highway for what seemed hours, and Sally finally nodded off, her chin on her chest, sitting between two of the four surly, burly escorts that came with Khull and herself on the plane. The flight had lasted several hours, the driving even longer, and now it was night.

She looked a little better. At least Khull figured she couldn't escape from a flying jet plane, and, reciting Santinelli's order to "preserve Roe's appearance," untied her and let her use the cramped little washroom to wash the dried, caked blood from her mouth and chin, change from her bloodstained shirt to a clean but sadly wrinkled blouse, and brush out her hair. She looked a little better—for a totally exhausted, manhandled, soon-to-die fugitive.

They were heading into the mountains, through tall forests of pine and fir that became monotonous after a while. Sally slept fitfully, jolting awake every few moments, but only long enough to see more trees going by the window, and then she would nod off again.

Some time later—she didn't know how much later—she awoke to morning light. The van was slowing down; Khull and his cohorts were looking around, trying to get their bearings. They were entering a village.

Khull, sitting in the front passenger seat, turned around to tell her, "Welcome to Summit."

Sally rubbed the sleep from her eyes and looked out the windows at a quaint-looking little town surrounded on all sides by snow-covered, sawtoothed peaks and thick, unblemished forests. Out the left window, just above the A-framed roofs of some ski lodges, the morning sun turned a distant waterfall into golden tinsel; out the right window, through a gap in the small inns and storefronts, the mountainside dropped sharply away to a flower-strewn alpine meadow. Patches of snow still remained everywhere, dripping and glistening in the low-angled sunlight.

Why have we come here? Sally wondered. It hardly seemed the setting for such gruesome business, and people like Khull and his bunch just didn't fit at all.

But then again, maybe they did. Sally began to notice some of the establishments and institutions in this village; she began to read some of the signs.

Taoist Retreat Center. Valley Tibetan Project and Monastery. Temple of Ananta. Library and Archives of Ancient Wisdom. Native American School of Traditional Medicine. Karma Triyana Dharmachakra. The Temple of Imbetu Agobo. Babaji Ashram. Mother's Temple Shrine of Shiva. The Children of Diana. Temple to the Divine Universal Mother. The House of Bel. The Sacred and Royal Order of the Nation.

She leaned toward the window. The big escort put his ham-sized palm in her chest and shoved her back. She twisted and looked out the rear windows as the building passed.

The Sacred and Royal Order of the Nation. The little gargoyle snarled at her from the front door of the black stone temple and from the building's facade. She could just hear it screeching, Welcome to Summit!

Destroyer had followed the hunting party clear from Chicago, and now, as the van came through the valley and entered the village, he was going to milk this moment for all it was worth. He dropped from the sky, alighted on the roof of the van, and stood there, his sword held high in victory, his wings trailing like banners behind him, his twelve captains forming his honor guard. Driving under the thick mantle of spirits was like entering a dark tunnel under a towering mountain; on every side, and thousands of feet above, demons cheered and waved their swords in a thunderous display of admiration.

Destroyer reveled in his victory and newfound fame. These vile hordes once ignored him, mocked him, cared not to know his name. Now listen to them! Let the *Strongman* listen to them! A better announcement of his arrival could not be asked for.

Guilo turned at the sound of wings behind him. The captain had arrived.

The cheers of the demons echoing out of the valley could only be for one reason. "They've brought her," Guilo reported.

Both he and Tal stayed low among the trees with their warriors. The swarm of demons below was nothing to tangle with before the right time.

Guilo pointed. "There! That blue van just entering the Summit Institute!"

They could see it only intermittently, as small as a grain of sand, appearing through the thinner parts of the demonic swarm and then disappearing again. It reappeared just long enough for them to watch it turn off the thin, gray ribbon of highway and slip out of sight under the mantle of spirits covering the Summit Institute.

"Well, now she's alone," said Tal. "We can't break through that."

"What about the fire you were going to start?" Guilo asked. "If ever we needed something to happen, it is now!"

Tal shook his head. "It will be a day late. For now, all we can do is wait for Nathan's signal and hope it comes soon."

The semiannual Global Consciousness Conference was getting underway; so the van's driver had to drive up and down the large, black-topped parking lot several times before he could find an empty parking place. Sally spent that time observing the Summit Institute for Humanistic Studies. It reminded her a lot of the Omega Center, except that it was newer and the architecture more modern. Stone was an abundant building material around here, and so was used in the construction of the offices, lecture halls, walkways and gardens. True to their religious devotion to Mother Earth, the designers of the campus did not supplant the natural environment, but let the campus merge with it, almost hiding it among the trees, rocks, and hilly terrain.

The hour was still early, so there were no people out walking. How fortunate for Sally's captors.

Khull turned to Sally, holding up his knife as a reminder. "All they paid me to do is deliver you here. If you get cut up in the parking lot, it's your fault and not my problem, understand?"

She nodded.

"Let's get her into Goring's place."

An observer standing at a distance would have thought an important dignitary had arrived and was now surrounded by Secret Service agents. Sally was barely visible within the tight cluster of bodies that formed outside the van's side door and then began moving up the path toward Mr. Goring's chalet.

Sally made a concerted effort to see around the backs and shoulders of her escorts and study the layout of this place. Right now they were passing through an expansive, meticulously arranged herb garden with sculptured hedges, stone pathways, and eye-pleasing reflection pools. In the middle of a carpet of moss, one lone man sat almost naked in the early-morning cold, eyes shut, legs crossed in the lotus position, totally entranced.

Leaving the herb garden, they rounded a corner, followed a narrow, natural stone stairway with tall evergreen hedges on either side, and then broke out into the open. To the right, the ground dropped away into a natural amphitheater, and beyond the amphitheater, a heart-stopping view of the mountains spread wider and higher than the eye could take in.

In the center of the amphitheater, a sizable group of people stood in neat, concentric semicircles around a blazing firepit, chanting, droning, and tossing flowers, grain, and fruit into the fire. On a small platform at the head of the circle, gawking down into the fire as if mesmerized by it, seven stone deities received the offerings and worship of these adoring early-risers while a gaunt, white-haired woman in a yellow robe sang a haunting song in Sanskrit.

Sally remembered the song and still knew some of the words, even though she hadn't heard it in ten years. She couldn't remember all the names of the seven little deities, but they were secondary gods anyway. This ceremony was to invoke the blessing of the Universal Mother first of all, and secondly to appease these seven dwarfs.

Then she caught a glimpse of some of the faces as they lifted toward the morning sun. No! There was Mrs. Denning from the Omega Center, and two of the Omega faculty! And was that Mr. Blakely, her counselor at Bentmore Teacher's College? She thought she recognized his face, and then his cracking, squawking chant identified him for sure. Close to the fire, her face washed with red light, was Krystalsong, a witch, scholar, and mother of four from the West Coast; she and Sally had worked together on a holistic preschool program.

Quite a homecoming for us all, she thought.

On the highway to Ashton, the mail truck continued to roll along, right on schedule. The morning mail shipment would be at the Ashton Post Office the moment they opened the doors.

"That has to be it!" said a spirit to his friends.

They were whirring and rushing along above the highway,

keeping pace with the truck and eyeing it curiously. The spirit leading them had been in a terrible fight; his wings were tattered, his flight was wobbly, and his face was misshapen.

"This time," he slurred, "we won't let any heavenly warrior stop us!"

"Destroyer will reward us!" said another.

"We will stop the truck and get that letter!"

They swept their wings tightly behind their shoulders and dropped like torpedoes toward the truck, cutting through the thin layers of morning mist, the wind whistling through their wings and whiskers. This should be easy enough. They could foul the engine, break the steering, flatten a tire. They could—

LIGHT! SWORDS! WARRIORS! The truck was full of them!

Nathan shot into the air and met the battered demon.

"You again?" they both said.

The demon dissolved into red smoke. Nathan spun to take out another one.

Armoth tore three spirits apart with one sword swipe, and then spun in a blur to bash two more with his heel.

A dozen warriors had burst out of the truck and now swirled around it, swatting and hacking.

Their picnic ruined, the remaining spirits fled like flies and the truck kept rolling.

forty

The saints were on their knees. The division was fading. Mark had devoted multiplied hours of his time and large measures of his personal concern to healing and restoring the hurting and wounded among his flock, steadily, prayerfully undoing the tangled mess that Destroyer and his hordes had created in the church. It had taken some real breaking, some repenting, some forgiving on all sides, but it happened, and was still happening, one heart at a time.

The Jessups were so hurt and dismayed that it took careful, loving appeals from the Walroths for them to come back into fellowship; Judy Waring was carrying a lot of bitterness against the likes of Donna Hemphile who had used her—and her mouth—to hurt God's people. But she had to admit that it was, after all, her mouth and her heart, and she started her turnabout with those two areas of her life. Every one of them had to totally reevaluate their opinion of Tom Harris, and they were still in that process even as they prayed.

It wasn't an easy restoration for any of them, but in the face of their revealed enemy they had a clear choice: rejoin God's army and fight the evil that was even now destroying them, their families, and their Christian faith, or . . . proceed with being destroyed.

They rejoined the army—with a vengeance.

The angels kept quiet, stayed low, and didn't talk much as they secretly placed themselves at strategic points around the country, waiting for Tal's "brushfire" to start.

Mota the Polynesian and Signa the Oriental had many points to cover all around the Bacon's Corner area, but they now had more than enough warriors, so carefully, methodically they covered them. Terga, the tender-egoed prince of the town, was getting edgy about the sudden tide of prayer coming from the reunited saints, but so far he did not sense the activity all that prayer was bringing about. Besides, he'd heard the news from the powers above him: the woman had been captured; the danger was over.

Cree the Native American and Si the East Indian had returned once again to the Omega Center for Educational Studies, and were now planting angelic warriors like explosive charges in just the right places all around the campus. It was tedious, dangerous work, the greatest danger being discovery. While they crawled along or under the ground, moved under the surface of the lake, stole from tree to tree, or spent hours totally motionless under rocks, boats, or buildings to avoid discovery, they could always see Barquit, the Prince of Omega, soaring to and fro, his eyes everywhere, laughing and exulting in any progress made in the classes and workshops, then growling and spitting at any clumsy moves by his demons or by his puppet-people below. He was still very much in charge and ruling his demon hordes with an iron hand. Now that the woman was captured, he felt no fears or worries at all, and obviously planned on remaining at his post forever.

On the surface, Bentmore University looked like the same old red-brick, permanently established alma mater it had always been, and classes were in full swing as usual.

In the spirit realm, however, Corrupter, Bentmore's rotund master of disinformation and fleshly indulgence, moved like a blimp over the campus, seeking out any damage the school may have incurred from that recent, violent exchange with Heaven's warriors. Ha! Destroyer was nothing but a status-anxious worrywart! Damage? There was none to speak of. Professor Lynch had been a bit ill lately, but he was getting old anyway, and there were plenty more where he came from. With the woman captured, the future was wide open.

Across the river, atop the North American Can Company, Chimon the European and Scion of the British Isles were back, hiding behind one of the factory's many ventilator stacks. Things looked quiet at Bentmore right now, but when Tal's brushfire started, there would be noise enough.

Chimon and Scion were looking for hiding-places and sending troops to fill them. The warehouse by the river could hold a myriad or so; the wharf on the Bentmore side would also serve very well, being closer to the campus. The troops moved silently and quickly. One false move, one ill-timed glint of light, could endanger them all.

At every point along Sally's journey, at every stronghold of Satan, the angels moved into position and then waited for the signal.

But they all knew they were waiting longer than expected.

In the peaks above Summit, Tal and Guilo watched and listened for any hint of what might be happening inside. Behind them, a hidden army lay in waiting, ready.

"Any time now," Tal said more than once. "Any time."

In purely a physical sense, Mr. Goring's chalet was an inviting A-framed structure built with rough-hewn timbers and a full-height glass front that commanded a marvelous view of the mountains. It could have served so well as a ski lodge or mountain getaway.

In a spiritual sense, it was a churning, frothing hornets' nest of evil, and Sally could feel it even before her captors led her through the front door. She knew she was being watched from every direction; she could discern the oppressive, smothering hate that covered the place like a leaden fog.

Destroyer was already in the chalet, shoving his way into the living room, brushing aside the Strongman's demons and attendants with rude boldness. Into the Strongman's lair he went, strutting down a narrow aisle formed by two straight lines of demon lords from all over the world, until finally he stood in the presence of the Strongman.

"My Ba-al," he said loudly, with a rather showy bow, "I bring to you Sally Beth Roe!"

The Strongman had heard the demonic cloud in an uproar, and now he could see Khull and his party bringing Sally Roe to the front door. He nodded in carefully measured approval. "So you have. So you have."

The demon lords raised their swords to begin a cheer.

The Strongman growled, his arms outstretched, "Hold!" They froze and stared at him. "First we will see if there is anything to cheer about."

The heavy plank door closed behind Sally and her captors. They were standing in Mr. Goring's spacious, comfortable living room. At one end was a massive stone fireplace; at the other end, a wall of glass brought in the mountains; the open-beam ceiling soared above them to the roof's apex, and from the massive ridge beam, rustic iron chandeliers hung on long chains.

Three men rose from their places by the fire. Sally recognized Mr. Steele, and it was obvious by his satisfied grin that he recognized her.

It was Goring who ordered, "Bring her here and sit her down."

Khull was after some glory. He grabbed Sally's arm and pulled her forward, keeping her constantly off-balance, then, with a cruel grip that bruised her arm, flung her down into a sofa. With just a few small gestures, he ordered his four thugs to stand guard around her.

"Gentlemen," he said arrogantly, "I bring to you Sally Beth Roe."

The three men stood before her, staring at her with great interest. The gray-haired man with the perfectly trimmed beard and the bone necklace looked at the tall, silver-haired executive type, and then both of them looked at Mr. Steele.

"This is she," said Steele. "Well done, Mr. Khull. We will settle our account with you immediately. However, if you are agreeable, we may still have need of your services."

Khull smiled, giving Sally a leering, sideways glance. "It would be my pleasure."

"Then please remain for a time, you and your staff. We'll try to settle this business as quickly as we can."

"Take your time."

With Sally placed securely on the sofa and under capable guard, the three gentlemen relaxed and took their seats—the two older men in another sofa facing Sally, and Mr. Steele in a large easy chair between the two sofas, facing the fire.

Steele opened the conversation. "Sally, let me introduce my two friends." He indicated the man with the perfectly trimmed beard. "This is Mr. Emile Goring, presently Director of Finance of the Mannesville Association, an international humanitarian and environmental think tank and mobilizer of global projects. He's a major stockholder and director in over forty global corporations dealing in oil, gas, transportation, exports, mining, and so forth."

Sally looked toward Goring, who nodded back at her with a grim but still fascinated expression.

Steele wanted to be sure Sally was impressed. "Consequently, what Mr. Goring desires to do, he has the means to do. He and his associates are major contributors and underwriters for such endeavors as the Summit Institute; this institute is part of their vision, and it wouldn't be here at all if not for their efforts.

"The other gentleman is Mr. Carl Santinelli, Senior Partner at Evans, Santinelli, Farnsworth, and McCutcheon, one of the most powerful law firms in the country and, in a sense, the flagship of the ACFA. He is a man of great causes in law and jurisprudence, a legal activist of the highest order, and definitely not a man to be tampered with."

Sally looked at Santinelli, and got a cold, probing stare back.

Then Mr. Steele turned to Goring and Santinelli. "Mr. Goring and Mr. Santinelli, I introduce to you Ms. Sally Beth Roe, former Director of Primary Curriculum Resources at the Omega Center for Educational Studies, convicted murderer, former convict, production worker at the Bergen Door Factory, and most recently, vagabond."

Goring and Santinelli continued to study her as if looking upon a real oddity.

Steele relaxed in his chair and studied her himself. "It has been quite an adventure, hasn't it?"

"It has," she answered.

"I see your hair roots are beginning to grow out. I do miss seeing your fiery red hair. And since when do you wear tinted glasses?"

She sighed and removed them, rubbing her tired eyes. "All a disguise, of course." Then she bitterly admitted, "And quite futile."

"Quite futile," Steele agreed. "But you do understand, don't you, why we had to track you down?"

The question angered her. "It is my impression, Mr. Steele, that you and your associates want me dead, and I would like to know why."

"Oh, come now!" said Santinelli. "A person of your brilliance and experience should have no trouble seeing how much you are in our way. As for that initial attempt on your life, we will not mince words. It was a blunder, an unfortunate fiasco perpetrated by some incompetents who thought they would please us. We were not pleased. Killing you in such a way was never our original intent."

"So what was your original intent?"

Santinelli smiled. "Our original intent was the lawsuit against the Good Shepherd Academy in Bacon's Corner, your current town of residence. Your stumbling into the middle of our project was a total surprise to all of us."

Sally needed to confirm what she thought. "*You* are the people ultimately responsible for the lawsuit against that Christian school?"

Santinelli nodded. "Lucy Brandon first contacted our local ACFA affiliate, the affiliate contacted the state chapter, the state chapter contacted us, and we decided the case could prove profitable. We immediately put our strength and influence behind it."

"But not for the child Amber's sake, of course?"

Santinelli exchanged a glance with the others. This woman was as sharp as Steele had said she was. "Obviously you have no illusions about our concern for the safety, rights, and welfare of children, especially since the ACFA regularly defends the interests of child pornographers and molesters." He sat back with his chin high, tapping his fingertips together, watching her eyes for a response.

She forced one corner of her mouth to stretch upward and nodded.

"As you may well imagine, the real object of that lawsuit is not the awarding of damages to the plaintiff, but legal precedent, the molding and shaping of law, even the rewriting of law, through an ideal test case."

Steele contributed, "Ms. Roe is quite familiar with our agenda for social change through state-controlled public education. She was a major contributor to that effort at one time."

Santinelli nodded, impressed. "So you do realize how great a deterrent to our cause the Christians are as long as they are allowed to raise and educate their children according to their Biblical beliefs. Even before your years at Omega, we were seeking legislation and legal precedent that could be used to stifle that deterrent. It's taken this long for that to develop."

"But it did," said Goring with a gloating smile.

Santinelli indulged in the same smile and continued, "The latest legislation for our use was the Federal Day-care and Private Primary School Assistance Act, and the Munson-Ross Civil Rights Act, each a rather muddled stack of laws that—as we had hoped—would require testing and clarification in the courts. The Good Shepherd Academy case seemed tailor-made for that purpose. It not only involved federal funds spent in a Christian school, and therefore government intervention and control, but also included the useful, inflammatory child abuse angle, something we could use to incite support in the media and in the public mind, getting them all on our side regardless of the real issues. And that, of course, was the object. With the public outraged and preoccupied with the protection of innocent children, we would be seen as no less than champions for children in establishing through case law the right and duty of the state to control religious education." He couldn't resist a laugh of delight. "Even after the initial trauma—real or concocted—against the child fades into the past and is forgotten, the laws will still be on the books, and the government firmly planted within the walls of the church.

"As you yourself taught and were taught, once such control of religious instruction is established, the methodical, gradual elimination of religious instruction altogether is only a matter of time. And then such people as you once were will have tremendous, far-reaching power to control and mold every segment of the next generation without resistance."

Sally nodded. She'd learned this catechism.

Goring picked up the narrative. "Well, it did look promising, of course. But that was before you happened along. You can imagine what a shock it was to learn you were out of prison and living in the very town where we'd brought the lawsuit. Worse than that was the way we found out: Our little prize, the very child in question, supposedly the pristine, totally innocent victim of Christian bigots and abusers, suddenly chose to demonstrate her true colors one day in the local Post Office. Ah! I see you remember the incident! Of all people to witness such an outburst, it had to be you!

"When Mrs. Brandon brought the incident to her attorneys' attention, they passed the word to us, and, knowing who you were, we saw a substantial risk that you would recognize the child's condition, especially since you wrote the very curriculum that caused it. We were aware that you could severely jeopardize our case should you decide to step forward."

Santinelli allowed himself a mournful chuckle. "But really, we hadn't yet decided what our course of action would be before a misguided member—uh, former member now—of our staff took matters into his own hands and secured the services of an assassin."

"That part you are quite familiar with," said Goring.

"Oh, yes," Sally answered.

"And that," said Santinelli, "brings us to why we've all been on this merry chase. Ms. Roe, had you died then, we could have absorbed the error and continued with our plan, none the worse for our friends' impulsiveness." He sighed. "But impressive person that you are, you not only lived, but a) you killed the assassin and left her there to create all kinds of questions should she be found, and b) you made off with a ring the assassin was wearing on her finger, a ring that could eventually link the whole wicked affair with us."

Sally said nothing, and tried to keep her face from saying anything.

"The assassin was a crafty sort. She was a paramour of that former member of our staff, and pilfered his ring, we believe, for the purpose of blackmail and manipulation. That ring could have told anyone who its owner really was—all it would take would be the securing of the Nation's rosters in which all the code names are listed. Both items are now, we believe, in your possession?"

"I'm prepared to bargain," she replied.

They all stifled a laugh and exchanged glances.

Steele ventured a question they all felt was unnecessary. "So . . . you are willing to relinquish the rosters and the ring in exchange for something? Just what would that be?"

Sally looked them all in the eye and spoke clearly. "Abandon the lawsuit. Leave the Christian school alone, and let Tom Harris have his children back."

This time they didn't stifle their laughter at all, but enjoyed her appeal thoroughly.

"And then," Goring asked, "you will release the ring and rosters back to us for our disposal?"

"We can certainly talk about it; I'm sure we can arrange something."

Santinelli leaned forward. "Is that a chain I see around your neck?"

Khull found out for sure. He forced her head sideways and grabbed at the chain, yanking it from under her blouse.

The gold ring dangled on the end.

With a vicious jerk that pulled her from the sofa and gouged her neck, he snapped the chain and tore it from her. She landed on the rug with a cry of pain, only to be gathered up by the thugs and flung on the sofa again.

"Here now, enough!" said Goring. Then he pointed to her bleeding neck. "Put a cloth on that. I don't want it staining the sofa."

One of Khull's men placed his handkerchief around Sally's neck.

Khull dangled the ring above Santinelli's palm, and then dropped it.

Santinelli examined the ring. "Mm-hm. The Ring of Fellowship in the Royal and Sacred Order of the Nation. A sacred object, to be sure." He glared at Sally. "Too sacred to be in your possession . . . and no longer in your possession."

Sally held the handkerchief to her neck, stunned and deflated in her spirit and wincing from the searing pain from her wound. "I see you belong to that group."

Santinelli looked at the gold Ring of Fellowship on his own hand. "Oh, the Nation consists of many brothers, all in vital places: in government, in banking, on the federal bench, on college boards and regencies. You were quite familiar with Owen Bennett, of course, and I'm sure you've already read an impressive list of names from those rosters you stole. Like any other secret society, we help all our initiates get established in the right places, and we see to each other's interests—provided, of course, that each man's interests conform to the interests of the society."

"Apparently James Bardine's interests did not."

Santinelli smiled. "Ah, yes, that 'former member of our staff' does have a name. Then it was you who called our office? I understand our receptionist recently informed an anonymous female caller of his untimely death." He dropped the ring back and forth from hand to hand. "Brotherhood is one thing; violation of sacred blood oaths of secrecy is another."

He looked out the windows toward the mountains. "There are some things that are best kept sealed, Ms. Roe. If you could have toured these grounds, or walked through the town of Summit and met some of the people that are here this week, you would have found many different esoteric organizations represented, as well as some very . . . unique . . . individuals. We're all one global family, you know; that is the unifying cry of every heart. We proclaim that idea here and everywhere, just as you yourself have proclaimed it, and we teach that all are equal." He paused for effect. "But we keep to ourselves the fact that some are more equal than others, and far more fit to rule."

He set the ring on the glass coffee table and then looked directly at her. "I trust that now you fully appreciate what the stakes are here, how ruthless and determined we are, and how desperate your situation is. We are not here to bargain, Ms. Roe, but to put an end to the threat you pose to us. Exactly what process will be necessary to accomplish this will depend largely on yourself." He looked toward Khull. "I'm sure you'll find little comfort in the fact that Mr. Khull and his four accomplices are members of the same secret order to which your assassin belonged, a Satanic cult known as Broken Birch. They're a ruthless bunch who thrive on bloodletting, torture, human sacrifice. Quite unsavory." He looked back at Sally. "Ms. Roe, we are decent men, and we desire no more discomfort for you than you may make necessary. To be blunt, your fate depends on your performance."

Nathan the Arabian and his small band of sentries continued to ride shotgun in the mail truck as it drew closer and closer to Ashton. Armoth the African had flown ahead to warn Krioni and Triskal, the watchcaring angels of the town—it was only a matter of time before Destroyer heard about the letter aboard that truck.

In the herb garden not far from Goring's chalet, a group of about thirty conferees gathered in the crisp, scented air for a morning workshop led by a well-known recording artist. The young, blond-haired man had his guitar along, and some songs were planned before his talk on "Ecology: The Merging of Earth and Spirit."

There was a certain giddiness in the group. These people had never been this close to such a famous person before, and he was not the only famous person sitting there amid the rosemary, thyme, and lamb's ears. Two newsmaking clergymen of global stature were also in attendance, as well as a director of mystical science fiction films whose name was a household word and whose film characters were now plastic toys in every kid's room in this country and abroad.

The blond singer strummed his guitar, and they all began to sing one of his well-known ballads. The moment was magical.

The demons among them were enjoying it as well. Such worship and attention as they were now receiving was like getting a good back rub, and they even twitched and squirmed with delight at every bar of the song's carefully shaded double meanings.

Huh? What was that? The demons twisted their heads around to look toward a disturbance.

Two demonic warriors were gliding in over the top of the Goring Pavilion, apparently heading for Goring's chalet. They carried between them the drooping, limp form of a battered demon, still whimpering and wailing in agony. With a soft, rustling sound, they passed right over the herb garden and then disappeared beyond the tall evergreen hedge.

The demons in the herb garden fidgeted, stirred, and muttered to each other. *What was that? Who was that? What has happened?*

Some psychics were in attendance, and the demons attached to their brains were just as stirred up as the others. The psychics could immediately sense it.

The blond man even stopped the song. "What is it?"

"A disturbance," said a woman attorney and psychic.

"Yes," said a fifth grade teacher, his eyes closed. "Some kind of bad energy. Something's wrong somewhere."

In the chalet, Destroyer was relishing the entire conversation, as was the Strongman, though the Strongman was getting impatient.

Why wait so long? he growled. *Make her talk, and then finish her! The Plan is waiting!*

"Destroyer!" came a gravelly voice outside the building. It was one of Destroyer's henchmen. "A warrior brings news!"

"Not now!" Destroyer barked, wanting to watch what happened to the woman.

Frank E. Peretti

"Go!" said the Strongman.

He went, ducking outside the chalet to hear from a most pitiful-looking spirit.

"What happened to you?"

The demon sat on his haunches on the ground, his wings spread like tattered black tarpaulins, wrinkled, limp, and full of holes. His head was battered, and he braced himself to keep from falling over. "We attacked a mail truck on its way to Ashton."

Destroyer stooped low. "*Ashton*, you say?"

The demon started to topple.

Destroyer grabbed him by the neck and jerked him upright. "Did you say *Ashton*?"

The demon slurred a faint answer. "Ashton. A letter is bound for Ashton, and the Host of Heaven guard it."

Destroyer shot a glance into the chalet. The Strongman was still watching the interrogation of Sally Roe. He was still impatient. He wanted results. If he didn't get results, and fast, certain heads were going to roll.

Destroyer could just feel his head rolling. He let the demon flop to the ground, then motioned to his captains who gathered around him. "There is a letter bound for Ashton, guarded by the Host of Heaven. They do not guard it for nothing!" His face crinkled grotesquely at the thought of it. "Sally Roe may have written to someone there."

The captains gawked at each other.

"Well?" Destroyer demanded. "Did you hear me?"

"Ashton!" exclaimed one.

"We can't go back there!" said another.

Destroyer shushed them with a quick gesture. "Just look into it, and do it quietly. I'm sure it's nothing to worry about, just one little letter."

They looked back and forth at each other. "Which of us should go?" they wondered.

Destroyer held back a scream and hissed instead, "How about *all* of you? And take some spare warriors with you."

They all went, gathering as many demon troublemakers as wished to go.

Destroyer hurried back into Goring's chalet. The Strongman was intently listening to Sally's interrogation and didn't ask what the interruption was about.

Destroyer had no intention of telling him.

In Ashton, Krioni and Triskal could see the mail truck entering the city limits, right on time. Unfortunately, the precious letter inside was one truckload and one day late.

Triskal looked toward the west. "All clear so far."

Krioni was not optimistic. "They'll be here."

forty-one

santinelli leaned back, relaxed, and with an instructive glance at Goring and Steele encouraged them to do likewise. Then he looked at Sally and became suspiciously cordial.

"Sally, I have always considered myself a gentleman, a man of dignity and honor, and respectful of the dignity of women. I sincerely desire an intelligent, productive dialogue with you, and I'm sure, given the alternative, you desire the same."

"I would prefer it," Sally admitted.

Santinelli nodded. "Then, having agreed on that, it might be well for us to consider your credibility as a witness against us. It seems to me that you've forgotten what you are."

Sally answered simply and directly, "I'm an adultress, a baby killer, and a convicted felon." They looked uncomfortable. She'd answered that question a little too easily. "I've been reminded of that constantly since the day it first happened, by seven years of prison, by spirit tormentors, and by my own conscience."

Steele said, "Sally, that's a shameful and disgusting set of labels."

She smiled, and that even surprised her. "Actually, those labels are marvelous and beautiful because . . ." She hesitated.

Goring completed her sentence. "Because of the Cross?"

She brightened at that question. "Yes, Mr. Goring. I'm surprised you would know about that."

Goring sneered a little. "We know about a lot of things, Ms. Roe."

Sally gave that statement no reaction, but went on. "I'm far from competent in Christian theology, but I do know I've met this Jesus personally, and I know I've been forgiven. Considering what my deeds were, I find that fact exhilarating, inspiring."

They didn't like that answer at all.

The Strongman didn't like it either, and let out a roar that filled the building and set the demons stirring. He shot a sideways glance at Destroyer, who looked away.

491

Santinelli tried to keep cool, but his face was getting a little pink. "So are we to understand that you've turned to antiquated religion in one final attempt to expunge your past?" He laughed derisively. "That, Sally, is a marvelous delusion for the fainthearted and weak-minded. The notion that your sins are forgiven is as much a fable as the sins themselves. You are God, Sally; you are accountable to no one."

"Then I should be free to go, shouldn't I?"

"That's a side issue," said Goring with a wave of his hand, "having no bearing on our present purpose. Sally, let me be blunt: Even if sins were real and this Jesus could save you from them, what you must face at this moment is that He cannot save you from *us*."

"I wouldn't presume that He should."

Now Santinelli even raised his voice. "Ms. Roe, I'm sure you know that this conversion of yours has placed you in even greater jeopardy. You could have done no better in assuring enmity between us, and even your own death, than by becoming a Christian!" He leaned forward and with a controlled rage pointed his finger in her face. "You have established yourself as a supreme enemy of this enterprise, deserving of our hatred!"

Just like Amber, Sally thought. *Steele, Santinelli, and Goring are showing the same demon eyes, the same diabolical hatred.*

She acknowledged Santinelli's words. "I know."

The Strongman could see the peace in her eyes, and it incensed him. *Strike her!*

Santinelli slapped her across the face. "You will tell us where the rosters are! What did you do with them?"

Krioni and Triskal greeted Nathan and his warriors as the mail truck reached the Ashton Post Office.

"So you've had some trouble?" asked Krioni.

"A little," said Nathan.

"Well, we're expecting more," said Triskal.

Armoth followed the driver into the building and watched

intently as he set the mailbag with some others on a receiving cart. Soon the mail would be removed and sorted, and that would be the most critical time of all.

A sooty, motley band of imps and troublemakers, led by Destroyer's loathsome twelve, made their way toward Ashton, flying low to the ground, pouring on speed, their swords drawn, their eyes bulging with anxiety. This battle would be their last, thought the twelve. It may as well be their best.

At the *Ashton Clarion*, it was time to get the morning mail; Bernice had her coat on and her car keys in her hand, but wouldn't you know it? She no sooner put her hand on the front door knob than the phone rang, and it was Eddy from Eddy's Bakery. The guy was a paragon of pickiness!

"Yeah, Eddy, we can give you those two inches. Well, yes, for free, but that's just for a one-month trial basis." More questions. "To decide if you like it that way and if we like it that way. We've never done it, and I thought we should try it." He kept talking. She shifted her weight toward the front door. "No, I think we can just blow up that coffee mug a little larger and it'll work out fine. Right, you won't have to change your logo." She made a face and rolled her eyes. "Listen, why don't you talk to Cheryl about it? Yes, she knows all about it."

He didn't want to talk to Cheryl.

ATTACK! The black spirits threw fear and caution to the wind and descended on Ashton in a torrent of chaos and evil, wings roaring, sulfur streaming, blotting out the light, clashing with angelic warriors all over the town. Up and down the streets they soared, tumbling, clashing, hacking with swords of fire and heat at Heaven's warriors, dashing through traffic, ambushing at corners, streaking through buildings and wreaking confusion, shrieking their war cries, fully abandoned to keeping the angels on edge, in battle, no matter what the cost, no matter what the loss. While the imps, harassers, and troublemakers stirred up the town like a whirl-wind, Destroyer's twelve went for that letter.

Bernice got to her little Volkswagen bug at last, but the door wouldn't open. The key wouldn't even turn in the lock.

WHOOOSH! A streak of light cut across the demon who had fouled the lock. He dissolved.

The key turned at last. Bernice climbed in.

Down the street, the traffic light jammed on red and the cars began to back up.

A small sedan eased to a stop right beside Bernice's car, and immediately a pickup rear-ended it. Both drivers climbed out of their vehicles and began to engage in a long battle of apologies.

Six angels flew abreast down 6th Avenue while four more dove out of the sky and shot up Miller Street. They converged in an explosive clash just above the traffic signal, hurling dissolving demon saboteurs in high arcs that created a fern of red smoke trails.

The light turned green.

But the traffic still wasn't moving, thanks to the fender bender. Bernice decided to walk.

Sally tried to sink deeper into the sofa, but there was no way to lessen the pain of the big thug's bruising, crushing grip on her shoulders. He was hurting her and enjoying it.

Steele was speaking slowly and deliberately to make sure she heard him; at the moment she seemed rather preoccupied with her agony. "I'm sure you're familiar with Satanic rituals, so I shouldn't have to go into the details. Sally, we don't want to see it happen; but if we have to, we'll turn you over to Mr. Khull and his people and let them do their worst until you tell us what we want to know."

Sally was about to answer, about to say they were going to kill her anyway, but she was stopped when something happened to her eyes, as if they'd opened for the first time, as if a dark curtain had been pulled aside. Maybe the pain was causing her to hallucinate.

She could see the spirits behind these men. They were

towering, warted, ugly things, glaring at her with murderous hatred. Throughout her occult experiences, good and bad, she'd never seen them so clearly; she'd never discerned such evil or such hate.

But she could tell their hatred was not for her. It was for the Savior within her.

And then she knew. She just knew, and she spoke, whether aloud in the present world or in her spirit in another dimension, she couldn't tell. "You were there! All of you were there! You gave Him your worst . . . you killed Him!"

That troubled the spirits. They looked at each other, indignity and outrage wrinkling their faces.

"And He defeated you by dying! He won!" The big, hulking spirit hovering high above bared his teeth and roared indiscernible curses at her, his wings billowing. She looked into those burning, yellow eyes, and to her great surprise she saw fear. In her spirit she laughed. "And whatever you may do to me, *I've* won!"

She cried out. She could feel all the pain again. The thug was about to break her neck. The spirits faded away with the rest of the world. She no longer saw, she no longer heard. She was sinking into a dream, into bottomless darkness. Santinelli yelled something, and the thug let her go. She thought she would float up from the couch. The pain lessened.

In a moment she could see and hear again, and she realized she was almost falling over. Her shoulders were throbbing. Santinelli was saying something about killing her.

Then Goring said, "The conference day is going to start; people might walk by the windows. We'd better continue this downstairs."

"Wait!" Sally said, and they all froze. She had their attention. She raised her head, gathered her strength and courage, and feebly muttered, "I do have an additional bargaining chip. You should know that I've corresponded on a regular basis with Tom Harris in Bacon's Corner. I've told him everything I know and everything I've done. If anything happens to me, somebody will know."

Goring smiled, and reached into a briefcase beside the sofa.

"Oh, you must be referring to these." By handfuls, three at a time, four at a time, one at a time, Goring pulled the letters from the briefcase and set them in a pile on the coffee table, giving Sally a slow, torturous revelation. When she had turned a satisfying shade of white, he continued, "We've put a great amount of preparation into our plan, and fortunately we were able to exert enough influence on the plaintiff in the lawsuit who is also the local postmaster. She's been forwarding all your letters to us; so needless to say, Tom Harris and his friends never got them. They have no idea of your whereabouts, or what you might know."

Santinelli added, "And yes, we have been watching them, and it's obvious that they have little information about you and are shooting in the dark. I would say they're getting rather desperate. But that doesn't matter now, does it? We have you, and we will deal with you as we see fit, as we find necessary."

Goring pointed to the coffee table. "So, we have you, we have all your letters, we have the telltale ring; it's time we firmly dealt with those stolen rosters. Gentlemen?"

Suddenly she was hanging from her arms. She pushed with her feet to lessen the pain, and stood on her own.

"This way," said Goring.

The men of Broken Birch forced her along, taking her toward a stairway that led down into the cold, concrete belly of the chalet. Goring led the way, turning on the lights and guiding them down the winding steps.

Steele followed behind, and after him Santinelli. Khull followed at the rear of the procession, reaching into his coat for his knife.

Then Khull hesitated. "I'll make sure the front door's locked," he said.

He went upstairs again, but passed by the coffee table to take a good look at all those letters. *Hmmm. Excellent!*

There, I made it! Bernice checked her watch and found it only took about ten minutes to walk to the Post Office. That wasn't so bad.

Now to get that mail.

High overhead, Destroyer's twelve henchmen saw her. They also saw the canopy of angels over that building. They let out a cry and dove to the battle, their wings screaming, their nostrils trailing sulfur.

WHOOSH! Three of them swept five angelic warriors from the Post Office roof and engaged them, tumbling, rushing, spinning, hacking. They would be busy for a while.

Two henchmen shot through the north wall. Nathan and Armoth ducked as they passed, swatted them soundly, and sent them through the south wall.

OOF! Four more dropped through the roof and struck the angels down with bared talons. The demons got a faceful of fiery wings and then saw the swinging blades too late.

Red smoke.

The young mail clerk carefully emptied the mailbag, sorting out the packages, envelopes, junk mail, magazines.

"Hi, Al!" came a call from the lobby.

"Hi, Bernice! The mail's a little late."

"Oh, that's okay, so am I."

Ah, here was some mail for the *Clarion.* He slipped it into the *Clarion*'s box, then looked to see if there was more.

Four henchmen exploded through the wall, wings a blur, Krioni and Triskal hot on their heels.

A red sword swept downward.

The letter fluttered to the floor.

Bernice gathered all the mail out of the *Clarion*'s box and dropped it into a shopping bag. She looked through the opening and called, "Is that it?"

Al looked through the new mail that had come in. "Yeah, I think I got it all."

"Okay."

Bernice closed the door of the box and turned to leave.

Krioni took one spirit by the heel, but the thing was so strong it dragged him through the Post Office wall and he had to let it go.

Triskal took a nasty blow from one monster, slashed away at another one, and kicked a third out over the counter.

Bernice didn't see the spirit sail right past her as she reached to push the door open.

Nathan ducked for the letter.

A black, taloned foot caught him in the chest and propelled him as high as the ceiling. Two more spirits closed in on him. He spun, sword extended, dividing one, catching the parry of the other with a burst of sparks.

Krioni was back, saw the letter, and went for it. Armoth covered for him, pushing two spirits backward, right into Nathan's blade.

Krioni slipped his sword under the letter and flipped it into the air.

Al didn't see Krioni punching two demons out of the mail clerk's way, but he did see the letter just coming to rest on the floor, address up. "Oh, hey, Bernice!"

The door was just about to close behind her. She heard him call and turned back, opening the door again and re-entering the lobby.

Good! Now the warriors could concentrate on the demons. There shouldn't be too many more—just the biggest and strongest.

Al handed Bernice the letter over the counter. "Kinda thick. Might be a card in there or something."

Bernice's heart almost stopped when she saw the return address: S. B. Roe.

In Bacon's Corner, Kate handed Marshall the phone. "On your toes, Marshall," she whispered.

Ben and Bev heard that and got close. "Who is it?"

Marshall spoke into the phone, "Yeah, this is Marshall Hogan."

"Mr. Hogan," said the voice on the other end, "this is Debbie Aronson. I work at the Post Office with Lucy Brandon. I need to talk to you."

The Post Office lobby filled with red smoke as Triskal shot sword-first right through two spirits and through the wall to the outside, shaking the dissolving spirits from his shoulders and wings.

Bernice tore the letter open and found a Post Office box key inside. Box 203. Here? In this Post Office? She quickly scanned the letter from Sally Roe.

She may not have noticed, but she began to bounce up and down on her toes.

Marshall grabbed a pen while Kate got him some paper, and he sat down at Ben and Bev's dining room table. "I'm glad you called, Debbie. I'd be happy to talk to you."

"Well, I don't have that much to say. I'm on my break, over at Don's Wayside."

"Can we get together somewhere, sometime?"

"No, I don't want to risk being seen with you. Listen, just let me tell you what I know, and then we'll pretend I never talked to you, all right?"

"All right."

Bernice found Box 203. She could see a large stack of mail through the glass panel. She put the key in the lock, and it fit perfectly, turning the latch.

"Lucy's been intercepting some mail; she's been forwarding letters that I'm sure aren't supposed to be forwarded. I've seen her doing it for weeks now, and I think Sergeant Mulligan is scaring her into doing it."

Oh man, oh man, oh man. Lord God, is this it? Marshall tried to keep his voice calm. "Okay. Do you know who the letters are for, or who they're from?"

Bernice opened the mailbox door. What were these? Manila envelopes, smaller envelopes, a plain brown package, a little box wrapped in paper.

"They've all been addressed to Tom Harris . . ."

Marshall could feel his eyes getting big.

" . . . and they've all been from that woman who's supposed to be dead . . ."

Marshall kept from saying the name. Debbie had to say it herself. "What woman, Debbie? Do you know the name?"

"Um, that Roe lady. Sally Roe."

Bernice's hands were trembling as she dug every last item out of the mailbox and stuffed it into her shopping bag. She couldn't wait to get back to the office.

Nathan ducked under a violent sword thrust of one remaining beast, then came back hard and fast with his own blade. The thing backed through the wall, and Krioni met it outside.

Red smoke. That was the last of them.

The rest of Ashton was safe as well. The attack, centered on the Post Office, had been met and defeated.

Marshall hung up the phone gently, then leaned back in his chair, threw his head back, and let out a roar that shook the windows. He didn't know what to say, what to do, how to express how he felt, so he just hollered while Kate, Ben, and Bev tried to get him to talk.

"Marshall!" Kate insisted. "What is it?"

He just hollered again, raising his hands toward Heaven.

The phone rang again. Marshall picked it up in trembling hands. "Yeah?"

The voice on the other end could hardly speak, and the pitch was ceiling-high. "Marshall, this is Bernice! Sit down whatever you do!"

Sally had lit the brushfire at last.

Nathan was the first to have his hands free. He shot into the sky over Ashton, cutting a brilliant swath through the ebbing smoke of the battle now ending, and put a golden trumpet to his lips.

The signal carried over the farmlands, over the prairies, from one end of the sky to the other; every angelic warrior could hear it and knew what it meant.

Still they waited. Not yet. First Bacon's Corner, and then the rest. They listened again. The signal from Bacon's Corner should come soon enough.

At the Summit Institute, the demons heard the faraway signal, and it was unnerving, like a deeply buried memory too horrible to face. Too many of them had heard that sound before and now bore the scars that came immediately after hearing it.

The Strongman cocked his head around for a moment. "Wait! Be still!"

Destroyer heard it, but didn't want to admit it. He immediately thought of his twelve henchmen and the hordes they'd led into Ashton. Wasn't that the direction the sound was coming from? Oh no.

Out in the herb garden, the psychics were gasping with fear.

"No . . . no!" said the demon atop the woman attorney.

"No . . . no!" echoed the woman.

"What is it?" said the blond singer.

The demon atop the fifth grade teacher concocted an answer he didn't believe himself. The teacher echoed, "It is fear and ignorance, bigotry and hatred, still rife in the land! The winds of change must blow it aside; we must stand before it and prevail!"

"Yes, yes!" they all replied. The singer strummed his guitar, and they began to sway with the melody of still another song of global peace and perfection.

In Bacon's Corner, Mota and Signa burst from hiding with a shout, swords flashing, wings unfurling like the crashing of waves, white light burning like the sun.

"For the saints of God and for the Lamb!" they shouted as the cornfields, the silos, the store buildings, the barns, the forests, the roads all around Bacon's Corner exploded with the white light of Heaven's legions.

Mota shouted, somewhat with glee, "Stand ready! We will begin with Amethyst!"

forty-two

The sound of Nathan's trumpet was still ringing in the Strongman's ears. He knew something was wrong somewhere. *Get on with this! Cut her, burn her, do what you must, but delay no longer!*

Khull spoke softly to the dignified, honorable, respectable men who were paying him for his services. "We can make her sing loud and long. Just say the word."

Santinelli took only a furtive, sideways glance at Sally, now bound and held in a hard, wooden chair in the middle of the basement, weak with exhaustion, pain, and fear. She was surrounded by Khull and his four cutthroats, who now brandished their implements of ritualistic torture and were all too eager to begin.

"Sally, to think it would ever come to this!" Santinelli muttered. "You should never have mentioned that Name; you should never have aligned yourself with our enemies!"

Goring reminded him, "We have much at stake here, Carl. I would say the situation forces our hand."

Santinelli replied in a voice hushed by his own disgust, "So now we have become butchers!"

Khull smiled. He almost laughed. "No, Mr. Santinelli. You pay *me* to do that. I'm not as dignified and respectable as you are. I'm just a plain little rotten Satanist."

The Strongman gave Destroyer a shove, and Destroyer spoke quickly to Steele's mind.

Steele offered, "We're talking about a commodity here. Sally Roe's only value is in what use she is to us. Let's get that information and be rid of her."

Khull did chuckle a bit this time. "How about it, Mr. Santinelli? It's your decision: do you want her tortured?"

Santinelli glared at Khull. "Do *I* want her tortured?"

Khull smiled. He loved to see a big man like Santinelli squirm. "Okay, I'll tell you what: Add two extra grand to my fee and I'll pretend that it wasn't you that hired me." Then he tilted his head the other way, his eyes full of mocking. "Maybe you're still a little too Christian, huh?"

Do it! shouted the Strongman. *Just do it!*

Sally closed her eyes and prayed.

"I can't come to work!" Lucy cried into the phone. "It's Amber again! She's beside herself! I'll call later!"

She slammed down the telephone and went after her berserk little daughter, following a trail of chaos and destruction: in the kitchen, the drawers were yanked open and the contents spilled all over the floor, including the knives Lucy had tried to hide; in the dining room, the tablecloth had been yanked from the table and the azalea centerpiece now lay broken on the floor, the potting soil strewn everywhere.

From the front of the house, the shrieking voice of Amethyst the pony continued to rant and rail against unseen enemies. "No! No! Leave me alone! My master will destroy you! Leave me alone!"

Lucy ran into the living room. The coffee table was upside down, the books and magazines flung everywhere.

Amethyst's voice came from the front entryway. "She is mine! I have a right to be here! Go away!"

Lucy ran and found her daughter cowering in the corner on the floor, her arms covering her head, screaming in fright.

"Leave me alone, leave me alone!" the pony screamed.

Lucy stopped in her tracks and observed for a moment. Had she ever heard Amethyst frightened before?

Mota and Signa stood in the entryway near Lucy, swords drawn, in full glory, their light washing out any darkness around them. In the distance, the dull thundering of angelic wings grew louder and louder, and the light of Heaven's Host began to stream through the windows.

They had chased and cornered the imp, the teaser, the liar named Amethyst—and Amethyst was not a cute little pony. She was a small, crinkled, warty lizard with toothpick arms and legs and a dragonlike face, cowering in the same corner, her body superimposed over Amber's, her arms covering her head.

"She is mine," Amethyst insisted, even pleaded. "She invited me in!"

Mota held his sword right under Amethyst's flaring, chugging nostrils. "Saints of God are coming, and they will deal with you."

"No . . . please . . ."

The doorbell rang. Lucy's first thought was: *No! Not now of all times! God, how can You be so cruel to me?*

But she could see the outlines of her visitors through the frosted glass of the front door. She threw the door open.

Marshall and Kate Hogan.

"Hi," said Marshall, "we're—"

Amethyst screamed, "No, go away! Go away!" Then she began to curse.

Lucy stepped back from the door and motioned for them to come in. "You may as well know everything!"

They stepped through the door.

At the sight of them, Amethyst leaped to her feet, her back flat against the wall, her eyes bulging with terror. "Stay away from me! I'll kill you! I'll kill *her!*"

It took only a split second for the Spirit of God to tell them what they were facing.

"You be quiet!" said Marshall.

Amethyst's head bumped against the wall as if she'd been thrown a punch. She glared at them through wide, glazed eyes, hissing through tightly gritted teeth like a muzzled, rabid dog.

"Just stay there now, and be quiet."

Kate stood by Lucy and held her. Lucy clung to her without reserve.

"Amethyst?" Kate asked.

Lucy nodded.

Marshall and Kate couldn't help staring. This was the initial cause of it all; the lawsuit, the heartache, the mystery, the gossip and division, *all* the trouble began with this imp now

505

trembling and cowering before them. It was like isolating a virus—or cornering a rat.

"Amethyst," said Marshall, "it's all over."

Amethyst glared back at him defiantly. "She's mine. I won't let her go!"

Marshall spoke evenly and firmly. "Spirit, my Master has defeated your master. He has disarmed all the powers and authorities, right?"

Amethyst drooled in defiant silence.

"The shed blood of Jesus Christ has taken away your authority, right?"

"Yes!" Amethyst hissed.

"And my Master, the Lord Jesus Christ, has granted me His authority over you, hasn't He?"

"Yes!"

"And *you* are defeated, aren't you?"

Amethyst put her clawed fingers over her own mouth and refused to answer.

Mota flipped the hand away. "You answer him!"

Amethyst could hear the angels everywhere, could feel the heat of Mota's blade, and could not back away from the authority of this believer in Jesus. It was no use resisting.

"Awww!" Amethyst cried. "I hate you! I hate all of you!"

"Come out of her."

"No!"

"I'm binding you right now, in Jesus' name!"

Amethyst cried out, writhing, struggling against unseen shackles that held her arms and legs. She couldn't move.

"Let go of this little girl. Come out, and go where Jesus sends you."

One claw at a time, Amethyst began to let go of the little girl, her eyes darting back and forth from Marshall to the angels and back again. Mota and Signa began to close in.

With an anguished scream she dropped the girl and made a break for it, shooting through the roof of the house. Mota and Signa made no attempt to chase her.

It wasn't necessary. Amethyst had no sooner cleared the

roof of the house than she saw an incoming wave of white fire rolling over the town, heading her way.

The Host of Heaven!

She let out a squeal and shot across town, heading for the big white house. *The spirits at LifeCircle! They got me into this!*

Amber slumped toward the floor as if in a faint, but Marshall caught her. Lucy and Kate knelt beside them.

"Mommy . . ." said the girl, dazed and exhausted.

Marshall gave the girl to her mother. "She's all right, but we'll have some praying to do. We'll have things to talk about."

Amber fell into her mother's arms, and then nestled there with no desire to leave. That was fine with Lucy. She had her daughter back, and she wasn't about to let go.

With tearful, weary eyes she looked at these two rescuers and whispered, "I'm sorry."

Marshall and Kate were in a terrible rush, but they had to be gentle about it.

Kate started. "Can you help us?"

Lucy couldn't answer. She was torn and confused, pulled from all directions.

Marshall spoke gently but quickly. "Listen to me, Lucy. We know Sally Roe is alive, that she's been writing letters, and that you've been intercepting those letters from some people who want to kill her. The last letter she wrote gave away where she could be found. If she isn't dead by now, she soon will be if you don't help us."

Lucy looked down at her daughter, peaceful though shaken. "It's been just awful."

Kate asked, "Where did you send those letters, Lucy? Please tell us. Sally Roe's life could depend on it."

Lucy looked at them, then at her daughter. Her mind was so confused; it was just so hard to know what to do anymore.

Destroyer was filling Khull's mind with some marvelous inspirations as Khull held his knife in plain sight, always sure that Sally could see its clean, keen edge. "Might as well face it, *gentlemen.* We're all made of the same stuff. All our hands are dirty, and we're all killers at heart. You want power, we want power, and we walk on the disposable people to get it. That's the name of the game."

Santinelli looked at Sally. Her face was still red from where he had struck her. "I will not have your blood on my hands, Ms. Roe. What follows will be your doing, not mine."

Sally spoke for the first time since being bound in the chair. "The responsibility is *yours*, sir. I appeal to you in the name of decency itself, in the name of all that is right."

"Law derives from power, Ms. Roe, not from morality. Spare me your newfound beliefs."

"The rosters, Ms. Roe," prompted Goring.

Do it, said the Strongman.

"She'll turn state's evidence, John. Yeah, and she's got an earful for you."

Marshall was sitting at Lucy Brandon's dining room table, on the telephone with John Harrigan, his friend in the FBI. Lucy, Kate, and Amber sat in the living room; Lucy was still holding Amber, who hadn't made a sound. Pastor Mark Howard was there as well, at Lucy's invitation.

"Ever heard of the Summit Institute? Well, let me give you the location. Sally Roe's letters went there, and now she's probably there too, if she's still alive."

Lucy spoke up from the living room couch. "They'll kill her. They want her for no other reason."

Marshall liked what he was hearing from Harrigan. "Yeah, right, those agents shouldn't be too far from there right now. That's good. Well, get them over there, and I mean now! Yeah, right."

Lucy told Kate and Mark softly and bitterly, "LifeCircle! They got me into this! The whole lawsuit was their idea! Claire Johanson and Jon Schmidt—the whole lot of them! They've done nothing but threaten me and coerce me since this whole mess started, and now where are they? Well, I'm not going down alone!" She called to Marshall, "Tell them I'm ready right now."

Marshall heard her. "John, you can send somebody over here right now. She's ready to talk."

This was it! The brushfire was catching on! From here it would burn upward—hot, hungry, inextinguishable!

Mota took a golden trumpet in his hand and shot through the roof of the house, soaring through the white light of his warriors still rushing over the town. Upward, skyward, slowly spinning, wings afire, he put the trumpet to his mouth.

In the mountains above the Summit Institute, the signal reached Tal's ears loud and clear.

"Done!" he cried, leaping to his feet. "They've set the fire in Bacon's Corner!"

"Better late than never," Guilo said with a shrug.

"It will reach Summit soon enough," said Tal, drawing his sword. "Prepare to attack!"

Amethyst was getting close to the big white house, the home of LifeCircle. The roar of Heaven's wings thundered in her ears. She whimpered, she cried, she fled before them. *My masters in LifeCircle! They will save me!*

Santinelli smiled a bitter smile as he looked long and hard at Mr. Khull, still brandishing the knife. "I believe you're right, Mr. Khull. I do see myself." He looked at Sally. "Power is power, whether it be wielded through legal decisions or . . . from the edge of a knife. And as for our gentle followers . . ." He looked upward, thinking of the hundreds of peace-seeking conferees now gathered from around the globe. "We *are* equal. We are devils, all."

He stepped back and took his place by the wall, out of the way. Goring and Steele joined him. He crossed his arms and with chin jutted out resolutely, said, "Teach us, Mr. Khull. We will learn."

Destroyer clicked his talons, and the spirits of Broken Birch moved the five Satanists like puppets.

Khull smiled with diabolical pleasure and nodded to his

men. Two of them immediately looped a chain over a beam and affixed a hook to it. The other two released Sally from the chair and yanked her to her feet.

The Strongman, Destroyer, and all their wicked lords and commanders gathered, moving in close, ready for the triumph.

Sally knew there was no more time. "The rosters are in Ashton!"

"Too late," said Goring. "Please proceed, *gentlemen!*"

They bound her hands in front of her.

"The rosters are in Ashton!"

Where? growled the Strongman.

"*Where* in Ashton?" demanded Santinelli.

"I sent them to a Post Office box!"

Santinelli put up his hand. Khull looked disappointed, but he motioned for his men to stop.

Santinelli stepped forward. "What Post Office box?"

Sally really did try, but . . . "I . . . I can't remember the number."

"Proceed, gentlemen."

They grabbed her arms and started lifting her.

"I planned all those letters!"

Santinelli held up his hand again, and Khull's men set her down. Santinelli exchanged encouraged glances with Goring and Steele. "My, how the revelations are beginning to flow!"

Destroyer didn't like the subject matter. He nudged Steele.

"She's lying," said Steele.

"I remember the mail room, Mr. Steele!" Sally cried with a trembling voice.

Steele only leered at her. He didn't know what she was talking about.

"I used to work in the mail room at the Omega Center, remember?"

Steele didn't leer this time. He remembered.

Sally spilled it out rapidly, desperately. "You told me how to intercept mail you didn't want the staff to read. You said it wasn't wrong because it protected our purposes. You said your people did it all the time! Remember that, Mr. Steele?"

Goring and Santinelli looked at Steele. He was silent because he did remember it.

The Strongman suddenly grabbed Destroyer around the neck, but he didn't start squeezing. Not yet. He was waiting to hear the rest.

"Go on," said Santinelli.

"It was the only way to find you. I figured whoever tried to kill me would have to keep anyone from finding out I was still alive, so they'd have to intercept my letters; and I knew from the papers that you were using the postmaster in Bacon's Corner for your lawsuit, so that's where I sent them, and . . ."

"And you addressed them all to the defendant in the lawsuit, Tom Harris . . ."

"I knew you couldn't let *him* see the letters."

Santinelli smiled. He was impressed. "So your letters were to be a trail to the people ultimately responsible for your . . . alleged death!"

"Professor Lynch knew about my concern for Tom Harris, and Khull knew exactly where to find me, and you all knew without my telling you that I'd embraced Christianity. That was confirmation enough that you'd stolen my letters, but of course . . . now you've shown them to me. You have them. Every one of them."

Destroyer tried to force a leering, cocky smile as he choked and gargled out, "So what?"

Goring stepped in. "Marvelous! Yes, the letters are all here, and so are you. Now you have the satisfaction of knowing who your would-be killers are. But you recall, of course, that no one else has seen those letters, and the world has lost all track of you!"

"That's why I made copies."

There was a strange delay, as if that sentence took a few seconds to reach their ears and register in their minds. They all looked at her dumbly.

She drew a breath and went for broke. "The copies are in the Post Office box too, along with the rosters and James Bardine's ring, the one I took from the finger of that woman who tried to kill me. The ring you took from my neck is the one I got years

511

ago from Owen Bennett. You can doublecheck his code name, Gawaine, on the inside of the ring if you like."

Santinelli came close, and he was even shaking a little. "What Post Office box, Ms. Roe?"

"It's empty by now anyway. I sent a letter to a lady who works at the *Ashton Clarion*, and I enclosed the key."

Now the Strongman applied the pressure, and Destroyer had to struggle for breath. "I never heard of any such letter! What do *you* know about it?"

Destroyer tried to answer. "I sent the twelve captains to Ashton to look into it—"

The Strongman began shaking him, making Destroyer's eyes look like horizontal, yellow blurs. "Where are those twelve?"

"They . . . they . . ."

"Wasn't the intercepting of those letters *your* idea?"

Suddenly Destroyer thought he was reliving his first feelings of doom; he was hearing the sound of a trumpet again, just like before. But this time it was louder. It was reverberating all around them. It was so loud he couldn't be imagining it.

He wasn't. The Strongman heard it too, and let out a growl that shook the room.

Then they heard a resounding shout from so many voices it sounded like waves of the ocean. "For the saints of God, and for the Lamb!"

The Strongman roared again and threw Destroyer to the floor. "The enemy! We are discovered!"

The hundreds of demons in the room—the Strongman's aides, the bloodstained murderers of Broken Birch, the lofty and conceited deceivers controlling Santinelli, Goring, and Steele—flew into a panic, reaching for their swords, jostling each other, shouting and shrieking.

The floor and walls began to shake with the rumble of heavenly wings descending from above like a violent storm.

It was exhilarating, thrilling, reviving, rewarding—everything an angelic warrior was made for!

The Host of Heaven had waited so long and had built up such fervor that when the signal finally came, they broke over the crests of the mountains on every side like a violent, shimmering ocean wave and showered down like hail upon the dark cloud of demons in the valley, scattering them like dust before the wind, routing, battling, swinging, and pushing down, down, down toward the Summit Institute.

Tal, at the crest of the wave, dove like a hawk, his wings straight back, his sword a needle of light at the end of his outstretched arm. His war cry could be heard above all the tumult, and his sword was the first to strike.

They flew into the heart of the black cloud, like piercing a black, boiling, thunderhead. The swords of spirits clashed, wings slapped and fluttered, red smoke fogged the air. Tal kicked, cut, spun like a scythe, and fought his way downward, downward. He could hear the roar of Guilo, the Strength of Many, just above and to the left, batting at demons and mowing them down, flipping them sideways to meet other blades, kicking and grabbing what hides he could find, cutting a widening swath, gutting the cloud at its core.

The Strongman slapped his demon lords about the room to bring them to their senses. "Are you commanders or not? To your posts! Defend us!"

The demons scattered to their posts, leaving the room almost empty except for the demons of Broken Birch.

The Strongman glared at Destroyer. "The woman has lit a fire that will consume us. There is nothing more we need from her. Finish her before *we* are finished!"

Destroyer shot a glance at Khull's demons.

Khull raised his knife.

"Mr. Goring!" came a cry from upstairs. "Mr. Goring! Something terrible is happening!"

Footsteps! People were in the chalet!

Khull grabbed Sally from behind, clapped his hand over her mouth, and poised his knife at her throat. His message was clear.

"Mr. Goring!" came the shout again.

Santinelli pushed Goring. "Answer them! Stop them before they find us!"

"My word," said Goring. "Those letters! They're right up there on the table!"

He hurried to the stairs, turning off the basement lights.

"Mr. Goring, are you here?"

He ran up the stairs. "Yes, right here! What is it?"

Amethyst cupped her wings open and came to an abrupt halt just short of the big white house. LifeCircle was under attack! Angels were everywhere! The spirits there, her masters, were fleeing!

Claire and Jon scurried about the office, finding documents, papers, anything and everything that might connect them with this miserable lawsuit and everything it entailed. They would deny everything, of course. It was all they could do. Maybe they'd get through okay, maybe they wouldn't—they didn't know, they couldn't think about it, they could hardly think at all; they were just too scared.

They'd gotten the tip-off: Lucy was talking; there were copies of Roe's letters in the wrong hands. The lid was coming off!

Jon jammed papers into a trash can until it was full, muttering angrily, "I knew we should have gotten out of this long ago! We've overreached ourselves!" He ran to find another container.

Claire had the telephone propped on her shoulder. She was talking to Miss Brewer, Amber Brandon's fourth grade teacher. "That's right. You'd better come up with some good explanations for what happened to Amber. Lucy Brandon's done an about-face, and she's blaming it all on you. Hey, don't blame *us*! You didn't have to select that curriculum; that was entirely your own choice, and we had nothing to do with it! No, I never heard of any Sally Roe; that's your concern, not ours!"

She slammed down the phone just as Jon rushed back into

the room with a garbage can. "Jon, what about that curriculum? Can that be traced to LifeCircle?"

Jon found some documents and held them up for Claire to see. "Not after I burn these!"

Overhead, the swarm of survivors from the LifeCircle rout turned tail and fled before a wall of angels. They flew toward the elementary school. Ango the Terrible would be there with all his mighty hordes! He would know what to do!

Goring reached the upstairs and found the two psychics from the morning discussion group all in a dither.

"Here now," he said, "what's all the commotion?"

"Bad energy," said the woman attorney. "I can't explain it, but all the psychic energy around here is horribly disturbed!"

The fifth grade teacher nodded in agreement, his eyes wide with horror. "We're being invaded! That's the only word I can think of to describe it!"

In the basement, Sally, Khull, and the others stood in the dark, overhearing the conversation. Sally tried not to stir; she could feel Khull's blade against her throat.

Goring was trying to calm them. "Well, just take it easy. Let me encourage you to combine your insights with others around the campus. Perhaps we can all learn and benefit from this experience."

"It's scary!" said the lady.

"I'm so disoriented," said the man.

Khull pulled Sally's head back so hard, she thought her neck would snap. He huffed into her ear, "They're feeling *you*, lady! You and your filthy Jesus!"

The cloud of evil spirits closed ranks and drew in tight, swords ready, as all around angelic warriors continued to thunder down the mountainsides like an avalanche and swirl around them like a cyclone. The Host of Heaven struck the cloud at the base, and it collapsed downward to fill the gap; they assaulted the pinnacle and it shriveled, bleeding a shower of stung demons; they shot like fatal bullets through its center, and the cloud's mass began to thin. They harried it, struck at it, sliced it into weaker segments. The cloud was thick, tough, and tenacious, but it was weakening.

Tal hacked an attacker, mowed through four more, spun and kicked another spirit aside, and then spotted a sudden, instantaneous gap in the demonic mantle just over Goring's chalet. He folded his wings above his head and dropped through it.

Sally and the others could hear Goring having a bit of trouble with his distraught psychics.

"Now, if you'll excuse me," said Goring, "I do have some urgent business to attend to."

"What could be more urgent than this?" said the man, his voice coming close to the basement stairway.

"Please!" said Goring, coming after him. "Use the front door! Go out the way you came in!"

Maybe, just maybe, that man would hear her. Sally steadily filled her lungs.

"Wow!" said the woman. "What are all those letters? Fan mail?"

Sally screamed, pushing the sound against Khull's hand with all the diaphragm she could muster. The scream came through Khull's thick hand a pitiful, muffled moan. No one heard it.

Khull had his excuse. He dug in with the knife.

"AWWW!"

"Khull!" said Santinelli. "What is it?"

Khull just moaned something unintelligible.

"Get the lights!"

"Where are they?"

Cursings, fumblings in the dark, tripping, stumbling, Khull growling, cursing, bumping into things, the wooden chair toppling.

"What was that?" said the man upstairs.

"Out!" said Goring. "Get out of this house!"

Steele found the lights.

"Khull!" said one of Khull's men.

Khull was holding his chest; his shirt was slashed, red with blood. He'd carved a wound across his own ribcage.

"Where's the woman?" he cried, his eyes wild with rage.

The Strongman and Destroyer were blinded for an instant. Something had struck them. They blinked and squinted, trying to recover.

"Where's the woman?" the Strongman howled.

Destroyer stared in horror at the spirits of Broken Birch— they were strewn about the room as if by a bomb blast, dazed, disoriented. The Strongman's aides looked this way and that, but saw nothing.

"There!" a spirit shouted.

The light of day hurt Sally's eyes. She was out in the morning air. She could see the herb garden and people gathered there.

A huge man held her, his face like bronze, his hair like gold. He set her down and pointed toward the mountains.

"Run, Sally! RUN!"

New strength coursed through her legs, and she ran.

The demons hurled themselves at Tal with suicidal abandon, their eyes crazed with bloodthirst. He darted, dodged, feinted, meeting their swords with his own, kicking whom he could, swirling, dashing, jabbing, keeping them back.

"YAHAAA!" came Guilo's voice behind him. Now Tal had some help. Struck demons began to fly across his vision, limp and dissolving.

He could see Sally Roe, still in the clear, still running. *Run, girl! RUN!*

forty-three

SaLLy ran like a frightened gazelle, her thoughts set on that front gate, her stride never breaking. She bounded into the herb garden and whisked right past the blond singer and his little group.

"Hey, who's that?" someone asked.

Then came Sybil Denning's voice. "Well . . . ! Sally! Sally Roe! Sally, is that you?"

Sally didn't look back, she didn't slow down; she just kept running, her long hair blowing in the wind behind her, her arms pumping, her legs grabbing up distance. She dashed out of the herb garden, across a lawn, down a pebbled path, and into the main parking lot. She could see the main gate.

Goring was just herding the two psychics out the front door against their protests when someone else ran up full of questions.

"Hey, who was that we saw running? What's going on around here?"

Goring asked directly, "Was it a woman?"

"Yeah. Man, she looked scared—"

"Which way did she go?"

"We're *all* scared! What's happening?"

"*Which way did she go?*"

"Well, toward the front gate. She was splitting the place!"

"I'll look into it."

Goring closed the door right in their faces and called to Khull's men. "She's outside, heading for the front gate!"

Khull's four hooligans were just bringing Khull upstairs.

Goring was indignant. "Don't bring him up here! You'll drip blood on my carpet!"

"Get the woman!" said the Strongman.

Destroyer shoved and swatted the Broken Birch spirits into action. "You heard him! Get the woman!"

Khull ordered his men, "Get her! Bring me the pieces!"

They bolted for the back door.

Amethyst was only one of a mob of hysterical demons who converged on the Bacon's Corner Elementary School, but there was no rescue here either. The Host of Heaven had already struck the place, and demons were scattering from the roof, from the playfield, from all around the school, like hornets from a burning hive.

Ango, the boastful lord of the school, was fluttering about the sky with half a wing gone, wailing, cursing, spitting his hatred and screaming for help; but all his hordes had forsaken him and fled. Out of control, he careened crazily into a cluster of brilliant warriors, met their swords, and exploded in several directions, vanishing in trails of red smoke.

In the school office, Miss Brewer was having a face-to-face confrontation with Mr. Woodard, the school principal.

"No way!" she said in a voice just below a scream. "I'm not responsible for selecting that curriculum, no matter what anybody says! You told me to teach it! You and that Life-Circle bunch were behind this whole thing, and I'll tell that to anyone who wants to know! I'm not going to take the rap for this, not for anyone! *You're* the principal! *You're* the one responsible! You can fire me if you want, but I won't be your patsy. Is that clear?"

"I'll look into it," said Mr. Woodard, looking pale.

Miss Brewer went back to her classroom. Mr. Woodard picked up the phone and dialed Betty Hanover, the Number One power-holder on the school board. "Betty? Bruce Woodard. Listen, I don't know what's going on here, but I want you and the rest of the school board to be clear on where I stand in these matters. I will *not* be left holding this thing, understand? I can be heavy-handed if I have to be . . ."

The demons from LifeCircle and now the survivors from the elementary school turned and fled before the pursuing angels. Terga, the Prince of Bacon's Corner! He controlled the school board! Surely *he* could stem this tide and stand against this attack!

Amethyst was not quick to flee, but indecisive. Where was Ango?

The demons rushed away, leaving her behind. She searched for Ango. Was he here?

STUNG! An angelic sword caught her under the arm and she went spinning, plummeting down toward the school. She reached toward that black tar roof, even pushed toward it with the power of her wings. It was a safe place. She'd flourished in those rooms before. Maybe someone below could help her, hide her . . .

The black roof slapped by her, then the rafters, the insulation, the ceiling, a classroom full of children—

SWIPE! A warrior finished her, and she fell dissolving to the floor, a smoldering heap just behind Miss Brewer, just below a crayon drawing on the wall, a marvelous picture of a purple, winged pony under a rainbow.

Sally ran toward the big stone gate. Right now that gate seemed like the gateway to Hell itself, but she was getting *out*, she was escaping, she was breaking free! *Come on, girl, get through that thing!*

Khull's men raced through the hedges and down an obscure pathway toward the highway to head her off. So far they hadn't been seen by any conferees, but that was due more to luck than caution.

"The woman!" cried the spirits, their attention diverted from the battle overhead to the fleeing figure on the ground. That diversion cost many of them their presence in this world. The angels were there, swords flashing, and no one could stop Sally Roe.

She reached the gate. There was no invisible barrier, no burly thug to stop her, no dirty hands grabbing. She passed through it like a bird out of a cage, her heart soaring. *O Lord God, my Savior Jesus, will You save me? Are You running with me now?*

She crossed the highway and ducked into the forest on the other side. First she would get some distance behind her, then perhaps double back to the village, get a ride, hike out, whatever. *Just stay alive, Sally, just stay alive! Hang on!*

Khull's men saw her cross the highway. They fanned out. The demons of Broken Birch stayed close to the ground and followed them, goading them on, filling their blackened minds with thoughts of blood and murder.

The cloud of spirits began to change shape. The base began to shift sideways, crawling up the mountainside, spreading a mantle over the path of that solitary, fleeing figure.

Tal shouted to his commanders, "Keep her covered, but let them follow!"

They understood, and backed away before the advancing demonic hordes.

The thick mantle over the Summit Institute began to pull away, leaving it open and vulnerable.

Demonically speaking, LifeCircle was a desolate ruin, the elementary school had fallen to the enemy, and now as the wilting, bleeding leftovers from those two defeats fled to the homes and businesses of the Bacon's Corner school board, they discovered Terga, their mighty prince, all by himself, flying in crazy circles over the town, screaming in rage.

"Cowards!" he shrieked. "Deserters! Come back and stand!"

The demon lords under his command were nowhere to be seen, but had fled before the advancing flood of heavenly armies. The Oriental, Signa, was right at Terga's heels. Terga was as good as finished and presently out of his mind.

Mota had already led a powerful contingent of warriors on a bold sweep through the home of board chairwoman Betty Hanover, routing the ruling demons of that household and leaving Mrs. Hanover feeling unsure of herself—especially now, when a federal postal agent was on the phone.

"Just trying to track down some information," he said. "We

understand your elementary school was using a curriculum written by the woman in question, a Sally Beth Roe."

"Uh . . . well, I don't know anything about that."

"We understand that Sally Roe lived right in your area."

"Really?" Betty tried to sound surprised, but never was much of an actor.

"Well, we're just trying to find her. We have to follow up on a complaint."

"Complaint?"

"Mail tampering, for one thing."

"Well . . . you might try talking to Claire Johanson . . ."

"Already did. She said to call you."

"She—" Betty buttoned her lip, but cursed Claire up one side and down the other in her mind.

"Hold on," said the agent. "I've got the name of the curriculum right here . . . Yeah . . . *Finding the Real Me.* Ring any bells?"

"The Omega Center!"

"Beg your pardon?"

"The Omega Center for Educational Studies in Fairwood, Massachusetts! They're the publishers of that curriculum! They'd know the author, I'm sure. We don't know anything about the author. All we did was buy the curriculum from Omega. They're the ones you should talk to. We don't know anything."

"All right. Do you have their number, address, all that good stuff?"

"Just hold on."

She gave him the information and hung up the phone, unable to stop shaking.

The phone rang again. It was school board member John Kendall. "Betty, I'm calling to warn you—"

"You're too late," she told him.

School board member Jerry Mason called right after she hung up on John Kendall. He wanted to know what she knew about the Sally Roe/mail tampering/lawsuit/curriculum thing, and didn't Sally Roe commit suicide a while back? She wanted to know what he knew, they both wanted to know what Claire Johanson knew, and both agreed that none of them knew a lot and that all of them wanted to know a lot more, especially what the *feds* knew.

The demonic powers and authorities of Bacon's Corner were scattered. Terga's best warriors fled elsewhere to find a new home for their mischief; Terga, alone except for the deserters who joined him on the way, set out for the Omega Center. Perhaps there was time to warn Barquit, Omega's prince. Maybe Barquit would have the strength to save them and stop this onslaught.

Far away from it all, in the city of Westhaven, the Circuit Court of Appeals, with all parties oblivious to the spiritual racket steadily growing and spreading out of Bacon's Corner, convened at two o'clock in the afternoon. Wayne Corrigan and Tom Harris took their places at the defendant's table on the right side of the courtroom, while attorneys Ames and Jefferson took their seats on the left.

"All rise," said the bailiff, and they all rose, and in strode the three appellate judges, one younger man, one older man, and one sagging woman. They sat down, the three lawyers sat down, the clerk and bailiff sat down, and the court stenographer poised her fingers over the little keys.

Tom looked around the courtroom. Apart from one reporter that had shown up looking a little bored with his assignment, the gallery was empty. Of course. The public was waiting for the real show, the trial.

"Ah well," Corrigan whispered, "it's going to be a short day anyway."

"No earthshaking surprises?" asked Tom.

"To be honest, I'm not expecting any."

The older judge put on his reading glasses and referred to his papers. "This is the case of *Brandon v. the Good Shepherd Academy,* the defendant appealing the lower court's ruling as to compelling a child witness to be examined by defense's experts and to testify in this case . . ."

Corrigan sneaked a glance at Ames and Jefferson. They looked bored. Boy, now there was confidence!

In Fairwood, Massachusetts, the Omega Center was in full swing, with classes in progress, fair weather on the campus, and—by their standards—nothing weird or unusual happening. A gang of young adults continued their good-hearted game of touch football on the playfield; on the Tai Chi plaza, two dozen practitioners moved in slow motion through time, space, and spirit; in the classrooms, high school kids, adults, and even senior citizens learned the latest westernized twist on Hindu mysticism; and in the quiet, cushioned meditation rooms, young transcendentalists watched with eyes closed as demons played cosmic movies in their brains.

Cree and Si, their armies in position, were ready and waiting. Any moment now . . .

Barquit, Prince of Omega, was troubled when he first heard the humming and whistling of frayed wings and then the anguished wails and laments of spirits far away. He took wing and hovered above the Omega Administration Building, peering westward until he saw the spirits from Bacon's Corner approaching, screaming with alarm.

Something was up. "Forces!"

FWOOOM! He covered his head, blinded by brilliant light exploding on every side, obliterating the forests and hills, washing out the blue of the sky, bleaching out the colors of the Center. Spinning about in panic, he drew his sword, but it was struck away before he even saw his attacker.

He fled into the sky, feeling the burning light of Heaven at his heels.

Telephones began to ring in every room on the campus, and every teacher, group leader, and facilitator got the word: the football game was over, classes were canceled, and anyone out in astral travel would have to come in for a landing. Mr. Tisen, the head of the Omega faculty, had gotten an angry call from

Betty Hanover, a threatening call from Claire Johanson, and last but not least a nosy and intimidating call from the FBI. He was clearing the campus, and that meant everyone.

Cree and Si led their forces through the campus like a flash flood, whipping through and around the buildings, flushing demons out of the rooms, chasing them through the surrounding woods, cutting them down out of the sky. The demonic deceivers were swamped and confounded. They called for Barquit, their crafty leader, but he was long gone. They had little time to lament about it before they were gone as well.

Barquit looked back only once, just long enough to know that Omega, his empire, had fallen.

The Strongman! This is his blunder!

"Classes are canceled," said Tisen over the loudspeakers. "Everyone to your dorms. Get your belongings loaded on the buses and be ready to roll!"

The classes ended so abruptly and the students were sent out so quickly that many thought it was a fire drill, or even an air raid. Some were still slipping on their coats as they hurried outside; others, still half-entranced, had to be led by the hand. The teachers were gathering up their coats, grabbing their briefcases, handouts, and curricula, shutting off the lights, locking up the rooms.

The football game broke up, and the players jogged back toward their dormitories full of questions.

Within an hour, the buses began to roll down the drive to the main road, carrying away faculty, students, even maintenance personnel, all chattering and wondering together just what in the world was going on.

Only a few noticed the plain olive sedan parked in front of the Administration Building. It hadn't been there long.

"I'm sorry," Tisen told the two federal agents now standing in his office. "You've come at a hectic time. We're just closing down for our midspring break. Hardly anyone is here now."

The two men exchanged glances.

"*Midspring* break?" asked one.

Tisen smiled. "We follow a rather unique calendar here, gentlemen."

"We'll have a look at it."

The other agent noted, "We saw the buses pulling out. It looked like an evacuation."

Tisen grinned sheepishly. "Well, most of them have planes to catch . . ."

The agents didn't waste time. "Like I asked you over the phone, this is the same Omega Center that published the *Finding the Real Me* curriculum?"

"Well . . . yes, it is."

"Then you must be familiar with the author, Sally Roe?"

"You mean me personally?"

"I mean you personally or any other way."

"Well, of course I'm familiar with the name . . ."

"Where can we contact her?"

"Um . . . Well, I'm afraid she's deceased."

"How do you know that?"

"Well, I—"

One agent consulted some notes. "What about an instructor here, a lady named Sybil Denning? Is she still on the campus?"

Tisen shook his head with just a little too much sadness. "No, I'm afraid she's gone."

"Do you see much of Owen Bennett anymore?"

Tisen looked shocked at that question. "*Owen Bennett?*"

"He used to be on the Omega advisory board, right?"

"That was a long time ago."

"How about the director of this place . . . uh . . . Steele?"

"He's gone."

"The *director's* gone?"

"He's away at a conference."

"What conference and where?"

"Well, um . . . Do I really have to answer all these questions?"

"Maybe now, for sure later. Suit yourself."

These guys were intimidating. "He's . . . he and some other people on our faculty are at the Summit Institute."

The two men nodded to each other. Apparently they already knew about that place.

Goring, Steele, and Santinelli stood in a close cluster near the big fireplace, trying to lay a contingency plan. They paid little attention to Khull, who still sat at the top of the basement stairs trying to tape up his wound with gauze, cotton, and anything else he could find in Goring's first aid kit. So far he was only making a mess.

"You know what she said in those letters!" said Goring. "She didn't leave out one thing!"

Steele asked Santinelli, "How would our chances be in court?"

Santinelli was grim but determined, and spoke in a low mutter. "There are many variables and contingencies. We should immediately inventory and eliminate any liabilities." Goring and Steele couldn't help a quick, sideways glance at Khull. Santinelli cleared his throat to correct them. "Any connections at all with the Bacon's Corner case must be eradicated. I can call my office on that. As for material evidence . . ." He shot a glance at the coffee table. "I strongly suggest we burn these letters!"

Khull pretended he didn't hear anything.

The telephone rang. Goring cursed, but decided to pick it up in the kitchen. He stepped out of the room.

"Power in the right places will also be a crucial factor," said Santinelli. "This will be a test of how much we really have."

"Mr. Steele!" Goring called. "It's your faculty head, Mr. Tisen!"

Steele motioned for Santinelli to follow him, and they joined Goring in the kitchen.

"It sounds urgent," Goring whispered.

Khull saw his chance, and struggled to his feet.

A sleek, blue sedan pulled into the parking lot, and three men in business suits got out, getting a good look at the place and acting just a little bewildered.

"They're going to think we're crazy," said one.

"Let's make this quick," said another. "I want to get back in time to see the Broncos game."

They encountered a beautiful blonde woman just getting out of her Mercedes.

"Pardon me, ma'am," said the group's leader. "We're looking for . . . uh . . . ." He lost his train of thought.

The second man stepped in. "We need to talk to the people in charge of this place."

"Oh," said the woman. "Why don't you try Mr. Goring? His chalet is right over that way, beyond the herb garden, see?"

She gave them just a few more pointers and then went her way. One man was ready to head for the chalet, but the other two just kept staring after the woman.

"C'mon," said the one, "let's go."

"You know who that was?"

"C'mon!"

"That was . . . you know, What's-her-name, from that TV show . . ."

Tal's brushfire continued to rage.

Far away, on the Bentmore University campus, there was quite a buzz about the School of Education closing down so suddenly. Information was scarce. There were isolated conversations here and there about the sudden death of Professor Samuel W. Lynch. No one seemed to know how he died, or at least no one was willing to talk about it. The only news being consistently repeated among the faculty and students was that he'd been found dead in his office and that the School of Education was suspending classes indefinitely. There were rumors, of course: Lynch may have been murdered, and there might be some kind of scandal afoot. There might be an investigation. Student reporters for the *Bentmore Register* were hoping for an exposé.

Corrupter, the bloated demon Prince of Bentmore University, was dethroned at last, and it was Chimon the European and his British friend Scion who batted him out of his position like a beach ball over a fence. The angelic forces had done their job quickly, and now homeless demons were aloft and wailing, most of them heading for Summit. Soon they would descend upon the Strongman along with all the other evicted and dethroned spirits, demanding rescue, answers, relief.

Immediately, with the slamming down of the phone, Goring, Santinelli, and Steele came dashing around the corner and back into the living room with one goal in mind.

And one huge shock waiting for them—an empty coffee table, and no Mr. Khull.

"The letters!" cried Goring.

"Khull!" said Steele.

"That devil!" said Santinelli, dashing out the door.

forty-four

SALLY'S heart pounded and ached in her chest as she scurried and stumbled over damp pine needles and patches of crusted snow, grappled and groped through prickly, dead branches, and tried with all her rapidly ebbing strength to stay ahead of the snappings, huffings, rustlings, and footfalls of the devils pursuing her.

Two were directly below, but invisible behind limbs and thickets; a third was to her left, and she'd seen him twice, so close she could read the demons in his eyes. The fourth was silent and invisible except for his eerie, intermittent whistling to let the others know where he was.

They were getting closer. *O Lord Jesus, help me run!*

"Hey," said one of the three visitors, "now who's that?"

His friends expected to see another celebrity. What they saw was a silver-haired man in a business suit running like a wild man across the herb garden.

"Guys, I just have this feeling . . ."

Khull, his chest still reddened from his wound, had Goring's briefcase full of Sally's letters in one hand and the keys to the van in the other. He stood by the van, unable to find the right key to open it. He could see the key to the door, but it kept falling out of his fingers and dangling from the key ring.

Guilo stood by him, flicking at the keys with the tip of his finger, making them dance, slip, flip, and turn every which way but where Khull wanted them.

Tal swooped low over the parking lot with a message: "They're on the way!"

"Splendid!" said Guilo.

Santinelli was gasping for breath and about to collapse when he reached the parking lot, but the sight of Khull holding Goring's briefcase fed his rage and his rage kept him going.

531

He got to the van in mere seconds, pointing his shaking finger.

"I'll . . . take . . . those!" he gasped.

Khull smiled mockingly. "Huh? You mean *these*?" It was a great joke to him.

Santinelli was losing all semblance of dignity. "You devil! How dare you betray us!"

Khull held up his hand. "Hey, just who was going to betray who? We're all devils, right? You said so yourself. I'm taking these for insurance: number one, to make sure I get paid, and number two, to make sure you and I always remain close, trusting friends!"

Santinelli had more rage than sense, and grabbed at the briefcase. Khull wasn't about to let go of it.

Guilo let them go ahead and tangle. He was waiting for the right moment.

All right. Good enough.

With his huge hand, he batted the briefcase free. It struck the pavement, flipped twice, then flew open, throwing the letters everywhere.

Santinelli—dignified, honorable, distinguished, high-powered attorney Santinelli—stooped to grab up the letters, but so did bloodthirsty, demonized, Satanist murderer Khull. They went to their knees, playing one on one, grabbing faster, grabbing more, shoving, jostling, grappling, ripping . . .

Until they came to the feet. Three sets of feet. Nice shoes. Nice suits. Three men.

One man held out his badge. FBI.

Destroyer braced himself, but the Strongman didn't roar this time. He didn't even slap Destroyer around the room. Instead, with defeat in his eyes, he looked above and all around, just watching his empire crumble.

The cloud of demons was so hacked apart by this time that the light of Heaven was shining down on the Summit Institute in alarmingly large patches, turning the Global Consciousness Conference into a shambles. The psychics were unable to get any readings, the channelers' spirit entities weren't speaking, the tarot readers couldn't remember what their cards were saying, and every "higher self" on campus was out to lunch and not answering.

In the meantime, word was getting around the campus that three federal agents had just arrested someone and were still checking around. Something big was going down, and few conferees had their minds on their own hidden potential and godhood, a shot in the arm the demons could have used.

All this was distressing enough, but then the other spirits began to arrive from Bacon's Corner, the Omega Center, Bentmore University, and other centers of demonic power disrupted by the spiritual shock waves. One by one, in various stages of dismemberment and injury, they tumbled into the basement of the chalet, screaming, scratching, clawing for rescue, for answers, for someone to blame.

Terga, the Prince of Bacon's Corner, was slowly withering, and pointed at the Strongman with his one good hand. "You brought this upon us! You and your ridiculous Plan!"

Corrupter, only half his original size, rolled across the floor like a lame rat and spit out his accusation. "Have we built our empire at Bentmore only to feed it to Heaven's Host?"

Barquit kept his wings tightly wrapped around him, humiliated by his defeat and now swordless. "Your Plan! Always *your* Plan! Is this why I was never warned of the woman's coming, *or* of this ambush laid against my principality?"

Then from all around, from every fanged, drooling, spitting mouth, came the big question: "What have you done about the woman?"

The Strongman had one simple answer for all the questions. He pointed to Destroyer. "*There* is your betrayer! If he had killed her when he should have, we would not be in this state today! It was *his* idea to capture her letters, and now her testimony is *in writing* and defeats us! He is the one whose harassments did not destroy her, but drove her to the Cross!"

The Cross! That was all the spirits needed to hear. Swords appeared. "You will pay for this!"

Destroyer met their murderous eyes with his own, drew his

blazing sword, and sliced the air with ribbons of red light.
"So you are better than I? Then show it now!"

They stood in their places, spitting and cursing at him from
a safe distance.

He huffed at them in anger. "To the Abyss with all of you! I
will finish what I have started!"

The Strongman shook his head. "You won't, Destroyer. She
belongs to the Lamb. He has redeemed her from our grasp!"

Destroyer clenched his teeth and growled, "I *will* finish!"

The Strongman spread his wings in Destroyer's path. "We
are withdrawing, Destroyer, and Khull's henchmen will not
go with you. Without men to do your killing, the *woman* will
have power over *you!*"

"She doesn't know that!" Destroyer pointed his sword
right at the Strongman's belly. "I will finish what I have
started!"

The Strongman studied Destroyer with probing eyes, and
then stepped aside. The hate-crazed demon shot out of the
chalet.

"We will not see him again," said the Strongman. He
turned to the battered, tattered assemblage. "Princes, we are
restrained! We will wait for a better time."

In a burst of black wings, chugging sulfur, and trails of red
smoke, the Strongman and his princes scattered in all directions from the Summit Institute, abandoning it like a sinking
ship, letting the clamor and smoke shrink into the distance
behind them.

Follow the woman, follow the woman, get her! The spirits of
Broken Birch thought only of the woman and stayed close to
the ground in hot pursuit, guiding and empowering the four
killers who now thrashed and clawed their way through the
forest looking for their fleeing prey.

There! The killers spotted her, struggling up a steep bank,
losing strength, stumbling, falling.

Tears streamed down Sally's face; her shirt clung to her
back, soaked with sweat. She clambered over some stones and
then flopped to the ground, her lungs heaving. Every muscle

in her body trembled and quivered; her legs and arms would no longer move. She couldn't see, she couldn't think; she felt she was dreaming.

The demons jumped on the backs of the killers. *Kill her! Kill her! Chop her into little pieces!*

There was a roaring sound behind them. The forest was flooded with light.

Behind them?

Some looked back. They screamed, and others looked back also.

They could no longer see the Summit Institute, their haven, their fortress—all they could see was the Host of Heaven!

Cut off! Ambushed!

"Take them!" said Tal.

Red smoke.

Killer Number One collapsed to the ground, gasping for air. He'd had enough of this mountainside.

Killer Number Two, further up the slope, turned when he heard Number One hit the ground. "Hey, c'mon!"

Number One didn't answer. He just wanted to breathe.

Number Three had just broken into a clearing and could see the Institute. He whistled at them. "Hey! Looks like feds down there! They've got Khull!"

Number Four saw the woman tumble behind some rocks. He took his knife in his hand. He was almost there. He paused just momentarily to look back, then cursed. "It *is* Khull!"

The Summit Institute looked like a model of itself from up here, with neat rows of toy cars lined up in the blacktop parking lot and rough shake rooftops nestled among the trees. Khull wasn't hard to recognize, staggering along between two men in suits with the front of his shirt all red and his hands behind his back. That guy behind him had to be Santinelli, being led along by a third man. There was no sign of Goring, but just seeing this was enough.

"Good-bye," said Number Three, heading back down the mountain.

Number One followed him. "Let's get into town. I'll hot-wire a car."

There was an immediate consensus.

Sally did not hear them go. She lay among the rocks in a dead faint. The Satanists had come within four feet of her hiding-place before turning back.

In Claytonville, former Police Sergeant Harold Mulligan locked the front door of coroner Joey Parnell's home and put Parnell's house keys in his pocket. He'd just dropped by the Parnell residence on a business call—but it wasn't police business. Mulligan was in civilian clothes, and was driving his own private vehicle, an older Ford. He did not linger, but got into that Ford, backed down the driveway, and drove out of that neighborhood, out of that town, and, for all practical purposes, out of existence. He would never be seen again.

Within a few days, the papers would report the mysterious gunshot deaths of Parnell and his wife, both found dead together in the Parnell home, apparently from a mutual suicide pact. Satanic literature would be found in the home, along with evidence linking Parnell to several unsolved murders in that part of the state.

Sally awoke with a start and stiffened. *Don't move! They might be near you!* She stifled her breathing and remained still, listening.

There was no sound except the cold breeze. The shadows were longer. It was the only way she could tell that any time had passed. She lay among some large stones, flat on her back. She raised her head slightly. She felt cold.

Then she felt fear. Steady. Pounding. Growing. Like footsteps behind her in the dark, like some . . . some *thing* lurking around the next blind corner, like a crawling, unstoppable monster approaching while she was unable to move.

She whispered so quietly she only mouthed the words, "Who's there?"

EYES! Scales! Blackness, power, sulfur, *hatred!*

It stood tall before her, a waking nightmare, a black, towering silhouette against a surreal, blood-red sky, the bulging yellow eyes leering at her, never blinking, never wavering.

She knew it was there. It was not material, and physical eyes could not see it, but she'd had such visitations before, and she knew it was real. She tensed, rose to her elbows, looking up at it while it looked down at her, the sulfur blowing in silken wisps from its nostrils, its fangs bared as it grinned with fiendish delight.

It spoke to her in her mind. *You know me.*

She did, and now she had good reason to be terrified. She pushed herself away, wriggling backwards on her hands and elbows, speechless, shaking.

The thing's words throbbed in her head. *You know me, Sally Roe, and you won't get away!*

The huge red sword came down like a meat cleaver.

Tal heard Sally's scream above the battle and shouted, "Guilo!"

"YAHHH!" came Guilo's answer as he shot up from the center of the ebbing cloud. He'd heard it too.

Side by side, with wings spread full and trailing fire, they dove like meteors for the mountain, rolled sharply to the right, then dropped into the forest, lighting up the treetops.

Sally tumbled over the rocks and rolled down the steep incline, arms thrashing, kicking up pine needles, dirt, and pebbles. The ground was washed red with the light of that huge sword as the thing glided down the slope after her, wings spread like a canopy. She could hear its huffing breath, the rippling of its leathery wings.

She came to a stop against a tree.

WHOOSH! The sword split the air once more. Sally ducked, scrambled down the hill, fell, and rolled again.

Tal banked to the left, Guilo to the right; they would strike from opposite sides. Tal shot up from the mountainside, chest just above the rocks and brush, then cupped his wings, swung his feet out before him, and doubled back.

He could see Sally tumbling down the slope with the black spirit pouncing on her like a murderous vulture, red sword flashing again and again. Beyond the spirit, he saw Guilo as a fast-closing ball of light. Tal hauled back his sword, ready to strike.

The loathsome spirit saw them coming and stood his ground, ready to meet them. They came at him like two colliding trains. With incredible power, he batted them both aside. Guilo went tumbling uphill, trying to come out of a spin, while Tal cannonballed downhill, passing through and between the pines, disappearing into the thick forest below.

You are mine, said the spirit, *and I will finish what I have started!*

"No!" Sally pleaded. It was the only word that would come to her mind.

ZING! The sword caught her in the leg. She fell against a tree, then to the ground. The sword came down again, just missing her shoulder.

Brilliant light! Two comets! Guilo from above, Tal from below, closing again!

Guilo struck first. The spirit batted him aside, but caught a stunning blow in the back from Tal's sword and teetered forward before spinning and meeting Tal's sword with a jolting parry that sent Tal fluttering into the forest again.

Guilo dove and struck the thing's neck. It elbowed him several miles out of the way.

Tal righted himself, gripped his sword tightly, and shouted, *Sally Roe! Stand against him! Turn him away!*

Sally didn't seem to hear. She was crying out, trying to get on her feet. The thing leaped upon her, digging its talons into her. She could feel them searing her flesh. She was choking on the foul breath. It raised the sword again.

OOF! A streak of light passed overhead, and the thing pitched forward. Guilo looped in a tight circle and came in for another pass, and there came Tal, straight down from above.

The spirit rose to its feet and faced them head-on, wild-eyed, sword ready. Guilo came in low; it kicked him aside. Tal dropped from above; it batted him into the treetops.

Speak up, Sally! said Tal.

"Stand aside," the thing roared. "The woman belongs to *me!*"

With that, it stomped its black, scaled foot down on the fleeing woman's leg, knocking her down, holding her there.

Tal shouted, "She is *ours,*" and dove for the demon again, at least to keep it diverted.

This time their swords met in a shower of sparks. The blow sent Tal reeling.

Take authority! said Tal.

You are mine, Sally Roe! said the demon.

"No!" said Sally. She'd found some words. "I belong to Jesus, the Son of God!"

That's it, that's it, that's it! Guilo roared, rushing through the trees with incredible fury.

His blow knocked the demon backward. The thing whipped his sword around, but Guilo pulled his feet in just in time and got away.

You do not belong to Jesus! the monster screamed. *He could never love you!*

Sally was distraught, groping for words. "Jesus loves me! The Bible tells me so!" A child's Sunday school song. It was all she knew.

Tal scored a hit and sent the demon tumbling into the trees.

Sally went running for her life, crying out, "Jesus, help me! Help me!"

The demon recovered and roared after her, wings thundering. *You will burn in Hell with me! I will drag you there myself!* He swung his sword at her, but his reach was short.

She fell, twisted, looked up at those yellow eyes.

He landed on her, knocking her flat with his knees, clamping her down.

Their eyes met.

"Jonas!" she screamed.

He broke into a wide, hideous grin, the fangs dripping, the

brow furrowed with wicked laughter. The sword went high over his head.

"Jonas," she said, extending her open hand toward the gnarled face, "STOP!"

The sword remained above his head. The eyes narrowed. *You are mine!*

She rose up on one elbow. She was gaining new courage. "I am *not* yours! I belong to Jesus!"

No . . . no, Sally Roe!

She was amazed. The sword teetered above the demon's head. He could not lower it. She spoke again. "I belong to Jesus now; He paid for my sins with His blood, and you can't torment me anymore!"

I will do what I wish! I am going to kill you! Suddenly the demon didn't sound too convincing.

"My Lord has defeated you!"

Destroyer stumbled to his feet, holding his sword limply, his eyes losing their fire.

"Get out of my life, Jonas! Forever! Do you hear?"

THUD! Tal came in with a blow that sent Destroyer spinning. The black demon righted himself and held his sword ready. Guilo came in from the side and assailed him again with a clash of blades and bursts of light.

"The woman belongs to *me!*" Destroyer roared.

"She is *ours!*" said Tal.

Sally's desperate, screaming voice came across the distance: "I belong to Jesus! Jonas, I *renounce* you! You have no claim to me! Get out of my life!"

The words hit Destroyer like poisonous darts. Then a revelation hit like a salvo, and Destroyer stood still, facing his archrival, the Captain of the Host.

"You *knew*, Captain of the Host! You knew she would do this to me, to *us!*"

Tal held his sword ready, but answered, "I knew what you would do to *her*—that you were commissioned to destroy her."

Destroyer's mouth spread open, and the fangs went dry. "*You* placed her there, in Bacon's Corner!"

"And you tried to kill her, as always!"

Destroyer began to wilt. "She . . . was *mine*, from her youth!"

"Ours—our Lord's," said Tal, "from her mother's womb."

"Get out of my life, Jonas!" Sally cried. "Jesus has conquered you—so get out!"

The sword quivered in Destroyer's hand. "She has taken away my name!"

With an agonized roar and a final burst of fury, the weakened demon dove at Tal, bringing his blade down in a fiery arc. Tal parried, jabbed, let him keep coming. The red sword swung from the side, came back again, cut through the air. Tal sidestepped it, struck it aside with enough force to throw the demon off-balance. He delivered a stunning kick to the demon's flank, jolting him, toppling him. The demon twisted about, swung at him; Tal met that clumsy attack easily, then brought his own blade down in a shining arc.

The air filled with red smoke. Destroyer wailed like an eerie siren, clutching his opened side, floating, withering, fading. He pushed himself backward with one foot, hovering on erratic wings. Tal hauled back for one more blow, but it wouldn't be necessary. As the demon's eyes remained fixed on him, ruby-red, bulging in hate, the wings fell silent.

With the dying, groping lips forming a silent curse, the thing pitched forward, sighing out sulfur, and slipped into oblivion.

The forest was suddenly quiet. Now Tal could hear the muffled weeping of Sally Roe. He sheathed his sword.

She lay nearby, facedown in the dirt, weeping, physically exhausted and emotionally spent. Guilo sat beside her, his wings spread over her, stroking her head and speaking soothing words to her soul. Tal approached quietly, knelt beside them, and spread his wings high and wide, joining Guilo's wings to form a canopy to keep out the world for a while.

"One more season of restraint," he said. "She has gained it for all of us." He touched her head, now scratched and dirty, and said softly, *It's over, Sally. You've won.*

In the valley below, the sounds of battle continued—rumblings, shrieks, clashings, flashes of light like distant lightning. But it would settle eventually. The outcome was certain and only a matter of time. For now, they remained with her.

forty-five

IN Westhaven, in the quiet, dull courtroom, Wayne Corrigan was just finishing his rebuttal to Gordon Jefferson's arguments.

"And so, we hope that the court will be careful to protect Mr. Harris's constitutional right to due process and his right to confront his accuser. We confirm once again that we have no intention of harming Amber Brandon or causing any further trauma. We only desire to get to the truth, and that, we believe, is the least our judicial system must allow any defendant. Thank you."

He took his place next to Tom Harris. Tom had been watching the clock. It was just about 4 in the afternoon.

The three judges had been watching the clock as well. The one in the middle, the older man, shuffled his papers together.

"Thank you, Mr. Corrigan, and thank you, Mr. Jefferson and Mr. Ames. Arguments were thorough and well-presented. Court will recess for the day. We'll have a ruling for you by Thursday, the day after tomorrow."

WHAM! The bailiff rapped the gavel and ordered, "All rise!" and they all rose, and the judges went out.

Ames and Jefferson seemed just a little somber, even angry, as they rose, gave Corrigan and Tom a carefully sculpted dirty look, and left the courtroom.

"Hm," said Corrigan. "I didn't think I did that well."

"I thought you did great," said Tom.

Corrigan shrugged. "Well . . . we've been praying. It's in the Lord's hands." He gave a weak smile, looked at the floor, and admitted, "But I don't know, Tom. Sometimes I wonder if I'm just a rotten lawyer or if God chooses to stay out of courtrooms. I haven't had much to feel good about lately."

Tom's smile came from deep inside. "Oh, whatever happens, God isn't mocked. He's Lord, Wayne. However He wants this to turn out, I'll accept it." He slapped Corrigan on the back. "Let's get some dinner."

Corrigan fumbled a bit. "I hope you have some money on you."

"Uh . . . I have three dollars, I think."

"Okay. I think I can match that."

"We'll make it McDonald's!"

The lake was calm, like a mirror, reflecting the trees on the shoreline with clear, unbroken lines and deep spring colors while just above the water's surface myriads of bugs danced in the sun like tiny golden sparklers. The lone fisherman sat in his aluminum boat, glad for the quiet, glad to be alone. He was somewhere in his fifties, with salt-and-pepper hair and a youthful face, dressed in jeans, flannel shirt, and a drooping fishing hat that had to have been his favorite for years. The fish weren't biting much, but he was getting the peace he'd come for, and he was satisfied. For now, he reclined lazily against a boat cushion, just floating, relaxing, and not thinking much.

Somewhere in the middle of the day, he heard the rumble and gentle splashing of boat oars, and looked out from under his hat brim. Yes, someone was coming toward him in a small wooden dinghy.

When the visitor drew nearer, the fisherman sat up. He knew that slightly rotund, bespectacled man in the straw hat. They weren't exactly friends, but they'd bumped shoulders on many occasions. What was he doing here? This was supposed to be the fisherman's hideaway.

The visitor looked over his shoulder, smiled, and kept rowing closer, not saying a word.

The fisherman had an eerie feeling about this encounter. If the visitor wasn't going to speak, then *he* would. "Jim?"

Jim looked over his shoulder. "Hey, Owen." With a few last oar strokes, he brought the little dinghy alongside. Owen used a short piece of tether to join the two boats together. "Ah, thank you much."

"To what do I owe this visit?" asked Owen Bennett. "I hope it isn't business. I'm out of the office right now."

"Oh, I figured this would be a great place to have a chat, just you and me." Jim looked back toward the resort. Some families were picnicking near the lakeshore. "But I'd talk quietly, Owen. The sound is really carrying today."

Owen lowered his voice and asked, "So state your business. I'm very busy doing nothing today and I'd like to get back to it."

Jim heaved a deep sigh, rested his forearms on his knees, and just looked at Owen for a moment. "I'll come right to it, but even that'll take a while. I suppose you've been keeping up on that case out of Bacon's Corner?"

Owen stared at him blankly, then shook his head.

"Never heard of the place?"

"No, afraid not."

"Well . . . I never heard of it either. Never cared to, except that the ACFA started a lawsuit there, and I know they were coming your way with it. They were going after a Christian school again, and thought they had all their ducks in a row, including you."

"Well, if it's a pending case, obviously I can't discuss it . . ."

Jim held up his hand. "Oh no, no . . . don't worry about that. We don't need to discuss the case, no sir. We can talk about other things."

"All right."

Jim looked across the lake, gathering his thoughts. "We can talk about a few personal items, I suppose . . . like a particular secret society, the Royal and Sacred Order of the Nation?"

Owen smiled. "Well now, if I talked about that, it wouldn't stay a secret, would it?"

Jim nodded. "So I've gathered. You know, I'm amazed at how many supposed friends of mine know everything else but what I want to find out about that bunch."

"It's just a lodge, Jim. It's really nothing to worry about."

Jim wasn't that willing to brush the matter off. "Ehhhh . . . you have to understand, a man in my position gets a little spooked when men in your position start protecting each other and keeping little secrets among yourselves. Well, I said *little* secrets, but I don't know *what* size they are, do I?"

Owen remained tight-lipped. This was Jim's meeting; let him carry the conversation.

Jim did. "I hear that Carl Santinelli's a member, and *that* would concern me, as much as his name gets around Washington. To think the two of you are bosom buddies in the same secret society curls my hair just a little."

Owen got a little tense, and his voice had an edge. "That raises an obvious question for me, though I doubt I'll get an answer: How did you find out?"

"I've been reading some mail, Owen. A lot of mail." Jim looked directly at him. "Letters written by Sally Beth Roe."

Paydirt. Jim could see a definite reaction all over Owen's face. Owen lowered his head and muttered, "Oh, boy."

"Aw, we've all got a few skeletons in the closet, Owen. You know that about me, and I know that about you."

Owen couldn't contain his curiosity. "What . . . Did she write to *you?*"

"Oh, no. She wrote to the headmaster of that Christian school—I guess to give him some inside information and help him out."

"Well . . . I hope you can recognize truth from vindictive lies."

"Mmmm . . . one of the first things she wrote was that she wasn't dead, and I was impressed by her truthfulness."

"Jim, I think you're talking in riddles!"

"Well, okay, stop me if you've heard this one: Sally Roe wrote a whole stack of letters to the headmaster of that school, I guess to help him out. The only problem was, he never got the letters because somebody tampered with United States mail and snatched them all. Turned out it was the local postmaster, also the plaintiff in the suit, but she agreed to cooperate and told us where she sent them all. You'll never guess where: the Summit Institute! Some FBI agents went there and found every one of them in the possession of—are you ready for this?—Carl Santinelli, Mr. ACFA himself. He's in real hot water right now."

"That has nothing to do with me."

Jim was a little shocked. "What happened to the old team spirit, Owen? I thought you guys were lodge brothers."

"That means nothing."

"All right, all right, we'll try not to place guilt by association."

"I would greatly appreciate that."

"But just for my own information, don't all you Nation guys have some kind of membership ring, some funny gold ring with an ugly face on it, and your secret code name on the inside?"

"I don't have any such ring."

"Well, I know you don't have yours. Sally Roe has it. Well, she *did* have it. Now we have it."

Owen just stared.

"Yeah, it's yours, all right. We checked your secret lodge name against the Nation's official membership rosters. 'Gawaine,' wasn't it?"

Owen's face was like cold stone. "What game are you playing here?"

"The game we all play, Owen. Sally says she learned it from you. That's why she saved your ring all these years. It's a nice ace for her to play, and it makes her story credible, especially since she happened upon another ring, this one belonging to some kid brother of yours in the Nation, James Bardine, a hotshot punk lawyer with Santinelli's firm. Bardine's ring turned up on the finger of a Satanist." Jim added with an appropriate, sinister touch, "A woman who was hired to kill Sally Roe." He quickly added, "The assassin blew it. She got killed herself, and now we have that ring too.

"So that sort of ties all four of you together in this thing: you, Carl Santinelli, James Bardine, and that Satanist lady—uh, make that woman, or something derogatory if you like."

Jim removed his straw hat and wiped his brow. "Owen, I'm ready to lay odds you already know the rest, the whole lawsuit over that little girl having some kind of psychotic, personality blowout of some kind, and the ACFA blaming the Christian school just to get the government through their door, and . . . Well, it was quite a plan, yes sir." Jim looked directly at Owen for his next comment. "A plan worth killing Sally Roe to protect—a plan worth covering up the fact that someone tried to kill Sally Roe to protect. A plan worth tampering with the mails and hunting down Sally Roe to protect."

Owen occupied himself with his rod and reel, and didn't look up. "Jim, I believe I'm growing tired of your company."

"That was your baby, wasn't it?"

Owen froze for a moment. If Jim was attempting to shock him, the attempt succeeded. He reached down and began to untie the tether between the two boats. "I think you'd better leave."

Jim placed his hand on Owen's to stop him. "You were on the advisory board at the Omega Center, and you got her that position at the Center after she graduated from Bentmore. You spent a lot of time with her, didn't you, every time you flew out for meetings with Steele and the others?

"Until she had that baby instead of aborting it. Now there was a wrench thrown into your career! She could have sued you for child support, laid the whole thing open in public, right? What better way to solve that problem than to remove the only tangible link between the two of you—and destroy the woman in the process?"

Owen straightened up defiantly. "Do you actually intend to argue that *I'm* to blame for Sally Roe's incredible delusions?"

"*You* believe in that spirit stuff, don't you?"

"That's my personal business."

"And at the time, *she* believed in it—with a lot of help from you and that Omega bunch."

"That establishes nothing."

"Who says the newspapers and networks ever have to establish something as juicy as this? They'll print it now and prove it later. You've slipped them some goodies yourself from time to time, you know that."

"And we could slip them some more—*you* should know *that!*"

Jim nodded. "Yeah, that's right. We could make life pretty difficult for each other, no question." Then he chuckled. "But I sure enjoy the picture I get in my mind of you hearing a case brought by some of your lodge brothers in the ACFA, knowing they tried to protect their case by killing a woman you once had an affair with. Top that, Owen!"

Owen Bennett looked across the lake and thought for a moment. "So what do you want?"

Jim smiled. "Have I done it, Owen? Do I really have a lever on you?"

Owen snapped, "What do you want?"

"The sound carries, remember." Jim stopped to think for a moment. "Owen, I think I've been a pretty good attorney general, and I think I could do an even better job if certain parties would take all their weight and push it around elsewhere. I want this leash off my neck."

Owen looked grim. "I didn't put it there."

"But you have pull with the people who did. You're one of their star players."

"I can't cross them, Jim. You know that."

Jim shrugged. "Well, you could always step down, I suppose."

"I can't do that either."

Jim was resolute. "I'm giving you a choice, Owen."

Tom Harris grabbed the *Hampton County Star* from his front porch and stepped inside to the smell of hot biscuits, eggs, hash browns, bacon, the works.

"What's new?" asked Marshall.

"Oh, quite a bit," said Tom, perusing the front page.

It was Friday morning, it had been a week like no other week, and the core group, the central players, were gathered in Tom's house for a big breakfast, just to be together: Ben and Bev Cole, Mark and Cathy Howard, Marshall and Kate Hogan, and Tom. Just Tom. If social worker Irene Bledsoe had heard of all the shake-up, she wasn't saying, and so far she wasn't returning Tom's calls.

Ben asked, "Any speeches from the ACFA boys about the court's decision?"

"Kind of a moot point now anyway," said Mark. "The lawsuit's been dropped. It's all over."

"Too bad," Tom quipped. "I was scheduled to give a deposition next week. Now I'll miss out on the wonderful experience."

"But it ain't over, not yet," said Bev. "I mean, we're talking 'bout a big investigation here. We're talking 'bout some arrests!"

Marshall smiled a weak smile and shook his head. "Probably not."

"Are you crazy?"

"Sometimes I wonder . . ."

Mark asked, "Well the authorities *are* going to look into this?"

"My FBI friend John Harrigan doesn't think so. There are cases and there are cases. Some you go after, some you don't. A thing like this is . . . well, such a big can of worms; there's so much of it going on in so many places, and you can't arrest *everybody*."

"Hey, listen to this," said Tom. "Here's a quote from Gordon Jefferson. There's even a picture of him here, standing outside the courtroom . . ."

"Wait," said Ben. "I want to sit down."

Tom read the quote from the ACFA lawyer. "'We sincerely regret this monumental breach of justice and of the rights of children everywhere. The clock of progress has been set back severely by this ruling. Had the court ruled in favor of the child, this lawsuit could have continued, and we could have fought against the scourge of religious bigotry and intolerance against our children. Mrs. Brandon wishes me to share her deep regrets and her thanks with all her supporters everywhere, and to express her heartfelt dream that the fight for our children will continue. For now, she has asked, and we have agreed, to drop the suit, pick up the pieces, and go on with our lives as best we can.'"

Kate was appalled. "What a pile of *lies!*"

"But what great PR!" said Marshall. "Official ACFA policy: No matter what happens, come out the hero!"

"Let me see that," came a voice from the kitchen. Tom handed the paper to Lucy Brandon herself as she came into the room. She perused the story and just shook her head. "I dropped that suit on Tuesday, *before* that hearing!" She passed the paper on to Ben and said angrily, "But they'll never tell, will they?"

Tom remarked, "Wayne Corrigan and I were wondering why Ames and Jefferson gave us such dirty looks. They *knew* the suit was dropped!"

"But they still wanted that ruling," said Marshall. "Every little step helps."

"Well to be honest," said Mark, "I think they did just fine. The judges handed down some pretty strict guidelines."

Ben searched through the paper glumly. "Nothing more about Joey and Carol Parnell."

Bev put her hand on Ben's shoulder. "Ben, you just got your job back. Don't go chasing another phony suicide. Leave that for the Claytonville cops."

But Ben was obviously frustrated. "I'm having a hard time being patient with all the inaction I'm seeing!"

"I should have warned you about this part," said Marshall. "It's tough to get action out of the authorities when the case is so vague and untraceable . . . and when the authorities are part of the problem."

Ben passed the paper to Marshall, still fuming. "Well, this is one authority who's going to earn his pay. There has to be a way to stop them!"

Marshall skimmed the first few pages and then smiled. "I think we did."

"No, we didn't! There's been no investigation, no arrests, not even truthful reporting in the papers about what really happened. We all know the kinds of things these people are getting away with!"

"Oh . . . we hurt them, Ben. We hurt them. We won this round." Marshall passed the paper to Kate. "And . . . well, I think we stand a good chance of recovering our POWs too."

"Josiah and Ruth?" asked Tom.

Marshall nodded. "Stomp a mole in your yard, you've killed your neighbor's mole too. We'll see."

"What about our MIA?" asked Kate.

"Sally . . ." said Marshall. The thought was painful.

"What did Harrigan say?"

Marshall hesitated a little on that one. "That's a tough situation. Khull and his people were apparently in the middle of some Satanic ritual in Goring's basement when the feds got there. They had to have had a victim, but there was no sign of Sally, and Khull isn't talking. The only thing they found was Sally's letters. She could have escaped, or maybe the Satanists—Khull and his bunch—killed her and disposed of the body before the feds got there. We just don't know."

Tom grew very somber. "We owe her everything. She's just got to be alive somewhere."

"We're gonna be prayin' for that gal, that's for sure," said Bev.

"And I want to meet her," said Tom. "After reading all her letters, I feel like I know her. No. I *do* know her."

"An incredible woman," said Kate.

"That she was," said Marshall.

Just outside Claytonville, a housepainter pulled his battered, laddered van to the side of the highway and let off a hitchhiker. "Sure I can't drive you further? You're out in the middle of nowhere."

"Thank you, no," said Sally Roe.

She remained there on the highway shoulder, a very tired, dirty, bedraggled vagabond in jeans, soiled blue jacket, and checkered scarf, watching the old van pull away, its rocker arms clacking, its exhaust pipe blowing smoke, its springs sagging under all the ladders and paint cans.

She felt just like that van. Her face was etched with the miles, her soul was weary from the pain, her body was bruised and dented from the abuse. But . . . she was still rolling, still chugging along, and at least now she had a good reason.

She crossed the highway as soon as she got the chance and ducked into the woods, following an old, rutted, surveying road she'd visited in the darkness of night . . . When was that? It seemed like years ago. She almost wondered if it was the same road, it looked so different in the daylight—inviting, peaceful, canopied in the fresh, new-growth green of spring, and not at all the horrifying, demon-infested hell it was the last time she was here.

She walked for some distance, following the meandering, rising, and dipping road through thick forest, tangled brush, and low-hanging limbs. She didn't remember it being this far. Perhaps she'd missed a turn somewhere. Maybe she'd hidden that truck a little too well.

Oh! There, through the limbs and leaves, she caught a familiar blue tint. Well! Still there!

Mota and Signa stood next to the old Chevy pickup, hands on swords, eyes alert, waiting for her arrival. Their warriors had closely guarded that machine since Sally left it there. The kids on dirt bikes, the hikers, the equestrians, and any would-be vandals had all passed it by, so it remained untouched, slightly overgrown with brush, but ready to roll.

Sally pushed through the new growth, pulling the keys from her jacket pocket. The door opened with its familiar groan; the smell of the cab was the same; she still remembered to avoid that small rip in the seat lest it grow longer. Her heart danced a little. This old truck was a blessing because it was familiar, it was hers, it was a piece of home.

It moaned a bit, hesitated, cranked over a few times, and then, with Sally's well-practiced pumping of the gas pedal— something that had to be done just right—it lurched to life!

Mota and Signa gave her a push, and with little difficulty she got the truck turned around. The two warriors hopped into the back, and they were all on their way back to Bacon's Corner.

forty-six

"I would like to know the real reason why I'm being fired," Irene Bledsoe demanded.

Her supervisor was an older woman with white hair pulled tightly to the back of her head and held there with innumerable pins; her hair was tight, her expression was tight, and due to her obesity, her clothes were tight. Everything about the woman was tight, especially her patience.

"You know your driving record better than I do," she snapped, hardly looking up from the work on her desk. "Such irresponsibility on the road, especially while transporting children, is a liability to this organization and cannot be tolerated."

Bledsoe tried to maintain her professional dignity, but she was definitely indignant. "Ms. Blaire, I have here in my hand the driving records of no less than a dozen other Child Protection Department employees; I even have some aptitude test scores—"

"I have seen them all, and do not wish to see them again."

"Ms. Blaire, you are tangling with the wrong person!"

SLAM! Ms. Blaire slapped her papers and pencil down on her desk and bored into Bledsoe with eyes of cold steel. "You just *said* that to the wrong person. Ms. Bledsoe, you are addressing, in essence, the state. We don't 'tangle' with anyone; we set our agenda and judge our employees by how efficiently they carry out that agenda. The fact is, you have been judged to be a liability to this department, and as such, you have been terminated."

"It's because of the Harris case, isn't it? That *is* the real reason?"

Ms. Blaire answered coldly and mechanically, "It is because of your driving record, Ms. Bledsoe. You—"

"I was only fulfilling the orders I received!"

"You simply can't be trusted to transport children safely, and that is my final word on the subject. Now finish out your duties properly, or I'll see to it that you forfeit your severance pay!"

"You . . . you can't do that!"

Ms. Blaire only smiled her cold, calculating smile. Oh yes she could, and Bledsoe knew it.

"All right. All right. I've cleaned out my desk and handed over my caseload to Julie and Betty. So what's left?"

"Drive the Harris children back to Bacon's Corner."

Ed and Mose were still sitting at their post in front of Max's Barber Shop, just taking in whatever passed before them on the Toe Springs–Claytonville Road.

Ed was looking through the latest *Hampton County Star* and making sure Mose was kept up to date on everything whether Mose was interested or not.

"The Big White House is for sale," he said.

Mose was watching a mud puddle across the street and wondering if maybe the Mercantile needed new gutters. "Heh?"

"I said the Big White House is for sale. That couple living in sin finally decided to move on."

"What? They splitting up?"

"It's just an ad for the house, Mose. It doesn't say anything about that."

Mose took a moment to spit into the street. "Yeah, probably doesn't say anything about Sergeant Mulligan either. He was living in sin too, I hear, him and that supervisor from the door company."

"You mean with each other?" Ed wondered.

"They're both gone, aren't they? Both took off at the same time. Somebody saw them together. I wasn't born yesterday, Ed."

Ed thought for a moment. "Eh . . . I don't mind them leaving. They were a strange bunch, them and their friends."

"Not a very good cop either."

"Jon Schmidt was a cop?"

Mose was astounded at Ed's dullness today. "No, friend, *Mulligan!*"

"Well, I'm glad to see him go too."

"Yeah, and that bunch at the Big White House, I'm glad to see them go."

"*Everybody's* going. Looks like the whole town's quitting."

"Who's quitting?"

Ed turned the paper toward Mose, and Mose adjusted his glasses. "See here? You've got . . . uh . . . these three folks on the school board, uh, Mrs. Hanover, and John Kendall . . ."

"John Kendall? That stubborn—! Who finally talked him into it?"

"And look here: Jerry Mason. That's three."

Mose was amazed. "Well . . . wasn't it just yesterday Elvira was telling me that the grade school lost the fourth grade teacher, Miss Beer?"

"Brewer."

"The same. She and that Woodard got into a fracas."

"Woodard's getting old, that's his problem. He's retiring."

"Say what?"

"He's retiring end of this month."

"He didn't seem that old."

"You been looking in the mirror too much, Mose."

Mose tilted his hat back. "Well I'll be. You're right. Everybody's quitting! Maybe they know something we don't! Hey! Hey, wait a minute there!"

"What?"

"Well, flip back to the second page there. Look there."

"Well, give me wings and call me an angel . . ."

"There's something going around, Ed. Something going around."

They were looking at a news item: SUPREME COURT JUSTICE STEPS DOWN.

Ed tilted his head back so he could read through his bifocals. "Who's this Owen Bennett?"

"Newest man on the Supreme Court. Hasn't been there long."

"'Bennett attributes his resignation to ill health and personal reasons.' But he looks kind of young, don't you think?"

"You been looking in the mirror too much yourself, Ed."

"Well now, that could be . . ."

Mose broke out laughing. "Hey, you know what, Ed? Maybe we oughta quit too."

Ed thought about that a moment and replied with great seriousness, "Mose, where would the world be without us keeping an eye on it?"

Then they both laughed, hitting and poking each other and having a great time; you could hear them for blocks.

Sally drove on toward Bacon's Corner, turning over and over in her mind just how she was going to present herself to Mrs. Potter, back from the dead as it were, and ask to continue renting the old farmhouse. Of course, that would be contingent on getting her job back at the door factory, and that was probably contingent on whether they would accept her excuse for being away so long without saying anything, and that raised the whole question of what she was going to tell them, and that was going to depend on what she could and couldn't talk about in public during the course of the investigation, and then again, she didn't know yet if there would even be an investigation.

She slowed as she approached an intersection out in the middle of the cornfields. She felt a slight tension in her stomach. This was the same intersection where that Bledsoe woman just about rammed her with Tom Harris's kids in the car.

Anyway, the first thing was to find out what was happening in Bacon's Corner, and how that lawsuit was progressing, or if it was still progressing at all. Bernice Krueger should have gotten that last letter by now, and she must have sent all that material to Tom Harris, so *something* should be brewing. She hadn't seen any newspapers in the last several days . . .

Well! What was this, a flashback of some kind? She had to be seeing things!

There was that same green Plymouth!

Irene Bledsoe made sure to stop carefully and safely at the notorious intersection that had cost her her job. Josiah and

Ruth were buckled in snugly this time. The intersection looked the same except that the corn was taller. It was almost like *déjà vu*, sitting here waiting for that . . . that blue pickup truck . . . being driven by the lady with the checkered scarf . . . !

Sally stared transfixed. She couldn't help it. This was Irene Bledsoe again! And there were the two Harris children!

From the back of Sally's pickup, Mota and Signa waved to their two comrades, Chimon and Scion, who rode atop the Plymouth. This encounter had timed out nicely!

Irene hesitated. She was the vehicle on the right, so she was supposed to go through the intersection first, but she just couldn't move. This couldn't be!

Josiah saw the woman too, and marveled. "Hey, look! There's that lady in the blue truck!"

"Yeah," said Ruth. "I remember her!"

So it wasn't a hallucination! Irene pressed the gas pedal gently and began to creep across the intersection, just staring at the woman.

"Hey," said Josiah, staring as well, "she's crying."

Sally watched the Plymouth pass in front of her and speed away, and then she wiped her eyes.

Lord, this was from You! You've used this to tell me!

Now she knew. This encounter, this scene before her, said it all: Somewhere, somehow, the darkness had been pierced; it was broken, fallen, its power was gone.

The children were going home!

From high above, Bacon's Corner looked downright cheery, warm, and inviting, like a little town from a model railroad, its brown, red, and black roofs bold against the surrounding patchwork green of the fields, and its silver elevators stretching toward the sky, flashing in the sun.

The skies were clear, both of clouds and of spiritual filth, washed with Heaven's light, freshened with prayer and praise to the Maker of it all. It was good to be back, good to see the place so clean. This was victory's reward.

Tal and Guilo began a gentle descent, their wings spread wide and motionless to carry them lazily over the town, high over Front Street with its cars and pickups jostling through the one intersection, over the Mercantile with its chimney smoking and red rototillers out on the sidewalk, over the small cluster of houses and garages on the Strawberry Loop, just over the top of the big silver water tower with the red light on top, steadily lower over some small farms—from up here the chickens looked like little white, black, and red triangles—and finally, at rooftop level, across the Pond Road and to the roof of Tom Harris's house.

They came in over Tom's front yard, pulled up, and stalled just above the peak of his roof, alighting upon it. They could hear breakfast in progress below; much chatter, sharing, rejoicing. Good enough. The others would be arriving any moment, and then that almost happy gathering below would be completed.

Guilo pointed to the northwest. Two streaks of light were descending rapidly out of the sky. Nathan and Armoth, just returning from Ashton!

Two more trails of light appeared in the eastern sky; Cree and Si were returning from the rout at the Omega Center.

Within moments, Nathan and Armoth passed over the house like two shining eagles, waving their swords in greeting. Tal pulled his glimmering sword and directed them to land on the left side of the front yard.

Cree and Si dropped steeply from above and cupped their wings to break their dive, settling like paratroopers to the right side of the front yard as Tal directed them.

Then they waited, every warrior in his place.

"Ah, here they come," said Tal, looking up the Pond Road toward town.

It was the green Plymouth, with Chimon and Scion still riding on top, their wings trailing like flashing, flickering banners. They waved their swords at their fellows, who waved back.

Irene Bledsoe eased the Plymouth to a stop out on the road in front of the house. She was about to reach back to help the children unbuckle and get their things, but there was no need; Josiah and Ruth burst out of that car like kids out of school and raced down the front walk without looking back.

Bledsoe turned her sharp nose forward, hit the gas, and got out of there. Chimon and Scion spread their wings, lifted from the roof, and let the car shoot out from under them. Then they settled to the ground on either side of the front gate.

The kids didn't knock or announce their arrival at all, but simply yanked the front door open and burst into the house, raising such a reaction from the people inside that Tal and Guilo could feel the noise through their feet.

In Heaven, reunions like this happened all the time, and the angels always found it absolutely riveting. Only human souls made in the image of God could fully know the soaring joy, the tear-stained ecstasy of losing a loved one and then, after a stretch of time that is always too long, feeling their warm embrace again, hearing their voice, sharing all their news. But moments like this were what the angels worked and fought for, and it was their fathomless joy, their greatest reward, to behold it once again.

The warriors in the yard could see through the front door. Tom was on his knees, clutching his children, weeping with joy. His friends were gathered all around, touching him, touching the children, murmuring prayers of thanksgiving and praise, asking questions, but getting no answers in all the confusion, and not minding at all.

The wings of the angels rose with their emotions, reaching high, spreading wide, shining like the sparkling joy that filled the house this day. They began to worship.

"Can we stay home now, Daddy?" Ruth asked through her tears.

Tom hesitated. He was afraid to answer.

Marshall touched him. "You can tell her yes."

Tom's eyes shone with deep joy and assurance. "We *did* win, didn't we?"

Marshall indicated the kids with his eyes. What more proof did they need?

Tom said, "You'd better believe it! We're never going to be apart again!"

More hugs. More tears.

A quiet squeak of breaks. Tires on gravel. A glint of blue.

Tom didn't notice, for obvious reasons, but Marshall did. He looked out the open front door.

He couldn't be sure. He couldn't believe it. He moved toward the door while the others stayed in their little rejoicing huddle.

There was a woman out there, parked across the street in a blue pickup truck.

Sally tried to keep low, tried not to be obvious as she examined Tom's house. She listened, and could hear the rejoicing through the open front door. She'd seen Irene Bledsoe driving off, and she'd seen the children run inside. They were all having such a wonderful reunion in there. She didn't feel she belonged. She didn't know what to do.

Mota and Signa hopped out of the back and stood by the cab, speaking gently to her. *They aren't going to hurt you, Sally.*

Hey, they won't mind the way you look.

I look awful, she thought. *I smell bad. What if they don't know who I am? What if this is the wrong house?*

C'mon. They'll be glad to see you!

She turned off the engine and sat there for a few more moments, just staring ahead and thinking. Her hands were shaking; she was so nervous her stomach ached.

They sound happy in there. They seem like a friendly bunch. I've just got to know how things turned out. They can reject me, I suppose, but I've got to know.

She opened the truck door and stepped out onto the shoulder. She walked toward the back of her truck—from this angle she could peer through the front door and see what was going on in there.

Oh, brother! They'll be able to see me too! I think that big guy did!

At that one, fleeting glimpse, Marshall thought he would soar through the roof and straight to Heaven! This was the Lord's work, all right! Oh, He does all things so well!

He moved carefully to the front porch as if approaching a timid deer, afraid of scaring it off.

Tal dropped to the porch and stood beside him. *That's her, Marshall. Don't let her get away.*

Sally hurried back to the cab of the truck and started to climb inside. She was going to bag this idea. Maybe she could write Tom another letter; this was just too awkward!

"Sally!"

She froze, her hand on the door handle, her right foot on the truck's running board. She didn't know if she should be Sally Roe or not. Who was this guy?

"Sally Roe?"

She remained still, just staring ahead. *If I turn my head, he'll know. Who is he?*

From inside the house she heard the children laughing. "Wow," said the little boy, "my own bed again!"

Am I safe? Is the running over?

"Thank You, Jesus," came a black woman's voice. "Oh, thank You, Jesus!"

You're safe, Sally.

She turned her head and looked at the big, red-haired man standing on the front porch. His eyes were gentle.

"Yes," she said, not loudly. Having said it once, she said it loud enough for him to hear. "Yes! That's me!"

Suddenly there was a crowd of people on that front porch, all looking her way—a lovely red-haired woman, a good-looking black couple, a kind-looking gray-haired man and his blonde wife, and . . .

Sally stared at that man as much as he stared at her. She'd seen his picture.

Tom had seen her pictures too.

You could cut the silence with a knife.

Marshall broke the silence with an invitation. "Sally, Tom

Harris—and all of us—would like very much to meet you. Would you like to come in?"

She relaxed just a little, but tried to hide behind the open truck door. "I'm . . . I'm hardly presentable . . ."

Tom replied, "You're among friends!"

Tal had to laugh. Hardly presentable! Wasn't it strange, the way humans looked at themselves with eyes of flesh and not of the Spirit? Certainly that dear woman had been through mire and filth of every degree; she was scarred, exhausted, ragged, and dirty.

But to the angels, she appeared as God Himself saw her, just as any other redeemed saint of the living God: pure, shining, clean, dressed in garments as white as snow.

With a little loving prod from Mota and Signa, Sally crossed the road, a tired, blue-jeaned vagabond coming home. She passed through the front gate, approached the front porch, and then, as angels and saints alike watched in tremendous awe, she extended her hand to the lone man standing between his two bubbly children.

"Tom Harris?"

"Yes."

"I'm Sally Beth Roe."

Tal clapped his wings just enough to return to the roof, then settled there in a comfortable sitting position, his sword at rest by his side.

Guilo asked the question for all of them. "What now, captain?"

Tal looked down at the laughing, praising group below. "I think we'll stay a while."

The warriors were glad to hear that, and moved in closer to listen to all that marvelous conversation, all that sharing and catching up.

Tal smiled and shook his head in wonder. "Redemption. It will never cease to thrill me."

If you enjoyed reading
Piercing the Darkness,
you'll want to get these
other Frank Peretti titles:

This Present Darkness

Ashton is just a typical small town. But when reporter Marshall Hogan and pastor Hank Busche begin to compare notes, they suddenly find themselves fighting a hideous plot to subjugate the townspeople—and eventually the entire human race.

A fast-moving, riveting thriller, *This Present Darkness* offers a fascinating glimpse into the unseen world of spiritual warfare—and the power of prayer.

This Present Darkness
AUDIO CASSETTE

You've never experienced this riveting best-seller in such a powerful way! *This Present Darkness* is available on audio cassette—and read by author Frank Peretti, who, besides his phenomenal success as a writer, is also a master storyteller. These two 90-minute tapes are packed with special music, stirring effects, and all the drama and excitement of the full-length novel.

Piercing the Darkness
AUDIO CASSETTE

Read by the author himself, this audio abridgment of *Piercing the Darkness* is fortified with dramatic sound effects and music that bring to life all the intrigue and spiritual impact of the beloved novel on two 90-minute cassettes. Great for listening to in the car, while working around the house, or to enjoy as a family.

Prophet

John Barrett, anchorman for the city's most-watched evening newscast, knows something is wrong. The facts don't add up. So he determines to find the real news—the truth. It won't be easy, though. He's caught his producer reworking a story to fit her own prejudices and then lying to cover her tracks. She also appears to be hiding something much bigger.

As he confronts the politically correct attitudes of the news team, Barrett finds that they are in league with desperate forces that will stop at nothing to keep the lid on the story, even if it means his job . . . or his life. Once again,

Frank Peretti has woven a prophetic tale for our times that penetrates to the very heart of a struggle that threatens to tear our society to pieces.

TILLY

Kathy and Dan Ross are just like any other young couple ... except for the secrets that lie buried in their souls. When Kathy is captivated by the simple name "Tilly" on a small grave marker, both her life and Dan's are changed forever.

Tilly is the deeply moving story of a woman's struggle to reconcile herself with a long-ago abortion, and a couple's efforts to ultimately move forward with their lives. This powerful tale of forgiveness will shake the most stoic soul.

The Cooper Kids Adventure Series

A four-volume set of Frank E. Peretti's "Indiana Jones-style" adventure series. Build sound values in kids ages 9–14 while keeping them glued to their seats. Nearly 2,000,000 copies sold!

BOOK 1: The Door in the Dragon's Throat

Jay and Lila Cooper have been on adventures with their archaeologist father before, but nothing like this! As they make their way through the dark and mysterious cavern called The Dragon's Throat, they can't help thinking about the other exploration parties that tried to open the Door leading into it. All fled in panic or died terrible deaths!

What really lies behind the Door? Incredible riches from a lost kingdom? Some ancient evil? Will they be able to overcome whatever force lurks behind the Door in the Dragon's Throat? Join them as they solve this dreaded desert mystery, which ends with a gigantic clash between the forces of good and evil.

BOOK 2: Escape from the Island of Aquarius

When Jay and Lila travel with their adventurous father to an exotic South Seas island to find a missing missionary, they discover some very strange things going on. It appears that the arrogant leader of the island colony is the man they've been sent to find. But if that's true, then why is he acting so strange? As the Coopers attempt to solve the mystery, they find they also must find a way to overcome the evil that holds the colonists in a death grip—before the entire island breaks apart.

BOOK 3: The Tombs of Anak

When Jay and Lila Cooper enter the cave-tombs of Anak with their father, they hope to find a coworker who has unaccountably disappeared. Instead, they stumble onto a frightening religion and new mysteries that soon put them all into incredible danger.

Who or what is Ha-Raphah? How does he hold the local villagers in overwhelming fear? The Coopers desperately search for answers and begin to unravel the mystery, but more peril lies ahead. Will they understand the truth in time to avoid disaster, or will they be swept away in a last desperate attempt by Ha-Raphah to preserve his evil powers?

BOOK 4:
Trapped at the Bottom of the Sea

When Lila insisted on leaving her father's teaching expedition to go back to the States, she never suspected that her flight would be hijacked! Now she is a prisoner, trapped at the bottom of the sea in a locked, top-secret weapons pod with no way of escape. Meanwhile, her dad, Dr. Jake Cooper, her brother Jay, and darling adventure-journalist Meaghan Flaherty are trying to pick up Lila's trail.

Pursued by angry terrorists, they island-hop in a remote corner of the Pacific, hoping against hope to find the plane. But will they reach Lila before her air runs out? Or before the pod is found by another hostile group searching for it?